The Tollkeeper

Mark R. Vickers

Least Tern Press
An imprint of Vigoré Publications LLC

LEAST TERN PRESS
Published by Vigoré Publications LLC

Vigoré Publications LLC
P.O. Box 16716
St. Petersburg, Florida 33733

Trade Paperback ISBN: 978-1-7322540-0-8
ebook ISBN: 978-1-7322540-1-5

Book cover design by Mario Lampic

www.thetollkeeper.com

Printed in the United States of America

For Cyndi

"To live is to war with trolls,
In the vault of heart and mind.
To write is to sit in judgement
Over ourselves."

—Henrik Ibsen

"They mixed honey with the blood,
and thus was produced such mead
that whoever drinks from it
becomes a skald and sage."

—*The Younger Edda*

Chapter One

"Who's that tripping over my bridge?" roared the troll.
—*The Three Billy Goats Gruff*

No one respects tollkeepers these days.

If people think of them at all, it's as a bunch of unskilled dead-enders barely pulling down minimum wage. Drivers especially disdain the odd-looking ones who remind them of creatures out of medieval fairy tales. I don't mean the monsters of 21st-century cinema: those alluring, brooding, forever-young vampires or those poetically surly werewolf types sporting six-pack abs and five o'clock shadows.

No, I mean the immense and awful ones. I mean trolls like me.

It wasn't always like this. Over a thousand years ago, when I was still a child, toll-taking trolls were a venerated lot. Everyone respected the Old Ones with their thick flaps of flab hanging over plate-sized belt buckles. People paid their tolls with deference, knowing the giants would just as soon eat their scrawny asses as take their paltry coinage.

None but glory-seeking fools would hazard them: short-lived fools, mayflies of men buzzing about the Old Ones with brave-sounding noises punctuated by impotent jabs and swipes of swords and axes.

The Old Ones—not dim, as the myths of men tell it, but merely bored—would swat most of these would-be heroes flat as a matter of simple reflex. The biggest and best of the warriors would get slivers of genuine attention before having their helmed heads pinched off as if they were so many annoying ass boils.

We kids called all these indistinguishable warriors by the same name: Olaf.

It was sweet to watch for us young ones, who had so often had our own noggins rattled by the stony backhands of our elders whenever they deemed us insufficiently respectful. To see the pitiful but not pitiable ways the humans were slain made us realize just how gentle the Old Ones were with us. Those grisly deaths made us feel loved.

I am reminded of my youth by this drunken douche in a Jag pulling up to my tollbooth in these wee, dark hours. He has the same bravado of those long-dead warriors, the same secret hope that his shiny, top-of-the-line equipment will protect him from a hostile universe. Trolls have always known this about men. It's not just greed or status that makes the boys crave their toys. It's feeble mortal fear deep beneath a gloss of fair-haired arrogance.

"Hey, boss, can you change this bad boy?" he asks, presenting a hundred-dollar bill between his index and middle finger with great flair, given his state of inebriation. I picture him as a teenage douche-in-training practicing the movement—and probably even the line he uses with it—in his old man's BMW in the driveway.

"I'm sorry, sir, a fifty is the largest I can change this evening."

"Too bad, dude," he winks and runs his fingers through his blond highlights as the engine revs. "Best raise the toll gate 'cause Billy Goat Gruff is coming through."

I don't know what sets me off. Maybe it's the remark, though I know it's just a lucky shot-in-the-dark from a dipshit who's already half-in-the-bag. I've been passing as human for centuries, so he can't know what I am. Or maybe it's those Nordic baby blues trying so hard to charm and bully at the same time, to wrest past me over the Bayway and onto the white, silken beaches laden with women, song and spirits. Or maybe I'm just peckish.

"The hell you are, Olaf," I say, taking a quick glance around to check for approaching headlights before I reach down through the low window and twist off his head like a grapefruit off a branch. Then I smile my crooked smile at his sweetly puzzled expression and take a bite from his noggin, the juicy goodness dribbling down my chin.

"I fuckin' love Florida," I murmur.

"Uck," I hear and nearly bobble Olaf's head away in surprise. "The salt, the sand, and the goddamned blazing sun. What's to like?"

Only then do I finally realize the little Polo-wearing puke had been showing off for a woman in the passenger seat the whole time. The sunroof rolls back and her head and bare shoulders pop up through it.

I'm not proud of what I do next, it being such a stereotype and all, but I roar at her, roar as only an alarmed troll cornered in the fjords can roar, with the kind of wounded fury known to freeze the blood of the most vicious Vikings of yore.

"Jeez," she says, shaking her head. "You disappoint. You seemed so cool a second ago."

And so I go stony silent instead, that other troll stereotype.

A black SUV with a couple of paddleboards strapped to the top rolls our way and I reluctantly prepare myself for more carnage, no longer in the mood. Luckily, somebody finds some coins and they veer into the exact change lane.

The young woman riding with Olaf has light brown hair pulled back in an all-American ponytail, a real cheerleader type. Her ethnicity is not quite identifiable. Eurasian, perhaps? She waves good-naturedly to the passing SUV from the Jag's sunroof, just a nice local gal hanging with her bud the tollkeeper. I hold Olaf's head under my change drawer.

"Now what?" she asks.

I consider yanking her fresh-faced, cover-girl head off as well, but we are somehow beyond that now.

"Car accident," I say.

"Allow me," she says brightly. "But be a sweetie and chuck Charlie in the back for me." So I flick the headless body of Charlie/Olaf over the seat like it's a wet beach towel. Then she slides into the gore-slick driver's seat, nods once as I raise the gate, and speeds away before I can utter an oath. I figure I've just been had, standing there like another dim-witted troll outsmarted by a quick-thinking beauty hurtling over the Bayway toward freedom and frozen daiquiris.

But just as I am envisioning smirking human children falling asleep to the sweet tale of my humiliation and demise, the Jaguar swerves hard up against the concrete barricade and spins like a robot dolphin performing for chrome fish.

There is a thrilling suspended moment before the car nails its entry with minimal splash, its taillights dimming into darkness as if it were waving goodbye.

Then nothing. By and by, I carry the head of Charlie/Olaf over to the scraped and cracked barricade, half-expecting the cover girl to invite me in for a swim. Still nothing. Not even bubbles.

She sure was a surprise. I'm not surprised by much these days.

I sigh and punt Olaf's bloody pate into the blackness. Then I go back to my tollbooth to mop up the mess, don a clean shirt, microwave some popcorn and call 911.

Around 5 a.m. or so, my boss Chen shows up to take over the booth for the coming rush hour. By then, there is just the one emergency vehicle left on the side of the Bayway and a small dive-boat anchored in the water. I see somebody in a wetsuit talking to a uniformed cop on the boat.

My boss is a trim, middle-aged Chinese guy who hates deviations from routine. Chen is annoyed that he has to initial all the paperwork I've filled out. He gives me grief for failing to wear my kitschy toll-collector shirt, replete with palm trees, swordfish, cartoony beach scenes and Florida landmarks, and he shakes his head at the shirt I'm now wearing, a tee that's way too tight and reveals an unlovely slice of belly hair. It has a silkscreen of an Old West poster showing a tabby cat and bearing the legend, "WANTED Dead and Alive: Schrodinger's Cat."

"The cops asked to see the video," I tell him. "You really ought to get that busted camera fixed." Meaning the camera I accidently-on-purpose broke almost a year ago. Chen's not one to sweat the small stuff, a quality I like in a boss.

"Klaus, you write worse than me," he moans as he hands me back the papers, "and I is a goddamned immigrant."

"Me too," I say, but he just makes some exasperated, disbelieving sound that dismisses me from my shift.

Good thing, too. Not long till sunrise.

Chapter Two

"In the forest dwell troll-women, who are known as Ironwood-Women.
The old witch gives birth to many giant sons."
—*The Younger Edda*

Too big for a bicycle or even a county-issued golf cart, I trudge on the asphalt highway shoulder till I come to a barely visible service road. The track of crunchy, broken shell quickly narrows into a brambled, tangled, palmetto-strewn path to nowhere-you-need-to-be. There's instant jungle that would gouge the paint and hack the doors off any lost tourist's truck. Everything else would bog down in the gullied, dun-colored sand that I kick to crap every day to maintain it as a tire-swallowing pit of tropical despair.

"Stay the fuck away" is my landscape motif. But for the dense hunk of humanity oblivious to my feng shui, there is plenty of signage: Private, Keep Out, Danger: Sinkholes, Beware of Dogs, and the like.

Of course, there are no dogs anymore. I ate those foul-tempered, mangy mutts long ago when they started wagging their tails at my approach.

The rest of the signage is true, though. Trolls don't bluff much. My *mor* taught me that long ago.

I remember how a chieftain's whelp rode up to the cave at the mouth of our favorite mountain pass. He'd been astride a fine, golden Fjord horse at the vanguard of other zit-faced high-breds sitting on lesser mounts.

"Hail, troll mother," he'd announced, with more courtesy than most others of his type. "We have dire need to pass quickly and unmolested. We pay in good copper."

My mor had not been an unusually recalcitrant troll, as our folk go, but the young prince had picked his posse badly. One who had an especially nasty dose of blackheads and sat a spotted gray pony piped up, "Save your coppers, my lord. This hideous witch cannot hinder us all, else we slay her and her spawn."

The prince told the cretin to be quiet, showing a controlled fury he must have learned from his father. But the bones had already been thrown.

"It's gold you'll pay, or I'll smash your fine horses with your lord's own legs and piss in his hollowed skull," Mor calmly told them.

"The troll bitch bluffs!" cried Blackheads, drawing his iron sword. The prince turned toward him—a serious mistake. My mother snatched the royal off the steed and, true to her word, ripped off his legs and then used one as a club to attack the other riders, who flailed at her with swords and axes.

I'm not saying they didn't hurt her. After all, the Norse whelps were kin of iron kings, whereas she was just a single dam feeding her family. She lost an ear that day and walked ever after with a limp, but she was true to her word: the prince and four of their horses died that day. As the eldest, I'd claimed the golden horse for myself, a feast I've not since forgotten.

"You were right to leave them to your mor," she told me after. "My honor was at stake, but next time you either join the fray or I eat you myself. This deed has long arms. We ain't seen the last of that clan."

She hadn't been bluffing on that score, either.

It is nearly sunrise. In the middle of the viny, creeper-induced claustrophobia I've cultivated rises a chain-linked fence with—contrary to ordinance—razor wire at the top. Within is an ugly, county-owned storage shed with a smallish efficiency apartment attached.

Once inside the fence, I ignore the apartment, unlocking the cinder-block-and-aluminum shed instead. Inside are my tools, including a big-ass, broken-down, riding lawnmower that I lift with one hand while reaching beneath to get a grip of the manhole cover I cast myself years ago. It is specially designed to fit my big mitt and too heavy for most humans to budge without machinery.

I've thought about trying to cast a few spells on the cover. Nothing fancy. Maybe just a heart-stopper, breath-taker and, for the sake of tradition, the standard kick-in-the-crotch charm. But I left magic behind me ages ago.

I lift the cover and crawl into the cold hole with the same sense of relief a human feels creeping under the covers in bed. My weird-ass day—that is to say, my night—is almost over.

Florida is essentially a gigantic sandbar, a land about as antithetical to my kind as axes are to trees. No stones to grind, no mountains to hide in, no caves in which to escape the deadly sun and moronic marauders. It's a death sentence, like transplanting a giant redwood into a salty swamp.

Except for one minor, little-known detail about trolls: we are excellent holders of breath.

It turns out Florida does have caves, lots of them, but mostly watery underground ones. Sinks and caverns and glens and springs, all plugged into an invisible network huge and labyrinthine enough to drown legions of hapless humans. A perfect troll haven.

We are also natural diggers, of course. I once saw a full-grown mountain troll use a combination of jackhammer kicks and spatulate hand gouges to completely bury himself in just a few minutes in the stony soil of Norway. I am not of that caliber, but I can easily dig through this soft dross.

My hole punches through a limestone ceiling into a cold, flowing river both crystal clear and utterly black, less a space than a secret dimension where I can forget the absurd terrors of being surrounded by the soft, nauseatingly sweet-and-sour larval swarms of humankind, mindlessly oblivious to the predator in their midst. They would mob me in all their gooey malice if they detected me, baring me to merciless Sól. But down below I am safe in the embrace of the Earth Mor.

Even so, I can't stay. Trollfolk must breathe by and by, so I follow my pitch tunnel to steps I carved long ago. They lead to another iron cover, above which is my lodge, pleasantly dark and hard and cool. There isn't room to stand but plenty to stretch out on the cement, which has been worn to the contours of my body after many years. I am home.

Wearing white silk pajamas, we sit in a circle on folding chairs, a spotlight shining down. I'm pleased to be here among friends, having been alone for so very long. For some reason, the actor George Clooney has us playing a theater game in which we make eye contact with others before throwing them an invisible object. "Red ball," I say, naming the pantomimed item and tossing it to my boss, Chen. However, as Chen mimes pulling it out of the air, it turns into a small pumpkin about the size of a navel orange.

Chen examines it with interest before chucking it to blond Olaf, who has had his head sewn back on with hairy-looking stitches. He fumbles the pumpkin from hand to hand, and I see it's become a jack-o'-lantern with sharp, gnashing teeth. Olaf bobbles the pumpkin into the darkness behind him, but a hand emerges to catch it. The hand belongs to Olaf's girlfriend, who steps into the spotlight, smirking. The pumpkin has transformed again, this time into a small version of my head. I recognize the thick russet brows over gray eyes, the square cheeks and the aquiline nose. Suddenly, I am seeing through the eyes of the disembodied head, my head. I am tossed to Clooney, who smiles at me mischievously before taking a bloody bite out of my cheek as I scream and scream.

When I wake, I sense dusk outside. Normally, I'd be cautious about leaving my hole until it's darker, but the dream has left me edgy and restless. I crawl up through a tunnel of my own design through the bridge abutment, leaving only a large reinforced block of seawall concrete hanging over me. With care, I lift the block, scanning the sloping seawall on either side and down to the water. No one. I squeeze out of the tunnel, moving quietly, and then softly lay the great block down again.

I lie back on the slanted seawall, feeling the warmth of the sun still radiating from the concrete. I hate that scarlet-haired bitch Sól, but do not mind a little cozy radiance left over from her big fat ass. I pull off my 5XL cotton plaid shirt and lie back again.

"You're not so bad, Máni," I tell the moon now up over the horizon. "Your hellion sister, Sól, though, makes the world's garbage reek and grass wither. May that sharp-toothed Sköll someday clip her rosy rump."

It's nearly high tide, a mercy to my nose. These days, low tides mean that the stinking mud flats spread out like an open corpse. There are worm burrows here and there, and a few small crabs crawling sideways in a desultory fashion, but compared to the old days—before they dredged the bottom of the bay in order to create million-dollar waterside properties out of the muck—the bay is a cadaver.

I am about to take another nap when I notice a skiff quietly approaching the wall about twenty yards away. It irks me that I hadn't seen it before. I'm getting careless in my middle age. Whoever is on it might have seen me crawl up. There are two fishermen, one sitting on the stern of the small craft and the other on the middle thwart. The second man handles the oars and then, as the bow slides up the concrete, jumps up onto the inclined wall. He carries a small anchor, which he wedges between some cracks in the concrete from which weeds are growing.

The fisherman says nothing, not even turning my way. That in itself isn't unusual. Some of the myths say that trolls can make themselves invisible, but that's bullshit. Our stony skins have some chameleon-like properties, I'd say, but even the Old Ones who'd learned a respectable amount of magic over the millennia couldn't pull off that irritating faerie trick of invisibility. No, it's just that we're practiced at blending into the landscape, at patiently waiting with so much stillness that humans just assume we are crags or boulders, patches of heather or clumps of mountain ash.

Or, in this case, part of a seawall.

"How are they biting?" I shout over at the anglers, trying to gauge whether they startle. The one still in the skiff doesn't move a muscle, making me suspicious. Maybe he's dozing, or maybe he already knew I'm here. As a troll, you learn from an early age that paranoia is a survival skill.

On the other hand, the one on shore flinches and swears softly in a foreign language. He looks my way.

"No biting," he shouts over in heavily accented English.

I rise and walk across, letting myself loom over him. He is a short, black man with gray stubble, wearing a tattered khaki bucket hat. I try to converse with him but he just looks up at me, shrugging and saying a few phrases that sound vaguely apologetic in his language. I think I catch a few familiar words. French patois, maybe? I'm thinking Haitian. My looming makes him uncomfortable. He starts feeling around in his pockets and removes a crumpled pack of Kools. I take the pack and pull out a cigarette. He waves a Bic at me and I kneel down to let him light me up.

I sit next to him, both of us smoking, him reeling in his line occasionally and then throwing it back out. Like he said, no biting. He offers me another cigarette, which I take. I'm watching his partner in the boat, who still hasn't moved a muscle, something you could expect from a troll but not from an antsy human.

"What's his deal?" I ask, pushing out my chin at the figure in the skiff.

The fisherman puts his hands together and lays his head down on them, pantomiming sleeping. Then, he has an idea. Through more charades, he urges me to wake his buddy. He's chuckling, clearly amused at the idea of me scaring the bejesus out of the deep sleeper. I don't move but he keeps repeating a word that I think I recognize: "réveille."

It'd be a dumb, cruel thing to do: have some humongous, ugly dude scare the living piss out of your friend, who might fall face first into cardiac arrest. It is the kind of mischief that young trolls got up to when I was a kid.

So, what the hell, I do it. I creep down to the boat, carefully put one foot on the center thwart, and yell, "Réveille, you old bastard!"

Nothing.

I start to get a little worried, not particularly wanting to get involved in a second scene with the paramedics in two nights.

"Hey, you little shit, réveille," I say quietly, shaking his shoulder. That's when his head falls off and I step back in alarm, losing my footing and falling into the water. I hear my smoking buddy laughing up on the wall but can't spot him. I am getting seriously pissed. This is yet another stupid-troll story for the books.

Though I'm in the bay, I can feel the submerged foundation of the seawall under my feet, a foundation made slippery by seaweed just below the low-tide mark. Grabbing it by the gunwales, I pull the boat toward me to steady myself, then see the faux angler's head rolling around.

It's a goddamned pumpkin.

"You motherfucker!" I yell up the incline toward the little Haitian, who seems to be long gone. As I start to pick up the pumpkin head, intending to smash it to pulp, the top comes off. Falling out is something heavy, though wrapped in paper.

"I'm an idiot," I say, stepping up the concrete incline and pulling the little boat along with me. My dream comes back to me, making me shiver. I carefully look over the body of the pumpkin-headed fisherman, half expecting it to be Olaf's. But it is a craftily cobbled together mass of driftwood, old fishing buoys and scraps of clothing.

Then I pick up the object wrapped in paper. It turns out to be a little silver jaguar leaping in attack. It's the screwed-off hood ornament from a car. Olaf's car, I'm guessing. I carry it over to where the little trickster had been sitting and use his abandoned Bic to look at the wrapping paper. It turns out to be a printed invitation addressed to "Tollkeeper" with a time, date and the name of a restaurant. The message "You'll love the Rakfisk" is elegantly hand-written on the bottom, though there's no signature.

Chapter Three

"We daren't go in, for here the Trolls live."
—*East of the Sun and West of the Moon*

The note reveals that someone is watching. Maybe they know I killed Olaf, or even about my tunnel to the seawall. I should have made damned sure that crazy girlfriend was dead.

It's been long years, decades even, since I've encountered any type of serious threat. My mind has been numbed by the routine of taking tolls, making change, expanding my tunnels and falling into the mind-deadening shadow realms of television. It's a kind of death, or at least a hibernation of spirit.

Mor would have clubbed me for my folly. She'd always seen danger coming, had never allowed her sharp mind to lose its edge.

She'd been right, for example, about fallout from the prince's death. We hadn't seen the last of the prince's clan, which was known as the Völsungs. She'd slain him for honor's sake, but the Völsungs had their own obligations of honor and vengeance. A more foolish troll might have been lulled into complacency as the days wore on, thinking she'd frightened away the humans for generations to come. My mor, however, knew a well-planned revenge when she smelled one.

Some of the peasants paying her tolls to cross the mountain pass looked suspiciously more well-fed and well-bred than usual, despite their rags and coppers. Although obeying her demands without question, they were sharp-eyed, sometimes casting glances into the nearby hills.

"Spies," she said. "They explore the terrain, plan an attack. See if you can catch one among the slopes."

The next afternoon, while lurking along a rough gorge path, I did. All was silent except for soft falling shale and trickles of water. The spy was an archer dressed in grays and browns to blend into the landscape. He was leery but moved quickly, trying to get far from our mountain pass before sunset. It was too late. He didn't grasp the timing of long shadows as well as I did. There would be no more sunlight in the gorge that day.

I was still young, by troll standards, and he a proper man, but my strength was twice or thrice his. The trick was to surprise him, avoiding his arrows. If he discovered me too soon, he'd easily slay or wound me from a distance. So I had to move at almost infinitesimal slowness behind a fallen slab of sandstone as he came down the mountain path in my direction. If I moved too quickly, he would sense the motion, but if I moved too slowly, he'd spot me from above as his line-of-sight shifted. These are the kinds of lessons you learn from your elder trolls—or you die.

I wasn't perfect. Just as he was coming into range, my foot edged out from behind the stone slab and he stopped dead, as if there were poisonous serpents on the path. The time for stealth was over. I charged him.

Trolls aren't known for their sprinting speed. We are built for ambush, our thick thighs tuned to the pounce, our torsos designed for grappling and pummeling.

The archer was good. He got off a shot into my thigh before I could snatch him. Then he reached for his long knife. If he'd had a comrade nearby, I would have died. As it was, I lunged at his knife arm, holding fast his wrist and biting through the forearm. He screamed, naming me a demon and horror. To him, no doubt I was. And so is a cat to a mouse, a wolf to a sheep. This is the way of the world.

Unfortunately, he quickly bled to death. When I brought him, my first human kill, home to my mother, she beat me into unconsciousness. She'd never been a gentle dam, of course. It wasn't her way. Yet never had she raged at me to such an extent, either.

"I told you to *catch* one," she erupted. "Not kill it! I can learn nothing from such meat. Catch means trap alive. Any troll can kill! Too few can think!"

I vowed not to let her down again.

"Strong but cunning," she urged. "Strong but cunning."

I thought deeply on this. To most trolls, cunning simply meant circling a boulder well, having a good eye for rich travelers, and using networks of tunnels to their advantage. For my mother, though, it meant something more. It meant what the humans call "strategy."

Rather than throwing away or eating the archer's corpse, I considered how I might use it in some cunning way. Would his comrades come looking for him or assume we had waylaid him? They couldn't be sure unless we left evidence. That night, I found and collected his broken bow and other items I'd left scattered about, and I erased signs of blood and struggle as best I could.

I considered posing the man's corpse in such a way as to make his kin believe he was alive, but the feeding ravens would quickly give that game away. So, I stuffed his clothing with heather and ferns, making a dummy archer, complete with a full quiver of arrows and a repaired bow. Then I skinned and stuffed one of his arms, using enough salt to keep away the birds.

Within two days, I spotted more Norsemen on the cliffs. They were calling out a name that I assumed belonged to the dead archer. They came in the brightest daylight, safe from the mad dam lurking in her cave. Although I couldn't attack them in the sun, I could prepare for the earliest time the gorge would fall into shadows.

Using our hive of caves, I called for help from various locations in the cliffs. This confused them, making them desperate enough to split into singles and pairs. I then carefully posed the dummy archer so it appeared as if he'd fallen behind some boulders from the cliff above. There was a nearby path below these rocks. When a man approached along it, I called out weakly and waved the stuffed arm.

The man, who was an elder clansman of some sort—perhaps the archer's father—was cautious. He shouted out to the dummy but didn't immediately scramble up toward it as I'd hoped. I waved the arm again in a way that only allowed him a glimpse of it, not wanting the unnatural state of the fingers to give my trick away. Instead of speaking, I only moaned.

He did ascend, though apprehensively. He could not give into his own well-founded doubts, mistaking them for cowardice.

When the elder was finally close enough, I picked up a log I'd placed nearby and hurled it at his legs. Although he approached with sword drawn, there was little he could do about the log, being neither fast nor agile enough to jump over it in time. It smashed into his right leg. A broken shinbone stabbed through the skin, leaving him at my mercy.

When I brought him home to Mor, he was panting like a wounded hare. He'd lost considerable blood. As I laid him on the floor of the cave, he vomited up his last meal. She looked him over and grunted.

"The blackness of his eyes grows and his heart trembles," she said. "Death stalks him. Lay him down on skins and cover him. Stem the bleeding. Keep him warm and out of smoke."

She touched the elder's white skin, incanting a healing spell she'd used before on her children.

"At least this one breathes," she said, stalking into the cave. That was her idea of praise.

She came back with skins in her arms.

"The human might yet recover. Use your soft ways with it."

My soft ways. Till that day, she'd only scowled at my "soft ways," by which she meant any signs of gentleness with my sibs or animals. As a child, she once caught me cradling a stoat that'd been injured in a trap. I'd looked into its eyes, smoothing its fur with thick fingers and speaking quiet words. She had snatched it from me, wrung its neck and thrown it at my feet.

"Soft," she had whispered disdainfully. "Like your *far*."

It was the first time she'd referred to my father. I'd always assumed my far was the huge mountain troll who came to visit in the dark winter months, dragging behind him a reindeer or other offering through the deep snowdrifts. He seldom spoke more than a word or two at a time. He had the hunched back, low forehead and fleshy nose so common among our people. It gave him a dim look, but I'd grown up in a landscape filled with such powerful trolls and knew better than to underestimate his intellect.

In our initial encounter, he'd held me high and sniffed me from head to toe. There was a low growl from Mor, which he ignored before flinging me across the cave into the midden. From that time onward, he paid me little heed and I stayed out of his way, admiring his classic troll stoicism from afar. Over the years, a crusted nodule started growing off the side of his neck, the sign of an emerging second head. My mor rubbed it in the firelight as the mountain troll sat silent and cross-legged. She felt pride in being mated with one ancient enough to grow a second head.

There was nothing soft about him. When Mor made her comment about my far, I realized that this mountain troll whom I so admired was likely the father of my sibs but not mine. I never spoke of it to any of them.

The human I'd captured didn't die of shock after all, though I'm sure he wished he had. My mor made the whole family—including my younger sister and brother—watch as she interrogated the elder.

"What clan are you from, human?"

He said nothing, only screamed as she held one hand and then another into the fire. I never shifted my eyes from the scene, not wanting to appear soft to Mor or my siblings. My sister was especially fascinated, feeling none of the scandalous pity I harbored. When the elder's flesh lightly caught on fire, she snickered, amazed at the fragility of the human.

It was hours before the elder gave up the name of his clan, a fact my mother already knew because of the tattooed runes on the back of his neck. It probably never occurred to the man that this torturing bitch of a troll-dam could read and, therefore, already knew the answer to a secret he was desperate to keep.

This was more of the cunning she valued. After telling many lies, the elder finally divulged his true clan name, so she knew she'd broken his spirit, dishonoring himself in his own eyes. Now he only wished to die, to be forgotten and have his bones cast into our midden. And die he did, but only after admitting he was a spy sent by the jarls of his people, gathering information about how to best avenge the young prince, whose chieftain father was away in the wars.

"When he returns, troll bitch," howled the charred old man, "your guts will be hung like garlands through our halls and we will piss in the skulls of your brood."

I admired his fierceness, though was careful to conceal the fact. When the time came, I was proud to eat his purplish heart.

Chapter Four

"The hardest thing in life to learn is which bridge to
cross and which to burn."
—David Russell

The baffling dinner invitation is for Thursday, my night off. Had
the sender known that in advance?

I try to think what Mor would do. She might just ignore the note,
forcing them—whomever they are—to make another move.

But ignoring the note would only raise my level of paranoia.
Already, I'm squinting with suspicion at every passerby, glaring if
they seem too friendly or curious or angry. A tollkeeper sees the entire
circus of humanity parade by every day. Bored, neutral equanimity
is the trait most valued among human and troll tollkeepers alike. I've
lost that essential quality. My calm has been damaged.

I could lurk nearby the restaurant to catch a glimpse of whomever sent the message. Trolls are born to lurk, so I would be playing
to my strengths. On the other hand, I'm far from the fjords of my
youth, where trolls could blend in so easily. What's more, I've long
stayed away from the beaches, laden with tender human flesh, lightly

cooked and slathered in oils. It is a brightly-lit smorgasbord of boozy, hormone-driven humans, such easy prey that they are a dangerous lure to an unchecked troll. Of all the things I fear most, losing control again is uppermost in my mind.

I could simply walk into what is likely a trap, trusting that they have some mischief in mind that doesn't include my immediate death. If they wanted to slay me, then wouldn't the Haitian have come armed with more than a fishing pole? Still, I don't like walking into a set-up without doing some reconnaissance.

So, lurking it is.

Trolls do not cross bridges, we guard them. We are the gatekeepers, the toll takers, the sentinels of the status quo, the defenders against transgression and discouragers of sojourns. We believe in staying put. We are suspicious of questers and heroes, especially epic heroes. They are merely meddlers writ large, interlopers trying to make a name for themselves. They are the quintessential unreasonable humans who, instead of adapting to the world, expect the world to adapt to them. They are, in short, a mortal pain in the ass.

It has been my curse to be forced among them, to go against the eternal troll grain, to be roughed up and sanded down by the calloused fingers of fate. Wasn't my original absurd odyssey to these lands enough?

I gird myself as I approach the tollgate. "Screw you, Vegtam, you One-Eyed Old Bastard," I say to a raven as it perches on one of the black-and-yellow lowered gates. "Wandering is for chumps."

Miriam is operating the right-side tollgate this evening in my stead, knitting a sweater for her daughter's child who lives in northern climes. She looks up, surprised, as I approach the gate on foot.

"Thought you were off tonight, Klaus," she says, giving me a gap-toothed grin. I like her. She reminds me of the more pleasant crones of the homeland, the ones able to lay tranquility down like wool fibers over the rough stones of long, hard lives.

"Just out for a walk," I say.

"Good for you," she responds, patting her crone belly. "I could use some of that myself."

I touch my own paunch hanging heavy over a thick, steel buckle wedded to heavy leather. I give her my best co-worker smile and wave, not stopping for more small talk. The sun will be up all too soon, and in Florida there are precious few troll holes in which to hide away.

It is an excellent bridge on which I tread, the first of two fine bridges before I come to the beach. As I pass by, I touch the scratched and patched concrete barrier where the car of headless Olaf spun. A tractor trailer blows by me, my clothes slightly sucked forward in its wake.

When I first arrived in this land, there was no traffic, no lights, no bridge at all. I was the area's first tollkeeper when there were little more than paths through mangroves. It was a flat, wet wilderness into which I'd been cast. Now it is barely recognizable, all stone and steel, oil and tar.

The scents of Boca Viaja Bay are also very different from times past. So many poisons floating like a sheen on the waves, poisons to which my troll nose has never quite grown accustomed. The humans, with their fleeting lives, don't notice the stench, though the aborigines of old would have choked from it.

The sea grasses are shriveled, the studded shoals of scallops gone, the oysters shrunken, the teaming mullet only a remnant of what they once were. From a troll's perspective, it has happened in the blink of an eye.

Despite the millions of automobiles that have swept by me over the decades, I've never owned one. My lair's sunk beneath the bridge. My kind seldom roam far without need, and there's been no need. I've had hordes of paying travelers, the clammy darkness of a hidden cave, and a nearby all-night Albertson's where I bribe a butcher to keep me in all the blood tongue, pigs' feet, pork rinds, griebenschmalz, and head cheese I can ingest—and I am a great, grand, even glorious ingester of meats. What more could a lower-middle-class troll desire?

So, here I am hoofing it to the beach. The bridge I work stretches from the mainland to Boca del Sól. From that condo-crowded enclave of geriatrics, there's another bridge to Saint Drogo Beach.

After crossing the first bridge of the causeway, my size twenty-four New Balance sneakers, specially ordered from 2BigFeet.com, are pinching my toes. So I take a shortcut across the golf course. It's deserted until I see someone on the ninth green standing in the darkness. The figure lifts the flag and peers down into the cup. I'm hoping it's just some greenkeeper working after hours. I despise bumping into other fabled creatures of the night, but it happens. Like attracts like: it is the way of *Orlog*, the law of the cosmos.

So, I guess I shouldn't expect anything less on this shameless slice of emasculated sod named after that irradiated bitch Sól.

"Fuck me," I whisper, getting a whiff of its stench.

"Yes, fuck you, you man-eating Si-Te-Cah hulk," says the *draugr*, or whatever its people's equivalent is. The undead thing is hairless and beyond just rotten, its ribcage concave with disintegration. "Go back to the Western lands where you belong."

I seem to remember that Si-Te-Cahs are Native American giants who supposedly lived in the Southwest. Red-haired giants, at that. Given my copperish locks, I can see where the draugr might get a little mixed up.

"Different branch of the family," I correct. "My brand of giants come from far east of here."

"Whatever," says the draugr. "Get off this burial mound, or I'll drive you mad."

No bluff. Draugrs are well known for casting clouds of crazy. I've got enough problems. But it's not easy getting on the good side of a putrid poltergeist.

"You're kidding me," I say. "Even Florida developers can't get away with building on ancient barrows, can they?"

We stare at one another a long moment and then both burst out laughing, him so hard that he coughs up something that squiggles on the ground.

"Hey," I say, "if you want to drive somebody out of their gourd, maybe it ought to be the plaid-wearing geezers who butchered the jungle to spread this feculence."

"Look around," it says, spreading its arms just as the sprinklers turn on. "Could I make these people any more deranged than they are?"

I can only shake my head, which brings another lull in the conversation. I get the sense that neither of us has exercised our social skills much in the last century or so.

"Hey," it says suddenly. "Want your fortune told?"

"Uh, sure, okay."

I don't, of course, but I also don't want to reject a semi-friendly offer from a draugr, not when he can still chuck some nasty piece of sorcery at me.

"Right, then," it says. "Here we go. Give me your paw, monster." When I hesitate to put my hand into its bony fingers, it just chuckles.

"At least you show some sense. Okay, here it is, then. Ready? You cannot escape the eye of Neptune," it proclaims. "No, wait, that's for a different guy. All right. Let's try this: you will be getting out more in the future. Beware the sun till you find the right kind of block. Drive safe and don't feed the gators. Beware strangers bearing gifts, practice safe sex and, uh, watch what you eat. And drink. Losing a few pounds would be good for you. You're pretty chunky, even for a Si-Te-Cah."

"Nice," I say, less than impressed by the string of clichés. "You ought to work for the State. You got some kind of pamphlet I could take with me?"

We get another laugh out of this, then I'm itching to go. It's best to leave draugrs on good terms when you can.

"Go on, get out of here," it whispers, starting to lurch away. "I still have to haunt the back nine anyway."

The last bridge. A red light flashes and a black-and-white gate comes down to bar the way in front of me. Then the drawbridge, which is essentially an enormous steel grate, rises up and up till it stands at attention like an immense guardian. There are no waiting cars. I pause to see what kind of sailboat is motoring under the bridge, but none appears. For some reason, this unnerves me more than the draugr did. I'll take blatantly supernatural over creepy portents any time.

Back in the day, the greatest of the Old Ones guarded the bridges into our most sacred lands. Before you could cross, they demanded your family name. They had long memories, often knowing your ancestry better than you did. If they quizzed you about your clan and found you ignorant, they'd turn you away—or worse. I wordlessly run through the many names I've adopted through the centuries. Hallr was, I suppose, the first name, the one Mor gave me to use in the wider world. I whisper it, superstitious fool that I am.

The drawbridge lowers and the gate lifts. No cars come from the other direction, either. I take a deep breath and start across. As I do, the lights on the bridge blink out. Ditto for those in the houses just across the intracoastal waters. I pause, trying to convince myself it's just a power outage.

The stars are suddenly sharp, dense pinpoints of gold and silver light. They have not seemed this bright for decades. I can even see the Milky Way rising like a cosmic tree, its dark, chasmal trunk canting to the left and outlined by clouds of radiance. It reminds me of Mor's stories of Yggdrasil, the mythic tree of trees whose branches extend into heaven. Pointing toward it, in the western sky, is the tiniest of red slits, a coming comet.

I look over the railing into the dark waters where a school of pale fish swim slowly in straight lines, like knives moving beneath the surface.

After I cross over the full span, the power comes back up and the bridge rises again. This time I force out a laugh. Hell, I work for the Florida Department of Transportation. Why am I surprised the bridges are screwy?

Chapter Five

"They killed giants, their conquering swords had brought them down."
—*Beowulf*

As it turned out, Mor had precious little time to act on the spy's confession. The Völsung clan's chieftain had just returned from war, according to the troll talk in our hills. Mor had to make a decision: fight or flee. The humans would know our strength, the mouths of our caves, and our toll-collecting habits.

It turned out their chieftain was a strong one, a king who ruled other local chieftains. He had waged many a battle and survived. He would not come with callow, overconfident cubs but with warriors braced with iron, schemes and a thirst for vengeance.

Most trolls would have fled, knowing the odds. Even Mor might well have done so if the hill talk hadn't reached her mate, Talvard, the mountain troll, whom I once considered my father.

It was still autumn, over a month before winter mating season began, but Talvard came with one of his younger brothers down from the heights of the Galdhøpiggen. They carried not only clubs but maces, axes and spears—the first troll spears I'd seen for many years.

I should probably call those spears "pikes" because they made the spears of men look like twigs, being twenty feet long and tipped with razor-edged stones. Talvard and his brother were prepared, wearing dense iron-studded leather armor with gorgets at the throat. Rather than the imbecilic beasts of human fairytales, they were terrible, warrior giants out of nightmares.

And so it was that when the Völsung king led his battle-hardened men against the defiant troll-dam of the western pass, he found that his spies had badly failed him.

The king's name was Alfr. He made no effort to disguise his moonlit march. From Alfr's perspective, he owned these lands, and our mountain pass was critical to controlling them. In the past, the king had never begrudged our toll-keeping. He might have considered it a service rendered since we not only kept the pass cleared of rockslides but allowed no outlaws to hinder commerce or easily sneak past the border. (Unless, of course, they gave Mor a sizable cut of their loot. She was not, after all, a zealot.) Back then, trolls were a vital part of the social landscape.

Alfr brought upwards of two score warriors with him, some of whom smelled familiar to me. I'd sniffed their tracks on the surrounding pathways when they'd scouted us.

The king looked solemn and yet, in retrospect, weary in his battle gear. I doubt he expected anything like the kind of bloodletting he'd recently seen in his campaigns against the other warlords. But he wasn't taking foolish chances, wearing silver mail armor over thick red robes. He also donned an iron helmet with a guard around the eyes, the first of the type I'd ever seen. His horse was a glossy black stallion, and a young man behind the king carried a pole with a red standard. On top of the pole was a lit torch.

Directly behind him were six archers on horseback, ready to slay us if we charged.

I'd never witnessed a human army before, not even one as small as this. I was particularly impressed by the array of Viking shields, colorful even in the dim firelight. Some sported black and blue swirls, others bluish crosses, and a few exquisitely intricate and interwoven illustrations of dragons or other beasts. I could feel their beauty weighing on my chest like a heavy stone. I had a sudden yearning to demolish them.

"Troll dam," Alfr said loudly, a kind of proclamation. "You murdered my brave eldest for no cause, according to many witnesses. You and your kin must answer for your monstrous wickedness. I am only sorry it has taken so long to avenge him, may he thrive in the halls of Valhalla."

"I defended my honor," Mor said simply, standing at the entrance of our lair, ready to jump behind a boulder if the arrows were loosed.

The king nodded, as if he'd expected this. He motioned with his hand and his warriors approached, a few on horseback, most on foot and carrying spears and shields. None charged recklessly toward our lair, as my Mor had hoped. The Völsung king had a disciplined group with him.

Still, they had underestimated her.

From either side of the steep, stony mountains plummeted Talvard and his brother. Lunging with their gigantic spears, they ambushed the mass of warriors as if they were a single great beast. Three warriors and two horses were skewered immediately as the mountain trolls roared in battle rage. It took precious moments before the warriors understood their predicament, flanked by foes coming at them from the astonishing direction of near-vertical walls.

It might have been a massacre if Alfr hadn't been a good field general. He shouted an order and joined his hands in a doubled fist over his head. Even as the swords rang against the hard wood of troll spears, the troop tightened, round shields turned outward. The warriors who'd been advancing toward Mor and me turned back. The standard bearer was waving his pole for some reason.

Mor didn't hesitate. Now that she knew she couldn't lure any of the fighters into the cave, she charged the king with a spiked club and stone knife. I had been keyed up and even afraid moments before, but now something broke in me, a savage exultation that made the whole world suddenly sharp. Possessed by this elation, I assaulted the warriors who defended their liege.

Four good trolls against forty armed men are decent battle odds, according to the lore of my people. Although I was puny compared to the twelve-foot mountain giants who'd come to our aid, I was around six and a half feet tall and a good three hundred pounds. Undersized for my age, sure, but more than a physical match for most humans. Mor had trained me in the use of maces and axes, and I was as ambidextrous as most trolls.

In two movements, I shattered the shield of one warrior with my mace—which amounted to little more than a heavy iron club with a spiked dome—and cleaved his skull with my axe. Then I jumped back to avoid the spears of his brethren.

I hated the damned spears. Once they were set properly, they neutralized my superior reach. Lacking a shield, I had to bat and hack at the spear tips.

Mor growled, "Slay the standard bearer!"

I had no idea why she would want me to waste my efforts on some stripling waving a lit pole, but Mor was our general, and I knew better than to question her judgement. The bearer was well inside the throng, three-men deep. While she attacked the front lines, I backed away behind her, trying to gain a little distance before dashing toward the lines. It is usually death to leave your feet in battle, especially when you're a target as big as a troll. If just one of the fighters had raised his spear at the right moment and at the right angle, I would have been instantly skewered. But this was the fastest way to the standard bearer and one that, I hoped, would take the Mor-besieged warriors by surprise.

I vaulted over one stunned soldier before bringing my mace down on the helmet of a red-bearded fighter who didn't have time to get his sword tip up. The black iron helmet might as well have been forged with tin for all the protection it gave him. By pushing against the now dead and falling warrior with the haft of my axe, I slowed my momentum and kept my feet. The stout man behind red-beard had the chance to adjust to my unconventional attack, raising his shield as I slammed into it.

I knew my time was short, that I would soon receive an axe in the back as they closed around me, so I continued to throw my shoulder into the big man's shield, forcing him to one side.

Reaching out with the spiked ball of my mace, I was able to yank the head of the stripling standard bearer into the edge of my axe, cleaving him through the middle of his face.

When the standard fell, the torch poured flaming fuel on the head of another one of Alfr's warriors. So, I'd succeeded in my task, but my maneuvers had left me unprotected from the stout foe I'd just pushed to one side. He must have been astonished that I still hadn't raised my weapons against him. Whatever he felt, however, he had used his time wisely, bringing up his sword vertically in the cramped space and slicing up and into my right breast.

I yelped like an injured wolf before feeling myself yanked backwards by the leather vest I wore. It was Mor, extricating her idiotic vaulting son from danger as she momentarily broke off her assault on the king. She was also bloodied, having been jabbed by the long spear of Alfr, who was still astride that damnable black horse. It was the largest horse I'd ever seen, a breed apart from the small, tawny Fjord horses that were common in that day. It had been well trained for battle, never panicking or rearing, keeping his master above the fray.

The calm-headed king was our biggest problem, as Mor well knew. Talvard and his brother had been slaughtering warriors at a great rate, having dropped their spears and drawn their axes. The men's shields were no match for the awesome might of mountain trolls, still charging with devastating force despite being peppered with arrows. They would win the day for us if only the ranks could be well and truly broken. To achieve that, we needed to kill King Alfr.

Mor feigned a retreat, calling me to her. Apparently, my previous acrobatics had given her an idea. She grabbed my arm and shoulder, shouting, "Use your knife to take the chieftain!" She spun me in the air as if I were still a child and threw me in the direction of Alfr.

The moment stretched long. It felt as if the club in my right hand propelled me toward the king, as if I were some troll-child's parody of Thor. In my left, I held a long obsidian knife that I had carefully knapped during long nights spent around campfires. As I turned toward the king at the zenith of the arc, I saw something from the corner of my eye, something that disturbed and distracted me, even as I tried to fend off the king's spear rising to lance me.

It was then that the damned horse reared, not in fear but because the king wished it to smash and slice me with its sharp hooves. And, indeed, it did connect with my right shoulder, spinning my knife arm away from my intended victim and bringing my legs flailing into the black nag's flanks. Though dazed, I knew only a lightning flash movement would save my life, so I struck out at whatever was nearest with my jagged knife. As the Norns would have it, it was the underside of the king's horse.

Now, to my satisfaction, that blasted war beast finally did panic, bucking and kicking and screaming its horse scream, so lovely to my ears. It flung the king to the ground.

Yet, even as our victory seemed near, some dark thought oppressed me. A split second later, I registered what I'd seen while in the air: more warriors.

I realized why my mother feared the standard bearer: he was not simply a carrier of empty banners of human pride. He had been giving a signal to others, more warriors hidden down the rocky road, awaiting a sign if they should be needed. The cunning Völsung had kept them in reserve.

Bearing their own long thrusting spears, the fresh troops hurled themselves into the two mountain trolls. At that moment, I became little more than a frenzied animal, all cunning and judgement lost in a haze of fury.

By the time I regained myself, the battle was nearly over. I still lived but couldn't stand, two arrows sticking in my sides, and legs so hacked with spear tips that they'd become nearly useless. A large man sporting a blue and gold tunic raised a two-handed axe over me, kicking his fellows away so that he might have the honor of taking my head.

He froze, though, spotting Mor before I did.

She was bathed in blood. One eye had been gouged out and an arrow was sunk deep in her left shoulder, another in a thigh. Yet, she held a knife to the throat of the Völsung king.

"Him," she pointed with her chin to me. "Him you will spare," she told the king.

The axe wavered.

"Nay, I will not, fierce dam," the king said.

Then she bent further toward him. I thought she was going to take a bite from his neck but instead only whispered something.

The king frowned but nodded. "He is spared... for now," he shouted.

The man in the blue tunic lowered the axe as Mor half-dragged and half-walked King Alfr to our lair's opening, using him as a shield from the remnants of the archers. Talvard was there, somehow still alive, breathing raggedly as if his lungs had been shredded. His brother had been slain and, I knew, his great head would soon adorn a spike.

Mor waved her mate into the lair and threw down the king. An arrow pierced her shoulder as she turned, but it barely slowed her as she disappeared into the cave.

To this day, I don't know if they survived. I'm sure Mor, always the apostle of cunning, had mapped an escape route and set traps for pursuers. But whether she evaded the warriors in her badly wounded condition and led my family to safety, I cannot say.

The king himself did not pursue his quarry. He had wanted a battle in the open, of course, which is why he'd arrived after sunset. But he didn't begrudge the chase to others willing to brave the tunnels. He gave them permission to go before looking down at me, a question in his eyes.

"Throw it over a horse," he ordered. "Bind it tightly and watch it closely, but let no more harm be done to it this day."

This order was too much for the man in the blue tunic, one of Alfr's captains. The humans had suffered much and lost many to the trolls that day. To spare one was an outrage.

"It must die, Alfr!" he said. "No matter what pledge you gave to spare your own life."

During the battle, the king had fought with a calm, grim determination. Only now did I see him turn truly wrathful.

"You fool, Dofri! I did not spare his life to save my own. If you believe that, then challenge me here and now!"

"Then why, Alfr?"

The king walked over to me, his sword at my throat.

"Do not hinder us, beast, and you won't be harmed."

I growled low but did not attack. For whatever reason, Mor wanted me to survive this day.

"Dofri, check behind its neck," said the king. "Do you see any markings?"

Dofri had two men yank me into a sitting position and pull down the leather vestment riding up on my neck. At first, he saw nothing, amid the blood and gore. He spit into his hands and wiped away the grime. He stared, then looked closer still.

"Odin's Eye!" he swore.

"So, she spoke the truth," said the king quietly.

Other men looked to Dofri for an explanation. He, in turn, regarded the king, who nodded his assent.

"There are runes from another age," explained Dofri. "Runes we have seen on stones and our most sacred weapons. What can it mean, Alfr?"

"It means the bitch dam spoke true. This beast belongs to our clan."

Chapter Six

"Heads, galls, domes, bogs, sogs, bays, baygalls, strands, and hammocks…"
—*Ecosystems of Florida*

I've never heard of a restaurant called *Snorri's*, which is strange because your average tollkeeper gets lots of absurd questions from tourists, as if we work for some state-run low-wage concierge service. Veteran tollkeepers either get good at giving drivers "the idiot stare" to indicate they don't know anything—a great way of speeding along the traffic—or they become adept at quickly giving directions to known hotspots, even if they wouldn't be caught dead in those places.

Snorri's isn't on my tollkeeper map and it doesn't have a website, but the address on the note indicates it isn't far down the beach. As I get closer, I see why it's off my radar: it's a theme-based joint embedded in one of the resort hotels. To get to it, I have to walk across a terrazzo lobby floor depicting cavorting dolphins under a smiling sun. I make a point of scuffing Sól's face.

Above the restaurant entrance, written in some faux-runic font, is the name *Snorri's*. To the right side of the entrance is a four-foot fiberglass statue of a scantily-clad, feathers-wearing woman dipping her toe into a fountain built into the terrazzo floor. It's such a sublimely tacky swan maiden, I wonder if the artist intended it as a sly parody. Anyway, it's hard to believe the Scandinavian theme isn't more than just coincidence.

I'm going to have a tough time lurking around this hotel lobby without being seen, especially given that I don't know who or what to look for. I walk up to the reception desk where a well-groomed but mauve-haired kid wearing a small, gold nose ring is typing on a keyboard. He looks up at my chest and then higher up into my face. "Wow," he says.

"Yeah, I get that a lot. Got any newspapers?"

He reaches somewhere under the counter and holds out a *USA Today*. "Got any *real* newspapers?"

He gives me nothing more than a smile and a shake of the head.

So, I plant myself in a snazzy-looking La-Z-Boy on the far side of the lobby, hoping to check out who is coming and going. I'm wearing chinos and the kind of touristy looking brown-and-beige long-sleeve shirt that serves as camouflage in these parts. My hair is growing peppery around the edges, a feature I hope helps me blend in with this crowd of middle-aged, middle-class, middle-brow Americans taking a mid-priced vacation midway up the Gulf Coast of Florida.

Aside from a couple of bar charts, I don't find much worth reading in this rag. I was hoping to get the local paper to see if they had another article about the wreck on the bridge. Last I heard, they'd only found one body, a guy named Charles Morin.

Putting aside my frustration, I adopt the frozen troll posture that dams teach their babes. Over the top of the paper, I watch people enter and exit. A kid aged four or five is hugging her father's leg as he stands in a line at the desk. She points over to me, tugging on his shirt, and says, "Is that real, Daddy?"

I guess this whole "blending in" thing isn't quite cutting it. Her dad, tired and sunburned in a floppy hat, glances over with disinterest and then does a double take. I shift my gaze toward him. "Jees-susss," he whispers as he realizes I am, in fact, real. He tells his daughter to stop pointing.

It is precisely then that someone at the lobby doors says, "Oh, *there* he is, exactly on time as usual." A slender business-type woman wearing a Calvin Klein print walks over to me in her quarter-inch heels. She's accompanied by a sandy-haired guy wearing a polo shirt, grayish slacks and a navy blazer.

"Oh, Klaus," she says. "It's so wonderful to see you again." She kisses my cheek before I'm able to stand. "Edmund, this is who I've been telling you about."

"Great to meet you, my friend," he says, extending his hand. I shake it automatically, my hand enveloping his like a shark swallowing a mackerel. "Hildy speaks highly of you."

It takes me a beat to respond, my mouth an oval. It isn't that I don't recognize her. I know damn well it's Olaf's girlfriend, the one who should be snail food at the bottom of the bay, the one I've been half-expecting to turn up again. Or, at least, I *think* it's her.

She seems older now, with darker hair and a few more lines around the eyes. And, even more weirdly, she looks totally Anglo. *Is* she really the same person? How could a human change the shape of her eyes? Regardless, I squelch my shock and try to play along.

"She'd have to, wouldn't she?" I laugh, holding my hand horizontally and palm down over the top of my head. Standing at seven feet, four inches in my socks, I learned long ago to make tall jokes a part of my repertoire. Self-deprecation is the best tactic for a troll determined to pass as human.

The restaurant serves a fusion of Norwegian, Danish and Swedish food.

"It is owned and operated by my dear friend," Hildy tells us. "He is a graduate from the magnifique Le Cordon Bleu of Paris."

She orders for us. I'm hard put not to roll my eyes at the pretentiousness of it all.

When the food rolls out, it's mostly fish, reminding me of my Icelandic days. This does little to raise my mood. Sensing her mistake, Hildy quickly orders me the most massive, indecently succulent pork chop I've ever seen in this country. For a moment, I'm able to put aside the menacing nature of the dinner invitation and the mystery of Hildy herself.

"Compliments to the chef," I say when there's nothing left but a gray, porous bone. I nearly ask for another. In truth, now that I've begun, I could eat a platter stacked with them.

"You should tell Andre yourself," she responds, waving over a skinny black man dressed in a white chef's coat. Just as I'm ready to commend the man, I recognize him.

"You!" I say.

Andre grins. He looks less grizzled than he did the other night, but it's definitely the Haitian guy who duped me on the seawall.

"Bonjour, monsieur. We are so happy you could be with us this evening."

I'm aching to stand up and snatch the smirk off his face, demanding to know what the hell is going on. Who are you people? But I don't. It would not be the cunning thing to do.

He gives us a little wave and disappears into the kitchen through a swinging door.

"So, Hildy was telling me how you're a senior guy in the Florida DOT," says Edmund, now on his third glass of a vino he ordered with a French accent off the wine list. I have a Danish brew that is a little sweet, though nothing like the cloying mead of the Old Country.

Having been aggravated by the sight of the cook, I have a barely restrained yearning to snatch up Edmund by the neck and squeeze. Killing Olaf at the tollgate woke something in me that needs tamping down. It's an ancient lesson that trolls and Norsemen alike once knew well: carnage is addictive. So, I raise my glass mug with a slightly trembling hand and take a long, slow draw.

"Yeah, I guess you could put it that way," I say to oblivious Edmund.

"Cool. Listen, Hildy's consulting with us about a government project. It'd be great to get the perspective of somebody who knows his way around the DOT from the inside. We've also got to deal with the Corp of Engineers. Hildy says you know a few things about that, too, given all the boondocks you folks have paved over in this state."

I glance at Hildy, who raises her eyebrows in an amused way as she sips her spring water.

"What kinds of issues are you having?" I ask, still with no clue what he's talking about.

"This," he said, touching Hildy's glass with a spoon, making it ring. "Water, the bane of this whole half-sunk hunk of swampland we call Florida."

Hildy keeps the libations flowing, pouring more wine into Edmund's glass and beer into mine. It turns out Hildy is some kind of environmental consultant advising him on a land deal. The more Edmund drinks, the more excited he gets. I watch as all the polish washes away from his prep-school manners, allowing a darker, frat-boy side to emerge.

"Shit, Klaus, between the feds and the state, you can't take a piss in this state without some regulator wanting to hold it for you. Know what I mean? Wetlands, springs, aquifers, shorelines, etcetera, etcetera, etcetera."

Hildy assures him I do, having lived in the state longer than most. This stokes his fires.

"See, that's what I mean! If we had all this wetland red-tape back when this state was first being developed, most of it'd still be underwater with the sharks and sea cows."

I wonder how much Hildy knows about my lair and how much she would share with a dimwit like Edmund. There's more than pricey perfume wafting from her. There's a subtle humming of something. A bit of the Old World magic, I'd say. *Seidr*, or maybe *galdr*. Whichever it is, it makes me simultaneously anxious and strangely nostalgic. It suddenly occurs to me she might be a *spaewife*. The idea makes me shiver. The last time I encountered one of those creepy *vala* soothsayers, things did not go well.

"I sure as hell miss Charlie tonight," Edmund says. "I wish that arrogant sonovabitch would walk through the doors right now."

Hildy sympathetically squeezes Edmund's hand.

"Charlie was Edmund's partner," she tells me. "He died a few nights ago in a car accident."

"Sleeping with the fucking fishes," Edmund erupts. "The goddamned fishes!"

As other diners turn to look at boorish Edmund, Hildy rubs his hand. I suspect he's hamming up the grief to get more attention from her.

"That guy, he was seriously connected, knew everybody worth knowing. The pols, the bean counters, the paper pushers, the muckety-fucking-mucks. I don't know if I can make a deal like this work without him, Hildy."

"Don't worry, dear," says Hildy, winking at me. "We'll figure it out together."

Edmund is eager to do a little barhopping along the beach. He treats Hildy like a prom date, entwining his right hand in hers, the gold band on his left hand occasionally glinting under the streetlights. I loom behind like a reluctant, neglected principal chaperoning a couple of middle school kids. It irks me.

We're in front of a local bar with a neon Schlitz sign in the window. Several motorcycles as well as run-down beach bicycles are parked out front. A hunk of cardboard on the entrance states, "No shirt, no top, no problem."

"According to his calendar, Charlie was supposed to talk to some guy here tonight," says Edmund, looking wary. I guess it's not the kind of place he was expecting.

"Looks interesting," Hildy says. She grabs the door and waves us in. A nimbus forms around her head where a light is reflected in the glass, and the mischievous grin I'd seen at the tollgate flashes.

The place is a dump. Beneath the stench of bleach is the reek of vomit and stale beer. Except for a couple of shadowy booths in the back, there are no tables. Just a rectangular bar taking up most of the space and a couple of lopsided pool tables squeezed over in a tight area to our right. A blonde woman wearing cut-off shorts, a muscle shirt and a puka shell necklace tends bar.

There are two open stools. Edmund and Hildy take them. I stand at the bar on Hildy's left. With a sidelong look, I scan her neck and arms for any markings suggesting she's a spaewife. Nothing, but who knows what's beneath that sheath dress?

The bartender, who I've mentally tagged Blondie, takes a quick look at me and then focuses on Hildy and Edmund. I get the feeling she's used to big uglies like me but doesn't see too many upscalers like Hildy. Blondie sniffs, rubs her nose on the bar towel, and asks what she can get us.

Hildy ignores her, looking around at the patrons, mostly men. Their heads all swivel toward her, as if they were compass needles pointing north.

"How about a mojito?" asks Edmund.

Blondie makes a sucking sound. "Outta lime juice. And limes. How about rum straight up?"

Edmund nods reluctantly.

"Schlitz draft," I say.

"Same," says Hildy.

When he has his rum, Edmund mutters something into his glass about a Florida bar without limes. He's got a good buzz on already but finishes his rum before asking Blondie in a quiet voice if someone by the name of Lucky is around.

Blondie has no patience with discretion. She yells to some guys in one of the booths, "Hey, one of you guys called Lucky?"

"Who wants to know?" someone shouts.

Blondie doesn't bother answering. Just points an elbow at Edmund while washing a mug.

The back of the booth is facing toward us, so we can barely glimpse who's sitting there. I admire its ill-lit seclusion as a good lurking spot. A couple of guys slide out to make way for somebody on the inside, presumably Lucky.

My eyes are drawn to his neck tattoo, which looks like a stylized F. A rune? Wish I could see the whole thing. It looks familiar, but then I've seen thousands of tattoos over a long lifetime. Lucky's in his mid-twenties, I'd guess. Medium height, spiky black hair. Trim build under a black t-shirt. He's annoyingly handsome with an oval face and aquiline nose. I instantly dislike him, though I can't say why.

He stands next to Edmund and sets down his open bottle of malt liquor.

"So," he says, still staring straight ahead, "something I can do you for?"

Edmund turns to Lucky, expecting the man to meet his gaze and press some flesh. Lucky doesn't move. Edmund makes a motion to get off the stool, then stops, still uncertain of proper etiquette in this strange land. It's not Edmund's idea of a business meeting.

"My partner Charlie was supposed to talk some business with you," Edmund finally says into the air in front of him, following Lucky's lead.

"I don't know a Charlie."

"Lam set it up. You know Lam?"

"Yeah, well, I just might know a Lam," he says, finally turning toward us. He gives me and, especially, Hildy the once over before pointing his chin toward the pool tables to my left.

"Let's step into my office," Lucky says. Hildy stands to join them but Lucky shakes his head. "Just us, girlie. You know how it is. Men's business and all."

Over in the empty corner near one of the tables, Lucky and Edmund start talking in low tones.

Hildy's eyes narrow. She drums the fingers of her right hand on the bar. I've no idea why their conversation should annoy and worry her. I start to ask her what the deal was with her bizarro dinner invitation.

"Shush," she says. "We can talk later. Listen to what they're saying."

Her words hit me hard, confirming that she knows what I am. No human would be able to hear two guys speaking in low tones eight yards away amid the clinking and clanking of bar noise and the bray of rock-and-roll pulsing through crappy speakers. But I can, of course. It's an irony of a troll's life that, even as humans snicker from a distance at my thick-lobed and ample ears, I can easily make out their whispered aspersions.

In the case of Edmund and Lucky, I was expecting little more than a minor drug deal. Lucky has that look. And I detect a sharp, sweet tanginess clinging to his clothes, an odor mingled with burnt carbon and sulfur.

But they're talking about land instead. Some crappy wetlands to the north. Lucky knows a desperate guy looking to sell, and Edmund says he needs another property for paperwork that's already in process. Hard to imagine why Hildy cares about such a dull conversation. Edmund ask about legal and technical stuff: acreages, ownership rights and something called wetland reclamation. Lucky says all that bullshit would be worked out later. Sounds like he's losing patience with Edmund's superior attitude.

Then I realize a tall, dirty-blond guy in a Black Sabbath t-shirt has slipped onto Edmund's stool.

"Y'all from around here?" he asks Hildy in a good-natured way.

"Near Orlando," she says.

"No shit," Black Sabbath responds. "I got an ex down that way."

Hildy giggles loudly, flirting with this guy in a weirdly distracting way. Edmund looks over. Lucky laughs and says it looks like he's got some competition. I suspect Edmund would prefer to ignore Hildy and finish his business dealings, but Lucky's goading him on. I can already see which way this is going. Some things about humans never change, no matter what century you're living in.

"You married to this pretty lady?" Sabbath asks as Edmund strides up.

"You're on my stool," says Edmund. "I was just having a quick chat."

"Y'all together?" Sabbath asks.

Hildy arches her eyebrows in amusement, looking at Edmund.

"Naahhhh, y'all ain't together!" Sabbath tells them, slapping the bar like a happy man.

"Tonight we are," Edmund says, stepping around and putting his hands on Hildy's shoulders. Black Sabbath stands up. He has a good two inches and forty pounds on Edmund. This would be your classic white-collar, weekend-warrior type against your blue-collar, weekend-partier type. I suspect that Blondie bartender has used her bleach bucket to squeegee up the remains of previous weekend-warriors before.

I sigh, thinking I'll never get answers at this rate. So, I wobble a bit, trying to look drunker than I am. I slip between Edmund and Sabbath and slide onto the vacated stool. Sitting with my back to the bar, I put my right leg up to the wall like it was a tollgate between the two men.

"Thanks, fella," I say to Edmund. "I could use a sit down."

Sabbath, looking less like a good-natured country boy by the second, says, "I don't see a ring on the little lady's finger, and she was looking my way like she just might be hankering for a genuine good time tonight. Am I right?"

"Look, dude," says Edmund. "We're just about to leave. I just need to…"

"You're not willing to defend my tarnished honor?" Hildy asks. "I thought I was with you tonight?"

"Yeah, bro!" Black Sabbath scoffs, loudly enough for the whole place to hear. "Defend the lady's honor."

"Screw you," Edmund says.

"Listen, Haircut. The only thing standing between you and a good ass-kicking is this drunken fat man," he says.

"If I got to break your knee, Jumbo, I will, sure as shit," he tells me, trying to shove my leg down with no success.

I put up my hands in a surrendering motion, but don't move my leg. That just confuses him. When Sabbath decides it'd be easier just to duck under my leg, I put my other leg down at a diagonal angle, blocking his way. This really pisses him off, enough so that he kicks at my leg, which might as well be stone. I give him my best goofy grin.

This is better. This is control, a squelching of the monster, replaced by the clown.

Spectators laugh. Sabbath has gone red in the face. Cussing a streak, he decides to go the other way around. The whole bar watches him circumnavigate the rectangle so he can get at Edmund.

Meanwhile, Edmund is frozen, stuck in an indecisive stupor. He's too drunk to retreat but not drunk enough to rush into a *mano a mano* with Sabbath. He looks to Lucky for guidance, but Lucky's leaning against the pine-board wall, enjoying the show.

"He's just a little wasted," I tell Edmund casually. "I'll calm him down."

"You sure, Klaus?" Edmund says, suddenly seeing a way out but not wanting to be viewed as a coward.

"Hey, I'm a government worker. I deal with hostile people all day long," I say. "Besides that, we don't want Hildy hurt in some brawl, do we?" Hildy grins, keeping her eyes on the fast-approaching Sabbath.

Lucky waves bye-bye as if Edmund were a child. Their conversation is over, just as, I suspect, Hildy planned it. I'm guessing she wanted to know who Edmund was meeting but didn't want any deal to actually get made.

"Let's go," Edmund tells her. This time Hildy relents, allowing him to guide her toward the exit. "Thanks, Klaus, I owe you one," he says, ducking out the door.

I stand here with an arm and leg spread toward the wall to keep Black Sabbath from chasing after them.

"Look, man," I say. "That guy has a heart condition. You don't want a murder on your hands, do you?"

He stares up at me with fierce blue eyes, the kind that make me think he was born into the wrong century.

"Bullshit!" he yells.

"True," I assure him. "He's got the heart of a chicken."

He gives me a bitter guffaw. For a second I think we might be friends, but he's suffered too much public humiliation. And there's something else, something about the way Hildy had been looking at him, something about that mojo I felt beaming off her at *Snorri's*.

Sabbath pulls a jackknife out of his back pocket, unfolds it and holds it over my arm.

"I don't want to hurt you, Jumbo," he growls, "but you'd better move. Now!"

"Fred, stop it," says Blondie the bartender.

One of his buddies in a biker jacket is coming up behind him, trying to talk him down. Fred, however, is committed. He feints at my arm. I don't budge. He jams the knife as hard and deep as he can into my meaty forearm. It hurts like a mother, a good hurt that makes me yearn for my younger days.

The bar goes quiet, and Fred goes still, just watching as the knife sticks in my unmoving arm, as if he can barely believe he put it there.

I reach over with my other hand and pull it out. Then I lick the blade.

"Iron rich," I tell Fred, snapping the blade off the handle with my thumb. "You should get one with better steel next time. We done here?"

Blondie has a phone in her hand, trying to figure out whether to call the cops. Some other guys, calling her Misty, are urging her not to. I shake my head.

"Just take care of Fred here," I tell her.

The spell has been broken. Fred sits down on a stool, looking at the broken blade on the dirty, checkered linoleum floor.

"Sorry, man," he whispers.

"No problem," I say, sucking at the wound in my arm. I smile at them, blood in my teeth. "It was fun."

Turns out Hildy made Edmund wait for me down the block. We walk back to *Snorri's* and Edmund gives me a ride across the Bayway in his Porsche. I squeeze into the back like a pickled herring as he and Hildy sit with their seats scooted up as far as possible. While going through the toll gate, Edmund asks me how much longer it will be before they completely automate the toll system as they've done in south Florida. I grunt something noncommittal but Hildy chimes in, "I hear it's coming soon."

They drop me at the twenty-four hour Albertsons when I tell them I want to pick up a few things before going home.

"Hey, thanks for your help back there," says Edmund, opening the back door for me. "That could have gotten messy."

I wrapped a couple of bar towels around my forearm and rolled my sleeve down over the wound, so Edmund figures I just talked my way out of the bar. Which, by my standards, I had.

"I like people who can keep their heads cool in heated situations," he confides. "I hope you agree to join Hildy's team so we can work together on this land deal."

From the driver's side, Hildy blows me a kiss as if we were old friends.

Chapter Seven

"Maybe you are different from others. Or maybe it's just a way to survive."
—Thale

King Alfr was from a long line in an ancient clan, the Völsungs, going back centuries. Literacy was rare back then and written records rarer yet. Nothing but the runes on my neck indicated I was linked with the clan. Some said I was an evil omen that should be sacrificed to the gods.

Alfr might have killed me if an elderly skald hadn't reminded townfolk of one of their oldest songs, one telling of a legendary Völsung chieftain who, while lost in the forest, stumbled on a beautiful woman singing by a stream.

As the song had it, the chieftain would not release the woman however much she pleaded. He brought her home, intent on wedding her. Whole stanzas described his love and lust and how he slowly wooed her. Then, on their wedding day, the women of the clan insisted on dressing her for her nuptials and discovered she had a cow-like tail.

"Huldrefolk!" the people cried. Forest spirit, she-troll, dark elf, Lady of the Forest, enchantress. They gave her many names and begged their chieftain to cast her out. He refused and maintained he would marry after making many sacrifices to Odin. If the legends spoke true, her tail would fall off, and she would bear him many strong children.

After the wedding, according to the song, the tail remained, but the chieftain, refusing to lose her, sliced it off with his seax. In the end, she bore him strong, intelligent children deft at wielding magic.

Then one day soon after bearing another son, the huldre mother disappeared with the newborn into the wilderness. Though her husband and sons searched long for her, she was never found. According to the song, she still plays with her infant son under the moon amid the happy huldrefolk, who honor them on an island lost amid mist-filled seas.

"We do not know the truth of things," said Alfr to his people. "But do we dare slay such a branded beast, one the Norns have brought back to us in ways none could have foretold?"

In the end, they spared me, though the angry whisperings continued among those whose close kin we trolls had slain. I was put on a chain like a bear and kept in a darkened pit as my wounds healed.

I gave my name as Hallr, so Alfr decreed me Hallr Halftroll. I didn't want to accept the "halftroll" designation as anything other than a fiction. A full-blooded troll is what I yearned to be. Perhaps, I thought, the runes were just another cunning trick by Mor to preserve her undersized trollson if ever captured by the sneaking, superstitious humans.

There were many times when I wished the ruse hadn't worked. Not long after my capture, they decided to chain me down during the dawn to test my "humanity." I will not forget how that blazing bitch rose over the crooked horizon like a jackal come upon helpless prey. The humans watched, many of them laughing, as I lost my silent honor to Sól, her rays mercilessly streaking over my graying skin like a barbed whip. At first, I roared, then screamed like a tortured child, and then whimpered. By the time the king had me unchained and thrown back in the pit, Sól had burned away my consciousness.

Days later, Alfr arrived at the edge of my prison.

"You survived, Halftroll."

"Trolls are known for surviving," I said, and then in a mocking tone, added, "my lord."

He smiled grimly. "The clan values courage, Halftroll, but not foolish pride. Do not offend the one who stems the killing mob."

I greeted this with silence.

"It might have been better if you'd turned to stone like other trolls. We could have wheeled your visage through the towns of the realm in triumph and then raised it on a pole as a warning to all your kin," he sighed. "Now we are linked, you and I. You must use the mind you clearly have. Consider your future, the one your mor wished you to have at the last. Do not dishonor her."

I growled and strained at my chains, wanting to squeeze off the impudent king's head. He watched with interest, which only antagonized me more. Finally, exhausted, I stopped and sat down on the floor of the pit, my chains falling all around me like an iron nest.

"Whatever else you are, you are different," he observed. "Sea-gray eyes, raised forehead, copperish hair. Your nose may be large, but looks little like the sausage snouts of the mountain trolls who fought with you. And you have a squarish chin, a troll feature I've not seen before. Were you aware of these things?"

"Mirrors are scarce in troll lairs," I replied.

"But even troll lands have pools of water, waters into which you've no doubt peered, wondering what you are, *who* you are."

Alfr was a canny bastard, more like Mor than I cared to admit.

"I will spare you, Hallr Halftroll, if you will pledge your loyalty to the clan that is your birthright and to me as your liege. You will not run away into the wilderness, and you will fight with strength and courage so the valkyries honor you."

I stood up in the chains.

"I will pledge if you come down to hear it," I said.

Alfr glared, considering. Even in chains, I might kill him if he complied. If he did not, I would mark him as a coward and swear to murder him one day.

He jumped into the pit. Would Mor have punished him for his foolishness or rewarded him for his courage? It didn't matter. The decision was mine.

I stood still, trying to draw him in. At the furthest extent of the chains, I might have just reached him if he'd come a bit closer. When I failed to lure him in, I sprang at him nonetheless, hoping to at least startle and humiliate him. He didn't budge.

"You said you would pledge," the king finally said.

"And you'd believe the word of a troll?"

"Yes."

In the end, I did. Mor had cast me out, abandoned me to these people and convinced them I was part of their clan. Perhaps I was. If I stayed, I might discover the secret to my identity. Besides, there was nowhere else to go.

I knelt before him, saying, "I pledge my loyalty to you King Alfr Völsung and to the people you lead. I will fight your battles, all except those against the trolls."

"If trolls attack, you will fight them," he answered with steel.

"Yes," I promised. Even among trolls, this was the way of things. "I will." But I would not march or conspire against them. This I didn't bother to emphasize. I had pushed my luck as it was.

"Rise, Hallr Halftroll. Only your honor will chain you now."

This was either the stupidest or the noblest thing I'd ever heard. Probably both.

And so my pit, which I could have easily escaped now the chains were gone, was transformed from a prison to a training ground. Although the king would check on my progress, it was his cousin Dofri who became my surly weapons master. Among men, he was large enough, taller than I was at the time, though also lighter. It was plain he would have liked to kill me, which he could easily have done in the course of our instruction, claiming an honest training mishap. He was not afraid to batter and even slice me. Yet, he was loyal to his king, even when they disagreed.

Although he was not one for deep strategy, Dofri was a first-class wielder of weaponry and a fine tactician. In contrast, my martial-arts training as a troll had been sporadic and dependent on Mor's shifting moods. Of course, like any troll children, my siblings and I had played with weapons, laughing as we bruised and cut one another. Sometimes Mor would jump in, teaching me hard lessons when I grew overconfident against my younger siblings.

But weapons training for humans was a different matter. Fragile and weak by nature, they relied on skill more than strength, on intellect more than instinct.

So it was that I learned to fight as a man fights, with care and cunning, forging new reflexes from long practice. I began to enjoy it, all except for the sword training. That was hardest for me to learn, to Dofri's delight.

There are tales of trolls fighting with long blades, but I had never seen a troll bear one in battle. Jabbing and slicing are less natural to us than smashing and crushing. Dofri taught me the many nuances of swordplay, from deceitful feints to life-saving parries and counter-parries. These skills were uncommon even among humans. If men used a sword at all, it was for little more than hacking away at the wooden shields of their opponents. Dofri taught me the foibles of blades and how to snap and shatter them. There were rules that, if not followed, could lead to death, even for a thick-skinned troll.

I kept trying to use my superior power against Dofri, but he could dance away and make me pay in blood. The only time he grew truly angry was when I shattered a sword, pushing it beyond its limits.

"Swords are expensive, troll! Only the wealthiest warriors can afford them. I do not ken why the king wishes you to learn this art when a club would suit you better. But wish it he does. And if your sword shatters in battle and you die," he growled, "you make your teacher look incompetent. I do not want my reputation tarnished by one such as you."

"I am glad, at least," I said, "that my master will find some reason to mourn my demise."

Dofri scoffed, "Ah, the beast learns wit. Now learn the sword, you damnable hulk."

Chapter Eight

"To Frey he gave the boar; stating that it would run through air and overseas, by night or by day, faster than any horse."
—*The Younger Edda*

After my night out with Hildy and Edmund, I track down Chen to ask if the Bayway tolls are really going to be automated.

"You mean like the turnpike down south?"

The Florida Turnpike in the Miami-Dade area has gone to an "all-electronic" tolling system with no booths, no tollkeepers, no gates, no cash and coins. People are automatically billed for the toll based on cameras that spot their license plates on the pike.

"Where you hear that?" asks Chen.

"Just check into it, Jo," I say. "When they went to the transponders and passes, we were the last ones to know, even though the axe fell on our necks. This would be worse."

"Maybe not so bad if you keep your head," says Chen. "Sit in air-conditioned cubicle, click on computer, drink coffee, go piss when you want."

"No more people not understanding your demented, pidgin directions," I add.

"Or shitting their selves when they see you are so big and ugly," laughs Chen.

"Yeah, good times. Night, Jo."

"Morning, Klaus."

I lie in my lair thinking of tolls. Mor jealously guarded her mountain pass, as if it were the embodiment of her honor. She needed no gate, standing solitary on the high trail like a tall runestone in the shadows—immensely strong but not at all hideous, even to human eyes. Mor had become stouter over the years, I'm sure, but there was still something lithe in her limbs. I remember her as erect, not hunched, in a gray linen kirtle and smock, holding an uncarved wooden staff made smooth over time through her touch.

She was the perfect tollkeeper, daunting but not terrifying, resolute but also fair. If travelers had no copper or silver, she'd accept barter for the toll. We received livestock and tools and sometimes even vegetables if the pilgrims were poor.

She seemed to have a second sight about what wanderers held, or could bear for their toll.

As much as a troll could be, she was respected by the humans in nearby towns. They traveled our pass with confidence, or at least a minimum of trepidation. Small children occasionally wept and howled at the sight of her, but most were cautiously fascinated, sensing her interest in them. If they were brave enough to approach her, she sometimes gifted them with chipped flints or rough-cut toys.

I know she would disdain my modern life as a tollkeeper, a cog in a state machine rather than a ruler of the roadways. "Exact change!" I roar at the motorists who throw the wrong coins into metallic baskets and expect me to open the gates. Exact fucking change. No live chickens or jeweled knife hilts or freshly baked bread. Only coins or dirty bills or, even worse, much worse, the sterile invisible blips of ones and zeros coursing through scanners and cameras and magnetic strips.

The humans and their machines. Together they dissolve not only the toll but the tollkeeper, ridding the world of its frictions, including its ancient relationships. More and more, the connecting nodes are solely in their thin cables of glass and light, in landscapes from which they've banished not only my kind but their own.

This is a cause for irony and black mirth, I suppose, as humans become endangered in a world where machines take the tolls, making no deals, offering no judgements except "yes" and "no." Humans are now the fleshy, dull beasts online, so stifled and outraged and outcast that they scream and rage in their wilderness of words. Internet trolls.

Another irony: I am a model citizen online. No threatening spear shakes, no heads taken, no scathing oaths. I am an older troll now, grown cautious, my edges worn. The mortals have yet to master such lessons. They're still just learning to build their own dark tunnels, to evade the Internet hunters and despoilers they themselves created, to escape from the burning sun of their own omniscient systems.

I suddenly feel trapped, as only a nearly extinct and entirely alone animal can. I will not survive their cubicles, their office politics, their HR demons, their clock-ins and fingerprint scanners and e-mails, their massive, black parking lots of stalled cars going nowhere, as frozen as headstones. It would be better to die in battle than live as a drone. Oh, sweet Aurgelmir, you lucky, dead bastard. If only one-eyed Odin would end me as well.

Restless and despondent, I take a stroll after sunset along the local seawalls. The tide has just turned, and the mud flats reek of decay.

Up ahead of me, also staring into the water, is a motorcyclist in black, a skinny little guy dwarfed by a huge bike with its front tire parked on the seawall. As I approach, he removes his helmet, and there he is again, his dark, grizzled face looking all too amused.

"Bonjour, monsieur. You look so sad this evening, like a woman with ennui."

"Careful, Cook," I warn.

He puts his hands together in a melodramatic fashion, leaning his cheek on them, and reciting in a mock female voice: "Like a sailor in distress, she kept casting desperate glances over the solitary waste of her life, seeking some white sail in the distant mists of the horizon. She had no idea by what wind it would reach her, toward what shore it would bear her, or what kind of craft it would be—tiny boat or towering vessel, laden with heartbreaks or filled to the gunwales with rapture."

I grab him by the scruff of his leather jacket, holding him over the seawall.

"You were annoying enough without English. Now that you speak it, you're pretty much intolerable. I'm not in the mood tonight."

He grabs at my arm to keep himself from choking. "You injure me, monsieur. Whose heart is not lightened by *Madame Bovary*? Besides which, I come with glad tidings and a gift."

"Yeah, your chum Hildy already gave me some glad fucking tidings the other night. You know how hard it is to find a decent tollman's job these days, Cook?"

"You could learn the art of the cuisine," he says.

I pull him close to my face. "I prefer to be the eater."

Despite his nonchalant manner, I feel him trembling. "Please, monsieur, I am an old man and grow weak with the hanging."

I put him back down, giving him a chance to catch his breath.

"I would be happy to cook for you again. You love boar, yes?"

"I'll give you that, you nutty little bastard. You do know how to sling swine."

He steps back and throws his arm out like Vanna White, displaying the motorcycle to me.

"Then how about a hog, made just for you?"

We must be quite a sight, a veritable circus act on a Harley-Davidson Electra Glide Ultra Classic. Andre is the midget sitting in front, and I am the comically helpless and helmetless giant in back, complete with relax-fit jeans and green suspenders. I'm astonished the bike's tires hold air.

He demonstrates the hog's operation in the empty parking lot of a closed SweetBay: the clutch, the foot lever, the accelerator, the brakes.

"Six-speed cruise drive," he shouts up at me.

"Whatever, little man. Let me drive."

So he does, once again sporting that infuriatingly amused grin. I stall the beast, then lay it down, ripping my jeans, rashing up my arms. I jerk it, pop it, and stall it again. Hate to say it but I like it.

"They make anything bigger?" I ask.

"That's the heaviest they have, monsieur. A cruiser. Even Freyr would ride it in pride."

Freyr was one of the few Norse gods I could stomach in the old days, the one who gave up his magic sword to marry the shining, sublime giantess Gerðr.

"What would the likes of you know about Freyr, Cook?" I ask.

"He was a romantic, no?" he asks, looking at me with sudden somberness. "Yes, yes, a passionate, stubborn one." Then he smiles again. "Oh, how he loved his boar!"

I drive it now, the machine humming between my legs like a living thing. Andre chirps away at me from behind, something about "leaning." He sounds more alarmed than amused now. He says Hildy wants to see me. I tell him to fuck off, that I have to go to work. He tells me he's already called me in sick.

I keep moving down the highway till I'm near the tollgate. I know it might be slippery, having seen bikes slide because of the sheen of oil that collects next to the booth. Even though I think I'm prepared, I slide nonetheless, turning it sideways, finally stopping inches from the gate.

Andre chitters more loudly than ever, sounding like an angry squirrel. I roll the bike back to the booth, waving in apology to a dumbstruck Miriam.

"Sorry, old girl. Still getting used to it."

"Klaus?" she asks. "Thought you were sick. I never heard of you being sick before."

"Yeah, well, not so much sick as a little roughed up," I say, showing her my hands and arms. "Actually, it's more of a family emergency. Long story. Right, Uncle Andy?"

Andre nods to Miriam even as he curses me in French.

"I hope everything works out okay, honey," a look of concern tempered by skepticism on her face. God knows what she'll tell Chen.

Once we're past the gate, Andre starts pointing at the handlebars, trying to tell me something again. I finally realize that there's a transponder holder there. Turns out that I could have zipped right through the SunPass gate, no questions asked. I hold that thought a while.

At the top of the second drawbridge, I stop the bike. Andre quickly pulls off his helmet, looking alarmed.

"What's the matter?"

This time, there is barely a hint of an accent. I wonder where he's really from, but I'm dead certain he knows where *I'm* from. I'm being played, and I've been played enough for one lifetime.

"You know," I said, "there's a draugr around here that gives advice. You should look him up. Know what he told me? To beware strangers bearing gifts. You, Cook, keep giving me stuff, and I think you're pretty fucking strange."

I pick him up by the leather jacket and hang him over the side of the bridge. Then I yank off his riding boots, tossing them into the bay. "So, old fella, this time it's you who are going swimming, turnaround being fair play and all that."

"I beg of you, monsieur. S'il vous plaît."

"Right. You're welcome, Cook."

"You know," he says, as I let him fall the twenty feet or so into the bay. "Even for a troll, you're a genuine asshole."

Interesting. No Haitian accent at all that time.

I figure that Hildy—who is clearly pulling Andre's strings—will be at *Snorri's*, where I have no intention of going. Now that I've seen their little cast of characters, I'm less afraid than before. Slaying or exposing me doesn't seem their main intent. So whatever they want from me, they'll have to live without it. Fuck her and Edmund and her cook, too. Fuck 'em all.

I cruise up and down the back streets where the locals live. Most of it is way too quaint and gentrified, but some is still quietly shabby: torn screens on porches, beer bottles in sand lots, rickety stairs ascending to garage apartments. I drive by the bar where I got knifed, and this time I notice that the name is *Grimm's*. It reminds me of a sailor I used to know in the Old Country.

Why not? Kind of enjoyed my last visit.

I park the bike next to a couple of others, fumbling with the kick-stand, probably looking less like a Hell's Angel than a fat, clumsy, Scandinavian farmer.

Not many patrons tonight, though it's still early. Misty's working the bar again. Somehow she's not surprised to see me.

"How's the arm?" she asks.

"Not bad," I tell her. "Fast healer."

She serves me up a Schlitz draft, saying it's on the house. Then she points to the back booth with her thumb, a signal I can't interpret. There are three biker types with their backs to me. One's a big guy with long, blondish hair falling over a black jacket with orange insignia. The other has familiar-looking spiky hair. The blond dude turns around and, sure enough, it's my favorite assailant, Fred. He gives me a short nod.

"I think me and him are okay," I tell Misty. She just shrugs like it's none of her business.

The third biker, a woman, turns around too, playing with strands of her henna-dyed hair.

"I'll be damned," I tell Misty. "She sure is changeable."

"Yep," she says. "Consistently good tipper, though. You gotta like that."

"Sure," I say absently, "gotta like that."

Leave. I should leave. Just minutes ago I wanted to steer clear of her, loathe to get mixed up with a spaewife witch. But I came here of my own accord, didn't I? This is *my* life. *My* decision. The Harley has kindled something in me. A sense of new possibilities maybe. And a sudden yearning as well. I've been hidden, silent and, let's face it, lonely for so long. Maybe there are other options.

Meeting my eyes, Hildy waves me over, and I go find out which version of her chameleon self is on tap tonight.

Chapter Nine

"Never give a sword to a man who can't dance."
—Confucius

Alfr's youngest daughter, Inge, was as bold as only the very young and very old can be. The township, then called Risør, was her playground. Because of her father's status, she knew few limits. My life, by comparison, was nearly all limits. I was, in essence, a thrall, though I was both more and less than that designation implies.

By some, I was considered an exotic kind of domesticated animal, and a dangerous one at that. At the behest of a jarl or other influential neighbor, Alfr would lend me out at night to do labor such as fell and lift trees, work plows through rocky soils, dig in the thickest swaths of turf or spread heavy heaps of dung to fertilize fields.

But I was also more than a normal thrall in that Alfr was training me to be a warrior. This was a controversial and potentially dangerous decision. Taking a deadly troll and making it even more deadly—as well as more knowledgeable about the ways of humans—struck many as reckless. Even members of his own clan would whisper that Alfr was a fool for trusting a demon with human weapons. Some said I had cast dark spells on the king and was regularly plotting their ruin with a covey of trolls in the forest at night. In this way, I learned how much wretched rumor and falsehood passes for truth among human beings.

Inge was, in contrast, almost universally seen as a clan treasure, as if she were the spoiled youngest child of every family in the realm. This was, in part, due to her beauty, even in the twilight of her childhood. Dark hair and blue eyes were common in the clan, but her tresses were as glossy as coats of the most well-groomed horses. She was not careful. Her eyes didn't lie, or even hide her thoughts. When she was happy or sad or angry, it was clear to all.

Although she had been warned away many times, she would sneak under the leather flaps of the "troll's pen" in which I was housed and watch me train with Dofri. At first, of course, it must have been a great novelty to watch her father's monster put through its paces in the pit. No other family in the realm had its own troll. But she continued to come as the weeks and months passed, and I realized she was learning the martial arts by proxy.

She took it seriously, or at least as seriously as anything else in her young life. Dofri would tell her to "begone," but she seldom complied unless he threatened to tell her mother, a woman who was impatient with her daughter's wanderings. After a time, Dofri began to make use of her.

He would sigh, having cut, bruised or broken me yet again in our lessons. "What has the clan's troll done wrong this time?" he'd ask her.

"He lost his footwork" or "he raised his shield too high" or "he kept his wrist too stiff," she'd shout down to us. When she was wrong, he would correct her, but usually she was right. In those cases, he would say, "You see, Halftroll, even a child can understand my lessons, and without being so battered about."

At first, it made me furious. I wanted to devour the pretty imp like so much veal, teaching her ilk not to try my patience and dignity. Long would live the legend of the princess-gobbling troll. Yet, even I had to admit she was studiously even-handed in her commentary.

"He got you that time, Cousin Dofri," she'd say when I managed to land a blow. Or even clap when I finally learned a lesson well. Sometimes she tried to console me, explaining that she had leisure to learn the lessons because no blades or axes were aimed at her. "I think the world looks different from down in the pit," she'd say.

Dofri liked that. He mentioned it to comrades, who picked it up. "Things look different from the pit," they'd tell each other in all sorts of circumstances, from warring to whoring to arguing with wives. But I could never say it to Dofri. It would reek like an onion of excuses.

I'd been training nearly a year when the rumors of another war began to spread. Harald Bloodaxe laid claim to Völsung lands in the west. He was intent on winning new fishing grounds, as well as an excellent and growing shipyard. The people of Alfr's kingdom were wroth, not only promising to defend its borders, but to invade Harald's coastal lands in return.

Alfr could not arm me as the jarls were armed, with swords, chainmail and helms. The freemen warriors wouldn't stand for a troll thrall being equipped better than they, no matter who my master was. I was given a two-handed axe, a round shield and a heavy spear.

"If you want a sword," said Dofri, "you'll need to take one in battle. Don't bother with a brittle one. A good axe is better than a bad sword any day. Do not dishonor me, Hallr."

I wasn't worried about the weapons. I preferred the axe, the most natural weapon for me. Nor was I especially afraid of Harald's troops. Dofri had trained me well, and I was proud of my new skills. The worse enemy, by far, was Sól.

We had prepared for Her, garbing me all in black, including a long, finely wrought iron hood made especially for me. The faceplate was a mesh of closely woven wire. When the war was still just a rumor, Dofri made me wear and train in the infernal attire, first in the pit at night, then in the precious minutes of twilight, and finally in bright sunlight. In the pit, the dreaded garb slowed me by fractions of seconds, giving Dofri more chances to punish me than he'd had in many months. The problem was less the clothing than the hood, which reduced my peripheral vision. It was like learning to fight all over again.

Eventually, though, I grew accustomed to the garb and could nearly hold my own against Dofri, especially with axe and spear. When I got to train in twilight, it was a delight.

Fighting after the sun rose, however, was like doing battle in mythic Muspelheim, the land of the fire giants. At first, I suffered fear rooted so deeply that there was no digging it out. Today, I suppose, they'd call it trauma. Even as my will strove to force it down, the surging panic would rise like a growing wave, cresting over me and smashing my resolve. I flashed back to when they had chained me down during sunrise, my skin burning until my very mind seemed incinerated.

Oddly, Dofri was more patient than he'd ever been with me before. He had, no doubt, seen what they called "battle dreads" in other warriors, even ones he knew to be honorable and brave. Or maybe his patience stemmed from the fact that he'd helped chain me in those early days, hoping the sun would kill me and end the clan's troll dilemma. At any rate, he only poked me a bit as I writhed on the ground under Sól's barbed coils.

It took time. King Alfr's tolerance must have been sorely tested. Eventually, though, the dread dissipated, leaving me mostly with a scorching in the eyes. Encouraged by my progress, they tried to help me with their inventions: narrower eye slits, veils of dark cloth, and even beeswax pressed into the mesh of the mask. All had their flaws, as the veils ripped, the slits obscured, the wax caked and melted.

Dofri trained me to obey voice commands. Although I'd never been aboard a ship before, his directional commands were based on seafaring language. "Swing aft," for example, meant I should turn and swing my weapon behind me. "Swing port" was the command to swing to my left, and "swing starboard" the command to swing to the right.

"Why not just use the words right and left?" I asked.

"On a ship, port and starboard are always the same, though right and left will change depending on the way you're facing."

"You plan to make a sailor out of a sun-shunning troll?" I joked.

"We serve as Alfr sees fit," Dofri said seriously.

In the end, it was Inge who helped me most to cope with Sól. Resting between bouts of eye-scalding duels with Dofri, I would sit in deep shade and watch her in the sun-drenched training field. She would lie on her back, her eyes closed, smiling into the sun, or she would dance and twirl, holding chains of flowers up beseechingly to the sky, practicing some rite her mother was teaching her.

I knew she wasn't taunting me. When that girl taunted, she did it flagrantly and with confidence. As I suffered under my tutelage, she would yell, "Dofri tickled your inseams that time, Hallr!" or "You hold the sword like it's a snake going to bite you!"

So, no, she wasn't taunting but, rather, reassuring. She exhibited human adoration for the sun in those northern latitudes, where it would nearly disappear during the long winter season, months in which trolls ranged wide and rejoiced. My affection for Inge deepened then, as she approached the young womanhood of those times. If I could see the sun through her eyes, if I could share, to even the smallest degree, her adulation for that heavenly ball of fire, perhaps I could face it myself; a troll learning at the feet of a pretty, precocious child.

It never became easy. I badly envied the humans, weak as they were, their ability to fight under the sun. I wasn't the same warrior in the light that I was in the darkness, but I grew better, tolerable, perhaps even proficient if I had on the right garb. It would have to do.

In the campaign against Harald Bloodaxe, I was nearly slain in the first minute of the first battle. Harald's most aristocratic warriors—jarls, hersirs and their kin—were eager to claim the head of Alfr's tame troll. Not only would it be a source of honor but, they thought, it would demoralize our people from the start. That second notion was wrong to the point of absurdity. Many of the Völsungs wanted to see me die. In fact, they were wagering on how many minutes I would last. The odds were long that I would survive the whole battle.

Although we all stood in a long shield wall, my fellows placed me on the outside and gave me as wide a berth as they could, as if I were a weak member of the herd soon to be culled. A hulk dressed in black, I was not hard to spot as the troll among men.

For that first battle, Alfr marched us as early as he could, with dawn barely a rumor in the sky. The men in Harald's shield wall still looked groggy.

Vikings didn't have cavalries. Usually, they rode their smallish Fjord horses up to a battle, dismounted, and then attacked. But on that first day, several sons of jarls and hersirs sped their horses toward me in what was clearly a race rather than a coordinated attack.

My fellows in the shield wall paid little attention to the riders. It was the foot soldiers with their spears and long Dane axes who were the real threat. The riders were my problem.

The winner of the race was a lithe young man on a tawny horse. His green tunic was richly embroidered, no doubt the sign of a wealthy family. As he approached, I didn't take a proper stance, trying to look like helpless prey. This made the jarl's son careless. Without dismounting, he veered his horse to the left and swung to the right with his sword, intent on slicing me through the chest.

Dofri would have chastised him for such rashness. It was child's play to plant my spear in his right breast as he reached out. However, his falling body dragged the well-lodged tip of my spear down to the ground, cracking the shaft.

Like many Norsemen of the age, I carried my axe behind my back. When it was twisted artfully in the belt strap, it would hang there horizontally until needed. Now I needed it.

Once I'd killed the lead rider, the next three dismounted at a proper distance so they could stalk their troll quarry. They circled like wolves. One carried a sword, one an axe, one a spear. The spearman looked to be the oldest of the three, sporting a full black beard. He was also boldest, his silvery, razor-tipped spear giving him the advantage of a long reach. As I fended off his jabs with my shield, the swordsman attacked from the right.

Before Dofri's training, I would have simply swung my axe out in an arc to keep the swordsman at bay. Instead, I grabbed my axe near the head, then briskly shot out the end of its long hilt into the face of the onrushing swordsman. He went down hard. As the next jab of the spear came over the top of my shield, I brought down the head of the axe, cutting off that evil tip.

Having smashed through the nose of the swordsman and temporarily disarmed the spearman, I charged the axe-bearer. Although he got his black-and-purple shield up in time, my swing dug the axe head deep into its wood. Remembering another technique from Dofri, I twisted my axe so that the blade split the wood. As it fell into two halves, I wedged the edge of my own shield through the gap, bashing him in the head with its rim.

Just as I was feeling a delicious jolt of victory, my legs were whipped out from beneath me. The spearman had swung the shaft of his tipless spear in a wide arc and expertly knocked me off my feet when I was off balance. Wasting no time, Blackbeard drew his sword and charged, intent on finishing me while I was still on the ground.

The first swing of his sword bit into my shield, which I awkwardly managed to get over my head. Seeing an opening, the man kicked me hard in the head, partly dislodging my black hood and hindering my sight.

I thrust out blindly with my axe, hoping for a lucky strike at his legs. I paid for that folly when Blackbeard sunk the tip of his sword under my armpit.

Feeling helpless and doomed, thinking of what a disappointment I was to Dofri, I curled as much of myself back behind my shield as I could. Expecting Blackbeard to target the femoral artery in my exposed right leg, I once again blindly swung my axe where I expected him to be. Nothing. The arc ended in the dirt. And yet I lived. The killing blow hadn't come.

Tearing off my hood, I saw Blackbeard dueling with one of Alfr's spearmen, a young man I recognized as Dofri's nephew, Leos.

The feeling of doom dissipated, replaced by an emotion I'd seldom felt before: gratitude. No, not just gratitude. Something more like comradeship, the sense that I wasn't as alone as I'd thought. The sense, however fleeting, that I was connected to another.

I skittered from beneath the battling soldiers and regained my feet. The axe wielder who I'd bashed with my shield was just getting up. I circled around the dazed man before sinking my axe into the back of his neck, all but decapitating him. Then, I located Blackbeard again, spun low to the ground and took off his right leg at the knee. Screaming, he went down backwards. Leos sent the tip of his spear up under the man's chin, finishing him.

I nodded curtly to the young redhead who'd just saved my life before reluctantly donning my hood again. The sun rose, and I fought on against other foot soldiers. It was clear that many of them were more farmer than soldier, not up to battling a well-trained troll. But it was exhausting. I remember huffing in the heat, my throat parched, my eyes seared, my mind dazed and wondering if I'd been killed without noticing and gone to Muspelheim. Bloody bodies littered the land.

The battle was over in less than an hour. Harald had tested our strength, found his troops overwhelmed, and then retreated to the local countryside that he knew better than we. Alfr gave us a speech about how this was the first of many battles to come. Bloodaxe was known for waging long campaigns and for slipping away before a conclusive victory could be won against him. The war, said Alfr, would not only be won by strength and courage but by patience and guile.

As he glanced my way at the end of his speech, he bore an expression that reminded me of Mor's, one that bespoke future schemings.

Chapter Ten

"In strife like this I take no delight, sweet though to me are the fights of men."
—*The Valkyrie*

There's no civil cheek-kissing this time. Hildy turns on her stool and looks up at me coolly, like I'm some long-time member of her gang. I almost ask her if she's auditioning for Grease but decide that people who look like Li'l Abner with road rash should hold their tongues.

"Andre?" she asks.

"I had to drop him somewhere."

"You met Lucky the other night," she says. Lucky gives me an amused nod.

"And I'm sure you remember Fred here."

"Good to actually meet you," Black Sabbath says, sliding off his stool to shake my hand. "Sorry I lost my shit. Drunker than I knew, I guess."

"Not a big deal. So, what's up?" I ask Hildy as if she'd summoned me, a possibility I fear might be true.

"We were just winding up a conversation," Hildy says, turning away from me and staring up at the boxy old television hanging by brackets over the bar. The sound is off, but we can see the images of the comet they're calling Loge. That's a reference to Norse mythology, a coincidence I find unsettling.

"Well, you got my number, girlie. Your boy Eddy does, too. Let me know if you want to do a deal," Lucky says. "*Any* kind of deal."

Apparently, he's decided he'll do business with women after all, as long as he can creep them out in the process.

Hildy doesn't respond, never taking her eyes from the television, but I get the sense there's something smoldering deep within. Everyone is silent for a few beats.

"So, what're they saying about the comet today? Still gonna miss us?" Fred asks no one in particular.

"Yeah," said Misty. "But not by much, a fraction of an AU."

"Listen to the bartender acting all erudite," says Lucky. "An AU is what, girlie?"

"Astronomical unit," responds a voice from behind us.

I sensed someone was squirreled away in the corner of the booth but I was too distracted by Hildy's little gang to give it much thought. Now, I look back and see a man's face lit by a dingy, hanging bar lamp advertising Schmidt beer.

Even from a troll's perspective, the guy's hideous. His eyes glitter like polished eight balls, the irises such a dark brown that they merge with his pupils. They stare out from deeply sunken eye sockets. His badly snubbed nose appears as if it were pushing up against a glass, and his mouth looks as if it were stretched to either side of his face with hooks and chains. There are a few strands of gray in his slicked-back black hair, yet it's hard to judge his age. Mid to late thirties?

"Oh, yeah, I forgot to introduce my cuz, the professor," says Lucky. "He's sort of my distributor in these parts."

The man nods slowly, like a snake inclining its head. I'd say the professor is wasted, though maybe not on booze.

"Dr. Jormund," he says. "Charmed to make your acquaintances. An AU is approximately the distance from this planet to the sun. My colleagues in our Astronomy Department assert Loge will pass closely but harmlessly antecedent to Earth's orbit. Their Newtonian calculations dictate thus, though I deduce they have steadfastly refused to entertain certain antinomies of computational reason."

He speaks in a phony mid-Atlantic accent, the kind used by posh American movie stars in the 1930s.

"Which means what?" asks Fred.

Lucky beams. His eyebrows are arched with a hilarity that gives me goosebumps. I remember that look once in the eyes of an arsonist on a winter night a thousand years ago.

"The experts think we're going to be okay," I interpret, "but they aren't admitting the data looks kind of screwy. So the Fates may still fuck us."

Hildy shoots me a look I can't interpret. Scorn, perhaps, but also alarm, as if I'd unintentionally touched a sore spot.

"An event of such promise," says Jormund, waxing into a stoner's lyricism. "When humankind is confronted with the impersonal nature of an apathetic universe. A moment when we may finally rise above our petty selves to become something greater, building final edifices of Will on the slopes of Vesuvius, our primal energies gathered before a cataclysmic event that unleashes *übermensch* humanity at last."

This time Fred just turns to me, as if I've been designated the snake-head's interpreter. There's a lull in the hard rock pouring out of the lousy bar speakers, a moment when we can hear the hum of the naked florescent lights overhead.

I stay silent. This part sounds like stoner nonsense to me, and I think back to a volcano I once saw erupt in Iceland. Lucky puts his spin on Jornund's ramblings.

"He means that when the shit storm hits, the wolves will finally be off the leash. Will to Power, baby. With that, the wolves can get the sheep to do whatever they damn well please, right cuz?"

Lucky rubs the palm of his hand over his spiky head to make the hair stick up straighter, a jet-black rooster's comb. Jormund stares from beneath the dusty bar lamp that eclipses his forehead. He gives a barely noticeable nod.

"Wielding power is never that simple," says Hildy.

"It is in my experience, girlie," says Lucky.

We order more beers and Lucky starts telling stories about him and Fred when they were in high school together.

"Freddy here was my numero uno wingman," says Lucky, trying to catch the eye of Misty, who has been subtly flirting with Fred all evening.

"These days we just see each other around *Grimm's* when Lucky's in town," says Fred. Translation: we definitely aren't pals anymore.

When I first walked in, I figured Hildy and Fred might pick up where they left off. But I'm not getting that vibe at all. For whatever reason, she was just using Sabbath to throw a wrench into Edmund's conversation with Lucky.

Lucky wends back around to the topic of Will to Power, trying to impress us with quotes—or more likely misquotes—from philosophers Nietzsche and Schopenhauer. He tries to bring Jormund into the conversation again but the professor is passed out, face down on a table strewn with crumpled napkins and empty beer glasses.

Hildy's bored and suggests we play a game.

"More of a leadership exercise, really," she says.

"What's the winner get?" asks Lucky with a lascivious leer.

"Don't know," Hildy says. "Bragger's rights. Maybe a job interview at my firm. We've been looking to fill a few special positions."

Lucky loves this idea. Fred and I are lukewarm about it, at best, but decide to give it a whirl. It beats listening to Lucky's string of bullshit.

"It's a three-part challenge," Hildy explains. "Challenge one is to convince Misty to pour you a beer ahead of anyone else."

Given the flirtation between Fred and Misty, I'm pretty sure he's got this particular challenge wrapped up, but I pick up a spoon and gently tap my empty mug to get her attention. Just as she's turning toward me, Lucky pulls out a small gun from under the back of his jacket. He points it directly at Misty and says, "Draw me a quick brew, will you girlie?"

Even I'm stunned, and I've seen a lot of cold-hearted shit in my day. Except for maybe berserkers at their worst, no one would threaten a cup-bearer.

There's a beam of red light, a laser I guess, coming out of the little pistol, targeting Misty's chest. Tears are forming under her eyes. Her hands shake a little as she pours a draft and puts it on the bar in front of Lucky.

"Thanks, girlie," he says, smirking as he tucks the gun behind his jacket again. "You shouldn't have worried none. I never even put one in the chamber."

Before he can get his hand out of his jacket again, I smash the side of his face with my elbow. His head ricochets off the scratched-up dark wood paneling wall before he drops to the floor. I reach down and snatch up the little gun.

I look to see if Fred wants any part of me. He doesn't. Instead, he's embracing Misty, who cries into his chest. He's shushing her and whispering the word "sorry" over and over. I consider calling the cops. Does Misty want that? It's her call to make, but she's a kid. They should at least have bouncers in this dump, though I suppose they only want to pay for security on the weekends.

"Nice game," I tell Hildy. "Truly inspiring."

Impervious to my sarcasm, she shakes her head wearily, as if the whole situation is too stupid to comment on.

Lucky lies on the floor moaning and mumbling about how he's going to kill me. It occurs to me he might have another gun, so I pull up one leg and check it for weapons. Then I do the other. I feel like an idiot but don't want to die at the hands of this little pissant. I even frisk the passed-out Jormund in case Lucky wants to borrow a weapon off him, but the professor's carrying nothing except some white powder.

When Lucky finally staggers up, I push him against the wall.

"You ever hear of the valkyries, asswipe?" I ask. When he refuses to respond, I get my face in close, nose to nose. "Have you?"

He shakes his head just a couple of degrees while staring defiantly into my eyes. For a moment I seriously consider jabbing my fingers through his eye sockets and into his brain. Humans are such feeble things.

"They were serious business in days past, junior. Chooser of the slain. In a battle, they decided who lived and died. They carried spears, rode flying horses through lightning, carried the dead to Valhalla. They were not to be fucked with. And you know what valkyries did for their day jobs? They served ale to the rowdy dead heroes who, despite being the biggest badasses in the afterlife, never, ever threatened their cup-bearers. 'Cause a valkyrie is a holy thing, a hand of fate, a weaver of magic, a lover of the bold. And if you screw with her, she will stick a spear up your ass and have the ravens peck out your eyes. So endeth the lesson, you rabid runt of a *flaggermus*."

I turn to Hildy. "That's my idea of employee discipline, by the way."

She drains her glass of beer and yawns, revealing a nettlesome lack of interest in my bravado. "Maybe we should take a walk. Let things calm down a bit," she suggests to me.

"Sure," I say. "Might as well give him a chance to re-arm."

The Gulf of Mexico is an ocean on valium. The waves are mild, the tides mundane, the shore birds well-behaved. It is the place to bring a family of young children, or girls afraid of the rough surf, or old men with tender hips. It astonishes me that I found my way here, of all places, from the savage storms, winter gales and deadly maelstroms of the North and Norwegian Seas.

Hildy and I sit quietly on a green bench in the darkness, the crests of small waves spilling white foam over light, fine sands. We are like an elderly couple far from home and dimly remembered beginnings. She shifts in a little closer so we're no more than six inches apart.

"So, thanks for the bike," I finally say.

"Glad you like it."

"You want to tell me who you are?"

She pushes the toe of her black motorcycle boot into the white sand of the beach, forming a little mound.

"Just someone a little different," she says, turning her face up to me. "Maybe like you."

I'm drawn to her, whatever she is. I was from that first moment on the causeway. Perhaps I was born to be. Many are the tales of tricked trolls wooed by beauties, of generous giants calmed by pampered princesses with cunning young lovers lurking in corners. Many are the sagas of sirens singing men to jagged coasts and gravelly graves. In my mind is a garrulous girl spinning a car into the sea to bury her dead lover, and an elegant woman leading her married paramour into a dark bar filled with dangerous suitors.

As we sit, on the horizon over the gulf are silhouettes of tall clouds barely visible in the night. The largest of them flashes in silence, with no forks branching downward or outward. Heat lightning only, a distant light show, or a warning from Thor to local giants.

"You don't need to be afraid," she says.

"The hell I don't."

Going back to *Grimm's* is insane. Unless he's suicidal, no troll should frequent a bar jammed with liquored-up loser warriors. It's like an alcoholic vacationing in wine country. Yet, I follow the siren back in, trailing her like prey, drawn by a fine ass swaddled and swaying in leather, yes, but even more by the kind of imminent peril to which I'd been accustomed in my idiotic youth.

I check my pocket for the Ruger. I don't know if I could fit my fingers into the trigger guard. To my chagrin, Lucky is still there doing whiskey shots. His face is swelling more by the second. A plastic bag filled with ice cubes sits on the bar.

Misty is still here too, washing mugs behind the bar. She's pretending she's okay but isn't making eye contact with anyone. Still shaken. She should have at least called her boss, gotten relieved, and gone home. Small businesses are a bitch.

Lucky greets us like long-lost friends, slightly slurring his words. "Hey, there they are! We thought you went home 'cause of our little ruckus," he says. "So very glad you didn't do that, you know. Not because of a little ruckus. A little ruckus is good, you know, for bonding purposes. Me and Fred, we were always getting into ruckuses as kids. We, you know, like ruckuses now and again. They help clear the air and such, don't they, bud?"

"If you say so," says Fred.

"I do. I say so," says Lucky.

I doubt he is as drunk as he seems, though it's possible he's self-medicating with pills or powders. I need to keep up my guard and not get lulled by his I'm-so-hammered-all-is-forgiven shtick. The kid's a viper.

"Three," Lucky's saying to Fred, his palm on the bar. "She said three. I won the first one. Yep, sorry, but I did. I won it. There's two more, or I win the whole challenge, right Hildy? Tell me I'm wrong. I don't think so."

Hildy silently assesses him, as if she's listening to radio waves only she can hear.

"Okay, here's the second challenge. With no goddamned weapons or violence of *any* kind, be the first to get Misty to pour you another draft."

Lucky's about to protest but then decides better. This time, Misty knows the game as all three of us drain our mugs and hold them out to her. Fred smiles confidently. Lucky is trying hard to strike the right balance between intimidating Misty with an I-can-always-kill-you-later stare and an I'm-so-loaded-you-can't-hold-this-against-me look. Me? I feel rotten that Hildy is doing this to her again, so I grin to make her feel better, clownishly using my superior arm length to extend my mug far past those of Lucky and Fred, making her laugh.

To my surprise, it works. I've somehow threaded the needle between Romeo and Iago and am rewarded with an expertly drawn mug of Schlitz. What's interesting is the sideways glance Misty gives Hildy, who grants her a small nod of acknowledgment. Maybe Misty is being given credit for guts in defying Lucky.

"The big man shoots! He scores!" slurs Lucky. "Ew, and bedroom-eyes Fred is shut out! We go to the tiebreaker!"

"Right. Last challenge," continues Hildy. "This time we turn to Fred, who is otherwise out of the running." Hildy takes her black biker jacket and ties its sleeves around Fred's eyes. Fred takes a whiff of the leather, going for laughs, and congratulates Hildy on her perfume choice. Then she gives us the rules. We both get the opportunity to place something in one of Fred's empty hands. Fred doesn't know who places which item in his hands. Whoever gives him the object he likes best is the winner. The object can't be something Fred already owns.

This whole three challenges thing is getting wearisome, like those endless folk tales from the Old Country jammed with three wishes or three kisses or three princes. This is the New World, goddammit, where decisions are made based on greenbacks and credit checks, pseudo-scientific psych assessments, deep data, and political hardball played by tight networks of financial titans. What in the fuck are we doing here?

A light shines in Lucky's eyes. Since he and Fred knew one another as kids, Lucky may have long ago figured out how to push his buttons. Meanwhile, I know practically nothing about him, except that he's a fool if he ever followed the lunatic Lucky around.

Lucky starts playing charades with me, motioning for me to give his gun back to him. I shake my head. He insists, motioning toward one of Fred's open palms. I pull out the little pistol and, after fumbling with it a while, remove the magazine. I hesitate before, on Lucky's behalf, I put the gun in Fred's hand myself. Maybe Fred is a gun-lover from way back.

Now I need to figure out what to put in Fred's other hand. I think of giving him a mug of beer, or perhaps a pool cue, or maybe the keys to my new bike. Easy come, easy go. In the end, I pull Misty aside and ask if she'll be my item. I hate to throw her back in the game, one she'd never agreed to play in the first place, a game in which the stakes are poorly understood, at best. She just raises her eyebrows and pushes out her lips as if to say, "Why not?"

She takes Fred's left arm and pulls it around her, then places his hand so that it gently cups her left breast. Lucky is annoyed, clearly feeling that this is a breach of the rules. Hildy, however, gives no sign.

"How do you choose?"

Fred hefts the gun and then gives Misty's breast a soft squeeze. I wonder if he thinks the gun was my idea since he knows I took it away from Lucky.

"Gotta go with the boob," he laughs, taking off the blindfold. He's not surprised to see Misty and gives her a kiss.

"For keeps?" he asks Hildy.

"Are you putting a ring on it?" interjects Misty.

We all chuckle at that, at least until I realize Lucky's got his gun back, having snatched it out of Fred's hand.

He's chortling, looking at the weapon, and then snaps it up to point at my head.

"I lied about not having one in the chamber," he drawls. "I always keep it ready to go. You know, just in case some fat, dumb giant steals the clip."

"You're a tricky one," I admit. I deserve this for being such a gullible, careless schmuck. I should have jammed my fingers through his skull when I had the chance.

"I likes my mischief," he says, backing toward the pool table and picking up a stick. "And I don't much like ass-kickings, unless I'm the one doing the kicking."

He transfers the gun to his left hand and then swings the pool cue, heavy end first, at my head. I have time enough to admire how expertly he wields it before it crashes into the side of my face, and I fall like a sacrificed bull onto the linoleum floor, replete with ashes, peanut shells, and sticky beer spills. It hurt, but I'm not unconscious, though I pretend to be. Trolls have hard skulls.

As if to verify the fact, Lucky whistles. "Whoo whee, look at how he splintered this old stick. Hey, Fred, should I kill the giant prick?"

I have the distinct impression he's aiming down at my head. My whole "playing dead" gambit could be a deadly mistake.

"I wouldn't," Fred says.

"What in the fuck are you doing, boy?" asks a surprised-sounding Lucky.

"When we were kids, you always used to tell me to grow a couple. Guess I have."

That's when I realize that Fred too was packing and must be pointing a gun at Lucky. Fucking Florida! The place is so awash in firearms that any asshole can get a permit to carry, if they bother with a permit at all.

"I ain't dicking around, Fred. You draw on me, you better be willing to put one in my eye."

"Up to you," says Fred. "You got one bullet, I got more. And mine is pointed in the right direction."

"You're gonna rue the day, friend Fred, rue the damn day. And you, giant, laying there like a potbellied possum, you're gonna rue it, too. You feeling me?"

He kicks me in the temple with steel-toed boots. I involuntarily groan, a hairsbreadth from being knocked unconscious for real.

"Yeah," says Lucky. "He's feeling me."

Chapter Eleven

After the first battle with Harald Bloodaxe, King Alfr realized it would be a long, punishing campaign unless he changed tactics. Harald's home base was closer to army encampments, his supply lines shorter and surer, his troops easier to replenish. Bloodaxe's long-term strategy was to wage a guerilla war when it suited him and to draw out the campaign until the winter season, when we would be low on food and in need of shelter.

But Harald had underestimated Alfr. He wasn't just another hot-headed chieftain who would order his men to pursue Bloodaxe into the forests, where they'd be picked apart in ambushes. Instead, Alfr quickly put together a reconnaissance team and strike force led by his cousin Dofri and made up of just two other men and myself.

Bloodaxe's troops were still recovering and plotting their next attack when Dofri, his nephew Leos, a man named Gudrun and I crept up on their camps in the night. I was a good scout for the little team, seeing well in the dark and spotting Harald's sentinels long before they spotted us so we could make our way around and between them.

Harald had spread his camps in a crooked line. Some had fires, others didn't. It was a crafty system, making his troops impossible to surround and leaving them with many paths of retreat.

When Dofri shared this intelligence with the king, Alfr decided to use Harald Bloodaxe's craft against him. The idea was to sneak into a single, isolated camp and make his men pay for their patient ways of war. And so we did, choosing a camp with no fire, where the men were more likely sleeping without fear of attack. We removed the drowsy watchers first, allowing our knives to do their quiet work. Then we did the same inside the camp, killing as many as we could before someone raised the alarm. At that point, we used axes and swords to slay as quickly as possible while making our way along the escape route we had laid out.

We killed about a dozen warriors, suffering only a few nicks on our side. Skulking and stalking was what I did well, and I admit to taking pleasure in it. By human standards, it was not the most honorable combat tactic, but it was a fitting way to battle slippery Harald. The problem was that Alfr had to guard against a similarly stealthy retaliation from Bloodaxe, even while preparing for a full-scale battle if Harald should be angered into a more direct conflict.

By and by, Harald did respond by having archers shoot flaming arrows into our lodgings, which caused some havoc but few casualties. Alfr was pleased to think he might be beating Harald at his own game, though he was far from content.

"Is there a way to get to Harald himself?" he asked.

"He will be well guarded," said Dofri, "especially now that they fear our little band. If we knew in which camp he resides, it's possible though dangerous. He's the type to anticipate and lay traps. The cat can easily become the mouse in these games."

"By your leave, my lord."

"Speak your mind, Halftroll," said Alfr.

"A single thrall is of little risk, one who knows their camp and is both trained and bred well in the art of skulking."

"You mean yourself."

"I do, my liege," I said. I was young and beginning to grow cocky. I'd gotten a taste of glory and wanted more.

"Although you've trained me well to fight under the eye of Sól, I battle best in darkness. More owl than hawk, I can hunt your prey as the others rest, wreaking havoc on the enemy. If I am caught or killed, you lose little, but if I can lay my hands on the Bloodaxe, I will squeeze his neck and swing him hard, letting him earn his name."

"Thrall though you be," said Alfr, "I am loath to lose you on a doubtful throw of the die."

"Though far from certain, cousin, this roll may be a worthwhile gamble," said Dofri. "Halftroll's nighttime eyes are owlish indeed, and despite his size our little team sometimes loses sight of him when he is still within sword reach."

"I will think on it," said the king, dismissing us with a wave.

When Alfr called me back into his tent the next evening, we spoke alone. He sat in a simple oaken chair made from two rough hewn planks. I admired the elegant simplicity of the thing as I stood before him.

"You have kept honor and troth with us, Hallr, despite many hardships. You might have kept a vengeful heart for your mother's sake, or have become a bitter thrall, enslaved to a people where so many mistrust you. Few men would be as stalwart. And now you offer to risk all for us."

"I do not deny the risks, my king," I said, falling into the kind of high talk that I, like any good troll, would have disdained before my capture. "But it is good strategy, and my heart thrills to the challenge."

He was quiet as the two lamps to either side of him sputtered. The wind was gusting just outside and one of the tent flaps behind me was still open.

"And yet my own heart has misgivings," Alfr finally said. "The men in camp are already singing of Hallr Halftroll who, with only a spear and axe, slayed four noble-blooded mailed men well trained in the art of war. It is a deed worthy of the skalds. Your fellow warriors, though they have maligned and rebuffed you in the past, acknowledge your courage and ferocity in battle. They will not again shun you. They'll defend you like a brother the next time Harald's jarls ride to take your head. I tell you this, Hallr, because it would be easy for you to despair and seek respite in a heroic death. That would weigh heavily on me."

Alfr overstated the esteem in which his soldiers held me. It was true that fewer spit in my path as I walked, and a few like Leos even seemed to respect me. But in the song they sang of me, I came off as a lucky oaf bumbling toward victory over arrogant jarls.

Nonetheless, I took pride in Alfr's approval. Mor had never been one to offer praise, and I was starved for it.

"I thank you, liege, for your words," I said, my head slightly bowed to avoid the tent pole above my head. "They do me honor, but I plan to survive this feat, if the Norns be willing, even while dealing death to Harald."

"This I pledge you, Hallr," he said, rising from his chair. "If you achieve this feat, I will release you from bondage. Now go and speak with Dofri. He and the rest of your fellowship are fain to help in your plot."

Released from my bondage. I wasn't even sure what that meant. Released to do what? I craved my freedom but had also come to value my role in Alfr's retinue. Partly to avoid this confusion of feelings, I focused on the assassination plan.

During the next new moon, we set off for the camps of Harald Bloodaxe again. Dofri stayed on the far perimeter, awaiting my reports. I prowled the outskirts of camps with great patience until I found the subtle signs I'd been seeking: a war tent a little larger than the others, an array of sentinels more alert and disciplined than the rest, and bodyguards who studied the tent itself rather than the dark peripheries beyond the firelight.

It was well and subtly guarded. I retreated into the wastes beyond, seeking Dofri. I found my comrades hunched and cold, impatient for action. After relaying what I'd seen, they agreed it might well be Harald's tent. We laid a plan for my entrance and escape, knowing countless contingencies might foil us.

Dofri crept back to the camp with me. Harald's men were no fools. Two of the sentinels kept an eye on one another, as well as on the perimeter of the camp. The idea was that if one disappeared, the other would raise an alarm. Our timing was critical. We tried to synchronize with silent counts but knew this was chancy. Dofri would attack his man first, and I would be in place to silence my man. Although we did it well, the fast dragging away of bodies into the dark could not be done in complete silence.

When the man tending the fire began whispering the names of the dead guards, the time for prowling was over. Now was the moment for pouncing. As I ran toward the tent, an arrow from Leos took the fire-watcher in the head. I threw a knife at the guard at the tent flaps, but hidden mail saved him. He cried the alarm as I drew my sword, feigned a stroke as Dofri had taught me, and then pierced his throat with a second knife.

I tore open the tent from the side rather than the entrance, knowing whomever was within would be at the ready. Inside, they had doused their lamps. It would have been the right response for foiling a human assassin, but it gave me an advantage. I could sense there were only two of them, the larger one ready to spring from the side as I entered. I was ready. He impaled himself on my sword even before I crushed his windpipe. If he was Harald, my job was done, though I didn't think so. His actions were those of a protector.

As the smaller of the two attacked, I knew it couldn't be Harald. Too soft and young. Trained in the martial skills but not yet experienced in battle. I had failed. I nearly dispatched the boy in my anger and frustration as he cut at me with a knife. But Dofri would label me a mindless monster, only good for thralldom. I needed to be cunning, as Mor had taught me, to think as men do.

And so I dazed the youngster with a cuff to the head, took a nearby shield, and strapped it to my back. Storming out the other side of the tent, I cradled the boy and hoped we would not be instantly met by sentinels I'd missed. I ran for the shadows along the escape route we had chosen, but I'd gone only a few steps when an arrow took me in the thigh. Another arrow stabbed the shield on my back.

Before I was aware of the thought forming in my head, I bellowed, "The troll carries the hostage prince! Hold your arrows!" Dofri was the first to take up the call, followed by Leos and Gudrun. Soon, the call of "hold your arrows" was ringing through the camp as I hobbled into the moonless night like the child-stealing monster I was.

Several warriors pursued. I was lucky we'd kept together our little band of brothers. Dofri used his knife to slay two who were bold enough to follow us into the woods from the left side of camp. Leos distracted another with a shout, leading him into the waiting axe of Gudrun.

When we got back to our camp, it was already alert and abuzz. Alfr had kept out a strong watch to cover our retreat. But we didn't know if my bluff about a "prince" held any truth to it. Was this the kin of Harald or only some unlucky jarl's kith?

The next day, which was tense as Alfr prepared for another full battle, we discovered the truth. The boy had wisely kept silent as a healer treated his wounds. Alfr looked thoughtful as two jarls approached the camp under a flag of truce. Using guile, Alfr was able to confirm what the jarls thought we knew already, that the boy was Harald's eldest son. They assumed we wished to negotiate. Alfr learned what he could and then sent them away, saying a king does not negotiate with jarls. He would only speak with Bloodaxe himself.

It took time, as these things do. Arrangements were made, counselors queried, truces extended, and negotiation terms vetted. The two kings struggled in this as if it were an extension of their war. Bloodaxe accused Alfr of being a dishonorable thief of kin, though such hostage-taking was common enough in those days. Alfr said his troops would be happy to engage with Bloodaxe in one winner-takes-all battle before the onset of winter. Harald made excuses, knowing Alfr led the superior army.

Bloodaxe seemed to want to draw out the negotiations as he had the war. At last they agreed to withdraw their two armies for the winter. King Alfr kept Halfdan Sunmane, the son of Bloodaxe, as a hostage and brought him back to Risør. Several other hostages were also exchanged, in the manner of the day. The two chieftains continued negotiating into the dark months.

Delaying the war felt like a setback to me. I began to think I should have simply crushed the boy's skull. Sometimes the old ways are best.

Chapter Twelve

"Understanding your employee's perspective can go a long way towards increasing productivity and happiness."
—Kathryn Minshew

Hildy's offices are as inconspicuous as an old troll on a bleak mountainside. In a tall building named for a defunct bank, she has a space on the fifteenth floor. There is a small brass nameplate on a nondescript door: *Hild Brands, Inc.* I push a button that buzzes someone on the inside. Out comes the receptionist, an attractive young Asian woman.

"Klaus Rise?" she asks.

"That's me."

She smiles and holds open the door. There in the lobby are two familiar faces. Fred looks up from where he's been chatting with Misty.

"Let the games begin," he grins.

I shake their hands, impressed with how well they've cleaned up. I picture Misty scrambling through her wardrobe, looking for those one or two items that might be okay in a job interview. She picked out a sleeveless, gray-and-white knit dress reminding me of a mountain in wintertime, ice and snow trim around the crest but flaring out smoothly at the base. Fred has donned a black dress shirt, respectable pair of jeans, and low leather boots. Probably the best he could do on short notice. Neither looks ready for the C-suite but, hey, they don't have to. They're a couple of handsome kids.

By comparison, I must look like some chunky version of Lurch from the Addams Family. I wear one of two dress shirts I own along with some super-sized dark trousers.

"You look very debonair," says Misty.

"Thanks," I say. "They say stripes are thinning, so I almost wore my pajamas. These were the next best thing. You look nice yourself. I didn't even realize you were an applicant for whatever craziness Hildy has in mind."

"Me neither, until they called. I need to quit *Grimm's* anyway. Not enough hazard pay."

"Yeah, well, maybe having a weapon aimed at you is some kind of qualification around here," I joke. Then wonder if it is a joke. Lucky's missing, so maybe it wasn't a test of skills hinging on wins—more like a test of character.

The receptionist leads us to a generic office meeting room, complete with white boards, long faux-wood table, and rolling office chairs. "Ms. Hild will be joining you momentarily."

After she leaves, I ask, "Does anybody have a clue what we're doing here?"

They shrug.

"Good," I say. "I thought maybe I missed something, what with these little bangs on the head and all."

Hildy enters, sporting a trendy briefcase, dark blue suit and a no-nonsense attitude. She shakes our hands formally, almost mechanically, as if she barely knows us. The approach pisses me off. There's no color in her hair, no face jewelry, no sign of the biker-chick persona at all. No small talk about *Grimm's*, or how easy it was to find the office, or even the weather, for God's sake. She just motions us to sit.

"You three are here to learn more about several jobs for which we are hiring," she begins, leaning forward on her elbows. "As you must already suspect, I have idiosyncratic ways of identifying and screening talent. You three have already been identified and, to some degree, vetted. Today, we're continuing that process.

"I intend to give you information about the work we do here so you can decide if you'd like to proceed to the next step. *Hild Brands* primarily hires biologists, engineers, and lawyers in order to help us carry out our primary function, which is to consult with enterprises and government agencies on issues related to Florida land and water usage."

Hildy hands around a glossy brochure complete with a logo, mission statement, customer quotes, and a list of employee benefits.

"Frankly, only Misty here is remotely qualified, with a dual degree in ecology and journalism."

Fred raises his eyebrows and gives Misty a look of surprise. I guess this is the first he's heard of her degree. It's probably not something you want to broadcast at *Grimm's*.

"But each of you," Hildy continues, "has unique talents and life experiences that may help you fill other organizational needs. Klaus, for example, has DOT experience, and Fred did a stint as military police."

Now it's Misty's turn to look surprised. They may have spent some quality time together, but it clearly didn't involve a lot of discussions of career history.

"These jobs are less reliant on technical expertise than they are other qualities."

"Such as?" I ask.

"Qualities considered old-fashioned these days: strength, courage, guile, and occasionally something else. Let's call it daring."

My BS detector is clicking hard. Too much happy talk here. It's either bullshit or another shoe will drop.

"We also need people who are willing to bend or break certain rules and yet have a keen intuition about which rules those are. You'd be doing things outside the scope of what we'd ask of our other employees.

"Of course, those same qualities inevitably raise the risks of recruiting for these positions, so we've also selected you because we know things that give us certain leverage as an employer. I need to emphasize that we are not in the extortion business. You are free to turn down the job today or, if you accept it, to leave it anytime. However, we do our utmost to prevent breaches of confidentiality and security. More to the point, we will not tolerate betrayal. That's why, for these particular jobs, we prefer to have information that encourages loyalty."

And here it comes. The other shoe.

"I'm handing you each a manila folder that gives you some idea of the type of information we've collected. Again, I do not wish you to view these as a threat, only as a type of informational collateral that we hold to encourage your discretion and allegiance. We would only share it outside the firm if you betrayed our trust. I'm going to give you a minute or two to glance through your folders."

Informational collateral. I pick up the manila folder with my name on it. There are four eight-by-ten black-and-white photos. One is of the manhole cover beneath the broken down lawnmower in my service shed. The second is a shot of a small gravestone with the name Klaus Rise on it: Born January 1962, Died February 1962.

A third is the kitschy Florida toll-collector shirt I wore the night I killed Olaf, replete with bloodstains. I guess chucking it into the dumpster at the Albertson's was a mistake.

In the fourth and final photo, I'm at the seawall staring like a dumb animal at a silver hood ornament in my hands.

I'm angry but not shocked as I view these photos. Even by troll standards, the last couple of weeks have been uncanny. Hildy has not tried to hide the fact she thinks she can yank my levers however she wants. But she's going too damn far with these.

Fred has his face in his hands. Misty stares at Hildy through narrowed, angry eyes. In contrast, Hildy's gaze is steady, just another reptilian CEO giving people heart-rending, life-altering news.

I came here to learn more about Hildy and to, just maybe, restart a life long gone dormant. Now it feels like a grand mistake. Maybe I should just walk away.

"We'll take a break and meet back here in half an hour," she says. "If you come back, we'll order in lunch. Any of you is free to go at this point. Your files will be destroyed and your secrets will be safe, at least as far as *Hild Brands* goes."

"You can't possibly know this stuff, you psycho bitch," spits Misty, standing up and storming out the door.

Fred's next. He's angry as well, though I think mostly on Misty's behalf. He stares hard at Hildy, then leaves without saying a word.

"Nice job winning hearts and minds," I tell her.

"And how about you? Will you be back?" she asks. She tries to sound neutral, but I catch a whiff of remorse, maybe even a hint of desperation.

"Not sure. The paid maternity leave sure is tempting, though," I say, walking through the door.

By the time I get to the hallway outside the Hild Brand offices, Misty and Fred are nowhere to be seen, so I take the elevator down to the underground parking garage. Should I stay or should I go? I try to decide as I lean against an ugly yellow wall outside the elevator alcove, letting the lyrics of The Clash reverberate through my mind.

I'm ambivalent about these bizarre, human-designed caves. It's comforting to be underground, but there's nothing here a troll would build. Polished metal, thrumming machines, humming florescent tubes, scores of yellow-painted rectangles set off against exactly the same number of concrete parking curbs.

Humanity is an invasive species obsessed with unnatural order, molding virtually everything—even the trillions upon trillions of grains of Florida sand—into the artificial geometry of its own outlandish mental landscapes. Cinder blocks, poured cement, reinforced concrete. It comes in all shapes and sizes: slabs, beams, columns and walls.

Foundations too, of course. They're always pouring another goddamned foundation to isolate themselves from the vagaries of Earth. I envision countless humans crowded onto one gigantic slab of concrete out of which sprouts endless rows of white porcelain sinks. Humans stand at the sinks compulsively scrubbing their hands in the vain attempt to cleanse themselves of the dust from which they rose, hoping to hell this fanatical separation will divorce them from their own inevitable deaths. Pitiful bastards.

This parking garage simultaneously magnifies and distorts voices, a kind of auditory funhouse for the sensitive ears of a troll. Car doors slam, conversations rise and fade, and footsteps reverberate loudly—especially those of women in their hard-heeled dress shoes. People come and go, most of them studiously ignoring me, a motionless, monstrous man waiting for god-knows-what.

Out of the garbled sounds, I finally pick out familiar voices and head in their direction. Fred and Misty are in the Employees Only section of the garage, sitting in a couple of orange plastic chairs next to the large service elevator. Misty is speaking intently, emphasizing points with emphatic gestures. I hang back, wondering if I should join them. They're not friends. I don't have friends anymore. Just acquaintances. Yet, I feel vaguely connected to them after the events at *Grimm's*.

Out of the corner of my eye, I see someone lurking behind one of the huge, blocky concrete pillars. He's as close to Fred and Misty as he can get without being seen. And he's still. So very still, with both hands resting on the pillar. As a skulker born and bred, I know a fellow professional when I see one. He's a thin man wearing a dark hoodie and, incongruously, navy dress slacks. Looks like quality material, imported wool with cuffs, cut to just the right length over black snakeskin lace-ups. Pricey, I'm guessing. A stalker with money and expensive tastes.

There's something suspiciously bulgy and bulky about the hoodie jacket. He could be toting anything, of course, with all the electronics people carry these days. But my mind goes to weaponry, given his weird behavior.

Just as I take a step forward toward the man, I feel a hand on my shoulder and startle, wheeling around, leading with my elbow. It's an instinctive and potentially deadly move I learned from Dofri centuries ago. Hildy ducks away without making a sound. She's holding her finger to her lips. I take in several things at once: that Hildy moves like a cat, has been trained in the martial arts, stands in stocking feet, wears a grim smile, and has a feral look as she flicks her eyes to the hooded man. At some level, she's enjoying herself. In her, I catch another glimpse of the young woman I met on the bridge.

She motions me to stay where I am, then sneaks up to within half an arm's length of the gawker. I get the sense she's prepared if he reaches for a weapon.

"Who are you?" she asks, her voice normal but magnified in this mondo grotto.

Looking surprised and annoyed, Misty and Fred turn in our direction.

The man, however, doesn't startle at all. Instead, he moves his dark, hooded head around slow as a sloth. Creepy. When he catches sight of Hildy, he freezes. Rather than go for a weapon, he darts away in a crouched position, slipping into the massive herd of parked vehicles. He's astonishingly quick, a stark contrast to his recent stock-stillness.

Hildy signals and we give chase.

This guy is good. Those snakeskin shoes click not-at-all. I've lost sight of him despite my height, which gives me a better angle to see between cars. Going to where I last saw him, I breathe deeply through my nose. The place stinks of oil and gas, but I'm a goddamned troll and can pick out the subtle stink of our hooded voyeur. He must be headed toward the exit on the west wall. I catch Hildy's eye and point to where I think he's going. She's smart. Rather than slapping her feet down in a sprint to the exit, she moves quickly but stealthily down a row of cars, disappearing from sight.

I continue tracking, a Baskerville-sized hound in a forest of rubber, steel and plastic. Suddenly, our pheasant flushes and breaks for the exit. He almost gets there before Hildy springs out, grabs his left arm and then slingshots him, back first, against the yellow cinderblock wall near the door.

He has a couple of inches on her, but she holds her right forearm up against his throat in a practiced way. She pulls down his hood with her left hand, displaying the hideous features we first saw at *Grimm's*.

"What are you doing here, Professor Jormund?" she asks.

"Pray tell, madam," he says with his phoney accent, "what crime have I committed that warrants such an assault on my person?"

"You were stalking my friends. I want to know why."

Right on cue, Fred and Misty arrive, panting heavily. They must have chased after us when we pursued Jormund.

"Stalking? Heavens no! I have business in this building, heard loud voices and investigated. It is only happenstance that I've made your acquaintances in the past."

Hildy pulls away her forearm.

"Yeah, that's likely," I say. "Before you let him go, Hildy, you might want to check to see if he's armed like his 'cuz' Lucky. He's sporting the same neck tattoo."

I push down his collar with a finger. Yes, it's a stylized rune after all, but it's woven together with the English letter D. I swear I've seen it before, and not just on Lucky. But can I trust my recollection? Even among humans, with their puny lifespans, memories are notoriously undependable. They should try living for centuries.

"I've had quite enough of this," he says, his eyes becoming hard, black marbles. "Holding a person against his will unlawfully is a federal offense."

"Something tells me you won't be speed-dialing the FBI anytime soon," I say, reaching into one of his bulky pockets. As I do, though, Jormund whips up his left hand.

"Fuck!" I yell, yanking back my arm as if I'd been stung by a scorpion.

Jormund ducks away from us and smashes through the exit door. We can hear him pounding up the concrete stairs. No one follows. We're all staring at a hypodermic needle hanging from my forearm.

"Damn it," I say, looking at Fred. "Why do people keep jabbing me with sharp objects lately? And what kind of professor packs a hypodermic needle?"

Hildy holds my arm appraisingly, then yanks out the syringe.

"You're lucky. A clean, empty needle," she says. She bends over and picks up a little bag of white power which must have fallen out of Jormund's pocket.

She's nearly hyperventilating, her nostrils pulsing with anger and adrenaline. Striding over to a nearby trash can, she snaps the needle off the syringe before hurling everything in the can.

Without another word, all four of us walk back to the elevator banks.

As we gather around the conference table again, Hildy asks if everyone has made up his or her mind. Fred and I turn to Misty.

"We got interrupted down there," she says in a surly tone. "Anybody know why snakeface was spying on us?"

It's the same question I've been asking myself. No one speaks up. We all turn to Hildy, who is clearly the keeper of secrets around this place. She shakes her head.

"Well," says Misty. "I need a smoke before I make a final decision."

"Sounds like a good idea," says Hildy. "Klaus, could you do us a favor and snatch down that smoke alarm on the ceiling?"

I reach up and twist it off, wires and all, like a tick off a dog. I hand it to Fred, who grins up at me.

Misty knocks a Lucky Strike out of a pack from her purse. Then, surprisingly, she holds out the pack to Hildy, who takes one. Fred and I decline. The two women smoke in silence. After they've taken the edge off the tension in the room, I ask the question that's been circling in my mind like a raven.

"So, you're saying we'd be here to do odd jobs, things your more 'conventional' employees can't, or won't, or shouldn't do. There may be rules to break and weird shit to be encountered. It sounds more like government spook action than environmental consulting."

"Do you have a question in there somewhere, Klaus?" she asks.

"Are we the good guys or the bad guys?"

"Yes," she says. "Next question."

Chapter Thirteen

"From what I've tasted of desire
I hold with those who favor fire."
—Robert Frost

I hadn't slain Harald, so I remained a thrall of the king. In return for the capture of Halfdan, however, Alfr played out the invisible chain of my bondage when we returned to Risør. The citizens did not resent me as much as they had before. In those days, people warmed to you if you were savage toward enemies but civil toward neighbors. Not all warriors could strike that balance.

I felt a conflicted mixture of resentment, pride and relief. Resentment at still being a thrall despite halting a war. Pride in the added trust and respect I'd won from Alfr and his people. And relief that I was still bonded to the king who had given me my new identity as... what? A purposeful warrior? A uniquely skilled servant? In the twenty-first century, maybe we'd call it Stockholm syndrome. At the time, though, I only felt a kind of inner conflict that ebbed and flowed but never quite went away.

In the days of long winter darkness, I trained young men in the art of war, carrying on the lessons hard won from Dofri. They tended to come from the better families in Risør, so I did not dare scar them as Dofri had done to me. I was still considered a beast, but their beast, like a prized warhorse or a tamed bear that would attack on command. So, rather than scarring my students, I would reveal my own scars, using them as a map of my many blunders. The tales of my humility never grew old for them.

After giving lessons, I acted as a ranger and guardsman, defending the darkened township as people slept. Smoke from small, smoldering fires often hung low in the valley where Risør was nestled.

This occupation of guardsman was dangerous in its own way.

Alfr had warned me, "If some gruesome deed occurs in the night, Hallr, you will be the first accused. Not I, nor any other, will be able to save you then if you lack a witness. For your own protection, you must stay with your fellow guardsmen."

And so I did, though the lingering distrust rankled me. Our job was to secure the countryside from invaders, bandits, marauders, spies, and beasts of all sorts, including plundering trolls. In truth, our duties more often entailed keeping drunken men from killing one another—or their wives and whelps. In the quiet hours, we mended community fences, found lost sheep and cattle, pulled fallen trees from snowy paths and the like. I grew to love those quiet hours under the stars. Sometimes we'd even see the Northern Lights swirling across the skies in luminous bands of orange, green and purple. The iridescent hues pulsed and undulated like beings living beyond the ken of men or trolls.

We made our rounds in pairs, with Leos my usual companion. I'd grown to respect him as a member of our small band of guerilla fighters in the war with Harald. He was sharp-eyed and tight-lipped, cautious but never cowardly, the fourth son of a farmer with more children than land. He'd been encouraged to learn the skills of soldiering and patrolling.

Although he had talents in these areas, he feared they would not lead to what he wanted most: a prosperous farming life with a large family of his own. Leos had no wish for the itinerant soldier's existence, nor for the fate of a poor farmer with rickety kids scratching a living off divided, rocky lands. He wasn't even enthusiastic about the prospect of hazarding stormy seas to go raiding or, as they called it, *i viking*.

"Don't you want to die a warrior's death, so you wind up in Valhalla rather than Hel?" I teased, as we laid tumbled stones back on a crumbled wall.

"Once I have a family and lands to protect, I'll gladly fight and die for them," he said, pondering it far more seriously than I'd intended. "Someday maybe we can farm together. There are some stonier grounds in the north my father uses for nothing but goat pastures. Together, we might be able to do enough digging, lifting and plowing to make good farmland of it."

I laughed at the notion. "I'm only a thrall, Leos. The king will lend you my trollish back if your family asks."

"You'll win your freedom one day in battle, Hallr. I've heard Dofri tell it in his cups. Why make a ranger of you otherwise? They know well you could bang me on the head and disappear into the high mountains. Alfr is showing them they have naught to fear from you."

This insight surprised me. Leos and I usually discussed matters that were more mundane. The thickness of the ice sheets, the sharpness of blades, the ownership of sheep, the best types of wood for fires. He was not much given to speculation and gossip.

"Or maybe he wants me to disappear," I said in a jesting tone, though half serious. The mountains beckoned to me some nights and I considered just disappearing into the darkness.

"Perhaps," he said. "Why do you think the Norns brought you here, Hallr?"

"Well, I'm quite a good stump-puller, after all."

"Aye, and leg-puller as well," he said, grinning. "But I expect the runes on your neck say more than that."

This stopped me. "Do you know what tale the runes tell?"

"Nay, only what the elders have said. That you're of the clan."

"Its chattel, yes."

"Few are the cows or goats I've seen with runes, Hallr."

"So a long-lost troll prince, then, eh? As told by the skalds?"

"Well," said Leos. "That would be a pickle for any king, wouldn't it?"

One day as I trained the lads in the pit, the king's daughter Inge visited, chaperoned by an older married cousin and accompanied by the hostage Halfdan Sunmane. She was obliged to be more demure now, wearing a tan shift beneath a sky-blue dress and two ornate brooches of polished bronze.

I had seen Inge walking through Risør with Halfdan before, but always from a distance. The captured chieftain's son had been accorded great courtesy and many privileges as a hostage. There was speculation that a peace treaty with Bloodaxe might include a wedding with Alfr's one remaining unbetrothed daughter. Indeed, now that I saw them up close, I realized they made a handsome couple.

The boy had been named for his long blond locks, but he was the paragon of a Norse prince in other ways, as well. An oval face with a yellow beard just beginning to grow thick. Blue eyes, a straight and noble nose, just a hint of acne. He was slender, yes, but it was the type of thinness into which strong men had been known to grow. On the front of his neck he bore a tattoo of a rune that looked a bit like a modern-day F.

These days, the British tabloids would go mad for them. There would be fan sites and paparazzi and posters for teenage bedrooms. We would have to see him shirtless on a private beach, his young chest pixelated with blurred distance. And she would be seen with her bikini top unclasped as she tried to sun her back.

In Risør, though, royals were a deadly serious business. Many feared Bloodaxe because of his reputation for expanding his territories through violent and devious means. One tale had it that, during a period of negotiations for peace with two other chieftains, he set fire to a manor where they slept at night. Once they were dead, he took their lands amid the ensuing strife among their heirs.

Inge was beloved, yes, but she was expected to keep the people of the kingdom safe. Some hoped a marriage would turn the armistice into a peace. Others wanted no part of Harald Bloodaxe, unless it was his head on a pike.

The young men I trained, however, didn't care about the affairs of state. They focused on glory and pretty women. So when Inge came to watch them train, some looked down, blushing like children, while others self-consciously puffed out their chests and reined in their breathing. I was hoping Inge's party would briefly look on and disappear. They lingered. It was not my place to chase away royalty, though I stopped to give her a questioning glance. "Please carry on, Hallr Halftroll," she said, a newly minted woman testing the blade of her power.

The lads forgot most of their discipline as they showed off for the ladies and foreign prince, foolishly flailing and chopping away. They didn't understand the young woman was a connoisseur who would appreciate good footwork and a deft parry more than boisterous thrashing. I was embarrassed for them and, I realized with chagrin, for myself as well. I had an urge to scatter them like pigeons or even, for a dark and fleeting moment, throttle one of the meaty boys and, on bended knee, present his corpse to the beauteous lady.

When I spotted Sunmane sneering at us, I called a halt to their awkward thwacking and pulled my two best to the side. "Boys," I whispered, "this lady is a royal who knows the moves well. She has a keen eye for the smart stance, the clever turn, the sensible strike. Show her what you've learned. No huffing and puffing like untrained farmers, eh?"

They took my meaning and did the dance, not all to my liking but as well as they could. I wished to be proud of them, these lithe, shining sons of jarls, hersirs and wealthy freemen. Instead, I felt envy as Inge watched them intently, judging and seeking out small flaws, as if I were going to quiz her as Dofri had done in the past.

At the end of the match, I gave both a nod. Otherwise there was silence. I couldn't expect her to clap happily like the artless lass she'd been a short time ago. I called two more boys forward, preparing to give them the same speech, though I knew they were more likely to fail me. Inge's chaperone whispered in her ear, and they rose.

"Well done, men. May Freyja bless you all in battle." She hesitated before looking at me, saying, "As she has done your teacher." Then they were gone.

Although trolls and dragons were featured in many a scary children's story, it was fire that most terrified adults. A true conflagration could ransack, maim and murder, making drunken berserkers seem tame by comparison. Fire could kill a kingdom.

And one night in Risør, it nearly did.

From a hillside on the outskirts, Leos was the first to notice that the perennial layer of thin smoke in the town was growing thicker. As soon as he said it, I scented the danger. What a dullard I'd become! Looking down, we could see the smoke billowing from near King Alfr's manor. Leos blew his horn to raise the alarm while I dashed down toward the township. Rather than taking the well-worn path that meandered past gardens and wells to the southern part of town, I made a beeline from the hill to the Hall, crashing through brush, hurtling fallen trees, smashing through a thicket of young oaks.

Still, it took too long. By the time I arrived, the longhouse just south of the Great Manor was engulfed in high flames that threw up burning cinders. It was a breezy night and the wind blew in the direction of the manor, which dwarfed every other structure in the township. A bucket brigade was starting to form, but men argued over how to use the precious water. Should they try to tamp down the blazing longhouse in hope of quelling the spread of flames, or should they try dousing the lower roofs of the Great Manor to keep them from igniting?

Before the debate could be settled, someone shouted that a spark had already floated up under the tarry eaves on the second-story of the manor, where it was nearly impossible to cast water. We tried. Leos, who had followed in the path of wreckage I'd left behind, lent his leadership to the chaotic scene, getting the brigade to focus on the manor even while others built an ad-hoc scaffolding made of barrels, grates, ladders and furniture so we could reach the second story.

Meanwhile, Alfr's household was roused, with the king himself directing the removal of key items, treasure and documents.

For a time, we were successful in dousing the smoldering roof of the Great Manor. Then a sudden gust sent flames surging higher in the burning longhouse, which shot a stream of embers up onto the third story of the manor. Although we did our best to build the scaffolding even higher to reach the spreading blaze, we couldn't keep the southern wing from becoming a veritable torch. It was hopeless. We even had to tear down the scaffold for fear that it too would combust. Our demoralized, cursing crew panted and wiped the sweat-laced ash from our blackened faces.

Amid the shouts and pandemonium, two groups were still and staring. The first were the hostages, negotiators, attendants and guards who had been evacuated from the burning southern longhouse, the original source of the conflagration. Most notable among them was Halfdan Sunmane, who was huddled with his fellows. Several guards watched them closely to ensure Sunmane could not be rescued amid the bedlam.

Not far from these guests were the women from Alfr's household, who huddled together and regarded the flames with a range of deep emotions, like characters in an epic Rubens painting. There were the weeping servants, the dignified grief of the queen, the screaming of several infants, and the stony glare of Inge, who stood apart from the rest, more angry than frightened. I noticed her eyes shifting to the son of Bloodaxe. Only then did it occur to me that Inge, who had spent more time with Halfdan than anyone had, suspected the fair-haired whelp of arson.

"Leos," I shouted over the crackling flames and turmoil, "douse me with your bucket. Then work with the others to soak as much of the structure as you can. Maybe we can save something yet."

To the lad's credit, he asked no questions. In fact, said nothing at all. Just poured his bucket over my head and began to rally the others. I borrowed an axe from one of the guards I knew, sprinted through the main entrance and turned into the southern wing. Though the high walls to one side were beginning to blaze, the flames had not yet engulfed the inside, which was supported by eight mighty staves.

A brief lesson in the architecture of the times is in order. The Great Manor, like many chieftain houses of the day, was built using enormous staves, many of them taller and stronger than the masts of the largest Viking ships. Like the renowned stave churches that have endured from medieval times, each section was supported by these huge masts. In the ever-thickening smoke, I hacked away in a frenzied pace at the main staves, starting with the ones closest to the flaming walls. After slashing through the first four, there was only creaking to be heard and little movement in the walls. Even I, capable of holding my breath for long minutes, was choking in the gloom and succumbing to the growing heat.

Then part of the south wall fell. As oxygen from the outside rushed in, the flames abruptly grew taller and hotter. My tunic started smoking. Half-blinded, broiled and gasping for air, I stumbled in the direction of the main entrance. When I emerged out of the burning hall, Leos and his men whacked at my smoldering clothes with the dampened capes and scarves they'd been using to beat back flames.

"It may not be too late," I told them, panting, "if we can just chop through the four staves on the north side of the wing.

There were only moments left. Wrapping one of their scarves around my mouth and nose, I blundered back inside, with Leos and others following. I pointed out the staves they should chop, pantomiming to them what I was trying to achieve. When only two staves were left, the whole wing was leaning outward, the outside wall ready to fall toward the ravaged longhouse. The men were suffering badly now, being cooked even as they worked. When the first flaming beams fell, barely missing Leos, I snarled and waved them out.

They fled, all but Leos himself.

"You've got to warn them away from the south side!" I shouted. "This whole tower will drop like a section of Muspelheim, raining flames. Get them ready."

He nodded.

The roof threatened to collapse as more burning lumber fell. When I was down to the last stave, I chopped around it so only a thin center was left. Reaching under it, I strained like Thor hefting the mythic serpent Jörmungand, though I barely moved it. There was a resounding crack as something separated above. The stave leaned, just a bit a first and then gained momentum on its own. I threw the end of the stave as best I could, then dove toward the exit, praying I could escape before being crushed.

When I finally got clear of the building, there was no hero's welcome. The brigades were busy trying to save the rest of the chieftain's manor now that we had sliced off the searing inferno of the collapsed southern wing. The bucket brigades were well organized now. Other men shoveled snow and dirt to create a firebreak between the fallen wing and the rest of the Manor. I didn't join them, merely stumbling away to a safe distance. Down on one knee, I feared passing out in front of the whole township.

By and by, though, I felt a hand on my shoulder. I looked up to see little Inge bidding me quaff ale from a copper drinking bowl, one that had no doubt been hastily removed from the manor during the evacuation. She wore a heavy and slightly oversized fur cloak over what was likely a nightgown.

"Thank you, Hallr, for striving valiantly to save our home," she said.

There was laughter from the Sunmane retinue. Someone had made a jest, I assumed at my expense. One of the Bloodaxe negotiators, who was clearly in his cups, continued the joke in the same vein.

"Aye, my lord, and they likely serve the beast winter hay on a silver plate," he said loudly.

At this, Inge turned toward them.

"The Völsungs, my lord, know better than most how to distinguish between men and beasts," she said.

"And how fare these shivering and unsheltered guests in her lady-ship's opinion?" Halfdan Sunmane retorted, playing the amused prince.

"That depends, sir, on how well they have responded to our hospitality," said Inge.

"No one can be as grateful as a loyal pet, of course."

I'd become inured to insults during my first months at Risør, but I ground my teeth as Halfdan taunted Inge amid this crisis. I could feel a low growl in the back of my throat, one quelled with difficulty. I scrambled for cunning, clever human words instead.

"Take care, sir," I rejoined. "Even loyal pets may maul faithless strangers."

"In our land, such animals are soon put to rest," answered the Half-dan easily, infuriatingly glib. His fellows chortled at his wit.

"And in ours," I said, slowly approaching him, "we know how to extinguish incendiaries."

At this point, several Völsung guards laid their hands on me, firmly keeping me from moving toward Sunmane. I was exhausted, burned and blackened, yet I started to shake off the guards. Then Inge appeared in front of me, her small hand on my chest.

"Stand down, Hallr Halftroll," she commanded. I ceased, allowing Inge to restrain me, even at the shudder-inducing sight of Sunmane, spawn of Bloodaxe, smiling into my eyes.

Chapter Fourteen

"These maids shape the lives of men, and we call them Norns."
—*The Younger Edda*

If "stay the fuck away" is the landscape motif for my own property, then the motif for Hildy's place is "nothing here to see." I tried Google-mapping the address and got zilch. I have to rely on her directions, which she's written onto my palm with a thin-tipped permanent marker. I'm fairly sure I'm on the right path, which I found behind a decrepit billboard off a county road. The path is far too narrow for a car, not even quite big enough for my street bike. For the first couple of hundred yards, I'm forced to get off the bike several times to pull the tires out of the sand. After that, I just push the bike along.

I've been working for Hildy about a week now. Everytime I've pressed her on what she really wants from me, she's put me off. Instead, she's thrown a bunch of corporate crap at me: orientation classes, online-training courses and the like.

When she invited me to her place in the central Florida wilderness, she said I'd finally get some answers. I'm hopeful but suspicious. The banjo music from the movie *Deliverance* reverberates in a mental soundtrack.

After a long time walking, I realize I must have missed the turnoff which, if the directions on my palm are to be believed, is marked by a stone. Actually, she has written "runestone." At this point, I want to toss the bike into the brush and be done with it. I don't, though. I double back and finally come across a hunk of rock mostly hidden by a scrub palmetto. It's a three-foot tall limestone boulder, one honeycombed with holes from underground streams. I've no idea how it could have gotten here. Usually, this kind of limestone is brought up by bulldozers near construction sites.

It would be easy to mistake the runes for natural etchings, but once I see the first one, the others slowly become apparent. Some are tiny, some larger. I was never very literate with runes but, even if I had been, I don't think I could have puzzled these out. They're carved just one or two at a time in locations that look random, as if placed for the sake of aesthetics rather than meaning. Maybe the stone is just an oddity left here by some Florida scrub hippie selling strange junk out of a truck on the side of the road. I'll probably find some wooden wind chimes made with twigs and bits of Spanish moss as well, or maybe a hidden swathe of homegrown reefer.

I finally see the path. I bash through some sort of thicket, maybe hawthorn, before the path widens a bit. I'm sweating now, the bike getting heavy even for a troll. Finally, there is a hanging oil lantern, glowing soft and yellow from a tree branch. Beyond it is a wooden porch lit by two similar lamps, one on either side of a door.

Once out of the brush, I realize there's an enormous structure towering over this porch, at least three stories tall, ringed with layers of steep shingles and multiple roofs. It's been a thousand years since I've seen anything like it. It's what they used to call a manor. Only kings and chieftains had them. In fact, it's not so very different than King Alfr's Great Manor, built around a series of mammoth wooden staves. The porch itself is an oddity, an incongruent slice of Florida rusticity annexed to long-lost Norse architecture. Gods help Hildy and whoever else lives here if a typical Florida brush fire tears through these woods.

Looming over and dwarfing the manor is a colossal tree, vastly different than any of the oaks, pines, palms, cypress, hickories, maples, hollies and the like. It seems to have grown right through the roof or, more likely, the manor was built around it. Looks like a mammoth ash tree. I wonder if it is even real or some sort of long-lost Disney attraction. Shaking my head, I go back to studying the porch.

Even in this crappy light, I can see the sheen of well-preserved wood, a kind of subdued varnish making it glow. On the roof over the porch, there is a carved balustrade, something I have never seen before. On the porch is a rocking chair and a porch swing. I park the bike and ascend the steps, which squeak but not in a dangerous way. The workmanship is solid.

Just before I knock, I hear someone approaching on the other side of the swinging screen door. I'm hoping, expecting actually, that Hildy will be answering, but the footsteps are heavy. She must have a husband, lover, father, uncle, something.

When the door first starts to swing, I have the impression of a menacing figure nearly as large as I am. For a split second, I wonder if Hildy collects trolls for a hobby. Then I realize the figure is a shawl-wearing older woman with skin the color of bronze—in her late sixties or early seventies, I'd say—who looks human enough, just unrestrainedly magnified.

Beneath the grayish shawl around her shoulders is a flowing black robe. Her expression is as stoic as some Okie character out of a Steinbeck novel. She turns around and shouts the language of the Old Country in a dialect I barely grasp, though her words are simple, "Hildr! The troll cometh." A statement of fact. No surprise, no urgency. I'm just the expected, boring prom date, nothing unusual in this fractured-fairytale stave castle with a black Okie giant grandma who speaks some long-extinct dialect of ancient Norse.

The old woman exits down the hall even as Hildy approaches. Her hair is down, the color of chestnuts this time, and she smiles impishly. Sporting a metallic-looking sleeveless blouse and a flowing blue skirt, she holds her hands behind her back and rocks a little as she looks up at me; the fresh-faced girl who I first met at the tollbooth is back, sans bloody corpse.

"Evening, Klaus," she says, reaching out to take my hand. "We're so happy you could make it to Haven. Care for a tour?"

She walks me through a variety of rooms on the first floor, all lit with oil lamps. It's still and peaceful. The rooms are decorated with wooden furniture, some of it ornately carved in the style of the Gripping Beast, the elongated head far removed from limbs and claws and tail, wondrously tangled, twisted and contorted, like an ancient saga in which heroes and villains merge and disappear into one another.

We don't ascend the steep stairs to the upper rooms. Instead, I'm shown into the enormous room in the back, which faces a river or stream of some sort. Incredible. The broad, high hall is long like the nave in a cathedral, though open to the outside through two massive, wooden sliding doors. They're like the doors of a barn but taller, heavier and more ornate. It feels as if the world outside were the presbytery. In the middle of the magnificent space is a gigantic truss that turns out to be the ash tree – yes, definitely a white ash, to be specific, far too tall for this Florida landscape. Its straight trunk is covered in thick, light-colored bark with a diamond pattern reaching up to the high roof and beyond. There are only a few branches with leaves within the hall itself. How could there be green blades without sunlight?

The impossible tree looks powerful, yet past its prime. There are patches of moss and places where the bark is thinning, as if eroded by beetles with sandpaper carapaces.

Maybe it's not insects, but I'd swear something's moving, as if the veins and swirls of gnarled bark were rising slowly upwards along the trunk. I blink several times, trying to rid myself of what must be an optical illusion, then look elsewhere.

Twisted roots visibly push up through the stone floor. In Florida, I've seen many a leaning old oak tree pushed over by a hurricane and then somehow surviving with its roots showing. But this is different. The tree doesn't lean. It sits atop the complex mass of roots. They remind me of cypress knees but are more, well, rooty—like tentacles reaching out, almost capable of movement. I get the feeling of tendrils nurturing themselves amid unseen forces in the air. There's one astonishing root in particular that looks as if it's the dorsal ridge of an enormous serpent diving into the stonework of the floor, fully submerging only at the end of the hallway, as if plunging into the body of water outside.

Several feet in front of the tree is a kind of fountain or, maybe, an inverted well. The water rises up through a broad cylinder of gray-and-white Fauske marble and then falls over a lip into a large stone pool bottomed with light-colored clay. Hints of green algae mar the lip of the marble and portions of the clay below. From the pool, a stream of water flows in a stone trough parallel to the dorsal ridge root.

"You've already met my great aunt Urdy," Hildy says, nodding to the woman knitting in an immense rocking chair facing toward the tree root. In the barest possible acknowledgment, she darts her eyes my way for a moment before fixing them again on the roots, staring as if there were a television glowing with a primetime cop drama.

"This is my Aunt Verda," Hildy says. "Verda the Venerable."

"So very nice to meet you, Klaus," says Aunt Verda, who sits in another rocking chair facing the tree from the other side of the room. She looks a lot like the other aunt, though maybe a few years younger and with lighter skin. Both are dressed in black except for their dun-colored shawls and embroidered white headscarves. It's all very old school, but Verda has a modern sensibility about her, speaking American English with barely a hint of a Norwegian accent.

"We don't get many visitors to Haven anymore," she says, smiling. "I'm afraid our family has dwindled over the years, and it's so difficult to make new friends. Hildy, make Klaus a cup of tea."

I think about asking for something else, a beer maybe. There's something in Verda's tone, however, that makes it hard to even consider anything else. Hildy takes a kettle from an ancient-looking wood-burning stove in the corner and fills it with water from the fountain. Then Hildy and I sit in large wooden chairs—everything here seems designed for the giant aunts—on either side of an old-fashioned, slender tea table made of what seems to be oak.

As we sit, waiting for the water to simmer, I realize that what I'm looking at isn't a river or stream but a surprisingly large fresh-water spring. The combination of moonlight and outdoor torchlight reveals a boil of water, a subtle but constantly shifting distortion of the surface making the reflections quiver.

Feeling intimidated, I search for something clever but nervy to say. *So I guess this is how the one percent lives*, or *Your flood insurance must be a bitch*, or *What were the Brothers Grimm smoking when they dreamt this place up?*

I decide on silence.

Hildy prepares our tea and we slowly slip into small talk. She says there is a third aunt, Skuldy, who is away at the moment. That explains the other rocking chair that sits empty between the two aunts.

"This is really nice," I say, looking back over the spring.

"Nice?" she responds, amused again.

"Yeah, well, maybe *very* nice."

Even as I grin at her, I start to realize that there's far too much seidr here, unsettling, spell-bindingly, dangerously old-school divinity magic. I sensed a hint of it when I first met Hildy at Snorri's. But this... this is more seidr than I've ever felt collected in one place, even going back to my childhood when there were some seriously fae creatures hanging out around the troll village.

Back then, the short, shrunken trolls were the worst. I once saw one of the mammoth hill trolls, drunk off his ass and staggering, step on a shrimpy unseelie and literally lose one of his three heads by falling perfectly on his own axe. You didn't mess with those tough little shapers of fate.

Unlike humans, we didn't view magic as black or white. Seidr and the incantation magic called galdr were simply other forms of power, like broad shoulders or a cunning mind. Part of becoming an adult was learning that magic was a razor-edged weapon, something you handled with care.

Mor had taught me some basic magic, but I was not a good student. My spells would often falter and fall apart, as if I were a dangerously clumsy child muffing his way through a back handspring. My mother would get angry and kept saying I was thinking too much. It turned out that the only kind of magic I was remotely proficient at was known as petitioning, the kind of spell where I had to call on some higher power to ask for help. It made my mother scowl. "A dangerous beggar's magic," she'd called it. As for the divinity magic known as seidr, I was hopeless except for being able to sense it.

Here in the place Hildy calls Haven, though, the seidr is as thick as black flies in a summer forest, starting to make my skin itch and crawl.

I'm getting tenser by the moment in Hildy's tainted Eden, ready for some shit to hit, knowing that a troll's strength can be a puny defense against high-voltage magic. I need to tread carefully, stay polite in front of these two old ladies while backing out the door as soon as possible.

I am about to cut to the chase and ask, as cordially as a troll can, why I was invited here. Then I notice Hildy has somehow multiplied. There are three of her now. So, either the tea is laced with something or...

Fuck me, I think, trying to make the three Hildies cohere into one.

"Did you say something?" they all ask. Did I say it out loud? Is she, or they, reading my mind? All three of her are looking at me but with different expressions. The older, corporate-looking one is coldly attentive, the younger cover girl is amused, and the third wild-haired, bar-chick Hildy just seems smug. They are all three starting to piss me off.

Too late to be cordial. "Look, Hildies," I growl, standing up. "I can snap three necks as easy as I can the one. What is in the goddamned tea!"

She coheres again, but I swear she's still wearing all three looks at once. "Sit down, Hallr," she tells me with authority. "There's nothing in the tea but water, water that many would give their right eyes for."

"What did you call me?"

"You heard me, Hallr Halftroll. It's a better name than Klaus, isn't it? Though still not your truest name."

I sit back down, though not because she's ordered it. No choice, really. My legs have gone wobbly. It's been a long, long time since I've heard that name: Hallr Halftroll. I try to give her a wry, puzzled grin, though I know I can't pull it off. I'm terrified, more afraid than I've been since being shipwrecked on this caveless hell of a sandbar called Florida. Maybe more afraid, since I don't remember being virtually paralyzed then. She can't know my true name, of course. Even I've heard it only once. Whatever she and her weird aunts are, it's appalling to think they'd have that kind of power over me.

True names are a mere fiction in the twenty-first century, a legend from fairy tales, a throwback as incomprehensible to most modern humans as blood sacrifice and ritual dance. Those things harken back to longer, darker, colder days when the wise knew secrets that could kill and control. Such secrets aren't the spawn of theory and experiment, like the nuclear knowledge of engineers. And they aren't the closely held and closeted whispers of scandal that are the stock in trade of extortionists and politicians.

They are more dangerous. To those who know the ancient secret of your true name, you are hardly more than a puppet.

"No, I do not know it, Hallr," she says. "But *they* may be able to divine it," she nods in the direction of the aunts, who pay us no attention.

The runes on my neck suddenly itch dreadfully. Even back in the Old World—where magic was familiar and trolls were fact rather than folklore—these beings and this place were mere legend. No, not just legend: religion.

"What the hell do you really want, Hildy?" I ask.

"We want what everyone wants," she says. "To be left in peace. You are going to help us with that."

Chapter Fifteen

"If you want to be a Viking, you will need to be a sailor as well as a warrior."
—*Viking: The Norse Warrior's [Unofficial] Manual*

In the spring after Alfr's manor burned, the two kings came to an agreement in which Bloodaxe gave Alfr access to his rich southern hunting territories. In exchange, Alfr gave Bloodaxe access to certain harbors and bays controlled by the Völsungs. It was widely seen as an honorable compromise. Through my friend Leos, however, I knew that Dofri had counseled outright war, arguing that it was inevitable and that Bloodaxe would only use the truce to consolidate his power and erode ours.

In the end, though, Halfdan Sunmane was sent home, to the relief of the kingdom and, especially, the Völsung clan. There had been no more talk of nuptials between Halfdan and Inge since the night of the fire. Though nothing was proven against him, the town of Risør viewed Sunmane as an arsonist.

The rumors about "Sunmane the Blazestarter" must have pricked the ego of Bloodaxe and his kin. Or maybe they simply used the insult to justify their own brand of slander. In any case, the noxious gossip about "Inge the Troll-Lover" spread through the countryside more quickly than any fire could. By the time I finally learned of it from Leos, who had been mightily reluctant to broach the subject with me, my own fate was sealed.

I was summoned to Alfr's chambers in the night, while the rest of the town and, more to the point, his own family slept. I had hardly seen the king since the night of the blaze. He had been busy with the negotiations, preparations for war, and the rebuilding of the Great Manor. Two members of his guard led me into the newly rebuilt wing. Although it had been well swept of sawdust and other debris, it was clearly a work in progress. Freshly cut planks leaned up against one wall, barrels of tar and varnish were clustered into corners, along with saws, axes, adzes, chisels and sundry other tools. The giant staves in the new hallway had already been set but were so recently barked and carved that the scent of the wood dominated all other smells.

As he inspected the new wing of his great hallway, Alfr looked pensive, waving off his guard but not yet acknowledging me. I knew little of human kings at the time, but I realize now how unusual he was. In that age, the people in parts of what later became Norway selected their leaders, though that selection process was usually messy and political, often determined by favors owed, land owned, and last-minute switches of loyalty. Brutal skirmishes and duels sometimes played a part. A chieftain did not become a chieftain merely through blood connections. He had to prove himself both on and off the battlefield.

In his prime, Alfr was not the strongest warrior in the country, or even in his own clan. Being of medium build, he relied more on quickness and technique in a fight rather than on brute strength. Nor was he the most comely or charming of men. His unremarkable brown hair had started receding at an early age, highlighting eyes that were a tad too narrow over a nose too sharp. He had the look of a bird, though a serious bird with a penetrating stare. A bird of prey.

As he turned those eyes on me, I could sense an inner conflict I'd not seen before. There was a reluctant resentment in his stare, a look that was foreboding, a look that was at war with the first words he said to me.

"Hail, Hallr Halftroll," he said, striving for a smile and sportive tone, "slayer of jarls, tutor of soldiers, snatcher of princes, battler of blazes. See what your works have wrought."

He raised and spread his arms as if to encompass the entire hall.

"I am sorry we were not able to save this wing, my lord," I said carefully. "This is beautiful construction, but it must come at a dear price."

He nodded, accepting the apology even as he refuted the need for it. "Nonsense, Hallr. Without your heroism, we would be rebuilding everything, rather than just one wing."

I stayed silent, merely bowing to acknowledge his words.

"And you halted a costly war," he stated more quietly, with a hint of the resentment I'd already seen in his eyes. "Or at least postponed it. Now, Hallr. I require your aid again."

"I am at your service, my lord."

Here Alfr hesitated. To his credit, I think he was loath to do what was necessary, to capitulate to the smears of Bloodaxe and send me into exile in order to protect the reputation of his daughter. Many a king would have concocted some reason to slay me and be done with it. From the very beginning, allowing me to live had been an unnecessary risk. Now, the risks had grown.

"I am sending you west, Hallr. I require that you crew on one of my ships in order to increase the lands and wealth of our kingdom."

"On a ship, my lord?" I asked.

"Yes, Hallr, a ship. It is the only path open to us now."

Putting a troll in the middle of the sea is like placing a garden slug in the middle of a desert. The mere prospect seems elementally wrong, an act of sadism by a dark, curious child. Viking ships of that age were as open to Sól as a blooming rose.

Yes, Alfr had assigned me to his greatest longboat, the *Ormen Vig*, a sleek and deadly vessel with twenty benches. Maybe sixty feet long and nine wide, it was grand enough for a chieftain in those days, though not among the true one hundred and twenty foot giants of later years. On its bow was carved a dragon's head, fanged and opened mouth, reared back and ready to strike. Its horns curved gracefully backwards above an ornately scaled neck, and wide, angry eyes looked down on me as I stood on a wooden wharf in the darkness.

I spat into the black waters. The dragon was oddly familiar and yet terrifying. I wondered if I'd seen such a creature somewhere in the dark tunnels of my youth. But no. I realized it had the look of a maddened stallion on the battlefield, ready to sink its teeth into whatever meaty part—shoulder, arm, unhelmed head—a steadfast foot soldier might present it. Whatever shipwright or artisan had made this thing had clearly been to war in foreign lands with large horses.

I wanted to attack it in a bloody rage, pull apart its facade, and rip to splinters its inspired carvings as if they were the time I'd spent in the company of weak, smelly, short-lived men. Yes, I was infuriated by Bloodaxe and Sunmane, but I also felt betrayed by Alfr and the whole of Risør. Though there was no logic to it, I even resented Inge.

"You have a black look," said Leos.

"It is a black world," I rumbled, with a hint of threat. Which was absurd. Leos, too, had been sacrificed by Alfr, commanded to go sailing and pillaging with the troll, to watch over the beast, to abandon dreams of family and farming and the homeland he loved.

"Yes," he said, trying to make light of my mood, "but it will be a light world again soon with sunrise. We must find the captain before then."

Leos and I had hiked for two nights, resting in caves and crevices during the daylight hours. We said little, the camaraderie of our nights as sentries of Risør strained by our new orders. Even so, we moved like a single animal, me taking the lead, slowing enough to allow him to keep up in the darkness, holding back branches so they would not whip him as I passed, warning him of holes and roots he could not see.

He, in turn, hunted and foraged in the daylight hours, feeding us both so we could make good time during our night marches.

Having found the wharf and longship, we soon sniffed out the captain's tent. Grim of Gokstad was asleep inside when we arrived, but a bleary-eyed boy of thirteen years or so sat outside by a low fire, apparently waiting for us. When Leos greeted him with a low voice, the boy startled but made no sound, glancing quickly around as if seeking out enemies. He'd been trained for war, at least as much as a boy can be. I wondered how he'd gotten the bruises on the left side of his face.

It wasn't till he looked past Leos up at me that he nodded assent to our request that he wake his master. After all, Leos could have been anyone, perhaps an enemy spy, but even in the dim firelight, there was no mistaking the notorious troll of the Völsung clan. He crept on all fours beneath a leather flap. Soon we heard a loud, ill-tempered boom of a voice curse the boy. Five minutes or so later, Captain Grim shoved aside a flap as if it had insulted him and stalked outside.

Leos was starting to greet him when he marched right past us and took a long, hissing piss into the low fire. Leos and I glanced at each other.

"So you're the troll's keeper," Grim said, his back still to us.

Leos didn't know how to respond. No one had ever called him my keeper, though we both knew it was true.

The captain turned around, pulling up his trousers slowly as we watched, making a show of his still-dripping organ.

"I am Leos, and my companion is Hallr. We are honored to be sailing with you, Captain, on King Alfr's flagship."

Grim spat as he tied his trousers and dropped his tunic over them. The man had a slight paunch and long blond hair starting to gray, but there was nothing decrepit about him. He had a scar across his right eyebrow where the hair no longer grew and another along his jawline, a botched stitching job partly hidden in a scraggly beard that had more gray in it than his scalp did. Compared to many other warriors I'd met, he was not burly but had the look of a man with stringy, tough muscles. If my mor had slain him, she would have made him into a soup.

"It is his lord's ship to do as he pleases," said Grim, hardly sparing me a look, "but bringing a troll thrall aboard her is not pleasing to its captain. You will control him, and I you. If there are any breakdowns in this order, you will both pay the price."

Grim turned and started back to his tent, raising his voice so we would hear.

"Kol will show you the trollbox. Make sure the beast is stowed by sunrise if you don't want it turned to a stone anchor, though that might be the best use for it."

The boy, who we assumed was Kol, came quietly out of the tent and walked past us, not even bidding us to follow. We followed anyway.

"I'm not sure he likes us," whispered Leos to me, trying to ease the tension.

Kol responded without turning. "My far is a live shark thrashing in a small boat. He hates us all the same."

Chapter Sixteen

"Earth there was not,
Nor heaven above,
The Ginungagap was,
But grass nowhere."
—*The Younger Edda*

In the beginning was the Void, at least as the ancient Norse told it. There was neither Earth nor Heaven. Nor sand, nor sea, nor cooling billows. There was just a huge yawning hole in the universe known as Ginnungagap, as unlovely as an urban mud hole bordered by rusty wire and broken boards.

The Void did not stretch on infinitely, though. To its north were the frozen wastes of Niflheim, or "abode of mists," a region where eleven frozen rivers flowed at a glacial pace from a primordial well called Hvergelmer. The place was like some poisoned, abandoned industrial park in a rust-belt town. Think Buffalo or Detroit in the worst winter blizzard ever.

To the south of the Void was an equally crappy but totally different neighborhood called Muspelheim, or "realm of fire." It was as hot as Niflheim was cold, as glaringly bright as Niflheim was dark. It was sort of like the city of Phoenix after yet another housing bust, except with fewer tracts of thistle and puncturevine.

As was bound to occur in a universe where shit inevitably happens, the poisonous floes of Niflheim's rivers started seeping into the blasting, blazing plains of Muspelheim. This is when it all hit the cosmic fan. The venomous rivers of rime exploded into hot clouds and poured a rancid, chemical hail down into the yawning void of Ginnungagap. It was the Norse version of the Big Bang.

As it happened, the gargantuan icy sleet congealed, then quickened into life, taking the form of the first being in all the universe, a giant— or, as they used to say, *jotunn*. Not just any giant. The most giant giant in the history of giants. Although the humans later referred to him as Ymir, his fellow giants called him Aurgelmir. When I was a young troll, Mor called him Arg.

Arg was a fertile fellow. From the sweat under one of his gigantic arms, there grew a slightly less gigantic son and daughter, and then he begat another son—on one of his feet, no less.

It apparently made for hungry work. Arg drank from the milk of an enormous cow formed at the same time and in the same way Arg was. She lived by licking the salt stones that were covered by the layers of hoarfrost all around them. With her stupendous tongue, the astonishing ungulate uncovered—or maybe carved out from briny crags—another being named Buri.

So there they all were in their salty, icy new neighborhood: Arg, Arg's kids, the cow and the cow-carved Buri. They were the first to take up residence in the now foul-but-fertile mud pit called Ginnungagap.

You would think these first people would get along, being created by the same mysterious cataclysm. But, the way Mor told it, Buri turned out to be an utter asshole, small and jealous and pettily pissed that he wasn't part of Arg's immediate family. He hid it well at first, so eager was he to woo and screw Arg's giant daughter. He and the daughter eventually had a horde of half-giant brats, but his new family only made things worse for Buri. He hated being the puniest person in the universe, smaller even than his own children. So, though he cozied up to his father-in-law Arg, he schemed and plotted, as the ones like him—later called the Aesir—were born to do.

By and by, covetous Buri became the granddad to three fuckwit grandchildren, one of them the future ruler of Asgard: Odin.

Despite the fact that they were partly giants themselves, these nasty spawn shared their grandpa's seething bigotry against and hatred of the titans. They decided, like some inbred gang of midget thugs, to take down the old patriarch Arg. And not in a gentle way.

Mor described the murder in great detail. Cunning Odin struck first, aiming his knife at the lower spinal column so that Arg wouldn't be able to stand. As the Great One fell, Odin's brother Vili tried to slit Arg's throat by coming from around the back, but Arg's neck was too thick and Vili's arms too short. Arg, as maimed as he was, was able to grab Vili by the balls and yank them clean off. As Vili screamed, his brother Ve swung a great axe into Arg's carotid artery, causing a flood of blood so terrible that it drowned all but two of all the many *jotnar*, or giants, in Ginnungagap. The universe has not seen such a blood bath since.

After the slaying and flood, the three murderous brats dragged the First Being's corpse into the middle of Ginnungagap and turned him into landfill. Today, we are all living on the colossal corpse of Arg. Buri's grandkids channeled Arg's blood to make the seas and cracked his bones to make the rocks and tossed his brains to make the clouds and raised his skull to make the sky.

"And that's why we call him Arg," Mor told us. "It was his death cry as he was betrayed and dismembered by the half-breeds. Even now, in the winding tunnels, you can sometimes hear his name roaring through the hollows, ever reminding us of the crimes by the cruel and crafty Aesir."

Mor said the great and holy body of Arg/Ymir was used to create all the realms, except for the primordial Niflheim and Muspelheim. She said even the great ash tree Yggdrasil, which connects the nine realms as a body connects its organs, was made from Arg.

I remember how puzzled I was when I heard those tales, trying to envision the substance of a Void, to gauge the girth of the great Arg, to comprehend the tangles of cosmic roots and branches and rivers and springs. Where exactly were the other realms? Could I travel to them one day? Were they in the sky or over the seas or in caverns below the stone mountains? Was the thick star stalk of the Milky Way actually Yggdrasil itself?

Mor would become impatient with my queries.

"No more stupid questions from you," she'd say, squeezing my face in the tight clamp of her thumb and forefinger. "No wisdom comes of questions. Wisdom is won through fearless onslaughts."

I nodded to preserve my pinched face but, in fact, her words only baffled me further. How could onslaughts on half-logical legends achieve anything like wisdom? How else could I learn stories if I were not properly told them? Only now do I realize that even as a youngster, long before my capture by King Alfr, I was thinking more like a human than a troll. It must have aggrieved poor Mor.

I am still sitting in the large wooden rocking chair at Haven. The moon has veered across the sky, and the mist over the spring has grown suddenly thick. Hildy still sits beside me. I sense that hours have rushed as I've sat here in a daze.

"I don't get this place," I say to myself aloud. Could the giant tree looming over this spring be truly linked to Mor's bizarre tales of Yggdrasil?

"You are a dumb troll," someone says, startling me. It takes me a moment to realize it's Aunt Urdy speaking in the Old Tongue. She and Verda have pulled their mammoth rocking chairs up behind us, as if the heavy rockers were just a couple of lawn seats.

"True," I say, glancing back at her. "The question is, what exactly are you? And what are you up to? Trying to turn me into some kind of roofied stooge to do your bidding?"

She makes a hissing sound of exasperation, as if I'd only confirmed her worse opinion of me.

"Shush, Klaus," Hildy says. "Do not tempt fate."

"Look," I say. "I may be just another dull troll, but even I know that this place can't be what it seems. This spring can't be *the* Spring, this tree can't be *the* Tree. Yggdrasil is most definitely not in the middle of bumfuck Florida."

"No," says Urdy and "yes," says Verda, weirdly in sync.

Hildy shakes her head in consternation. "It's like a network, Klaus. It's... complicated. What you most need to know is that it's under attack by something dangerous and insidious, something encroaching even in sanctuaries like this one. If you're discerning, you can feel it, smell it, taste it, catch glimpses here and there."

"Whatever. I don't really care. It all gives me the heebie-jeebies anyway. Just tell me, why am I here?"

"To aid us, dear," says Verda.

"Aid you? A bunch of tough broads packing enough seidr to drop a bevy of berserkers dead in their tracks? Who or what is going to mess with the likes of you?"

The three women look at each other. Urdy folds her giant arms, clearly not deigning further responses to a fool such as myself.

"Let me guess," I say. "It's complicated."

Hildy nods.

"So give me the Cliff Notes version," I say.

"There are Powers within Powers, dear boy," says Aunt Verda.

"Yeah, okay. Now how about a version even a 'dumb troll' can get?"

Aunt Urdy mumbles something.

"What'd she say?" I ask Hildy.

Urdy reaches over to put her huge mitts on my shoulder. When I turn, she grabs my face between thumb and forefinger as Mor used to do. She puts her nose up close to mine. In a heavily accented English that she enunciates slowly, she says, "Fucking Florida real estate assholes."

I nod at her. When she lets me go, I rub my jaws like a child.

"Well hell, ladies," I finally say. "Then I guess even the likes of you got trouble."

As Hildy tells me their tale of woe, the night sky shifts in eerie ways that I can only assume is the result of the tea they gave me. The moon rises, and then suddenly slips into the middle of the sky. The stars move quickly, then slowly, and then reverse themselves. It's hard for me to keep track of what Hildy is saying. The night sky changes again, only this time I don't even recognize the constellations. The Milky Way seems so deep and rich, like a rainbow across the heavens. I'm no longer sitting in a chair but, rather, up against some sort of red bank of rich dirt. Behind me, there is no hallway and no aunts, just a giant looming tree, its leaves browning around the edges. Starting to die, maybe?

One of my arms rests on a huge root reaching through the bank of dirt and into a dark pool of water below. I can't decide what it is: a sinkhole, a dried up lake, some kind of well?

"Are you tired, Klaus?"

Whatever kind of cuckoo teleportation trance I'm in, Hildy is the constant. She leans against my shoulder, also staring into the pool, as if we were sharing a single thought.

"I don't know what I am, or where I am. I'm not sure I'm even awake."

"You are," she assures me.

"What's that smell?"

"Eucalyptus."

"Like the cough drops," I say.

"Yes," she says, smiling. "Like the cough drops. You always have to play the clod, don't you? As if it's a role you've played so long you no longer know how to give it up."

"You're one to talk. You've got more faces than Big Ben."

"I contain multitudes," she says in accented English, a much lighter version of her Aunt Urdy's. "But there is a core, Hallr Halftroll. This I believe. If there were not, then who is it that is so lonely?"

I don't say anything to this, wondering where the camouflage and line of bullshit ends. These roots feel real enough, rough, gnarled and hard. The twisted threads making up the roots could be letters or numbers, equations or incantations, if I could only read them. Another Yggdrasil in some other place? She said something about a network. I gaze up into the tree and wonder what it hides.

"They call it a Tasmanian Blue Gum," she says.

"So, I guess we're not in Kansas anymore. Or Florida, either, for that matter."

"It's a part of our legacy. Did you know a Viking ship once made it to these Australian shores?"

"I don't think Howard Zinn mentioned it."

"They were lost, battered and overwhelmed."

"I know the feeling," I sigh, leaning back.

The Blue Gum is gone, though I don't remember moving away from it. The night is somehow spent. In the dawn, the mist over the spring curls, stretches and steams. I'd swear there's a meaning to these ghostly wisps, one that barely eludes me. It reminds me of the roots of the Blue Gum tree and the motile bark of the ash, except in a kind of time lapse. In the spring, there are some sort of large waterfowl, swans I think, diving in nearby weeds and preening themselves.

"Care for a swim in Aunt Urdy's spring, Hallr?" asks a half-seen form in the billows below. Hildy's voice.

"Sun's up soon. I'm a bit, um, sensitive."

"Not here, you're not."

I don't quite believe her but, then again, belief has become a quaint concept since yesterday. I'm absurdly self-conscious as I shed my clothing, feeling more like a timorous teenager than a middle-aged troll. Still, even leaving aside the draw of Hildy herself, there's something alluring here. Something both primordial and fresh.

As I enter the water, she takes my hand and draws me further in. The water is cool, not cold.

"Come," she says. "There is an omphalos, a core where all connects. Believe in this if nothing else. It is the beginning of wisdom."

As she looks up at me and leads me on, I see a darkness just below the water in front of her. Before I can warn her, a tendril reaches out from below and wraps itself around her neck. It's like nothing I've ever seen before, just dark green goop that stinks. Hildy's eyes widen as she is yanked down by whatever vicious, spumy scum lurks in the spring.

Not thinking, I reach down into the darkness even as it reaches for me, a cold slimy muck wrapping around my arm. I try to pull it up but, Jesus, it's heavy. I can only lift the top of whatever it is a foot or so out of the waters. It doesn't yank me down so much as simply grow heavier, so heavy it sinks back into the darkening waters, threatening to drag me in after it.

Hildy and her aunts mentioned something insidious, but this shit is as subtle as a stone hammer to the head. It's a full-on assault.

I'm terrified, of course, but also furious, affronted by the idea that algae's uglier brother is threatening to kill me, me, who may be the last living troll in the wide world, the son of Mor, the slayer of great warriors, the direct descendant of mighty Aurgelmir! I shout in outrage and yank up my right arm with the help of my left. I pull it a foot, two feet, and three above the surface, roaring with effort.

Up comes a head-shaped glob, followed by a shoulder and a torso that I assume are Hildy's. She is wrapped in a yellowish green tangle of noxious dross. As I try dragging it all backwards toward the banks of the spring, a beam from the rising sun hits like a spotlight, the rays slowly dissolving the slime. A nose emerges from beneath the mass. Just when I think we're going to make it, I start stumbling in the water and recognize that whatever-nasty-ass-evil this is has begun tangling around my legs. I can't believe I'm going to die like this in four feet of water.

Then, of all things, three fat swans soar out of the sky and barely touch the water surface before diving beneath. There is suddenly a swirling mass of white battling the darkness below. One swan's snaky head pops up out of the water, dragging a twist of riverweed in its mouth, points its beak into the sky, and swallows the damned stuff down. It goes back under the water for seconds at a time.

Never have I been so happy for the gluttony of waterfowl. One after another, the swans repeatedly dive down and rip away the muck from my legs. Soon, I'm able to move again and drag my exhausted ass onto the shore, where I snatch the green scum from around Hildy's head and the rest of her body. Water dribbles out of her lifeless lips and I bend down to give her mouth-to-mouth when suddenly one of the damn swans bites my hand and another nips my cheek.

"Fucking birds," I shout. "I'm trying to help here!"

All three of them erupt into a cacophony of high-pitched honking as they try nuzzling Hildy with their orange beaks. And it actually works. Hildy opens her eyes and spews, throwing up sickening globs of green gunk in mucousy liquid. And if that weren't enough, all three swans start doing the same thing. I'm about to retch myself amid the steaming clumps of goo when Hildy, still a naked, wretched mess, takes my hand in hers and squeezes.

It feels good and awkwardly erotic. With as much gentleness as I can muster, I return the squeeze and try to come up with some quip to lighten the mood. Then I happen to look up to the deck, where both of the giant aunts stand, just staring down at us, silent as stones, eyes glinting in the morning light.

Chapter Seventeen

"My feet were pinched by the cold,
shackled by the frost in cold chains,
while anxieties sighed hot around my heart."
—*The Seafarer*

The trollbox was like an extra-long coffin, except made with less care. Its rough oak planks were hammered together by a motley assortment of nails and hinges, some rusty, others newly smithed. It was longer than I was tall.

Since there was no room to waste, even on this largest of all ships in Alfr's fleet, the box doubled as a long bench for two oarsmen. It also contained compartments—to which I wouldn't have access from inside the box—that held miscellaneous tools, weapons and dried foods.

In the minutes before dawn, Leos and I stared down at the trollbox in stunned silence as Kol threw it open. There were manacles inside. I hadn't worn chains since my very first days in Risør. Alfr had bound me with my word. Grim clearly preferred iron.

"Odin's Eye," Leos finally said, shaking his head. "Hallr…"

"A very practical crypt. Am I to wear the jewelry?" I asked cold-eyed Kol. The boy nodded. I thought hard about running off into the forest. Would they chase me? Probably. Catch me? With sunrise approaching, they'd have had a good chance. Still, the urge to flee was strong. I didn't know if I could maintain my oath to Alfr in the face of this humiliation.

"I'll talk to the captain about that," Leos said, picking up the rusty iron chains with distaste and attaching them to my arms and legs.

"Sure," I said. "He seems like a reasonable type." Then I climbed into the rough box, trying to smile sardonically though filled with dread.

I had brought the black leather garb and wired hood that allowed me to fight in Alfr's army, but I wouldn't wear it in the box. I anticipated that not only would it be hot and suffocating, but seeping water would saturate the cloth, making the box feel even more like a tomb. So I removed everything but my trousers and undertunic, trusting to the wood and my robust nature to get me through.

The first day was a taste of Helheim. Before the dawn, it was merely frosty. Not long after we made our way into the open water, however, the remnants of cold waves breaking over the gunwale began sloshing up through the porous and portable deck, saturating the bottom of my box. Even for a troll accustomed to dank and dripping caves it was frigid, the ocean waters having barely warmed in the early spring. A thin layer of arctic chill descended on everything from my ankles to the back of my head.

After sunrise, the slanted rays of Sól sliced between the boards of the box, burning me like thin, hot wires. I was the incarnation of Ginnungagap, cleft and tormented between the icy rimes of Niflheim and burning rays of Muspelheim.

The physical torment lasted for hours. It was the middle of spring, so the days were long and growing longer. The winds were against us. Captain Grim should have waited till they were more favorable, but he was an impatient man, so we ended up humping slowly over hostile gray waves.

Ornolf the Oaf was the hulking simpleton who shared the top of the trollbox, which doubled as a thwart, with Leos. On that first day, I learned that the oaf was a lightning rod for ridicule, had god-like powers of flatulence, and was a magnificent machine with an oar. He was a metronome propelling the king's ship through the dark waves with something more than just force—with a kind of inevitability. It was beautiful in its way, the swing of that oar. When I first started to doze in that accursed box, I thought it was hypothermia setting in, representing the slow, lingering, and ignoble death of a troll in a box on a fucking boat. Then I realized it was being lulled by the perfect cadence of the oaf's oar, never out of sync, never pulling air or losing his grip or going through the motions to appease Grim.

So there I'd be, just starting to doze off despite the burning and the cold and cramping and humiliation. Then the oaf would let one rip, literally shivering the boards above me with a string of farts. The first few times, I smacked my head on top of the trollbox as I was jolted awake, causing the crew to laugh uproariously at the idiotic dialogue between oaf and troll.

"Looks like breaking wind excites the troll slave, Ornolf. Make sure he gets his fill!" said one of the crew. Whether the oaf took these as words of encouragement or not, I don't know. I do know that on that first day, every ear-rending oaf fart would be followed by a storm of laughter and comments about the big, ass-sniffing noses of trolls or how the explosions would be music to troll ears. Grim quietly encouraged such jibes, once telling them to properly respect the "king's idle troll lord."

By the time it was dusk, the crew not only considered me a fool but, even worse, a useless one that had been inexplicably foisted on them by an out-of-touch, capricious king.

When Leos finally opened the trollbox, I had the appearance of an ill-kept beast: wet, disheveled, exhausted, still suffering red welts from the sunlight that had found its way into the crate. There was no pity in the crewmen's eyes, only combinations of curiosity, mirth, resentment and a kind of repressed fear to which I'd long since become inured in my time with humans.

"I've seen bigger trolls," said a balding man with a black beard.

"But none that stank so much," joked his thwart-mate, cuing the rest to laugh. Most had a hand on their weapons, ready in case the unleashed troll should charge. Indeed, I was sorely tempted to do so, laying waste to Alfr's ship of fools in revenge for my expulsion from Risør.

I didn't, of course, not only because of my pledge to Alfr but because any attack on these men in the middle of the sea would be suicide, and certain death for innocent Leos.

"Halftroll, I hope you're well rested because now we put your brawn to the oar. Take over for Leos. The rest of you prepare to make landfall and set up camp."

So, still chained and poorly clothed, I took an oar for the first time in my life and tried to synchronize my rowing with the steady Ornolf's. In short order, I wished I were back in the hellish box as I flailed away with the oars. At first, I wasn't dipping deeply enough, thereby catching mostly air and falling backwards off the thwart. This gave rise to more hilarity and jeering among the crew. Grim, who manned the steering oar, cursed as the ship corkscrewed and fishtailed.

"Dig down deeper, damnable troll!" he yelled.

In trying to dig deeper, I nearly threw myself overboard, again to much merriment by some but muttered consternation to those who were unpacking the gear we'd be using to set up camp. Grim used the wet blade of an oar to hit me upside the head.

"Captain, sir!" yelled Leos, who was no doubt afraid I'd jam that oar up Grim's ass, "I'd be pleased to take over for a time to show him the proper swings."

"Nay," said Grim. "He'll learn like every other landlubbing suckling who has ever gone to sea. The oaf learned and learned well through my tender tutelage, didn't you, Ornolf?"

The dim giant smiled and farted in response, never relenting in his mighty, pendulous swings even as I blundered along. By and by, despite my floundering, we brought the ship in along the coast and landed near the sandy mouth of a small river. Only once we hauled the shallow-bottomed ship up onto the beach did I realize that Grim knew this landing well and had found the place in near darkness.

The tired crew worked mostly in silence, knowing the routine of setting up their cooking pits and sleeping spots by heart. They briefly livened up as they devoured their stew of fresh eels and salted cod around a large fire made of driftwood, but then they threw themselves down onto their thin mats and promptly went to sleep. Leos and I sat together outside the ring of firelight. By this time, I was sick of the chafing, demeaning chains. Leos assured me he'd speak with Grim before the captain turned in, but Grim approached us first.

"You will stand ship-guard tonight," he said, addressing Leos. "You can stow the troll back in its box or chain it to the mast, whichever suits you. Just make sure it doesn't escape, or you'll take its place."

Despite myself, I softly snarled, causing Grim to reach for the knife on his belt. I spun when my friend lightly touched my shoulder. Leos quickly raised his arms, palms out, in a placating gesture.

"Can we speak privately, Captain?" he asked, standing.

"No, farmboy, we can't. You will control the beast, or I will do it for you."

"Captain, Hallr was never chained in Risør, as the king himself dictated. Hallr Halftroll was a trusted part of…"

Grim interrupted. "We are not in Risør, boy, and Alfr has no say in how I run my crew. Watchdogs need chains. You will do as ordered, or we will slay the monster and leave you to rot on some slimy seal rock. Do you understand me?"

Even in the shadows of the dimming fire, I saw Leos color. He turned and walked back toward the beached ship.

"We have a boat to guard, Hallr," Leos said, knowing that calling the *Ormen Víg* a "boat" was an insult to its captain. "Take care you don't trip and break those chains. Without them, our brave little crew will be too anxious to sleep this night."

I expected Grim to scowl and bluster at such mockery but saw the hint of a smile instead. Did he admire Leos's show of spirit, or was he entertained by the thought of our coming demise? Whichever it was, I decided to follow my friend's lead.

"We will, of course, attend to your wise commands, good Captain Grim," I said, putting on all the airs I'd learned among the Völsungs. "Our only wish is to serve you in all the ways that properly reflect your nautical prowess and esteemed beneficence."

As I bowed, I parted my arms, pretending to forget about the chains and bending one of the weaker links open. The manacles were feeble stuff, made for men rather than trolls.

"Forgive me, Captain," I said, holding up the chain and showing him how that link had started to part. "I can easily mend this." I put the link between my thumb and forefinger and squeezed it back together so that there was no longer an opening. "I shall endeavor to take more care with your irons in the future."

With that, I turned and followed Leos.

Chapter Eighteen

"Gianelli made a personal visit to the Corp's Florida headquarters to tell them to get out their rubber stamps."
—*Paving Paradise*

Like the sneaky Aesir who later called themselves the Norse gods, human beings were doomed from the beginning to be conflicted creatures. The legends say that the three grandsons of Buri created the first humans from an elm and an ash log. What the legends fail to point out is that the logs were originally made from the hair of Arg the First One.

Odin breathed life into these first two mortals, his brother Ve gave them senses, and brother Vili provided them—rather ineptly, I'd say—with brains and feelings.

And so it was that the first man Ask and first woman Embla were carved from the flesh of the greatest giant—maybe even carved with the same weapons used to assassinate the First One. These so-called gods taught the humans that all giants were evil. Their bigotry freed up the mortals to commit terrible crimes against us without remorse. Why else do their ancient tales celebrate thieves and murderers such as Jack the Giant Killer? We trusting jotunn-types finally wised up and started distrusting humans, consuming them as comestibles when the sneaky little cretins were caught burgling treasure, grabbing golden geese and the like.

Trying to live in a world dominated by the foolish, frightful, fast-breeding descendants of Ask and Embla is tricky on the best of days. Now that powerful seidr-swinging oddballs such as Hildy's aunts have entered my life, the world becomes an even more treacherous tangle of pits and snares where it pays to walk warily.

My mind swirls with myths this morning. As I wait for the staff meeting with Fred, Misty and Hildy to begin, I think about the legend of the Norns. Mor called them the *Nornir*. The way she told it, they were tough old jotunn biddies who took shit from nobody. They lived under Yggdrasil near a spring, and they determined the destinies of gods and mortals alike, with the possible exception of old one-eyed Odin himself. Mor liked the Nornir, seeing them as kin to the trolls.

But, in typical Mor style, she never worried about consistency. In some tales, the Norn sisters wove the web of fate according to their whimsical tastes, as if they were a team of Coco Chanels churning out designer lifetimes for every person in existence. In other tales, though, Mor portrayed them more like sweatshop workers, spinning away night and day under the stony eye of Orlog, the eternal law of the universe and true designer of destiny.

Later, I discovered that these weird sisters were not only the stuff of Norse religion. They showed up as the Moirai of Greeks, the Parcae of the Romans, the Sudice of Slavs and the Fates of today's popular culture.

The way I understood it, the Nornir weren't just weavers of the future but caretakers of the Tree of Life. Without them, Yggdrasil would become just another dead, decaying eyesore on the neglected front lawn of the universe.

Hildy kicks off the meeting with an annoying crispness, wasting no time on small talk.

"I have briefed Klaus about situations I want investigated," she says, back in her role of CEO of *Hild Brands, Inc.*

She displays no hint of trauma, gratitude or intimacy. If she hadn't mentioned our "briefing," I might have convinced myself that my night with her unfathomable aunts had been an exceptionally surreal dream.

It seems to boil down to this: Hildy's aunts are under attack by some elusive nexus of enemies, both mystical and mundane. About a year ago, they started receiving government notices in their PO Box, which had heretofore been used only for receiving shipping receipts. Apparently, even giant fairy tale crones have the occasional need for a new pair of Nikes or Pottery Barn knick-knacks.

The government notices explained that their property was going to be seized by the state of Florida under the law of eminent domain and that they would be fairly compensated for it. The aunts were, to put it mildly, unaccustomed to surprises. Baffled, they enlisted the help of their niece Hildy. She moved into the empty bedroom of her third aunt, Skuldy, who reportedly left behind her two older sisters in order to pursue some sort of science education out West. Stanford University, I think. Is she looking for answers to the slow decay of Yggdrasil?

Anyway, Hildy found that the Florida Department of Transportation was planning to build a new road through the middle of thousands of acres of state forest, connecting one small town on the forest perimeter in the northeast with another small town in the southwest.

After poking around, Hildy discovered that a bottling company was involved. There was the promise of hundreds of new jobs in Florida if the company was given access to sources of fresh spring water. And there was even talk about expanding the commercial use of new forest properties to build some sort of ecofriendly condos.

That's where the lecherous frat boy Edmund and his deceased partner, Charlie, came into the picture. Hildy had learned that they were consultants on the project and she'd seduced them into telling her more about it. Edmund clued her into a couple of congressmen, one of whom was also a real-estate magnate, but Hildy and her aunts believed there was more to this than mortal greed. The attack in Urdy's spring confirmed those suspicions. Some mysterious, magic-wielding type is making a play for their place.

"My aunts cannot clearly divine the hearts and destinies of the politicians and business people involved," Hildy told me when I was at Haven. "That lack of insight is unheard of. They thought maybe their collective skills were slipping because Aunt Skuldy had left. She's always had the best foresight of the three. Yet, Urdy and Verda still clearly see into the lives of other humans, so the murk somehow hangs over these particular events like smog over a city. Something's making the smog, and it's not just a couple of backwoods Florida politicians."

Despite Hildy's efforts, the bureaucratic wheels had continued to grind. It had gotten to the point where the U.S. Army Corps of Engineers was involved.

I obviously can't get into all this myths-and-legends mystic crap with Misty and Fred. All I tell them at this point is that we're looking into some fishy land deal that one of Hildy's clients is caught up in. "We're just trying to sniff out what's what," I tell them, which is true.

Since I'm somehow in charge of our little band of misfit investigators, I give Fred a choice: tag along with me today or stay with Misty, who is going to start digging through public records with the help of one of the on-staff paralegals. He looks torn, wanting to stay with her but not wanting to sit in a cubicle and do any kind of mind-numbing computer work. He opts to go with me. Our job is to take a field trip to the local Corps of Engineers office downtown.

When we meet in the parking garage, Fred looks at me like I'm insane. I've donned my black and highly tinted helmet, black leather jacket and a special-ordered, custom-tailored, supersized pair of Harley-Davidson leather and textile overpants.

"You ain't gonna ask me to come over to the dark side, are you?" he asks. "'Cause I'm pretty much already there."

"Fuck you, Luke," I say, starting my bike.

The U.S. Corps of Engineers doesn't even have its own building in this burg. Just one floor in a crappy edifice that formerly housed a now-defunct insurance company. Judging by the signage, it's desperately looking to lease more offices. The floor is covered by what was once a fluorescent-blue shag carpet, long since dimmed to a dingy weave. The receptionist at the desk was young when the carpet was. She gives us a cold stare, not at all intimidated by us. Which is saying a lot.

"We called ahead," I tell her, showing her my state government worker ID, which I still rate since I'm technically on unpaid leave from my tollbooth job. "We're here to see John Cragger."

Cragger is a balding gnome of a man, looking all wrong in some kind of skinny jeans and plaid shirt, which I'm betting he considers stylish. His beaked nose and a gentle indentation on his shiny dome makes me think of a carrion-eating Kappa emigrant from Japan I once met in a retention pond.

He hesitates when he sees us, as if he wonders if there's been a mistake. We don't look much like the representatives of the Department of Transportation, which is how I'd introduced myself over the phone. Nonetheless, he gives me a smile as his mushy hand disappears into mine when we shake.

The nuances of modern office behavior—especially etiquette—remain nearly as foreign to me as suntans and surfboards. When I lived in Risør and my life depended on the ability to interpret human intentions, I often felt as if I were traversing a high mountain pass on a thin and crumbly ledge. Even these days, when I'm operating outside my normal spheres, I sometimes find that interpreting human behavior requires all my white-knuckled concentration. I can sympathize with Arg, who no doubt got a shiv in his side even as Buri's grandkids beamed at him with all the good nature of serenading songbirds in lilac branches.

Trolls tend to be simpler to read. They roar when angry, grin when pleased, scowl when they dislike you, pummel when they really dislike you, and slay when they hate you... or are hungry... or are just in a pissy mood. Beware trolls having a shitty day.

Cragger's smile is the frozen type that doesn't light up his eyes. There is something else there. I smell the familiar scent of human fear. Of course, Fred is big and, despite attempts to tone it down, still looks like a guy who could kick the crap out of every cast member of *Sons of Anarchy*. And me, well, I make Fred look like a French Poodle. But there's more to this guy's expression. Suspicion, to be sure. But also, perhaps, annoyance, with just a taste of human cunning.

"Thank you for seeing us, Dr. Cragger," I say, having found on LinkedIn that the man is a PhD and, therefore, a doctor in his own mind. This brightens him up a bit. Since we're from a government agency with which the Corps often works, he gives us the "nickel tour," as he calls it.

There's not much to see. In a few of the larger offices, there are groups of mostly middle-aged men gathered around densely scripted flipcharts, detailed maps, or large computer screens. In one room is a long table with a miniaturized model of a forest and pastures, complete with river, roads, phone lines and train tracks. There are various types of toy-sized heavy equipment and unidentified widgets in the scraped-out middle section of the model.

These men are the engineering-types, Cragger assures us, sounding oddly in awe.

"They are busy as little bees, as usual, with many wonderful projects," he says loudly. None of the men pays him or us any attention. They stay serious. They are groups of grown boys having fun, being responsible for dredging waterways, building dams, operating locks, and otherwise screwing the landscape with their gigantic Tonka toys.

Feeling unwelcome, we move down another hallway. Cragger shows us into a space that, it turns out, is his own small domain.

"These are our regulators!" he says, as if he were a proud uncle. A man and woman look up from their computers just enough to acknowledge us. Otherwise, Cragger is getting the same non-response as with the engineers. Still, the feel of the room is different. There's no subdued boy-like excitement here. It's a place where men, along with a few women, sit in their cubicles alone, looking as if all their animal vitality is being slowly and painfully sucked out of them.

Cragger invites us into his small office, from which we can see into the regulator bullpen. I explain about the DOT's plan for a new road, giving him the construction details as well as I can understand them. He doesn't have a clue I'm just a tollbooth operator. We've led him to believe we're some kind of mid-level flunkies acting on behalf of someone higher up the government food chain, someone who is better off unnamed.

"Thanks very much for the tour, Dr. Cragger. Looks like you have a tightly run ship here. So, as I said, I just wanted to get a feel for the status of the permit under consideration. We know you may have reasons to reject it," and here Fred and I share pained looks, "so we were just trying to get a feel for the lay of the land."

Cragger frowns. It must seem downright weird to have representatives of the government agency that is seeking a permit telling him there are reasons to reject it. These kinds of subtle human machinations are not really in my wheelhouse, even after centuries of trying to understand them.

We're here for two reasons: to quietly undermine the permit request if possible or, failing that, to at least try to figure out where it is in the process and who is working on it. Hildy thinks the Corps will just rubber-stamp the permit, so she wants intel about the status and the names of the players involved.

"That's a rather unusual inquiry," he says. He's probably wondering what would happen if he just blows us off. He'd like to ask who we are repping, but he's a cautious type. It may be better, he thinks, if he has less rather than more information.

"Let me see what I can find out about your permit request," he says, with a hint of superciliousness.

Fred and I watch through the glass as Cragger makes inquiries among his staff. We see him frown as a pale woman with wilted-looking, shoulder-length brownish hair explains something that annoys him.

When he comes back into the office, he still carries that hint of irritation. "I wish I could tell you more," he says. "It appears the regulator in charge of this permit request is out of the office. In fact, he seems to be in the middle of investigating the permit in question, so I'd say you'll have your answer soon."

I look at Fred, who is nodding and trying to look thoughtful. I may only be a tollbooth guy, but I probably have a better idea of how government works. We need to be careful here, lest Cragger realizes he should clam up.

"Sounds like you're doing your due diligence," I say, trying for a neutral tone.

"It appears so," Cragger says.

"Pardon the question, Doctor. We're always trying to maximize our resources at the DOT. Do you investigate all your permits by doing on-site inspections?"

Cragger gives a curt, humorless laugh.

"Hardly. I wish we had that kind of personnel but, well, you know," he does an exaggerated shrug with both arms. "We usually just read over the forms carefully and make our determination from those."

"So, your office is doing an unusual amount of scrutiny of this project?" I ask, doing my best not to sound as if I really object to that.

Things are getting even trickier now. If they are thinking about denying the permit, then that's good news, and our presence here could seem like pressure to expedite approval, which means we are doing more harm than good. My real plan was to have a chat with the regulator, subtly calling attention to some of the reasons he should turn down the permit.

It would have been easier to just send in an attorney to advocate on behalf of Hildy's family. She tried that, but the Corps refused such a conference, saying that was against protocol.

"Oh, I wouldn't want you to draw any premature conclusions," says Cragger. "Actually, Brad hasn't checked in for a couple of days now. He's gone a bit AWOL, probably just taking a little undeclared vacation."

I badly want to dig further. What's Brad's last name? Is this typical for him? Just where did he go? But there's something in Cragger's demeanor that says I'd be pushing my luck. I don't want him calling the DOT asking about us.

I thank the doctor for his time, saying we'd keep in touch. Then, on the way out, I motion Freddy with my chin to engage the little man in conversation. After he and Fred walk into the hallway, I lag behind in the bullpen and stop by the cubicle of the wilty-haired girl.

"Hey," I say, "excuse me. Dr. Cragger mentioned you to us but, sorry, I forgot your name already."

When she introduces herself, I ask if the empty cubicle next to hers is Brad's. She shakes her head and points me to his desk. I tell her I'd like to leave him a quick note. I wind up writing him a faux message while scanning the papers on his desk. One is signed, giving me Brad's last name.

When I make my way out the door into the hallway, Dr. Cragger is coming back down the hall looking for me.

"Sorry, guys," I say, limping. "Bad hip's acting up. Growing old's not for sissies."

When Freddy and I are finally out of the offices, he says, "I did my best to distract him. You find anything?"

"Maybe, thanks. You're a good wingman, just like your demented buddy Lucky claimed."

"Demented, yeah, but he's no buddy of mine anymore," Freddy mumbles.

I wonder about that. The creatures of Odin's kin are such magnificent liars. Still, this is no time for paranoia, not when I'm going to need all the help I can get to track down Brad Lauder.

Chapter Nineteen

"His men rushed forwards without armour, were as mad as dogs or wolves, bit their shields, and were strong as bears or wild bulls, and killed people at a blow, but neither fire nor iron told upon themselves. These were called Berserker."
—*Ynglinga Saga*

Captain Grim of Gokstad cursed, bullied and disparaged every member of his crew, spewing the least amount of venom on Ornolf simply because the oaf didn't care. He wasn't putting on a show of being a hardass. He truly despised us. If any other member of the crew had insulted his fellows the way Grim did, the decks would have been slick with blood.

Yet, the crew let the insults pass, and not just because of his rank. The crew admired his seamanship. In those days, Norsemen distinguished between captains and skippers. Captains were usually the owners of the vessels and controlled the steering oar. Skippers were the navigators, and their encyclopedic knowledge of the seas was legendary.

Although Alfr owned the ship, he was seldom on board, so Grim was both captain and skipper. Not only did he have a masterly knowledge of all the treacherous seas in that part of the world, he was a top-notch warrior. The crew valued his canny ways of planning pillages, his basic fairness in dividing out the spoils, and the ruthless way he went into battle.

One afternoon, along the coast of what is now Scotland, Grim led the men in a raid of some no-name village in order to scavenge supplies. There wasn't much to take. The villagers had seen our ship coming and fled with everything they could carry, leaving behind some scrawny animals in the hopes that the people wouldn't be chased into the wilderness.

Lagging the other fleeing farmers was a stout, middle-aged man helping a crone, a pregnant woman, and a couple of toddler girls to safety. Grim led his men on a fast, loping walk and then single-handedly made a short, bloody massacre of the whole lot. The crew watched, knowing better than to get in range of the captain when he was in a bloodlust. Grim did not roar or curse. He just dispatched them and then, in a grunting but controlled rage, hacked them into pieces like a butcher preparing choice cuts. Afterwards, Grim strolled back to the shore to wipe the viscera out of his beard, hair and clothes. Leos (I was stowed in my trollbox, of course) told me there was a child's finger, which must have gone flying during the butchery, still stuck in a crevice between Grim's belt knot and tunic as he walked away.

I wondered if word of such deeds ever made their way back to Alfr. Would the king have cared? I couldn't imagine Alfr acting like this, but he was no fool. He might have preferred that Grim establish trade routes rather than pillage. However, Alfr knew hungry men would take what they needed if they had nothing to trade, or if they wanted to conserve their wares for well-defended towns.

In fact, Grim was a damnably fine trader as well, knowing the worth of goods and how to intimidate traders into lowering their prices. That barely-controlled, ever-simmering anger served him well. In truth, he would have made a good troll.

I think my endurance irritated Grim. He wanted to murder me, yes, but in a crafty way that would not outrage King Alfr or necessitate the death of Leos. Dofri's nephew was my only true friend, the only one not to see me as monster or threat or opportunity or weapon—as just another person trying to survive in a universe ruled by cruel and capricious gods. The young fool should have loathed me, especially after I caused him, the troll-keeper, to be banished from home.

Leos was no saint, of course. He'd been a soldier, a damned good one. He'd killed men and wooed women and drunk too much on many occasions. I'm sure he resented me at times. In the evenings, he'd sometimes chide me when he was cold, hungry, stung by insects or soggy with sleet.

"Look at the shambles of my dream, you damned troll," he would say laughingly. "No women, not enough food, the wind always whipping through rotting clothes. Your fault, you know. You just couldn't keep your mouth shut in front of spidery Sunmane. Gods, I wished we had just slit the throat of the pretty boy the first time we laid eyes on him."

What could I say? I'd chuckle, telling him nubile wenches would all come flocking to his skinny, pirate ass when he returned with enough loot. "You'll woo some soft, fat daughter of a rich landowner and finally die as a well-heeled, old fart boring his grandchildren with the same, ceaseless tales of his misspent youth."

We'd dream together, his dreams becoming mine, even though I knew I'd never marry or own land or be accepted as anything other than a dangerous, though useful, beast.

As the weather warmed, the days grew longer, and I, the demon in the box, didn't die, Grim came up with a new idea: he would harness my misery for his own ends.

By then, we had joined a tiny fleet of five other ships, two from Alfr's kingdom and three smaller ones that Harald Bloodaxe had contracted our shipyards to build for him. It irked Grim's men that Bloodaxe was allowed this privilege but, in the end, it had been part of the peace accord. The little fleet made up of "allied" forces was a kind of trial. If the ships and crews could work together, larger fleets would be formed.

Grim despised the idea of sailing with the Bloodaxe troops, one of the few areas where I agreed with him. As the captain of the flagship *Ormen Vig*, however, Grim served as the improvised leader of the small flotilla. This gave him ideas and opportunities.

This was years after the infamous Viking pillaging of the monastery on the Holy Island of Lindisfarne, the one that had first struck fear into the hearts of the Northumbrians and surrounding kingdoms. The pickings were no longer so easy, even on the east coast of Ireland, where our people had settled in various strategic locations.

It was on that coast that Grim decided to plunder a township that had refused to engage in trading with any Norsemen. It wasn't a huge town, but the residents were especially enterprising for peasants. Maybe their farmlands were unusually rich, or their local lord was unusually proud and effective. Whatever the reason, they built inner walls to which they could retreat if under attack. This fact had discouraged any determined raids in the past.

Looking back, my guess is that they didn't have anything Grim particularly wanted. They just pissed him off with their haughtiness.

He formulated a plan. Under cover of darkness, the crews from the other ships would land to the north and south of the town, then creep up to the inner walls carrying scaling ladders cobbled together from tree branches gathered in the surrounding forests. Shortly before dawn, Grim's crew would approach the town in plain view, carrying goods to sell. He would haggle with the overweening townspeople, drawing their attention forward and away from the raiders.

In pidgin Gaelic, Grim spoke to the bleary-eyed locals who were starting to set up their stalls for the outdoor market. I couldn't understand many of his words, but I'd never heard Grim speak in such a gregarious, good-natured way. I was inside the trollbox, which had been stood up vertically in front of the merchants.

I'd been told that I would be part of the raid, released from the box when Grim sprung his surprise. All of it was supposed to happen before sunrise. Leos was among the men standing with Grim, a fact that gave me some comfort. Nonetheless, I was preoccupied by three dismaying facts: I still had no weapon, was not wearing my iron hood, and sunrise was fast approaching.

The plan was that Leos would give me an axe and be able to find me shelter from the daylight once the wall was breached.

In my anxiety, I barely registered that Grim, still using his most affable tone, used the word "troll," for which there was no Gaelic word. "Sonovabitch," Leos whispered. "I think he's pretending he's going to sell you to them."

Before I could digest this, the lid of the box swung away and there I was, face to face with a middle-aged man wearing a silver-embroidered yellow tunic and some sort of purple cloak of expensive-looking material. He made an urgent, instinctive gesture with his hands that, though

I'd never seen the sign of the cross before, I recognized as a motion to ward off evil. To his credit, the man—perhaps the mayor of the town—swallowed his terror and spoke in a harsh, angry tone to Grim.

Grim cast off his amiable facade and loosed a torrent of pent-up obscenities at the man. He reached over and pounded me in the chest with his fist to display my fitness and power, as if I were a prized piece of livestock. As they argued, I realized that the horrible hag of the morning, red-clawed Sól, was about to creep into the sky. Just as the first burning rays slashed across my forehead and into my eyes, a horn bugle sounded from atop the town's inner walls, signaling our attack.

"Berserk, you damned troll!" shouted Grim. "Kill anything in your path to the dark wall, you ugly bastard, or the sweet sun will char your blasted hide to slag."

This had been his plan all along. To wait till sunrise, then use Sól's rays to whip me into a frenzy. I turned, sorely tempted to slay the treacherous Grim. But the crafty captain was gone amid the rising glare. Instead, I heard Leos's voice, trying to calm me.

"Hallr," he said, "I know it burns, but we will soon get you to shelter. I'm going to put an axe in your hand now. I'd appreciate it if you didn't lop off my head with it. Follow my voice, and we'll get you to the wall."

So I did, growing less and less rational as the sun rose higher, becoming the berserker Grim wanted me to be. A blind one at that. Without veil or visor, I was barely able to make out shapes. Leos tried to keep me in the shade of overhangs as best he could, but this meant I went smashing through posts and support beams, wooden carts, low walls or whatever else was in my way. I swung my axe wildly at whatever forms seemed to threaten, though most of the townspeople gave me a wide berth.

"Almost there," Leos panted.

I saw it. A high wall shielding the core of the town from siege and fire, casting its long shadow to the west. Just as I was about to step into that shadow, Leos shouted, "Swing aft, Hallr!" That command had long since been drilled into me by the pitiless Dofri, so I reflexively pivoted, twisted and brandished my axe to the rear, defending myself from the glare-blurred enemy behind. The assailant was good, dodging backwards so that I either just grazed him or missed him completely. When he disappeared, I swung the axe in wide arcs, hoping for a lucky hit if the sonovabitch tried to strike again.

As I turned toward the wall, I heard a nearby clash of weapons and a groan.

"The gate, you damned troll," Grim shouted from in front of me. "Smash the fucking gate!"

The trained soldier in me responded, dashing forward at the command. Following Grim's voice and able to see a little better in the shade of the wall, I found the huge wooden door and unleashed my rage on it. Not just rage against Grim but against all of them: a frenzied, kaleidoscopic vision of all those who had abandoned, banished, deceived, hated, chained, ensnared, and entombed me. All of them cleft and smashed and demolished into splinters. Soon the door was no more. Inside the walls, I continued to hack at any who opposed me, and even many who did not.

Chapter Twenty

"They took Mimir, therefore, and beheaded him, and sent his head to the Asa-
land people. Odin took the head, smeared it with herbs, so that it should not rot,
and sang incantations over it. Thereby he gave it the power that it spoke to him."
—*The Younger Edda*

Misty was able to track down the wife of Brad Lauder, the missing
Corps of Engineers regulator. It turns out Brad had been gone for
two days, even though he told his wife as well as his office mates that
it was just a day trip. Mrs. Lauder had filed a missing person report
after the first day. Law enforcement had been alerted, but there'd
been no sign of him.

"He was going to Vandriller Junction," Misty said. "Sheriff up
there hasn't seen him."

"That near Petticoat Junction?" I ask. They give me blank stares.

"Never mind. Old-guy joke. Terrible one at that. If you give me
the GPS, I'll go have a look."

"Road trip!" Fred says.

"Nah," I say. "You stay here with Misty, and let her give you a lesson or two in scouring databases and government records. Put those
military-cop instincts to use. We've already got leads that Hildy—or
I guess it's Ms. Hild around here—gave us. Now we need to dredge

up as much gunk as we can on the political and business assholes linked to this deal."

I go home to change and pack. Since my trip out to Hildy's, I've felt a headache creeping up on me. At first, I thought it was just a hangover from whatever mind-bending tea the weird sisters were brewing. Then I figured it was too much exposure to daylight. Now there are sharp pains, as if it was a skulking ninja whose knives are finally unleashed. A quick lie-down is in order.

A pumpkin head bobs in the water of my den.

"What do you call a guy with no arms, no legs, floating in your subterranean lair?" it asks.

"Shut up, Olaf," I say, "or I'll take another bite." Even in my dream, my head is murdering me.

"Answer the damned question, troll!" it shouts up at me with an authority that is very unOlaf-like.

Wait, I know this one. Don't I know this one?

"Bob," I say.

"The name is Mimir, you cursed affront to giantkind," it says.

This pisses me off. It's hard enough to be a troll amid the human swarms without having the blood-curdling head of a mythic jotunn piling on.

"Listen, you ugly…"

"So now the sisters are allowing dimwitted, heinous half-breeds to drink of the Well? How desperate they must be! What terrible price did you pay, half-troll?"

"Nothing," I say, "they just gave it to me. I didn't want the silty dreck!"

The head of Mimir explodes into laughter. I vaguely wonder how it does this without any lungs.

"Idiot!" it finally says, after filling the lair with its foul giant breath. "If the Allfather gave up his eye for a draft, what must the likes of you pay?"

I've nothing to say to that. Was it really the same well from which Odin purportedly drank? Somewhere out in troglodytic Central Florida?

"Screw you, Bobby. You're just a bad dream borne of some nasty spring-water bacteria. Or maybe it's from bad street-vendor food. There's more of chilidog than Norse god about you."

This cracks Mimir up again. He exhales a foul stench.

"Dude, breath mint!" I yell.

"A fool who persists in his folly…"

"Gets wise," I finish. "Now get the hell out!"

He laughs again. Even louder this time. Much louder. I can feel my brain about to shatter into shards.

When I wake, the headache is worse, not better. For the hundredth time, I ask what I'm doing. Why help the ominous old aunts, even if they are the Norns? What have the Fates ever done for me?

Which leads me to remember the runes on my neck, the reference to the "horse of the hanged." There are also the photos, the threat about my true name, the massive amounts of seidr sparking like a ruptured power cable. And, lord help me, I remember the feel of cradling the terrified Hildy. Guess I'm every bit the idiot Mimir said I was.

So, despite the needles in my brain, I drag my sorry ass out of the lush darkness of my lair, don my Darth Vader get-up, and start hauling my increasingly beloved hog through the primeval morass of my property. Just as I'm about to break through the brush onto the pavement, I spot a shadow amid the vines.

"You sure are shitty at the art of ambush, cook," I whisper.

"Guess it's true about trolls seeing in the dark," says Andre, keeping his distance. He puts on no pretense of a Haitian accent tonight.

"I smelled you first, dude. You always reek of fish and dead pig. Don't you guys serve anything other than svinestek? Maybe a nice dyresteg or something?"

"Pearls before swine, Klaus. I deliver whatever the mead-drinking cretins want. I'm a culinary genius. I can squeeze the nectar of gods out of goat udders. But braised boar is all the rage, and who am I to argue?"

"Yeah, you're a real martyr, Andre. Or is it Andy? Now get out of my way. Bizarre shit happens whenever you show up, and I could use a break from it for one night."

"Maybe because of a pounding headache?" he asks, only half-smiling. Nervous.

I step toward him and he steps back, raising his hands.

"Whoa, big fella," he says. "I didn't do it. I'm the solution, not the problem."

"Which means?"

"It means I'm still bearing gifts, man. Just don't dump me in the bay this time, okay?"

Chapter Twenty 139

"No promises," I grunt.

"Look," he says, holding up what looks like a necklace. "It's from Hildy. A thank you gift. Whatever you did for her, she's like, appreciative." I look hard at him for a hint of smirk. I could rip out his tongue easily enough.

"Just toss it here, cook."

It's a pendant. I try to make out the features, then realize it's a face rendered in silver, a familiar face at that.

"Mimir," I whisper.

"Yeah, trollman, good eye. Try it on."

Its appearance after that crazy dream scares me, but I'm not going to let it show in front of sketchy little Andre. With as much nonchalance as I can muster, I lower it over my head and around my neck. And the moment I do, the agony dissolves. I feel a wave of deep relief and even gratitude.

"Not bad," I tell Andre. "Now hit the road, cook. I don't take too kindly to trespassers."

Like Hildy's place, Vandriller Junction is out in the boonies of Florida. But it's a whole different kind of boonies—surface-of-Mars boonies versus Amazon-forest boonies. I roll by one earthen pit that looks as if a giant scraped the green, lush surface of Florida with an ice cream scoop, revealing nothing but ugly reddish-brown sand and clay. And not just one scoop. Many scoops, chaotically crosshatched and bordered by sloppy mounds of marl. At the bottom of the pits is filthy black water, which I imagine is some shade of gray in the daylight.

I've shut off my bike and quietly straddle it. I hear the steps coming up from behind but don't bother to turn. I know that tread by now. And that singular scent beneath the fragrance of the day.

"Welcome to Bone Valley," she says, stepping up beside me. It's henna-haired, biker-chick Hildy, of course, sporting a new nose stud this evening. Small emerald stone, I think.

"Seriously, that's the name?"

"Oh yes, Klaus, the area has the biggest phosphate mines on the continent," she says. "Most of the phosphate in the United States comes from Bone Valley."

"Hmm, thought I smelled a shitload of death."

She reaches into her left pocket and pulls out a new pack of cigarettes. Kools. I wonder if the cigarette that Misty gave Hildy has reignited an old habit. With a practiced movement, she tears off the top of the cellophane and knocks one half out of the box.

"Ancient death, at that," she says, lighting up. "Millions of years old. Right here was a mass cemetery for trillions of swimming, skittering, creepy crawling sea creatures, a boneyard colossal enough to be worthy of Ymir himself."

"His name was Aurgelmir."

"Potato, potahto," she says. "Either way, the ever-inventive humans rob the ancient graves to fertilize their wretched lawns."

"And big-ass farms, I imagine."

She considers the point as she exhales a lungful of smoke. "True," she admits. "They've got to feed their billions, the great global anthill of Midgard."

I just nod, her bleak, weary-sounding humor resonating with my own. If I ever thought she was merely human, her tone makes it clear she's not. Which makes sense. Not even the most talented spaewife is likely to be rooming with the Nornir.

"You despise them?" I ask.

"Not really," she sighs. "Well, sometimes, looking out at a scene like this. They are the great despoilers, and their depredations run deeper than they know."

I look down at her, thinking about the yellowing leaves of the great tree by the spring. I have to fight the absurd urge to stroke her hair. The moment passes.

"How about this Brad Lauder guy?" I ask. "You know why he came out here?"

"How well do you understand this country's 'no-net-loss' policy?"

"Not well," I admit. "I've heard DOT types whining about it. And didn't your well-manicured little buddy Edmund go off on a drunken rant about it?"

"'No net loss' is pretty much what it sounds like," she says, flicking ashes onto the ground. "Let's say a slice of wetland is destroyed when someone builds a Wal-Mart or a set of condos or whatever. They're supposed to reclaim or restore some other wetlands so that the total acres of wetlands in the country doesn't decrease."

"So I'm guessing that, like all government policies, it works to perfection."

"Easier to show than to tell," she says, pulling out a smartphone and reading something. A text? GPS coordinates? "We're not in the right place yet. It's in this direction."

We walk, me pushing my bike. She must have parked her own around here somewhere. As we tramp along the edges of these phosphate pits, I realize I'm seeing the landscape with an unnatural clarity. It's not the kind of hallucinogenic visions I experienced at Haven, more of a hyperrealism. Trolls always see well in the dark, of course, but now I see every blade of grass, every grain of sand, every cracked piece of shell or discarded sandwich bag or scraggly weed. When our path starts to curl around another large gouge in the landscape, it strikes me as remarkably ragged, as if there's been no time for erosion, something that happens quickly in the flimsy soils of Florida.

"It's here!" I say suddenly, surprising myself.

"What's where?" Hildy asks.

It's as if there's a voice whispering nearby, or maybe from inside of me. Eerie.

"This gouge, it's new," I say. "Why would it be new? What were they scooping up?"

We look across the shattered landscape toward the silhouette of the most enormous mobile machine I've ever seen, some kind of uber-crane lurking in the darkness like a monstrous emblem of approaching apocalypse.

"That's a dragline," Hildy says. "Seven million pounds of digging demon."

"Is that bucket thing big enough to scoop up a car?" I ask.

"A car would be nothing. It could eat a whole truck," she says.

"Like a truck driven by a Corps of Engineer regulator?" I ask. "As easy to hide in one of these huge mounds as a toy truck in a sandbox. But maybe I'm being paranoid."

"Maybe," she says, reaching up and fingering the pendant of Mimir resting on my chest. "But I doubt it."

We walk over to a man-made hill of debris and come down on a broad expanse of flatland that leads to a massive swampy fenland. I can see a figure up ahead. Long before we get there, I recognize Andre.

He's standing stockstill, not even acknowledging us. Hildy stands next to him and seems to fall into the same spell.

Finally, Andre breaks the silence.

"Do you feel that?" he whispers to her.

"Of course, I'm betting even Klaus does."

I almost tell her to go to hell, but she's right. It's not nearly the intense seidr I felt crackling around Hildy's aunts. But it's there, something thick, slow, and noxious, like a spiritual pus oozing from the earth.

"What's causing it?" I ask.

Hildy shivers.

"I don't know," she says. "I wish Urdy and Verda were here."

"Even leaving aside the bad mojo, this place doesn't look or smell right," I say.

"That's 'cause it's *not* right," she says, casting down her smoldering cigarette butt and stomping on it with her boots. "According to records, it used to be a vibrant place, a true sawgrass prairie. Now it's not much more than a giant retention pond, one larger than the original prairie, I'd say. Looks like they're constantly expanding it once the phosphate is out of the ground. This must be what the government wants to swap for the wetlands around our spring. It's 'no net loss' in action. I'm guessing it's what Brad Lauder came to see."

The prairie that they destroyed, she explains, contained many plants besides sawgrass: bladderwort, periphyton, and other types of rushes and sedges. It was a living thing, with water slowly flowing over it most of the time.

"This place is mostly marsh," she says, "maybe two to four feet of standing water out there. It doesn't flow much if at all. It's little more than a soggy corpse compared to what it once was."

She's righter than she knows. The stink of death wafts toward me on a changing breeze. It's much worse than just the usual rot of a fen. There's something else as well, the scent of human blood freshly spilled and sweet as candy cane.

The soldier, says the voice in my head, which I now think of as Mimir's. He must mean Lauder, since the Corps of Engineers is technically a U.S. Army command.

"Goddamnit, are you sure?" I ask aloud.

"Sure of what, troll?"

"Not talking to you, Andre. Looks like I'm going for a dip in this piece-of-shit swamp," I say, pulling off my boots and then handing my jacket to the cook.

Hildy's silent. I see her green nose stud rise and fall quickly. She's spooked, which makes sense given what happened to her in Urdy's spring. Maybe the same muck slithers here. Of course, she's the dame that spun a Jaguar into the gulf and came away without a scratch. If she's scared, then what in hell am I thinking by hazarding this stinking fen?

It is not what she fears, but something does lurk, Mimir whispers in my mind.

"Shut up, you pain-in-the-ass pate," I tell him as I start wading through the tall weeds that thrive in this slime. The water is just knee deep here and, nasty as it is, I only need to go out twenty yards or so before I start seeing the carnage.

It's everywhere. To my left is the corpse of a kingfisher, its azure head hanging on a thread, its red breast torn open and hollowed out. To my right is a blue heron, literally rotting amid the sedge, maggots squirming over aqua feathers. And there's a lot more: a decapitated painted turtle, a slew of frog corpses skewered on broken cattails.

Set up like a screen in the sedge is an enormous eagle whose half-rotted skeletal wings have been stretched as far as they will go in either direction. Its head is gone, replaced by that of a large raven whose eyes have been plucked out.

In the center of it all is what seems to be the half-submerged trunk of a large, hewed-down tree. I'm guessing it's a cypress because part of the trunk rests on the busted remnants of tree knees rising from the swamp like a model of city ruins. There's something wrong with this tree trunk but I don't have time to figure it out. On the tree is an unconscious, skinny guy lying on his back. He's a bloody mess, with long, ragged lacerations showing through his ripped up, checkered shirt. I presume this is our missing regulator, Brad Lauder. He's breathing fast, like the injured animal he is.

His arms are out of kilter, dropping down into the murky soup.

I'm getting cautious now. This freaky slaughterhouse scene reeks of loathsome magic, a lot of it emanating from Lauder or, rather, from beneath him. What I thought was a tree trunk is actually an enormous root, one that's been scarred and hacked as if it were a Jurassic Park chew-toy. This increases my dread, so I'm practically creeping toward him when I hear splashing behind me.

I'm relieved when I see it's just Hildy and Andre, eyes wide as they enter the circle of gore. I give her credit. It hasn't been long since she nearly drowned in her own backyard, yet here she is. Tough broad, just like her aunts. Their appearance not only makes me feel safer, it brings out my swagger. I give them a confident, lopsided grin before boldly and, I suddenly realize, stupidly stepping into a submerged hole that's deeper than I am tall. What a moron, I think, as the dark water closes over my head.

Don't panic; trolls are not so easy to drown. But just then I feel the jaws of some dragon-sized beastie snapping down on my head and neck. Time to panic after all! I try to bring up my right arm, realize I can't move it, then start flailing with my left. Just as I connect with something, I start spinning. Or, rather, the beast starts spinning, trying to rip my head off. Part of me thinks, "Oh, yeah, this must be one of those gator spins I've seen on the Nat Geo channel," and another part of me is thinking, "Spin, Hallr, spin in the same direction or it'll tear off your ugly troll head!"

So I do spin and spin and spin some more. Although I'm thrashing for my life, trying to elbow my way out of its jaws and blindly pound at where I think its black-marble eyes should be, I'm also strangely calm. I remember being a child lying on my back under a tall maple tree in the autumn, watching hundreds of yellowish seeds helicoptering to the ground as the wind blew, each seed a wonder, elegant as it gyrated down diagonally toward an earth covered in a thick blanket of rotting dead leaves. Spinning and spinning and spinning.

Chapter Twenty-One

It was blessedly dark. After the siege, I'd found my way into a stony storage room. I could hear my comrades looting, drinking, laughing, and even, much to my distaste, raping. After a while, I barely registered it. These men, the Norsemen in their prime, were alive, their enemies vanquished, their riches increased. Life was brutal but, for the moment, good.

If I wasn't rejoicing in the same way, it wasn't because I disdained them as savages. No one had been more savage that day than I. I'd helped Captain Grim wreak his revenge on the haughty Celts.

No, I felt low because I was sorry for myself. Grim's ploy angered me, of course, but I couldn't hate him for that alone. Good leaders showed guile. Odin himself could be a tricky prick, according to myth, walking the world in many guises, tricking giants and gods alike to get what he wanted.

What bothered me was the underlying premise of his trick: that I was most useful as a gullible, savage monster. If that were always the assumption, then I'd never become my shipmates' comrade-in-arms. Making matters worse, even my best and only friend, Leos, was nowhere to be seen. He could at least have dropped by to check on me before going off with the others.

It never occurred to me that he'd been injured during the siege. He'd led me all the way to the wall, and he was far more skilled in combat than most humans. So, when a group of my shipmates found me in the dark room and told me Leos had been slain during the battle, I was baffled.

"Do you remember, troll?" asked Broddi slowly and loudly, as if I were deaf or an imbecile. He was a stout and boisterous man, one of the more vocal troll-taunters on the ship.

Maybe I really am the imbecile they believe me to be, I thought. I tried hard to remember the battle and the last time I heard, if not saw, Leos. Nothing would come.

"When? How?" I finally said.

Most looked down at their feet. Even Broddi had a hard time meeting my gaze.

"You don't remember, then," he said. "Grim said you might not."

I was quickly moving beyond being stunned into being outraged.

"Just tell me!"

The men startled and moved backwards. That's when I noticed they'd brought their shields and weapons with them. They were either going to attack me or were worried I'd attack them. Given their fear, I assumed it was the latter.

"No one blames you, troll. We took a vote," he said, trying to appease me for some reason.

"Blame me?" I asked. "Why would they blame me?"

Then, before he could respond, I got it.

"You mean, I did this thing? I killed Leos?"

Broddi nodded.

"You couldn't see," he said. "Everyone knows you couldn't see. Yet you killed over a score of their fighters, troll. You helped win us the battle. We will not forget that."

"Get out!" I yelled. Then, more quietly, after they'd stumbled backwards through the door. "You cowardly, fuckwit humans."

I scarcely remember what happened after that. They must have coaxed me back to the ship and the trollbox. All I recall is lying in it for days, not wanting food or water, unwilling or unable to leave the box even at night. They put Grim's son, Kol, and Ornolf the Oaf in charge of handling me. At night, after the others had left the ship, Kol tried to convince me to get up or, at least, to eat. If I refused, he had Ornolf pull my lips apart while he poured water in my mouth. Sometimes Ornolf would even yank me up into a sitting position while Kol took off my shirt and cleansed my back with fresh water.

"There's more sores here again today, troll," he told me. "You're starting to get eaten up by them. And they're starting to stink. If it gets worse still, Far will have us roll you into the sea just to be rid of the reek."

I'm not sure why Grim left me alive. He could have jammed his sword into my neck as I lay there, and I wouldn't have lifted a finger to stop him. Maybe it was because he came away from the battle with an infected wound that kept him subdued. Maybe it was because, this time, I showed every sign of dying on my own. Or perhaps he didn't want to tamper with the loyalties of his crew, many of whom now told tales of my part in the battle and had stopped making me the butt of their endless jokes.

For whatever reason, I was still alive and being cleansed by Kol and Ornolf when a large ship appeared on the horizon, one that was every bit as impressive as our own *Ormen Vig*. Grim was cautious. Neither he nor any other members of the crew had heard that Alfr was building another Busse-class dragon ship. He asked the captains of the Bloodaxe ships if it belonged to their clan. They swore it didn't. Grim just scowled at their pledges. The unknown ship continued to trail.

Rather than beaching the fleet, Grim had them sail all through the night in order to lose the ship. He would have given battle if he trusted the Bloodaxe ships. As it turned out, he was right to distrust them.

Despite my listlessness, I became marginally more attentive from within the trollbox as the tensions grew. Grim gave the order to sail in a tight formation. In the darkness, though, two of Bloodaxe's ships suddenly veered off course and tried to simultaneously smash into the *Ormen Vig* from both the starboard and port sides. They had rigged their spare masts like lances on their bows so as to stave in our hull. We were lucky their timing was slightly off. One of their lances hit the mark but the other glanced off us.

Before the crew could react, the three turncoat ships sailed away in all haste. Grim unleashed a flood of curses as the *Ormen Vig* took on water. Our other two ships came to our aid, serving as pontoons on either side and keeping us afloat. Grim realized it had all been a set up. The Bloodaxe ships had attacked not in order to destroy but to cripple so that their new Busse-class ship could sink or, more likely, capture us. The attack was either a prelude to an approaching war or war itself. For Bloodaxe, neutralizing or acquiring Alfr's flagship would be a major coup, rousing the spirits of his warriors.

Captain Grim was short of options. He could either limp along in the seas, hoping the crew could repair the torn hull while still afloat, or he could make a run for shore, where they'd have a better chance of making the repairs. Neither plan seemed like a good one, so Grim concocted a third. He turned his waterlogged vessel away from the coast and out to the open ocean, gambling on his dead-reckoning skills.

Kol convinced me that Leos would have wanted me to help my ship-mates in their hour of need, so, for the first time in days, I rose from my grimy, wet coffin and went to work opposite Ornolf. The ship was heavy with water and still sinking, the surface of the sea only a couple of feet or so from the gunwale. We pulled so hard that Ornolf and I broke our oars. Grim bellowed and threatened but, in the end, gave us new oars. Without us, the ship barely moved.

Grim's gamble paid off. We found what he was seeking: a small chain of islands—barely more than seal rocks—where we had a chance of hiding while making repairs. His plan was this: pull the ship up as far as we could onto the biggest of the rocks, then send away our other two faster and smaller ships so they could lure Bloodaxe's vessels away from the *Ormen Vig*. After we made repairs, we would rendezvous with the others and turn on our pursuers.

The rock on which we landed was a huge trapezoid. The "beach" was just a stony, slippery slope onto which we could just barely pull the ship. I remember how my joints, which I hadn't used for days, audibly creaked and popped as I hauled on the waterlogged hulk. The crew did what they could to make repairs in the darkness. By morning, everyone was spread out over the flat top of the rock like so many exhausted seals.

I was, of course, back in the trollbox. No one had even bothered to chain me. I was awakened by the sound of the ship's keel scraping on stone. Still dopey with weariness, I at first assumed the crew was pull-ing the ship up further onto the rock to protect it from the rising tide.

I knew they'd planned to stay for a day and empty the vessel of all the waterlogged equipment and let it dry in the sun.

There were whisperings nearby and I realized the ship was being hauled down the rock, not up. Had Grim changed his mind, deciding to abandon the rock already? I decided I didn't care. In the daylight, I would be useless to them anyway. The grinding continued.

But then I heard a man swear groggily before starting to shout.

"The ship," he yelled, "they're thieving her away!" It was the voice of Broddi, who had taken the the morning watch. I heard a man running, followed by a struggle and the clang of metal on metal. Next was a confusion of sounds: nearby men cursing and urging each other on, the renewed grinding of the ship's keel, *Ormen Vig*'s sailors raising an alarm and racing toward us, then the splash of the ship being launched.

I heard a tumult of clanging objects, which I imagined were weapons or stones hurled toward the ship. An arrow suddenly shot through the top of my trollbox, the head stopping only inches from my neck.

Laughter erupted as men pulled at the oars and shouted insults at Grim's crew. They fell into a chant of "No Valhalla for you!" I did not sense anyone sitting on my box, so I raised the top by the smallest possible crack. Amid the glare, I could see a nearby sailor standing on the gunwale and making the universal "fucking you in the ass" sign, taunting the men left to die on the seal rock.

I eventually learned from their conversation that they'd trailed the *Ormen Vig* by some of the items we had tossed overboard in order to lighten our load: broken oars, extra shields, soggy clothes, anything we didn't absolutely need. The captain of the *Naorbita*, as the Bloodaxe ship was called, was sly and lucky enough to guess Grim's plan from the string of debris.

They could have outright attacked Grim's men, of course, but it would have been risky. Grim's crew held the high ground and, once alerted, would have been formidable. So their captain had his men pull the *Ormen Vig* down the rocky slope and into the sea, stranding Grim's disgraced and helpless crew.

The hijackers on the *Ormen Vig* were short-handed, of course, being less than half of *Naorbita*'s original crew, so they had little time to investigate their new prize. If they had, they would have discovered that the long box that served as a thwart amidships housed an exhausted, emaciated troll who didn't really give a damn about which set of assholes were currently crewing the ship. It's not that I had decided to turn traitor on Alfr. I just didn't care about much of anything since I'd murdered my only friend.

I remained a stowaway on my own ship until nightfall, when the scanty crew slipped it up the narrow confines of an Irish river where Captain Bjor felt they would be hidden and safe for the night. It was a sanctuary where they had previously stored supplies, including ale and mead. It wasn't long before the crew was celebrating their great victory with songs, tales of their exploits, scornful imitations of the look on the faces of *Ormen Vig*'s original crew, and the occasional drunken fight.

Caring little about them, I continued to lie in the ship. I had no plan. Maybe, when they were asleep, I would crawl out of the box and disappear into the countryside. Or maybe I would just wait until they found me.

As the revelries continued, I heard soft steps on the deck. So soft. I wondered if they had known I was there all along and were now getting ready to surprise me in the depths of nighttime. But no, no men could step that lightly, and even through the box, he had a familiar smell.

"Troll, can you hear me?" whispered young Kol, Grim's son. Apparently, I wasn't the only stowaway. I remained silent.

"I know you can," he said. "You're just being stubborn again. We've got to go back for them, troll... Hallr. That's your real name, yes? They can't last long. They'll all die on that rock, you know."

I didn't care. Humans died all the time. These particular humans had never been friends. I had been their laughing stock and chained beast.

"Hallr, they're not all bad. They didn't turn against you after Leos was killed."

Even while he whispered, I could hear frustration and fear making his voice crack. He was on the cusp of adolescence. I idly wondered if he'd ever make it past the cusp.

"There's something you don't know, Hallr. Something important about Leos. Do you want to know what it is?"

Did I? Over and over, my mind had replayed the part of the battle during which, according to my shipmates, I'd killed Leos. I knew what happened, I grunted for the boy to get the hell away from me.

As quietly as he could, Kol raised the lid on my box.

"If I tell you, will you help me?"

"Maybe," I rasped, "if I don't kill you instead."

That silenced him. I could practically hear his keen, little mind whirring, wondering if he should just sneak away into the Irish forest rather than take his chances with the likes of me.

"Just stay quiet," he said finally. "You'll kill us both if you bellow like a berserker, Hallr. Here's the secret: it wasn't you. You didn't kill Leos at all."

I reached out of the box and grabbed his right forearm with a speed humans somehow never expect from a troll. I squeezed slowly, knowing that even in my weakened condition, I could turn his little arm to pulp.

"Who then?" I croaked.

"Stop," he whispered. "Please stop. You'll make me scream."

"Who?" I repeated, still tightening, though slowly.

"I was going to tell you anyway, damned troll," he said, pushing out his words between clenched teeth. "It was Far. He kills everything. He loves it."

Despite what happened to the *Ormen Vig*, it wasn't usually easy to steal a Viking ship out from under its crew's noses. But we did have some advantages. Kol was exceptionally stealthy for a human, and he knew everything about our ship. Even in darkness, he was able to locate tools, weapons, and a full jar of the stuff we called flameteaser. It was a kind of tree fungus boiled in human piss, dried and then pounded into small pieces. We'd need it.

My first job was to swim unnoticed down the river a ways so that I could sneak into the wood unseen by the half-drunken, but still quite attentive, two crewmen on guard duty. It took time. Even for a troll, moving quietly through an unknown landscape is difficult. Still, my time as a guerilla with Alfr's army had honed those skills.

Luckily, they were having a whispered conversation, which made it easy for me to come up from behind, grab them together and cut both their throats with a single swipe. As I did it, though, I felt more remorse than I'd ever felt when killing humans in the past. These were young men, no older than Leos, men who would never again see their families or work their farms or embrace a lover. Mor would have approved of my cunning and efficiency but not my contrition. "Soft," I could hear her say, "like your father."

I sent up a silent prayer to Arg, asking him to make me into a hard troll, remorseless, vengeful, cold as the frosts of Niflheim. I made Grim my murderous muse, stoking the fires of hatred by imagining his death.

I waved to Kol, who stealthily moved from the *Ormen Vig* to the *Naorbita*. I thought what a cunning little prick he was, much like his own far.

As Kol prepared to set multiple small fires aboard the Bloodaxe flagship, I slunk down into the water and used a large awl to bore three holes below the water line in the bow, stern and amidships. I was sorely tempted to put my fist through the hull, but there was no way to do that quietly. Besides, these smaller holes would not become apparent until they were offshore where they'd have a harder time plugging them. If the fire didn't destroy the *Naorbita*, perhaps these would sink her. At the very least, they'd slow them down.

I signaled Kol that the holes had been bored. Next was the hard part, the part I wasn't sure could even be done, at least not in my current state. I went to the *Ormen Vig*, braced my back up against it, and pushed as hard as I could with my legs. The damned ship barely moved as my feet sunk into silty shoreline. I noticed that small fires were already starting to glow on the *Naorbita*. If I couldn't launch the *Ormen Vig*, Bjor's crew would soon be hacking me to pieces.

The quick-witted Kol, finished with his arson, dragged a thick piece of driftwood over and put it under my feet. I stepped on it, which provided the leverage to give the ship another push. This time it backed up farther, though the wood cracked under my feet.

A cry went up. Someone had seen the growing flames flickering in the other ship. The sailors ran to the ship and started throwing wet sand onto it in an attempt to quell the flames. Blinded by the fire, it took time for someone to notice me pushing at the bow of the *Ormen Vig*. When he did, he assumed I was a member of the crew.

"Hey now, what the fuck are you doing?" he shouted.

In desperation, I pushed once again, feeling the ship finally starting to ease into the river. Joined by one of his crewmates, the man started running toward me. I pulled my knife from my belt and strained against the dragon ship again. When my first attacker was still several yards away, a figure rushed out of the shadows and, knees down in the sand, thrust a knife into the charging man's soft abdomen. The man went down, tripping over his assailant, Kol, while the other one charged me. I was pumping my legs, trying to maintain the momentum of the vessel, when the ship disappeared from behind me, throwing me on my back. The sailor launched himself at me, aiming for my throat but only skewering the flesh just above my collarbone.

There was no time. The *Ormen Vig* was being carried away by the current. With the knife still in my flesh, I threw the man off me as if he were a rabid animal and jumped for the gunwale. I made it, but the hull smashed the handle of the knife deeper into my neck. Only after I managed to pull myself up and onto the deck did I pull out the knife. Within minutes, I was woozy with blood loss, then passed out completely.

I would have died if it hadn't been for Kol, a thirteen year-old child who had more grit and smarts than most adults. I don't know how he was able to scramble onto the ship, only that when I regained consciousness, he was using a bandage to tie a damp wad of scratchy wool over my wound and screaming at me to get the hell up.

He had managed to steer the ship away from the shores, but we were approaching the mouth of the river, where we would need either oars or sail to make our escape. Although I still felt light-headed, I was able to raise the heavy sail just as the *Naorbita* came into view behind. Their ship was still smoldering, but the furious crew had managed to quell the fires and man their oars. They were pulling furiously after us. If the wind had been blowing against us, they would have caught us despite the holes I'd left in their ship. As it was, however, we outpaced them.

Kol cupped his hands to his mouth and called out, "Your sails are cinders, you morons!" They might have been too far away to hear his exact words, but they got the gist. In case they didn't, Captain Grim's Viking prodigy gave them the same obscene signal they'd given the crew of the *Ormen Vig*.

In a month of trying, I would not have found those rocks on my own. But Kol? It only took him about a day. We could hear waves crashing in the darkness but didn't dare approach until the sky started to brighten. With just the two of us, maneuvering the ship was difficult. Smashing the ship onto the rocks was a serious risk, especially as the winds had picked up and created a sea of white caps.

I had rested in the trollbox throughout that day of sailing. After sunset, I went through Leos's belongings and discovered my black garb and wired hood. I didn't know if it would be enough protection as the sun rose, but I couldn't go back in the trollbox. At least not in chains and at the order of the murderous Grim.

We made our approach to the leeward side. They had seen us coming, of course. Gathered on one corner of the trapezoid rock, which seemed smaller now that the tide was higher, were several bodies piled on one another. It had only been about a day and a half, not long enough for healthy men to succumb to exposure and dehydration. They must have died fighting over the small amount of fresh water on the rock. I could imagine why they'd kept the bodies rather than giving them to the sea.

Grim stood on the edge of the rock, having crowded out the others. He didn't wave.

"You're going to kill him," said Kol, who was handling the steering oar.

"Yes," I said, "unless he kills me first."

"You should use an arrow. Kill him while he's on the rock. He's too dangerous up close," he said.

I thought about it. Was his suggestion a ruse? A bow would do me little good in close-quarters fighting against the crew if they decided to defend or avenge their captain.

"I'm better with an ax," I said. "Don't get near enough for them to jump. Let's luff the sail the best we can so I can talk to them."

As we approached, they signaled for us to come in closer. The ones still standing looked desperate, frustrated and angry. I shook my head, no doubt appearing as an enormous ghoul all cloaked in black. It wasn't quite dawn, but the sun would be up soon. I lifted the hood to speak.

"Line up. You'll jump down one at a time, according to my signal. If anyone jumps before I signal them, I'll toss them into the rocks. Do you understand?"

Not one of them nodded. Some looked stunned. Most had never heard me speak a full sentence. Troll thralls are expected to listen, not talk. Others looked as furious as I'd ever seen them, including Captain Grim. He was shouting angrily and waving at Kol to bring the ship in closer. Kol didn't respond at all, which I took as a good sign. My life was in his hands. If he decided to swing the ship in at the wrong time, he could knock me overboard or allow the crew members to jump at once and overwhelm me. We were drifting away from the rock, so I signaled Kol to bring us around again and circle it.

We went through the same routine on our second pass, me making the same speech and asking the same question. I got many nods, but none from Grim, who only glared at me and clenched the hilt of his sword. I told them that everyone needed to nod their agreement, or I'd leave them to molder on the damned rock. This time everyone nodded, even Grim, though just barely.

Kol and I brought us around again.

"Captain Grim, you'll be the last one on the ship. Agreed?"

Again, he nodded, and we started bringing them off the rock. After the third sailor was aboard, a man named Kori decided he would jump out of turn. As he hit the deck, he tried to stare me down with his fiercest look and held up his axe. I grabbed the arm with the axe, wrenched it till the weapon fell, and, as casually as I could given my injuries, threw him overboard against the side of the big rock. He smacked with a sickening, wet sound. Then, as if nothing had happened, I motioned for the next man to jump.

When Grim and one other sailor were the last ones left standing, I told them to start handing down the men who were unconscious or just too weak to jump. This took longer and required the help of some of the crew who were already on the ship. I supervised, keeping a careful eye on the captain.

Finally, it was just Grim, standing on the rock and staring at me.

"Move aside, troll. I'm coming down," he declared.

"Not unless you want to die quickly, you murderous bastard," I growled.

I turned to the crew.

"This man killed Leos!" I shouted to them. "His own crew member, and my friend."

None said a word, or even looked surprised. I realized they already knew, or at least guessed. Grim just smiled.

"Of course I killed him, you dense beast!" he shouted. "The fool warned you against my blow, which would have ended everything quietly. And he gave me this festering cut. Attacking his captain. I didn't murder the troll-lover. I executed him!

"Now take him, men. Kill the ugly, wounded monster!" he roared, unsheathing his sword and shaking it at me.

And then, nothing. Not one of them charged. Only a few reached for their weapons but, seeing no movement from the others, hesitated.

"Your choice, Grim," I shouted up at him. "Stay on the rock and rot or come down and let me take your head."

Grim was many things, but a coward was not one of them. He sprung down at me, his sword drawn, eager to cleave me in half. Fiery Sól had raised her head above the horizon by then, causing a million points of lights to glare up at me from the flickering sea. I stumbled in my robes backwards, nearly tumbling off the other side. Somehow my left foot found the gunwale, and I regained my balance just as Grim, crouched on the deck, stabbed upwards.

One of Dofri's expressions suddenly came to me: "Better wounded than dead." I twisted away from his thrust enough to ensure he didn't stab me in the gut but not so much I'd be thrown off balance again. His sword sliced over my ribcage, but this gave me an opening. Up came my knee into his head, dazing him, and then down came my axe, cleanly severing his head.

Oh, gods, how I wanted to bellow my triumph, pick up his head and, in the grand tradition of trolls, take a large bite from it. I didn't, though. The crew could still have turned on me in the blink of an eye.

I held up his head by the hair.

"Kol, son of Grim, your father has died a valiant death in battle and will be welcome in Valhalla. He has honored your family and deserves our prayers and full funerary rights. You must decide how best to send him into the afterlife."

I don't know what Grim had done to his son. The captain had treated Kol like a servant, seldom acknowledging him and never, to my knowledge, showing him any particular regard. Indeed, the fresh bruises Kol exhibited some mornings suggested there was no father-son tenderness in their private affairs, or perhaps only some horrific corruption of it.

Kol silently stepped over the thwarts to where I stood. He cradled the bloody head in his hands and requested that we build his father a funeral pyre. Then he ritualistically began to wail and pull at his hair. He was a smart kid putting on a good show, but I suspected that, in his heart, he'd just as soon use his father's brains as fish bait.

Chapter Twenty-Two

"Odin sends them to all battles, where they choose those who are to be slain, and rule over victory."
—*The Younger Edda*

*M*imir's head is floating in the swamp like a beach ball, quivering with laughter.

"What's so funny, you bodyless freak?" I ask.

"You, troll, you thought the libation was free, remember? Now look at you. You gave up a lot more than just an eye, as I predicted. Look around, troll. See the price paid in full."

So I do. I thought it was the same swamp I was in before, but it's different. I'm standing among reeds that aren't reeds at all but rather an assortment of people's bones growing out of the muck: long and sloping vertebrates, bristling stands of femurs and fibula, ulnas and radiuses with skeletal hands still attached. And the lily pads aren't pads at all, but rather the tops of skulls, thousands of them, some of them floating so high I can see the ridges of eye sockets hovering at the water's surface.

"Hell, that's not good," I say.

"Helheim, actually," says Mimir.

"So I'm dead, then."

"Let's just say you are exceedingly gray around the gills."

I feel more weary than frightened. Although I know it's not the same place, I look around for the huge root on which Brad Lauder had been lying. It'd be nice to take a long nap there. Alas, it's nowhere to be seen. So, I just close my eyes and fall backwards into the swamp, floating there like a turtle sunning itself. Except there is no sun, never any sun here. Lovely. I can feel myself sinking slowly, soon to settle peacefully under the surface, my noggin destined to be just another bony lily pad among millions.

"Not so fast," says Mimir.

"What now?"

I open my eyes to see Hildy's face. It's gigantic, covering the whole gray sky, or whatever that is up there. Her hair is auburn and streams below a winged helmet of polished bronze.

"Nice hat, Hildy," I murmur.

She ignores me, moving her lips in prayer or chant or something. She looks serious, stern even.

"So," says Mimir, who rises like a balloon, partially eclipsing Hildy's visage, "you interested in a get-out-of-Hel free card?"

"Maybe after a quick nap," I say.

"Answer the question, troll!"

"You sure have a bossy streak for a dead guy, you know that? Anyway, what's this free card gonna cost me?"

"Now you're learning, troll!" he says with enthusiasm.

He rises higher and higher above me, transforming into the sun. No, not the sun. It's a large, golden wheel with engravings that are familiar, though I can't quite place them.

"Wakey, wakey!" shouts Mimir just as the wheel explodes into a billion golden shards.

I sit up and whack my head on something. I hear an obscenity that, puzzlingly, doesn't come from me. It's Hildy, wincing and holding both hands to her forehead.

"Idiot, idiot, idiot," she says in the Old Tongue.

"Sorry," I murmur. "Guess you should have kept your helmet on."

At first she just stares at me with a blank look. Then something clicks.

"That's okay, Hallr," she finally says. "I'm the hard-headed type."

"Oh my God!" exclaims someone else in the room, an unfamiliar woman's voice. As she comes near, I see she's youngish and wearing some kind of lab coat. A doctor? Yes and no. It's a hospital, but something's wrong with it. Smells funny.

Hildy ignores the doctor.

"Hildy?"

"Yes?"

"Why is there a flea and tick poster in my hospital room?"

"Beggars can't be choosers, Klaus," she says. "There weren't any real hospitals around. And these people know how to deal with big animals that do dumb things."

"I can't believe he's alive," says the woman in the lab coat. Dark hair, large eyes. Hispanic, I'd say. "If the injections and compressions were going to work, they should have worked a while ago."

"I've always been a late bloomer," I rasp.

"Though hardly a rose," says someone else. Andre. He's sitting on an ugly orange vinyl bench, flipping through a local newspaper. "And with all those stitches they plugged into you, you're a whole new kind of ugly."

"A couple more gator maulings, and I might get as homely as you, cook."

He stands and grins down at me

"Nice way to treat the hero who dragged your immense ass out of the bog," he says. He looks at Hildy. "Or, at least, helped drag it."

A few minutes later, an ambulance shows up to take me to a real hospital. They greet the vet first. Apparently, they and an MD had walked her through emergency procedures over the phone after Hildy and Andre lugged me into the place.

It turns out the two paramedics can't lift me. Andre and Hildy look amused. I guess they're done hauling trolls for the day. The ambulance guys recruit several vet techs to help heft me onto the gurney, which is definitely not long enough. Then my weight crushes the gurney, so they can't easily load me into the back of the ambulance. That's when I call everything to a halt.

"I appreciate the effort, boys and girls," I say, still hoarse, "but I'm gonna take a pass. I just need a good night's sleep."

They argue with me, even threatening to call the cops, but they leave me alone after I sign a form and promise I'll make my way to the ER by myself. Once they leave, I lie down in a grassy patch out in front of the vet's place and take a nap. By the time I wake up, Hildy and Andre have got my Hog. I can barely walk, so Hildy winds up driving my Electra Glide while I hold her waist from the back. Andre gets a huge laugh out of it.

"Looks like you're being mauled by a black bear," he yells to Hildy, who flips him off.

"Stay awake," she shouts back to me, "or we'll both wind up road kill."

"Awesome bedside manner," I shout.

About two hours later, we make it to her aunts' place in the woods. I barely get to one of the bedrooms before I crash again, just awake enough to strip off blood- and mud-caked clothing. At least the bed is big enough. It pays to be the houseguest of giantesses.

I groan, more sore than I've ever been before, which is saying a lot when you've been alive for over a millennium.

"You're hurting," says Hildy, startling me. She's on the other side of the bed though and, unlike myself, she's on top of the covers. She's wearing a long, blue, linen shift, very Nordic old school, and her hair is back to a dark chestnut color.

The lights are out, and they've closed the heavy drapes, but I can still see well enough.

"Guess it could be worse," I say, turning on my side to face her. "In fact, I'm thinking it was worse. So, thanks."

With her right hand, she makes a gesture I've not seen for centuries, one that used to mean something like "it was nothing" or "no problem."

"I owed you one. Besides, it's what I do. Or used to do."

"So, valkyries have a retirement package, then?"

The corners of her lips quirk upward, though her eyes remain sad.

"Not so much retired. More like fired."

"Yeah?" I say. "I guess you annoyed that one-eyed boss of yours."

According to legend, Odin had twelve handmaidens called valkyries. Sort of like Charlie's Angels, except way more deadly. On behalf of their monoptic Charlie, they decided which soldiers lived and died on the battlefield.

"You might say that," she says. "He wanted me to choose one warrior to win a duel, but I chose the other. Odin's choice was a cocky old guy and my heart went out to the brave kid fighting him, a real underdog type."

"Then what happened?"

"Odin made me mortal as a punishment," she says, shrugging. "I didn't take it well. I felt betrayed and angry. I wasn't just a mortal but kind of a mortal bitch after that."

She looks up toward a ceiling made of polished wooden planks.

"You're not so bad," I say. Growing up with Mor has made me pretty tolerant in that area.

"I'm sure my ex would have a different opinion."

"Bad breakup?"

"Well, I did have him assassinated in his sleep, so yeah."

Is she kidding? Somehow I don't think so. It occurs to me that sharing a bunk with a fallen valkyrie could be an extremely poor convalescence strategy.

"Maybe he had it coming," I say.

"Not really. I wish he had. The truth is, he was a good guy, not to mention strong as a grizzly bear and brave enough to walk through fire—something he literally did for me once. The greatest warrior of his time and so handsome that he made Adonis look like some prepubescent boyband singer."

"Pretty sure I'd hate him," I say. "What happened?"

She tells how he'd pledged his love to her but married another. There were rumors that a sorceress had cast a spell on him so he would forget her, but she couldn't forgive him.

"I thought it was just an elaborate brush off," she says. "Later on, I found out he deceived me in another way, and I completely lost it.

"When he was dead, I was so filled with self-loathing and sorrow that I threw myself on his funeral pyre. Talk about your drama queen. Even at *his* cremation, it was all about me, me, me," she says, striking her fingers on her breastbone.

I search for a good response. Bupkis.

"I couldn't even die properly, not being as mortal as I had been led to believe," she says with a bitter laugh. "I just crawled away from the ashes blackened and scarred, barely recognizable as human."

She tells the tale of how her body healed before her mind. Her moods would shift erratically from day to day or even hour to hour. There were many fractured selves, though three were most prominent. One was a carefree, graceful and impish young woman, temporarily unburdened by her past. Another was a ferocious and feral hellion looking for action in seedy inns and raucous taverns. The third was older and more responsible, a healer and apothecary, a kind of mother to the other two.

"But she wound up being trouble as well," Hildy says quietly, almost to herself.

"Addiction," I say.

She turns over, puts her elbow on the bed and props her head on her hand, looking down on me.

"How would you know that?" she asked. I remember her deftness with that needle and the anger directed at it. And there was something else at *Grimm's* after Lucky's insinuation, a kind of seething resentment directed inward.

"Just a guess," I say. "Occupational hazard among the apothecaries, right? Analgesics, soporifics, laudanum, morphine."

She nods. "I was one of the original opium eaters back in the day," she says, "when immortality felt like a curse and a burden."

A mythic figure out of the Dark Ages, one at war with herself and everlastingly sick of that war. Seeking refuge in isolation and oblivion. A story familiar to me.

"And these days?"

"Day to day like the rest of the world's dope fiends," she says. "Remember when you walked into the Vandriller swamp? Just before Andre and I followed you, this man walked up to us, asking what was going on. He was smoking a doobie laced with black tar. I can still smell it. I wanted it so badly I could barely think. It was…"

"Overwhelming," I say.

"Something like that."

"You came in after me anyway. I appreciate it."

She nods in acknowledgment. We lie there silently for a while.

"I didn't know trolls were good listeners," she says softly.

"One of our many charms."

The next time I wake, the room is darker yet. Dusk is approaching, Hildy is gone.

I get up, naked, and walk over to an antique full-length mirror set in a gilded-gold frame. The stitches on my body are black and thick, made for livestock, not humans. There are long lines of them on the right side of my face, on my left shoulder and arm, and then more running like tracks from my chest to my belly. They look like huge, hairy centipedes.

"You are changed, troll," she says in the Old Tongue.

I nearly jump out of my newly stitched skin. It's Aunt Urdy, standing in the doorway and carrying a wooden box with a handle.

"Damn, old lady," I say, snatching a sheet from the bed to cover myself.

"Yet I see the malice striker did not bleed you of all foolishness and conceit."

"Look, I know this is your house, but could you please take your picnic basket and get out of here? I'm not feeling so hot."

"Hildr requested I examine your battle wounds, which may start to fester. We old ones still know something of weaving and stitching."

I go into stony troll mode, hoping that if I'm still enough, she'll go away.

"Sit, troll!"

I do, immediately, as if I'm a puppet and someone cut my strings. As I sit on the bed in the sheet, she holds up my arm and examines it with professional curiosity.

"Shoddy, hasty work," she says. "This area here," she points to my shoulder, "needs cleansing." She does something to the wooden box and it slides open, becoming three shelves' worth of antique sewing equipment. She picks up a pair of little scissors.

"I think I'm fine," I tell her.

"Hildr, tea!" she yells out the door, ignoring me.

I follow her scissors with my eyes as she deftly cuts a number of the black stitches on my shoulder.

"Thanks for the offer, but your tea doesn't agree with me."

"Mimir will protect," she says absently, making me flinch by fingering my wound.

"I lost ole Mimir in the swamp."

She looks deeply into my eyes, still with that doctorly air.

"No, he's still there. You, troll, ignore your gifts, reject them, yet *use* them, too, more often than you know."

Hildy brings in a bone-china tea set on a serving tray. I give her a "help me" look, but she only places it on a side table, gives me a wink, and leaves.

The old giantess doesn't serve the steaming tea but, instead, dips a linen cloth into the pot and starts washing out my wound with it. I recoil. The water is just a notch below scalding.

"Ease up there, Aunty Urdy," I say. "Remember that good ole 'first do no harm' dictum. You sure tea water is the right remedy?"

"Some water is dirty, some clean," she says in the Old Tongue as she works. "Clean water grows rare in these dark days. The dirty hurts the roots, sickens the tree, brings closer the end."

This explanation baffles me.

"Am I the tree in this scenario?" I ask.

She just shakes her head to indicate I'm hopeless. Then she plunks me hard right between the eyes with her middle finger.

I fall silent, only half recognizing she's just used her mojo on me.

Suddenly, I'm not on the bed but, rather, swimming. No, not swimming, just dunking my head underwater. Though the water is a foggy green, I can make out a scattering of eelgrass undulating in the current. It's flowing away from an underwater pit, at the bottom of which there is a small boil of water nudging up grains of sand. It's a spring, one of hundreds in the area, the highest concentration of them on the planet. But it's not me who knows this. It's the swimmer. I'm in her mind, a passenger of sorts. My butt floats nicely, allowing my head to swivel with an exhilarating freedom.

I'm a female bird, a swan to be precise.

I hover over the spring, tasting the water. There's more salt than there should be. A bad sign. A sign that the freshwaters of the aquifer below are being sucked up fast by a million greedy straws, allowing salt water from even deeper underground to seep into and contaminate the once-pure underground river. The greenness of the spring water also bodes ill. Too many nitrates causing unnatural algae blooms. There is a nasty tang of cattle, pig and human shit, with a metallic smack of auto exhaust.

I pop my head above water, mentally rating this spring as in danger, possibly dying. I spread out my white wings in annoyance and then fold them back up again. I look around for my companion, my sister, a sleek white beauty like the ones I saw the other night in Urdy's spring. She gives me a honk and starts flying, skimming over the greenish water for a few beats and then ascending, ascending, and I'm with her. Astonishing!

From the sky, the Florida landscape looks liquid. There's water everywhere, one lake after another, like the footprints of a giant walking through a soggy field. It feels so transient, as if the tide is about to roll in any second, submerging all the green in sight.

We're seeking another spring. I sense my sister's frustration in the way she turns her head as she peers downward. The springs should be obvious, their clear, quickening waters standing out against the millions of lakes and retention ponds. Distinguishing them has become harder. Then we see one and descend. A gentle boil barely roils the surface. We land, gratefully dipping our beaks into the water and then raising them to swallow. It tastes better than the last spring but still saltier than it should be.

Another bad sign: there's hardly any eelgrass here. Instead, there are dense mats of the brown muck covering the bottom. Must be two or three feet thick. I panic, thinking back to the living sludge that attacked Hildy and me. But there's no hum of seidr or galdr here. I dive and take a little in my beak. No, this particular stuff just tastes of human stupidity and hubris. That's strange because this spring run is out in the middle of a state forest, protected from the drainage of farmlands and highways.

Maybe it's the motorboats nearby. I can smell the gas on the water. Ducking my head under again, I hear the noisy thrum of internal combustion engines. That could have chased away a lot of wildlife that might have helped control the algae. There are sulfurous bubbles languidly ascending from the mat of muck. The longer I float here, the more nauseous the smell makes me.

This spring is also sick. I feel a wave of despair. The whole world is sick, turning yellow and brown like a tree with diseased roots.

This time I honk at my sister, signaling my need to get out of here.

After another few minutes, we see a third spring, but this time we don't even descend. We've been there before and know it has stopped flowing. The algae mats have become tall gray columns reaching to the surface—that is, where the surface isn't covered in water hyacinths, with their thick and glossy leaves floating on the skin of the spring. Little is left alive beneath those leaves, but atop them are hundreds of gorgeous violet blossoms, flowers on the grave of the spring.

"No, troll, you not the tree," I hear Urdy answering, this time in her broken English. I'm abruptly back in my own body, sitting quietly on the bed. She is restitching the slice on my shoulder. It takes me a second to figure out that she's responding to a question I feel I asked hours ago, though it must have been just moments.

"We are all the tree," she says.

Asleep again. Then awake. Middle of the night. Very dark in this house in these woods. Hildy's not here, but her scent is still in the bed.

I check an old walnut bureau and then the closet. Neither contains my clothes, though the latter does have a blue woollen robe, one large enough for a giantess.

I throw it on, then sneak toward the doorway into the great hall. Sure enough, both aunts are there, even at this hour, rocking in their enormous chairs. As far as I know, I've been silent in my approach, but Urdy says loudly, "Hildr goes outside, troll. Even the nurse can tire of the sickbed."

I enter the surreal hallway, trying not to tremble in the face of the pure and powerful seidr here. Aunt Verda looks up at me, nods politely and smiles. Urdy stares at my bare feet, a storm threatening in her eyes, but then sighs resignedly at my boorishness.

In my absurd bathrobe, I walk with as much deference and dignity as a troll can muster past the marble well, along the tree root and through the enormous doors.

Outside the air is fresh and cool, the spring radiating a serenity I didn't properly appreciate the last time. Máni the moon is in his waxing gibbous phase. I give him a friendly nod. Trolls love the moon, seeing it as the mind of Aurgelmir.

I see the approaching comet Loge as well. It's growing larger in the night sky. They say that, because of its size and trajectory, it will be visible for a couple of months.

It doesn't take me long to locate Hildy. In truth, I now know her smell so well that I could track her through the deepest, most labyrinthine cave systems of Jotunheimen. Is this creepy or romantic? I don't know. Merely a fact.

She lies beneath a nearby oak tree. Ordinarily, it would be the largest tree in the vicinity, but it is a shrub compared to the incredible ash tree of the aunts. It's restful, though. There is little thrum of magic here, just the homely glamour of dried leaves beneath the mighty, gnarled limbs of the oak, spread up toward the moon like an ancient worshipper.

"Looking good in Aunt Skuldy's robe," she says.

"Thanks," I say, deciding to join her in sprawling on the bed of leaves. "So, what did you say happened to her again?"

"She's just grown restless over the last several decades. She has always been, let's say, the most excitable of the three. Maybe because she has the keenest insights into the future. In every culture, diviners tend to be a bit twitchy, and she is the greatest of them all. Things happen so fast in this age. Can you imagine what that does to someone like her?"

"So, what, you're saying she's on holiday?" I ask.

"More like a sabbatical. She went to study quantum mechanics. I don't know why, exactly. It's something to do with predicting quantum events, which I guess is supposed to be impossible. She's totally engrossed in it, and she's stubborn, which is why her sisters can't get her to come home, even in the face of the current craziness."

"Maybe she already knows how it's all going to turn out and isn't worried."

"I hope so," says Hildy, watching the moon.

"What do your aunts say about the comet?" I ask, pointing up to it.

"It worries them," Hildy whispers, as if it's a secret. "It's another thing they didn't foresee."

All that unfathomable power, yet the sisters are finally stuck in the same dark boat as the rest of us, not knowing if it's shoals or rocks or open sea ahead. Should I be amused or terrified?

"You haven't told me what happened to Lauder," I say.

She doesn't say anything. Her eyes are closed and I wonder if she's drifted off.

"Hildy?"

"He didn't make it," she finally says.

"He was still alive."

"He was in deep shock, dying."

Dying. And what was I? If me, why not him? I'm a monster, a literal monster, and he was that rarity among humans: a curious, responsible and diligent guy going the extra mile because something in that CoE paperwork didn't sit right with him. It reeked, and he investigated and paid the price. What is it they say? No good deed goes unpunished.

An image of my old friend Leos flashes in my mind. A good man slain, cut down in his prime so I could be spared.

"Yeah, but…"

"I had to make a choice, Hallr," she snaps, sitting up. "That's all I can do, all I've ever been allowed to do!"

"That poor guy was just bait, though," I say, even though I know I should leave it alone. "Bait to draw us in."

"Not just bait," she says. "Sacrifice. Even if we'd never found him, he was still sacrifice. That place, it was…"

"I know what it was, Hildy. I just don't know who goes around sacrificing human beings anymore. It's really, really old school."

She laughs. A bitter sound, almost a cackle.

"Do you believe that, Hallr? Old school? Don't you see that these people, these 'modern' people, love a good blood sacrifice as much as any Norseman ever did? They live for it.

"You've spent decades in a tollbooth. How many of their fellows do they sacrifice each year to their worship of their cars and convenience, their own self-serving yearnings for status and speed? Thousands die on their roads, yes? Tens of thousands, even, every single year.

"How about the blood sacrifice of their children? Leave aside the destruction of so many of their unborn, if you like. In this nation, how many children are slaughtered in their schools by maniacs wielding terrible weapons? Their lives are forfeit by nothing more than a senseless wrath, a lust for gunmetal, a wallowing in paranoia and an idolatry of archaic words."

She is standing up now, voice quivering, eyes wide, face a mask of fury. I've never seen her like this, a woman nearly deranged by despair, threatening to tip into madness.

"And their wars, Hallr, their never-ending wars, feeding their magnificent youth into the maw of military misadventures. I was born to love battle. It's in my blood. But all my long life I've seen it. Nothing changes. Greed, fear, conceit, pride, zealotry. It's always the same. Always more sacrifices, always more terrible choices, always their death-dealing, infantile faith in their own righteousness. It's the history of humanity writ large. An endless, crimson river of terrible, rending, mostly futile sacrifices."

I could offer arguments against her torrid rant, but there's no point. This isn't about logic. She had to make a hard choice between me and the Corps regulator. I'm grateful it went the way it did. The sacrifice wasn't just Lauder's, but hers.

It occurs to me that maybe Odin didn't demote her for insubordination, after all. Maybe he just knew she'd had enough. Maybe it was an act of mercy to a dutiful, damaged daughter.

Chapter Twenty-Three

"It was dueling law at that time that if a man challenged another in any matter and the one who issued the challenge won the victory, then his due as victor was whatever the challenge had been made for. If he were defeated, he was obliged to ransom himself by an agreed sum."

—*Egil's Saga*

No one on the ship challenged my leadership. Most simply didn't care who was captain as long as we were, as I promised, headed home at all speed to warn the king and make war on the Bloodaxe traitors.

I had reached a decision. Never more would I allow myself to be shackled like an animal. King Alfr had promised that I would be chained only by my honor. I'd hold him to it. Otherwise, I reasoned, my pledge to him was void and I'd make for the mountains to search for remaining kin. Until then, however, I'd do my level best to kill Bloodaxe and win my freedom outright.

This didn't mean I had a clue about how to get us back home. While locked in the trollbox, I'd learned precious little about sailing. Most nights were spent ashore or anchored just off the coast. So my specialties had been those of the thrall: hauling the ship onto and off shores, pulling up the anchor, and manning the oars when possible.

Grim's son, Kol, on the other hand, knew as much—or likely more—about the proper running of the ship as any of the other crew. He and I were an unsettling pair: the child and the savage who slew his father, working with an eerie synchronicity. It was as if the spirit of Grim had been cleaved in half, and we two constituent parts had been freed. Kol was the incarnation of the skills, knowledge and intuition of the master mariner. I was the man's inner demon sprung to life, lurking in darkness, capable of hacking others to splinters on a whim.

We stood the trollbox up vertically in the stern. I had the ship's carpenter cut a horizontal slot near the top so that I could see out and a hole so I could shout commands at will. Even empty, the box had an ominous look to it.

There were slides inside so I could close those slots if I chose. I also added an extra plank of wood to the swinging door of the box so an arrow or even a well-thrown spear wouldn't easily pierce it.

"Same ship, same rules," I told them. "Just be careful of baiting the troll these days."

I smiled grimly, letting them know I was joking—sort of. I needed them to see me as more than a dimwitted monster. No matter how dangerous I was, they would not willingly follow a fool.

We sailed through the short nights without bothering to anchor or beach. This was not only because we were in a hurry to get home but because, at night, I could see all the landmarks, rocks, shoals and other signs as well as Kol could in the daylight. The crew would huddle under furs as I took the steering oar in hand and sailed the course set by Kol, who slept like a hound near my side. I'd sail it via landmarks, seamarks and the Pole Star, waking him when the universe was misaligned.

"Kol," I'd say, shaking him awake, "those shoals shouldn't be there."

He'd have a quick, bleary-eyed look and then tell me whether to hold or change course.

I did what I could to man the ship by myself at night. My long, strong limbs were often an advantage. For example, I tied the mainsheet to my boot, drawing it in or letting it out with my left leg.

Over the next few days, I had leisure to evaluate the crew. There were relatively few members of King Alfr's retinue, or *hiro*, as they called it. His hiro was packed with highborn men, many of them from the Völsung clan itself, who served as his bodyguard. For now, since Alfr still didn't trust Bloodaxe, he tended to keep his hiro close rather than send them out on the flagship.

On this crew, many were farmers who, if they had their way, would only raid till it was time for harvest. About two thirds were men in their twenties, probably the second, third or fourth sons in their families, not unlike Leos. They wanted to make their fortunes, or gain enough prestige to become part of Alfr's hiro.

The older sailors were driven more by suffering: failed crops, a bad marriage, gambling debts, a bloody quarrel. But there were also those who'd started young and become ill-suited for any type of conventional life. They not only savored the trading and raiding life, they were addicted to it: the variety, adventure, peril and sporadic bouts of brutality.

There were five men I had to watch closely: sadists who wanted, above all, to squeeze the sufferings of the world into a cup and drink deeply. They would kill and maim to satisfy a nearly sexual yearning. Brutality and fierce bloodlust were common among trolls. Sadism was not. It is a perversity more common among the human hordes.

Only once, though, did I act against the sadists. It was during the dreary, drizzly voyage home. As we crossed the North Sea from the Orkney Islands, the winds were favorable and constant, so the men curled up in furs under tarps we stretched between the gunwales.

As I operated the steering oar in the night, I heard moaning on the wind. Storm-stressed stays and shrouds, I thought at first. But, no, it was a human sound. Perhaps one of the sailors was having a nightmare or was ill. I sent Kol to scramble over and under the tarps to find the source.

He discovered that two of the sadists, Engli and Bersi, were carving images of Thor's hammer into the broad back of Ornolf the Oaf. The joke, in their eyes, was that Thor—the great half-jotunn destroyer of giants—had struck the giant Ornolf time and again with his famed weapon, Mjolnir. They knew that Ornolf wouldn't resist. Despite his great strength, he was useless in a fight and feared defying his crewmates.

As I've said, I was poor at most magic but reasonably good at the form of galdr known as petitioning. I'd seldom used it, shamed by Mor's description of it as a beggar's magic, but now my ire was roused. I felt a tiny seed of magic bloom in my chest, thrusting upward and out in an incantation. A reverser spell. I called on the power of the sea giantess Ran, who loves little more than snacking on the fleshy flotsam of drowning men.

As the ship lurched, Engli's knife slipped upwards into the arm of Bersi, who held up the undertunic of Ornolf so his comrade could work. Bersi cursed as the blood spurted from his forearm like water from a spring. He clenched his arm to staunch the flow but to no avail. It was a nasty arterial wound. Engli cut a strip of cloth from Ornolf's tunic and bandaged the wound, slowing but not stopping the blood.

"Find me a stick for a tourniquet!" Bersi demanded.

"Fuck you," Engli called back. "You ain't hurt so bad you can't get it yourself."

Bersi was in no position to argue. Not finding anything in the cavity where they crouched, he tried scrambling over the forward tarp to get to the next cavity up. Just then, the ship unexpectedly rolled to starboard. Bersi slid down the blood-slick tarp and shot out into the sea as if the ship itself were expelling him from her body.

I waited to see if anyone would raise an alarm. Kol wordlessly stared at me with a disconcerting intensity. Engli raised his head to watch the floundering form of Bersi quickly recede behind. I barely heard a strangled cry from the drowning man. Engli hesitated, then met my eye and smirked. In the end, Kol bandaged the oaf and settled him down as Engli curled up and went to sleep.

I instantly regretted the incident and felt Mor had been right—if you asked favors of gods, even the giants and giantesses, you never knew what they'd ask for in return. But there was no going back. I tamped down my emerging sense of dread and sailed on into the darkness.

Despite our urgent voyage home, we arrived too late to give warning. Bloodaxe had already struck, though in a typically underhanded way.

About a week before we arrived on the scene, Alfr and a sizable entourage had been inspecting weapons in one of the coastal townships near the border with Bloodaxe's lands. The king was there to gauge and ensure the loyalty of the citizens.

As Alfr was scrutinizing an impressive-looking Ulfberht sword, a harmless-looking local merchant came up behind him and stuck a knife in his side. The man, who was clearly no warrior, was quickly cut down by Alfr's guards. Alfr was not seriously wounded, but the attack raised worrisome questions. Why had a merchant, of all people, attacked a king? And why didn't he use something more deadly than a rusty carving knife?

An investigation revealed that the merchant's wife and two daughters had disappeared just days before Alfr's visit. Rumors grew like mushrooms in the night. One was that the merchant had gone mad and murdered them. Or, while planning his treachery, he sent them away into the forest to keep them safe. The most interesting rumor, and the one to which Alfr's clan gave greatest credence, was that Bloodaxe had taken them as hostages and would only spare them if the merchant—who would not be seen as a threat to a king—assassinated Alfr.

This attack was the final straw. Alfr quietly began to prepare the kingdom for war, but soon after grew ill. At first, it was just a headache but within a couple of days, he was wracked by a fever, followed by wretched, clenching spasms of his jaw and, later, spasms throughout his body.

This was the state in which I found the king when I returned. Dofri escorted me into the bedchamber, where the haggard king was propped up on pillows. The king said nothing, just looked at me stonily.

"I've already told the king your tale," said Dofri. "You've gambled with your life, Halftroll, returning here after committing mutiny on the Alfr's own flagship."

"Not a mutiny, sire," I say, staring at Alfr rather than Dofri. "Justice, arrived in a fair dual. Grim murdered Leos, a loyal member of your clan, without provocation or explanation. It was not an official execution but a murder he attempted to conceal."

Alfr spasmed and shook but managed a hand signal I interpreted as a command to be quiet.

He sat there and stared, trying to decide what to do with me. He looked toward Dofri.

"I side with the troll on this," Dofri said. "We both know, Alfr, that Grim was a savage son of a bitch. But Leos was also my nephew, so perhaps my judgement can't be trusted. Still, if Halftroll is a mutineer, he is an exceptionally bad one, having rescued your ship and then returned with all deliberate speed. For what it's worth, Grim's own son supports the troll's story and does not condemn his actions."

Alfr had closed his eyes as Dofri spoke. Once again, I'd unintentionally put the king in a bad spot. If he condemned me as a mutineer, some would see it as an unjust punishment of a loyal subject who had fought against Bloodaxe. If he didn't, he'd be seen as weak, absolving his rebellious troll slave.

Just when I thought he might have fallen asleep, he opened his eyes and made an angry gesture dismissing me.

Dofri walked me to the exit.

"He spares you once again, Halftroll," he said. "You remain in his debt. The time may be coming soon when you'll need to repay it in full."

I said nothing, only turned and walked away, angry. I felt I should not be in anyone's debt. All I'd done was serve the king despite the chains, humiliations, betrayals and even torture. At the same time, Dofri's words haunted me because, in a sense, they were true. My fate was not yet my own. My life was pledged to a king who could have, and perhaps should have, executed me. And yet there I walked, still only bound by my damnable honor.

I was told to keep the king's illness a close secret. Alfr's wife, Queen Sassa, wanted to make a public accusation of poisoning and witchcraft against Bloodaxe. Alfr refused. He did not want outsiders, especially Bloodaxe, aware of his condition. So his clan stayed silent.

They didn't realize that their silence was a critical part of Bloodaxe's trap. Even as Alfr convulsed uncontrollably in his rooms, falling in and out of consciousness, Bloodaxe unleashed a slanderous stream. He publicly labeled King Alfr a coward and liar, a breaker of oaths, a defamer of reputations, a practitioner of seidr, a patron of trolls and worshipper of Loki. At the end of his tirade, he demanded a duel, which the Norse called *holmgang*.

It was a masterstroke. If the Völsung suddenly announced the king was ill, Alfr would appear weak and indecisive. He might even be declared *nioingr*, a man without honor, and assigned the status of villain. If the clan put forward a substitute champion—and my old weapons master Dofri volunteered—Alfr would seem cowardly, unwilling to fight his own battles. And Bloodaxe might refuse Dofri, since he was not of the same rank as Alfr.

If Alfr tried to fight the duel himself, he would almost certainly lose and, assuming he survived at all, be obligated to pay *weregild*, which would add up to an immense amount of land, property and manpower.

As the clan argued internally about what they should do, they played for time. They negotiated that the holmgang would not occur for a full week from the day of the challenge, an extension that was on the very brink of seeming dishonorable. This would give Alfr time to recover or die, depending on which fate the Norns determined.

As it turned out, the Norns were indecisive. Alfr did not die, but he recovered very slowly. The fever and convulsions continued, though his lucid periods grew longer. When he was conscious, he demanded to participate in the discussions of the clan. The king desperately wanted to evade the trap by declaring war, but his jarls warned that many of the freemen might refuse to enlist as soldiers, figuring Alfr for a coward.

In the end, the king decided. Two days before the holmgang, he dragged himself from his sickbed and began, as best he could, sparring with Dofri.

I went to Leos's family, told them an edited version of how bravely my friend had died, and volunteered to be a farmhand if they'd grant me a place to stay in their barn. To their great credit, they accepted, never once blaming me as I blamed myself for their son's death.

They were good, gentle, hard-working people. When I sicken of humanity—despising its heedless, maggoty befoulment of Midgard and its absurd, dishonorable, Buri-like conceit—I strive to recall the faces of Leos and his family. Those humble people, who have long been forgotten by humanity itself, represent the best the species has to offer. It is for their sake that I give the humans as much leeway as I do.

But I digress. The evening before the holmgang, I was summoned to the Great Manor and shown into an antechamber to the main hall. Dofri was waiting for me. He wasted no time, quickly relating what had happened with the king. He also informed me of the rumor that Bloodaxe wanted my head for daring to attack his flagship.

"Do you understand what I'm telling you?" he asked.

"You're saying King Alfr may be slain and that, if he is, Bloodaxe will almost certainly demand me as part of the weregild owed him. Then he'll murder me at his leisure."

"Yes," he said.

"Thank you, Master Dofri, for informing me. I know you must have more important matters to consider."

"I do. Still, your lordship has a request of you."

I stayed silent.

"If Alfr is slain and you survive the day, then kill Bloodaxe, as was once your mission."

He didn't need to point out that I would likely die in any attempt, successful or not, to assassinate Bloodaxe. It would no longer be a matter of hunting him through dark woods, supported by a king and band of warriors. This time, it really would be a suicide mission. By calling it a request, Dofri was giving me a choice. If I chose, I could flee for the mountains during the night, leaving this vicious human circus far behind.

"I understand," I said.

He looked me in the eyes, wondering if I'd pledged my agreement or just acknowledged the request. But he didn't ask.

"You're dismissed," he said.

I saluted, turned and walked toward the exit, wondering if anyone would try to stop me. I was nearly at the door when Dofri said, "Bloodaxe will be prepared for you next time."

"Alfr will kill him," I said, not turning.

"We all pray for that," said Dofri. "But prayer is not a battle plan, Halftroll, and serves less well than a sharp blade."

The holmgang was held in the morning on a nearby knoll that had been used for duels for as long as anyone could remember. In the middle of the knoll they'd staked a large ox hide that was about ten square feet. Three black borders were drawn using charcoal around the ox hide. Each border was a foot outside the previous one. Ornate staves made of hazel wood were placed in the four corners of the outermost border.

The rules were simple. If one man stepped outside the outermost border, he lost the challenge. The winner would otherwise be determined when one man conceded, was incapacitated or killed. Each combatant had access to two weapons and three shields.

Because he had made the accusations, Bloodaxe was obligated to fight the duel in Alfr's territory, though he could bring his retinue with him. Of course, he abused the privilege by bringing what amounted to a small army of hard men. Although I wore the black, wired hood that nearly blinded my peripheral vision. I knew a number of his men had formed a semi-circle in back of me. I could smell their fear, antagonism and loathing, so I turned to stare them down. All carried crossbows, which were not yet common in that part of the world. To me, their little machines stank of human guile.

Bloodaxe sauntered onto the ox hide first. I had never seen him up close. His hair was black, face thick, forehead wide and torso stout. He was more beetle-browed than most humans, and I wondered if there was a hint of troll-blood there. He wore a naturally surly look as he stared toward Alfr's side of the hide. Toward the front of his neck, he bore a tattooed rune like the one on Sunmane.

When King Alfr arrived, the crowd started murmuring. The man had never been as stout as Bloodaxe, but now he appeared almost skeletal, as if he had aged twenty years since the last time I'd seen him. His skin had a distinctly yellowish cast, and his eyes had sunken into dark cavities. As he waited for the opening preparations and rituals to take place, we could see him suffering from sporadic fits of trembling. If anyone had doubted the rumors that he was ill, they would no longer. I could hear whispers of witchcraft, though some of the more experienced warriors labeled his condition as the "dread wound fits," recognizing it as the disease we now call tetanus.

Still, I felt a flicker of hope as I looked on. Whatever else those shifty bastards had done to him, they couldn't extinguish the king within that wrecked, wretched body. There was an almost amused grimness in his eyes and the set of his mouth.

This man—who had attacked my family to avenge a slain son, who had spared my life at the cost of his reputation, and who had freed me from chains based solely on a monster's pledge—this man was, for better or worse, the closest thing I'd ever had to a father. I resented and admired him in equal measure. The very sight of him caused a war within me. He could die a thousand times, and I still wouldn't be able to extinguish him. At that moment, I felt so angry that I wanted to kill him myself, and yet wished for nothing more than to protect him. Alfr the raider, the defender, the upholder, the betrayer, the cunning man, the noble fool.

A flag was waved, and the two kings clashed.

Alfr threw up his shield as Bloodaxe madly hacked away at the top edge of it with his sword. His strategy was to slice the round, wooden shield into slivers, then do the same to Alfr before the sick king had time to regroup. It nearly worked. Alfr was thrown back several feet in the initial clash, doing everything he could to defend himself from the swift assault.

But Alfr knew well how to take advantage of the kind of bold attack that necessarily leaves a duelist open. The only question was whether the mind of the trained warrior could get his damaged body to react.

Alfr held up his shield, pivoted on his right leg, swung around and smashed into Bloodaxe's back with his elbow as the stout king was carried forward by his own momentum. If Alfr had been physically well, this one movement might have allowed him to draw first blood. As it was, however, he only won a short respite before Bloodaxe launched his next, slightly more controlled, attack. Alfr soon had to replace his first smashed and shattered shield with a second. Meanwhile, Bloodaxe's shield was barely gouged.

Bloodaxe could have used his superior bulk and strength to push Alfr outside the boundaries of the holmgang and so win the match. But he wanted more than mere victory. When Alfr realized this, he backed close to the outer perimeter and then, as his enemy charged, performed a pirouette and pushed with his shield, trying to use Bloodaxe's movement to force him outside the boundaries. It nearly worked. For just a moment, the beetle-browed king stood there windmilling with his arms like a man on a precipice. Yet he regained his balance before stumbling Alfr had time to give him one last push.

The crowd moaned. Alfr had so nearly won.

The Völsung king looked too exhausted to go on. Maybe it had been the adrenalin and movement, but since the battle had been joined, he'd shown few signs of convulsion. Now he did, wobbling on his feet, the muscles in his neck visibly tensing and trembling. Bloodaxe saw his opportunity and rushed. In a desperate gamble, Alfr fell to his knees at the last moment and thrust his sword up to get under his opponent's shield.

And it worked. Alfr cut upwards into Bloodaxe's chest and then sliced into his left cheek. It was not, however, a killing blow, and his enemy's bulk crashed into the kneeling king, flattening him onto his back. From that moment, it was over. Finding himself on top, Bloodaxe clubbed Alfr in the head multiple times with the hilt of his sword, then stood above the dazed king and thrust his sword through Alfr's breastplate and into his chest.

There were a few cheers for the victor, but mostly the crowd was hushed. The strength in my own legs failed. I sat down on the ground, thinking nothing at all except that I was suffocating in the black, wired cage of my hood.

Chapter Twenty-Four

"Green were the moorlands,
And blooming behind her.
Out of her gold locks
Shaking the spring flowers,
Out of her garments
Shaking the south wind."
—*The Longbeard's Saga: A.D. 400*

When I open my eyes, I see only the latticework of oak branches silhouetted against a brightening sky. Dawn.

Then a face obscures my view. Déjà vu. Didn't this happen before, recently in fact?

"I need to beg your pardon, Hallr," Hildy says, hovering in the sky. No, not in it. Below the boughs.

"Okay," I say, still more asleep than awake. "How come?"

"Because I've been more of a grumbler than a healer since we've arrived. I guess things have dredged up memories that would be better lost."

"Yeah," I say. "Know what you mean. It's okay. I kind of like it."

"Like it?"

"It's nice to know you're not perfect, some omniscient type who holds all the strings, including mine."

"A girl can dream," she teases. "Go for a swim?" She looks almost happy. In fact, now that I'm studying her harder, I'm pretty sure this is a new look. Not the CEO, the biker chick, or the cover girl.

"Sometimes you look sort of Asian, other times you don't," I say, sounding stupid and quasi-racist even to myself.

"Not Asian," she says, smiling. "Sami. You know, indigenous."

That clicks. The Sami people. Reindeer herders from the Scandinavian North. I remember them always moving, a mystery people. They'd grin at us, the trolls, and wave as they passed. We never harbored them ill will, and they never seemed to revile us in the same ways other humans did.

"You didn't answer the question," I say.

"You didn't ask one," she says, standing up. "But I did."

"Swimming? That didn't work out too well last time."

"Come on." She gestures, walking toward the spring. "My aunts have made the sanctuary safe again."

So I stand and follow her. She just looks so cheerful, as if she's on vacation. As she slips off her clothes and enters the water, the sun rises. I startle, my first impulse to run for cover, but I remember that it's different here. Sanctuary, she called it.

I take off the missing aunt's robe and enter the spring.

Several swans come in for a soft landing a few yards away, barely making a sound. Hildy dives underwater. I hold my breath, remembering what happened last time. But she emerges near me smiling, her long hair slicked back.

She stands, her bare breasts rising like revelations in the morning mist that drifts over the waters. I suppose I'm gawking. She smiles, takes my right hand and gently guides it to her breast. There are no words. All those hapless fruit metaphors. I cup it in my hand, unable to imagine another curve or texture or weight. It is the Platonic ideal of the breast, the one by which all others are measured.

We move deeper into the water and kiss. Her lips are cool from the spring, making the warmth of her mouth and tongue more vivid. A fine, slow kiss. It's been a long time since I've loved a woman, so I savor rather than hurry the moment, folding the fingers of my left hand into her wet hair.

As I pull her closer, I feel the rough stitches brushing up against her soft, unblemished skin. I start to pull away, but she'll have none of it.

She pulls me tighter, as if revelling in the brambly sensation. My hand drops from her breast to her backside. As I cup it and pull her closer yet, I let the stitches on my arm touch her, scratching not hard but enough so she can feel them brushing by.

She moans. A good moan, I think. I'm still enough in my head that I wonder if I should moan as well. A troll moan can be more than a tad unsettling to others.

Screw it. You're a troll. You're a primal beast of legend, a symbol of chaos and fury, an incarnation of the Freudian id. Give in. Stop thinking like a human.

I moan. A moan that reverberates over the surface of the spring, one that causes jagged ripples to spread from our epicenter.

She doesn't flinch, though I think there's a little laugh trickling through her kiss.

I'm erect, of course, bursting with it, as if half my being has flooded into my cock. She reaches for it, so I pull her upwards, letting her guide me. But gently. Hildy is tall and strong but still, whatever else she is, she's not a giant like her aunts.

Her aunts, shit, don't think about her aunts. For fuck's sake, not those spooky old biddies.

But she takes me in. All of me. And the moan comes again, causing birds to take flight, sunning turtles to dive from embankments, and gators to seek deeper water.

And we begin in earnest. True lovemaking now. Me lifting her again and again to meet me, her propelling herself over and over, her muscles taut, hungry. As I lose myself in her, the visions come.

Thick, dark Florida thunderheads ride on winds, fast approaching, inevitable and awe-inspiring. Lightning flashes, crooked streaks of pure white bending toward the earth—over and over, every time a unique formation. Appalling, disturbing, thrilling, sheathed in gorgeous dark deluges that connect thunderhead to earth. There is no division, only affiliation and then union. The sky, water and land are one.

Then she and I are in the middle of it, disappearing into the same sky-earth union, thick droplets of water rushing over us and cascading into the spring, an immense waterfall dwarfing all others. Dwarfing me, the descendant of giants.

I see from a great, holy height, our bodies—Hildy's and mine—a mere dot on an immense, tropical landscape. The water pours in sheets for miles around, pool-

ing everywhere: fields of dry grass, expanses of palmettos in scrublands, forests of cypress, thickets of pine. The sky-water pooling, then seeping through the sands and soil, trickling over vast layers of porous limestone, then individual beads calmly, leisurely winding downward through intricate networks.

We slow now, Hildy and I, taking our time, relishing these moments of pleasure, and preparing ourselves for the next phase.

The sky-water reaches a great underwater basin, each droplet joining its neighbors, part of a pulsing arterial flow. Earth-water now. The underwater river undulates past stone formations, moving languidly as it expands into immense caves, then pressing urgently forward in the narrower reaches. One channel rises upwards again. We are coming full circle, surging now, ascending toward the fountainhead, the source of green and light and life.

The vision clears, and we are heaving our bodies together, groaning in unison. She screams words in the Old Tongue, and I let myself climax, the upswell immense, a euphoria I've never known. I explode into a full-throated roar, the type of thundering bellow certain to freeze the blood of mortals braving the mountains of Jotunheimen.

And Hildy laughs. Not derisive or demeaning, not forced. A laugh that is almost a giggle, a sound of amusement and joy.

Chapter Twenty-Five

"For a noble warrior slain
Vengeance now on king is ta'en:
Wolf and eagle tread as prey
Princes born to sovereign sway.
Hallvard's body cloven through
Headlong in the billows flew"
—*Egil's Saga*

At first I thought the feminine voice was a hallucination.

I had been alone in the darkness for over two weeks. Other hallucinations had already come and gone. One was of my mor, who'd tunneled through the rock wall of the root cellar to mock me. She looked distastefully at the small mounds of turnips, parsnips and carrots that were stored beyond the reach of my chains.

"Why were you even at the duel?" Mor asked, haranguing me. "Why didn't you flee to the mountains?"

I had no answer. She was right. I hadn't even resisted the crossbow-armed bodyguards who had taken me after the duel, securing me as property as part of the weregild won by Bloodaxe.

"I tried, didn't I? Tried to teach you cunning? Tried to at least give you a survival instinct! I knew you were soft but thought there was a chance you weren't stupid. Just another dumb troll. What a surprise!"

After that, she bricked up the opening in the cellar wall again, streaming insults until finally she placed the last brick, and I was thrown again into silence.

Alfr eventually showed up as well, still looking skeletal. He sat down just out of reach of my chains.

"I asked you for the head of Bloodaxe, and you delivered me a golden-haired serpent," he said, looking exhausted. "If only I'd killed you the moment I saw you, recognizing those damnable runes as nothing but your evil mor's trickery. I could have been spared this humiliation. What a fool I was."

"You were a great king," I said.

"Hah! Great king. Undone by an ignorant troll, an evil child and a guileful glutton."

"Great songs will be sung of you," I said.

The shadow smiled sadly and faded into the blackness, saying, "Thank you for that, at least, Hallr Halftroll. Your lies, if not your actions, do you credit."

So when I heard the girl's voice, I supposed it was yet another ghost formed of my growing madness. Her face appeared, lit by a thin candle casting a small circle of light.

She was saying my name again, growing impatient.

"Did they kill you as well?" I asked the princess Inge.

Her face went from impatient to solemn.

"No, Hallr, we still live, you and I. Still alive and much to do."

It took her time to convince me she was not a shadow. She spoke to me softly, as if I were a wounded cow that needed to be tended. At last she trusted me enough to approach with a key, freeing me from the thick locks and chains.

She took me by the hand and led me up the stairs to the door of the root cellar, which had served as an improvised prison. Opening it slowly and quietly, she peeked through. One of the guards, who occasionally brought me dirty water in a pail to drink and threw me the odd crust of bread or rotten piece of fruit, was twitching on the floor, staring at the ceiling with dilated eyes. There was a blackish stew spilled on and near him.

"Nightshade," she murmured as I stared, impatiently motioning me to follow. We slipped into and then out of the small wooden building, which had originally been a stall for selling the root vegetables stored below. She blew out her candle. The streets of Risør were quiet and dark under a new moon, but I'd been without light for so long that the Milky Way itself made me blink at its brightness.

Inge led us toward the boundary of the township where it abutted the surrounding forest. Never had the thickets around Risør called to me as they did then. I stood still, my eyes fixed on a dark, inviting gap among the trees. Inge stopped, sensing I was no longer following.

"You want to escape into the woods, don't you?" she whispered.

When I said nothing, she said, "You are, of course, free to go. I could not stop you if I wished. But I have one request before you do, Hallr Halftroll."

"No more, Princess," I hissed quietly. "No more requests or pledges or oaths or assurances. I'm a troll, not a hero in your ceaseless sagas. I need to get out of here!"

"Please!" she said, taking my enormous hand in her own. She was at least fifteen years old by then, maybe sixteen, a woman by the standard of the day. But she was also a child, a desperate one, beginning to sob. "Please help me kill him, Hallr. You don't know him, how horrible he really is—a dishonorable, lecherous, disgusting sorcerer. I need to avenge my father's death. Please, please aid me."

My hand still in hers, she was kneeling before me.

"I beg you, Halftroll. I beg you as I have never begged anyone before. Please help me get my vengeance, our vengeance, on Bloodaxe."

I pulled her up.

"You should have led with that," I told her. "Where lies that oozing human pustule?"

Despite all the advantages he'd had, Bloodaxe had been seriously wounded during the holmgang. As the victor, he'd won the right to convalesce in Alfr's Great Manor as a group of noble-born counselors worked out how much of the dead king's properties were owed as the price of weregild. The son of a bitch took up residence in the newest wing of the Hall, the one constructed after his son's act of arson.

The guard was one of the most dutiful and lethal servants of the Völsung clan. He hadn't been informed of any assassination attempts but, before he began his shift, Dofri had told him to be "compliant in the extreme" if someone in authority asked him to do something unusual. So, when the princess emerged out of the darkness and told him to walk the perimeter of the manor rather than guard the front entrance, he obeyed. But I could see he didn't like it. Like any guard, he feared being held to account if some crisis occurred on his watch.

He hadn't spotted me. I was lurking beyond the torchlight. As he trod away with an indecisive step, I considered killing him. If he decided to show fealty to Bloodaxe, he would get us killed. I didn't know, however, how Inge would react to my taking his head, so I decided I'd be gambling either way. He turned a corner, I caught up with her, and we quietly entered the manor together.

Once in the grand foyer, I didn't need to look down the passageway to the rooms where Bloodaxe lodged. I could smell and hear the breathing of two more guards. They would be Bloodaxe's men, and I couldn't imagine how we were going to get past them without raising an alarm.

Without giving me warning, Inge crept to the passage's entrance and whispered, "The sun will soon rise."

Considering dawn was still hours away, this struck me as the weakest of ruses. Did she really expect them to knock off early just because some suspicious voice told them their shift was up?

To my astonishment, it worked. Without saying a word, the two guards marched straight forward without even turning their heads to glance at us. It gave me the willies. Had they been bewitched?

Inge wasn't the least surprised. She wore the intensity of an animal on the prowl, eyes slightly squinting and forward focused. She eagerly slipped down the hallway. At the door to Bloodaxe's chamber, I touched her shoulder, signaling I'd go first.

The door wasn't locked. If I'd been half the troll my mother wished me to be, that would have made me more cautious. As it was, I just assumed Bloodaxe's victory had made him sloppy. Pride goeth before the fall and all that.

The door opened with nary a squeak or groan. *Nice workmanship*, I thought, just before going utterly rigid from head to toe. It didn't scare me at first. I was just puzzled, wondering how I could suddenly forget how to walk or move my arms. Was the floor tarred?

"So, that works good," said Bloodaxe from his bed. I was so frozen that I couldn't even follow him with my eyes, only with my peripheral vision. The room was lit solely by the dying embers in the room's fireplace.

"You never know for sure till you put it to the test," he continued, grunting as he stood. Taking his time, he took embers from the fireplace with a pair of iron tongs and used them to light a wall torch.

"That's better," he said. "Eyes ain't what they once were."

He reached under one of the down pillows on the bed and grabbed a long, silver-hilted knife.

"Didn't see that one coming, did you, beast? No, didn't see that coming at all. When I was a boy, my far caught a cow-tailed huldr in the forest. But, unlike the perverse and weak-minded Völsungs of yore, he didn't fall in love with it. He was too hard for something as soft and feeble as love. Maybe he fucked it some, but mostly just forced it to yield secrets."

He hobbled toward me.

"But he was no good at the magic it taught. Couldn't do no seidr at all, just a little galdr. But me? I was young. She could teach me, especially runes. Not many humans can do galdr good as me. It pissed off father something awful. He said magic was for women. I said Odin did magic. He thrashed me for my cheek."

Standing in front of me, he raised the torch to light my face.

"My boy, eh, the one you grabbed? I never thrash that one. See, he's right clever with magic. His lovely mum disappeared after he was born, and I've sometimes pondered if maybe she had a bit of the fae in her as well, the way she had with runes. I've high hopes for that boy.

"This bit here," he said, pointing toward my feet with the knife. "Protection magic. Protection from trolls. 'Cause I knew you might get out, or some wild troll might come for you. Now, I got to kill you, of course. Too bad. Was hoping to flay you till you learned me more galdr. But fuck it."

He really did look a little regretful as he raised the knife to jam into my throat.

Inge darted out from behind my giant bulk, jabbed her own knife into Bloodaxe's side, then spun backwards behind him. It was beautiful. Truly. It was close to the same movement Alfr had tried during the duel, but Inge was healthy and lithe, a young, beautiful predator resolved to annihilate an aging, ugly one.

But predators don't get old unless they are good at what they do. Bloodaxe was very good and, in this case, lucky. Inge's blade had hit the top of the king's hip bone, drawing blood but doing no great damage. He turned with a speed belying his size and pursued Inge as she backed into a corner of the room. She was prey now. She clambered over furniture and threw what she could at Bloodaxe but he was, despite his wounds, many times stronger than she. He put his knife between his teeth to free up both hands.

Inge feinted left, then right, then left again, and still the stout king caught her. Bloodaxe snatched her knife arm, smashing it on a table to jar loose her weapon, and then picked her up by the neck. He held her with his arms straight out, trying to protect himself from her kicking legs. Even though he was bleeding badly from her knife wound and had a blade in his mouth, he was smiling broadly, like a farm boy who had caught his first chicken. That grin was particularly ghastly because of the flaming face wound Alfr had given him.

He held her out to me, as if she were a gift. An idea struck him. He let go of her neck with one hand, lowering her to the ground so that her toes could barely touch. With his free hand, he removed his blade from his teeth.

"Good opportunity to try some healing magic here. Watch, fae creature, as I sacrifice this here virgin."

I don't know exactly what he planned. Runes cut into flesh? Incantations, a sliced throat, a chalice of blood? I never learned that kind of galdr. Even trolls have a sense of decorum.

But he made a mistake in allowing Inge's toes to touch the floor, on which he had painted runes with tar, mud and dirt. Although I could not see, I suspect one of her feet smudged a character, weakening the spell. But I've never known for sure. Magic is the art of changing another's consciousness in accordance with your will, I've read. So, maybe his will simply slipped as he focused on his new sorcery. Or perhaps my consciousness just imitated his in a kind of hideous sympathy. All I really know is that something suddenly gave way, and I could move again.

Not all of me. I was like a calving glacier, deeply frozen and yet shifting in a swift, deadly fashion. My arms reached out and encircled Bloodaxe's neck in the same way his had encircled Inge's. Then I squeezed. Squeezed as hard as my hamstrung resolve would allow.

Bloodaxe lurched into an incantation, which I choked off with pleasure. That's when he started hacking at my forearms with his silver-handled knife. It was the smarter move. My grip loosened. Suddenly his fierce eyes bulged. Inge had fallen to the floor and found her knife. Now she was piercing him in the back. They weren't arbitrary stabbings, either. She refused to miss his vital organs a second time. She targeted first his kidneys, then reached around to skewer his liver, and then riddled his lungs.

I saw flickers of terror and pain in his eyes, followed by an amused ruefulness before they finally dimmed. He was dead long before I was able to unclasp my hands from around his neck. When I finally did, he hit the wooden floorboards with a hollow thump. Inge dipped her hands in his blood and covered over the runes near my feet with it, which made it easier for me to move again. Once I had bandaged my forearms with torn sheets, she motioned me over.

"Drag it over to the bed, please, Hallr," she said in an eerily polite voice.

I obeyed. After he was laid out, she yanked up his tunic to reveal his genitals. Without hesitation, she castrated the corpse. She bade me open the shutters in the room, then flung the crimson mess out the window.

"Let the feral dogs have them," she said.

If they ever discovered what she had done to a king, not even her royal blood would protect her. I reluctantly picked up the corpse by the hair and bit as deeply into the skull as I could. I couldn't force myself to swallow the goulash of bone, hair and brain matter. I spit it out the window as well, wondering if even the wild dogs would revile it. Seeing this savagery, no one would doubt the guilt of the king-killer troll.

After that, Inge stabbed the corpse again, held the flat of her bloody blade up to both her cheeks, and painted symmetrical red arrows pointing upward toward her eyes. Such pitiable, glorious, celebratory savagery. Even my mother would have been impressed.

Chapter Twenty-Six

"[T]he greatest destroyer of the wetlands in Florida is the state itself—
or rather, one agency: The Department of Transportation, commonly
known as the DOT."

—*Paving Paradise*

Back at the office, everyone gets a look at the Frankensteinian set
of stitches along the right side of my face. Fred whistles, gently pulling down my collar to reveal how the tracks go down my shoulder
and beyond.

Misty starts to cry and follows up with a hug, which I accept with
all the wooden grace of an oak tree.

Fred has hunted gators in south Florida and is suitably impressed
by the bite patterns. "Must've been one big lizard," he says.

Hildy introduces Andre to Fred and Misty, and we scatter ourselves around an eight-foot-long, walnut-laminate conference table.
I'm uncomfortable as I squash into one of those rolling, black-leather
office chairs, hoping the wheels don't snap off and collapse under
my weight.

With furrowed brow and pursed lips, Misty studies Hildy. She's
never seen this version of our CEO, who is wearing a white jacket
over a floral-pattern skirt rather than her usual uniform of a navy-
blue business suit. But it's not just her clothes that are different. Hildy
looks younger and her eyes more almond shaped.

Hildy ignores Misty's suspicious stare. She stands at the whiteboard, which runs nearly the length of the room, and calmly briefs Misty and Fred on most of what happened at that swamp.

"So, what do we know at this point?" she asks, holding a black marker in her right hand.

"That there's at least one very sick, very slick, bird-mutilating maniac up in Vandriller Junction," says Fred.

"But that's not related to our case, is it?" asks Misty. "I mean, wasn't the attack on Brad Lauder just a gruesome coincidence? Nobody's going to murder anybody over some backcountry Florida swampland deal."

Hildy frowns, showing a flicker of annoyance.

"Okay," she says. "Two things. The land we're trying to protect isn't swampland. It's sixty acres of original wetlands and virgin forest centered around a fresh-water spring. It would be worth millions on the open market. Second, for now, let's keep our minds open about what is and isn't related."

Misty stares at the table in a tight-lipped way, vexed and embarrassed by the mild rebuke.

"We know that a Corps of Engineer regulator was skeptical enough about the no-net-loss proposal that he went up to check on the land himself," I say, trying not to take sides but probably sounding like a suck up.

"Which means he might have been considering rejecting the deal," Andre chimes in.

"Which means that anyone in favor of the deal might want him removed from the scene, allowing some other regulator to step in," says Fred, getting serious and starting to think like the military cop he used to be.

"Or," says Misty, "he might have just been in the wrong place at the wrong time. Maybe he was just a chance victim of the same gator that almost killed Klaus."

I nod, knowing she's wrong but seeing it from her perspective. She wasn't there, never caught the vibe of the place.

"Okay, I need to tell you guys something. This land deal—it involves my family, specifically my aunts," Hildy says, looking at Fred and Misty.

"Why keep that a secret?" asks Misty. It's her turn to be annoyed.

"I didn't know if the land was being targeted because it's pristine, or because someone wanted to hurt my aunts. They come from an old

Florida family that's rather well-known and well-connected in certain circles. I wanted you to see it as objectively as possible."

"Why tell us now?" asks Fred.

"Because somebody sent them a clear message. Somebody is making a power play, intentionally trying to injure them and everything they stand for."

"Which is what, exactly?" Misty asks.

"Let's just call it conservation," says Hildy.

Misty looks dissatisfied with that answer.

"Getting back to the subject of the swamp," I say, hoping to head off more questions from Misty about the aunts, "I wanted to ask about the pothead who showed up after I started my ill-conceived traipse through the muck. You think he was just a bystander at that hour of the night?

"Seems like a murderer would have made himself scarce," says Fred. "That whole 'return to the scene of the crime' stuff is pretty much a myth. And that's assuming there really was a murder. So far, the papers have just been calling it a gator mauling."

"What did he look like?" I ask Andre.

"Like a huge, white country boy," he says. "Well over six feet, wearing a baseball hat. Kind of musky smelling, as if he ran a dog kennel. Bloodhounds are big business in that part of the state."

"He was wearing a t-shirt with something written on it," Hildy adds.

"Yes, something about dust and planets," Andre says, his eyes narrowing in concentration. "I thought maybe it was song lyrics. That's what I told the county sheriff when he took my statement."

Misty starts typing into her smartphone.

"*In the Dust of the Planet?*" she asks Andre.

"Could be."

"That's a book by a philosopher," she says. "Somebody made the title into a t-shirt. Looks like Jay-Z was photographed wearing one."

"Ah, so close," says Andre.

"It has something to do with horror and philosophy," Misty says, still reading.

No one knows what to make of this. It feels like just another random fact.

"For now, I guess we can let the sheriff look for him," Hildy says thoughtfully, seeming only half convinced by her own conclusion.

"Let's focus on the land deal part of the puzzle. I've found out that the phosphate-mining company sold part of the swamp to a private party. So far I haven't been able to reach the owners, but I might have a line on them. Leave that to me."

She hasn't mentioned this to me before. I wonder if it could be related to her conversation with that menacing little Lucky. Maybe that land was in Vandriller Junction and she's going to reach out to him again. After our experiences with him and his ghoulish cousin, I'd prefer she stay as far away from them as possible. But what if Edmund already closed the deal with Lucky? Then we've got to connect those dots.

"What did you find out about the people trying to push the deal through?" asks Hildy.

Misty looks over at Fred, who says, "Go ahead."

She looks well-prepared, with a thick sheaf of computer printouts in front of her. Flipping through them, she launches into the particulars of two state congressmen and a state senator who support the deal as an effort to create jobs and bring a little East Coast, Boca Raton panache to the Central Florida boondocks. But, as far as Misty can tell, none of these people is the driving force.

"It's really the DOT that has a serious hard-on for the project," she says. "They want a road through there, and only there, bad. I guess your aunts must have already gotten the Notice of Intent to Appraise."

Hildy nods. She has already hired the best attorneys she could find.

"Your family is apparently arguing that the state isn't giving just compensation for the land," Misty continues. "So the government is set to adopt a Resolution of Necessity at an upcoming public hearing.

"From what I can tell, that hearing keeps getting delayed. When I call around to ask why, nobody seems sure. Just looks like an ongoing mess of misplaced paperwork, lost computer files, and other bureaucratic screw-ups."

Misty looks up at Hildy to see how she reacts to this, but Hildy just motions her to continue.

"The only people who seem to have their shit together are the guys at the DOT, who are setting up the no-net-loss land-exchange deal. That's even before the public hearing at which the state formally announces it's going to snatch up the property, whether the owners like it or not.

It's strange that the DOT is trying to get the Corps of Engineers to approve it in advance. Like I said, a serious hard-on."

"Not bad research for a potty-mouthed barmaid," says Fred admiringly.

"Yeah, well, you can take the barmaid out the bar…"

I still don't get how Hildy's aunts—who do an otherwise damn good impression of the Nornir of legend—can't control their own destiny here. I'm no expert in Nornology or fate or Orlog or whatnot, but I imagine you need to have very serious mojo to defy these ladies. Right now, it sounds as if the best the aunts can do is mess with the fate of paperwork and computer files, which seems beneath the great fate-weavers of my mor's tall tales.

"So," I say, "we need to know who's pushing this thing from the DOT side and why they're doing it. And we need to know if they have a specific grudge against your aunts or if they're working with some-body else who does. Leave that part with me. I have a little more pull than your average tollman and a connection that may help, though it probably means a trip to the state capital."

"That's good, um, Klaus," says Andre. "Once we find them, we need to figure out how to change their minds."

"That's going to depend on what's motivating them," says Fred as he drums his fingers on the table. "Any cop knows there are two reasons people mess with one another: to gain advantage and to get payback. Which reason are we dealing with here?"

"Couldn't it be both?" I ask.

"Yeah," he admits. "Sometimes it is."

"What about love?" Misty asks.

"What about it?"

"Isn't that a reason people mess with each other?"

"Sure," he says, winking. "Love is the ultimate advantage."

Chapter Twenty-Seven

"The princess asked the Giant again where his heart was, for she said
she would so like to know."
—*East of the Sun and West of the Moon*

After Inge and I finished desecrating the corpse of Bloodaxe, we
wiped the floors, furniture and anything else that might indicate she
was involved. I knew that at least three guards were aware of Inge's
role, but Sunmane had good reasons for protecting her and focusing
all the blame on Alfr's escaped troll.

After making sure we didn't trail any blood on our shoes, she led
me through the winding halls of the Great Manor and ultimately into
her personal chambers.

Inge lit a lamp, which in those days were just oil-filled bowls. Four
shallow pinches of clay held the wicks. A corona of light caught her
face and hair, giving her a holy appearance. But when she cradled
the lamp and walked toward me, the bloody, blade-shaped designs
under her eyes made her look sinister. Putting down the lamp on a
dresser, she showed me three large wooden buckets, two of which
were filled with clear, clean water and one of which contained a pile
of woollen rags.

Not saying a word, she undressed in the lamplight, showing no signs of shyness. She dipped a rag into one of the buckets of water and slowly began sponging the blood and grime from her arms, legs, torso and neck. She even wetted her hair where she felt streaks of drying blood. Then she held up lengths of her tresses and wrung them out, holding her head over the bucket to catch the drips.

Hundreds of years later, I opened a Degas folio filled with French women bathing themselves, often using nothing more than small basins, sponges and towels. Those paintings brought memories of Inge flooding back to me. Although more beautiful than any model Degas used, Inge was just as practical and frank as she went about the business of cleansing herself. There was nothing brazen or lewd in her movements. She paid no more attention to me than to a beast in a barn.

I was stirred, of course, but there was little lasciviousness in me. As stricken with her beauty as I was, I was also keenly aware of her tragedy. Fate had thrust her into these dire and degrading circumstances. Killing kings and bathing before trolls. The charming adolescent was gone, broken by the death of her once-great father and the humiliation of her family.

The Inge in front of me was someone else, a person from whom any sentimentality and convention had been burned away, a person forged by a cataclysm into tempered steel, a human weapon. I wondered what kind of wife this newly born woman could possibly make.

Then it hit me.

"It was a code, wasn't it?" I said. "The sun will soon rise."

She stopped washing for a moment. Without turning toward me, she said, "Yes, of course."

Of course. And it wasn't the sun that would soon rise. It was the son.

"Sunmane," I said.

"Yes, part of our agreement."

She stood, naked and clean except for her face, which retained the two dark carmine blades. Still the warrior. That paint would come off last.

"Take off your tunic," she said. She nodded over to a wooden chest, one that I realized was mine. She must have had it delivered from the barn where I'd been staying. The chest contained another tunic as well as my battle gear, the only other clothes I owned.

"You should dress yourself first, princess," I said.

"No," she said. "You're as bloody as I, and I will first tend your wounds."

I removed my tunic and undertunic before kneeling in front of her. Even when I was on my knees, she was not much taller than I. Taking one arm at a time, she rinsed my wounds. The depth of the cuts concerned her, so she stitched them with white thread from her sewing kit. Afterwards, as I washed my chest and stomach, she sponged my back and shoulders, which were not bloody so much as dirty from my days as prisoner in the cellar.

Next she motioned me to stand and, as casually as if I were a two year-old child, untied the drawstring on my trousers and pulled them down around my ankles. Before I could even object, she ordered, "Step out of them."

I did, it being too late for me to maintain anything like dignity.

Much worse, of course, was the erection. I was over a hundred years old but not much more than an adolescent by the standards of my people. I'd had little sexual experience. It was I rather than she who blushed.

She ignored the erection, unsnapped the buckles on my boots, and took each off as I clumsily stood on the other foot.

"Please princess," I said, "this isn't right. Allow me to bathe myself now."

Without saying a word, she stood up and slowly backed away from the glow of the lamp. I felt like an idiot. If I turned my back to her, I would only be showing her my huge, hulking ass as I bent down to wash my legs. But if I didn't, then I would not be able to hide the humiliating erection. Finding neither alternative acceptable, I opted to step outside the circle of the lamp. But it was only dim rather than dark where I stood. There was no escaping her gaze if she chose to look.

Partly to draw her attention from my nakedness, I asked, "Can you tell me about your agreement with Halfdan Hallburner?"

"If he allowed me to wreak my revenge on his father, I would agree to marry him," she said without emotion.

"You grant him much," I said, bending to wash my feet, "considering it is you who are doing him a great favor. With his father gone, he not only becomes king but inherits all the weregild still owed to his family by the Völsungs."

"Do you think that fact escaped me, Hallr Halftroll?" she said coldly.

"No," I said, feeling anger of my own, more than enough to make my tumescence disappear. I finished with the sponge, then turned to face her. "I suspect you were well aware of it."

Just for a moment, I could see she wanted to argue, to have a full-blown temper tantrum of the kind befitting a frustrated girl approaching womanhood.

The moment passed like a cloud on a breezy day. She could no longer indulge that part of herself. It was, in fact, her intent to smother that girl inside.

"He will forego the weregild but collect a handsome dowry," she said quietly. "This war will kill no more of our people, and my family will retain its standing. Sunmane is cunning and not a coward. He will conquer many kingdoms before he is done, uniting them into one nation. And my first son will inherit that great nation."

It was a convincing vision. With her help, Sunmane might well become a great conqueror. Where he was crafty, she could bring wisdom. When he was vicious, she could sometimes temper it with mercy. Where he would inevitably be selfish and arrogant, she could strive for a measure of benevolence and humility. It wouldn't be because she loved him. It would be because it was required of her.

"It's time for me to go," I said, walking toward the chest with my things in it.

"Not yet," she said. "I have papers and tokens I must give you so you can make good your escape."

"I won't need them," I said. "The mountains will suffice."

"I don't think so, Hallr," she said, walking toward me. "I will give you a crew and ship loaded with stock and trade goods, and an embarrassment of silver. You will be rich and master of your own destiny. You will sail to the new world called Iceland, free from the spreading tyrannies of Halfdan Sunmane or any other would-be king. You will live long and be happy, and I will think of you often in the coming dark days."

She stood directly in front of me.

"We could go together, princess," I whispered.

She smiled grimly, raised her hand to my chest and pushed me backwards till I was at her bed. Then she pushed me again, harder, and I sat.

"This is a bad idea, Inge," I said.

"No," she said. "This is my right. They whispered, chortled and accused us of being lovers. This is our vengeance on them. And it is a mercy you can do me. Sunmane will have my hand, but I will not give up my maidenhood to him."

"So, you would spoil yourself with a troll and a thrall just for vengeance," I said. A statement, not a question.

She slapped me. Hard. Then again. Still not satisfied, she punched me in the chest.

"You think so little of me now? Don't you realize I want you? Have long wanted you. You see yourself as a troll. They've convinced you that you're a monster. But I see a man, Hallr. A strange and mighty man, yes, but a man."

She reached out to stroke my auburn hair, then ran her hand over the runes on my neck. I brought up my hand and laid it over hers.

"You are beautiful, Hallr. And you are mine this night. You will grant me this last, earnest, ardent request."

Chapter Twenty-Eight

"Not dead, not living; all slimy; misty.
Not so much as a shape!"
—*Peer Gynt*

I'm sailing on a ship and playing out a thin, golden line into the water. The line is invisible to others, I know. It must be. It is a filament that ties me to Inge, who grows farther away with every second. As long as I hold the line, I can see her. She transforms into a fierce queen, beautiful but with two red fangs she keeps hidden from others. She has a whip she uses to lash Sunmane. As it flays his skin, spots of blood flick back onto her face. She seems satisfied and grows big with child.

The child is born as a troll but has a face like Bloodaxe. He is as fierce as his mother, and he looms over his father, who cowers in fear. Sunmane desperately feeds the son a stream of tiny men and horses and buildings. The trollson grows larger still. The father can no longer satisfy the son and whimpers as the boy grabs him up and plunges him head first into his gaping jaws. Inge the fiery queen laughs, revealing her red fangs. She hums, and her son joins in. Their humming becomes a low, thundering rumble and roar.

I wake inside a tiny dark room reverberating all around me. There's a fleeting moment of panic before I recognize the sound as the dull roar of a jet engine. I'm on a redeye flight to Tallahassee, my first airplane flight in over a decade. I've always hated flying. A hollow aluminum tube hurtling through the sky, jam-packed with hundreds of the hairless chimps jabbering and clambering and masticating and pissing thousands of feet above ground. The noise and stench of it alone is terrifying.

To make it remotely bearable, I've bought three first-class seats: my own, one behind me and the one next to me. Not only does that give me some more room to stretch, it safeguards against ugly accidents. The last time I flew, the backrest of my seat broke and smashed into the laptop-tapping businessman behind me. His nose will never be the same.

My goal is to get through this with a minimum of human interaction. My headphones and sleep mask tend to ward off flight attendants and chatty passengers. When those items don't work, a low growl usually does.

I adjust my pillow and try to get back to sleep. This flight is not a long one, but the less time I'm conscious in these confined quarters, the better off everyone is.

There are clouds in the first-class cabin. They drift and slowly curl over the seats, growing denser as if a storm is gathering. They block my view of the other passengers. All I hear, aside from the jet engines, is a woman's voice calling, "You're there, aren't you?"

She's way back in the cabin. I don't know if she is addressing me, so I stay quiet.

"Hey, troll!" she shouts, from the front of the cabin this time. I don't answer. Whoever she is, she's hunting me, and now I'm afraid.

"I hate that you're so hazy," she says, her voice coming from the opposite aisle. "You're like a hair in my eye I can't quite reach. You chafe my vision, troll."

I hear her brush by seats, one after another. Then, to my horror, I feel her grip my hand with the strength of a giant talon.

"There you are," she says. She pats my hand. "Don't worry, my boy, I'm only going to murder you."

"Why?" I ask.

"You are an impediment," she says cheerfully. Her face seems made of mist. "To what?"

"To change, to discovery, to a long-awaited elusive knowledge, the things that an anachronistic earth spirit such as yourself can't fathom."

"What kind of change?" I ask.

"This kind," she says.

The plane begins to tilt, sliding downward with a suddenness that makes me lightheaded. Fellow passengers hidden by the clouds begin screaming. The plane spins sickeningly, plummeting toward the invisible, dark ground below. We erupt into a ball of fire.

I suddenly wake to the pilot's announcement we will be touching down in Tallahassee in a few minutes. I struggle to remember the dream but it's mostly slipped away. I recall my fear muddled with scenes of fog and fire. A woman, wasn't it? At least an unseen enemy. Trolls know well that they tend to be the worst kind.

Jake McDermott's office is located on the seventh floor of the Florida Department of Transportation headquarters, which is an enormous ugly bunker of a building with long vertical black gashes for windows. Jake has thoughtfully closed the vertical blinds, knowing that I suffer from an extreme case of photosensitivity.

I first met Jake about twenty years ago, when he was still an up-and-comer in the DOT's Right of Way office. He had become the keeper of the lease deal that I originally made with the state government back in the 1920s.

As far as the law knew, of course, it wasn't me but a now-deceased ancestor of mine, one crazy hermit who had long owned an enormous strip of land along the mainland where the government wanted to build a bridge to the barrier islands. His name was Troels Gravesin, and he was a royal pain in the ass.

Back in the 1920s, the state didn't mess around if it wanted your land. The governmental Powers That Be wrote you a note and, a few days later, they showed up with men and machinery. You took their money and got out, or you stayed and got the shit kicked out of you.

Back then, a local partner and I operated a ferry from the mainland to the nearest barrier island. He ran the legal traffic by day, and I ran the more questionable traffic by night. I owned the land. In fact, I owned huge swaths of it up and down the mainland. The government had few options but to go through my land.

But Troels Gravesin was an ornery old cuss who refused to take the government money when they finally found him. He said he'd lease them the land but not sell it outright. The local Florida officials who'd been tasked with dealing with the weird giant of a man laughed at the idea. If Troels wouldn't take his money, that was his business. The state would do what it wanted.

Except the state didn't count on its equipment getting demolished night after night. Nor did it count on its night watchmen getting stalked, beaten up and thrown into huge canvas sacks. No one could track down the assailant. His footprints would literally disappear in the middle of the Florida scrub.

Everybody suspected that Troels Gravesin was the maniac behind the sabotage, but no one could prove it. The state even hired a couple of imported Pinkerton detectives to track Gravesin down and make the giant hillbilly saboteur see reason. After the Pinkerton dicks came back half dead inside canvas sacks, the project overseer was replaced by a man who was willing to make a deal with the devil. And so they signed a hundred-year lease that began in 1925.

Why did the crazy old Norwegian want a lease? Partly because he didn't like the attitude of the government fuckheads. More importantly, he wanted the state to literally owe him. It would keep them off his back. Besides, he knew there would eventually be a toll-keeping job, one the state would be happy to give him.

Troels Gravesin remains a legend at the DOT to this day, his name used to refer to any particularly recalcitrant property owners who got in the way of their road projects. I've created many human identities and personas over the centuries. Troels is among my favorites.

Twenty years ago, McDermott's job was to try to convince me, Klaus Rise, to allow the state to pay off the rest of the lease and take immediate control of the property. He was smart enough to recognize early in our interview that I'd have none of it, so he did the next best thing: tried to make me his pal. I'm not the sort to make pals, of course, but I have grown to like Jake's worldly-yet-good-ole-boy attitude.

"Hello, Mr. Rise," he says with his best Tallahassee twang, vigorously shaking my hand. "Long time, no see. You need to come round these parts more often."

"Hi, Jake. Well, you know how I hate to fly."

"So how goes the battle? Hope you're okay. Looks like you got a stitch or two there."

"Not so bad, Jake. This could have been worse. You know what they say: sometimes you get the bear…"

"…And sometimes the bear gets you," he says, laughing. "But, seriously, aside from looking like you fell under your own mower, you look good. In the last twenty years, I've turned into a fat, balding old man but you, you just seem to get younger over time."

"Wish it were so, Jake. I guess your eyes are getting old, too."

As Jake laughs, in walks another man.

"Klaus Rise, this is Peter Gunty."

Gunty and I shake hands as he gives me a suspicious look. Then the three of us sit around a black-veneered, small, round table in Jake's office.

"Pete's the man in charge of the Welacoochee Forest initiative you were asking about. Pete, Klaus here is a friend of the organization and our very own lessor of some damned valuable properties down there on the west coast."

"Lessor?" asks Gunty, suspicion turning to puzzlement.

"You ever heard of the famous Troels Gravesin case?" asks Jake.

"No, can't say I have," says Gunty.

"Pete's only been here a couple of years," Jake tells me, almost by way of apology. "He hasn't quite caught up on all the stories we tell around the cracker barrel in these parts."

Jake outlines the tale for Gunty, who seems outraged by it. I suppose that making deals with blackmailing saboteurs is not his idea of how good government works.

"Interesting," he says. There's a brief moment of discomfort while Jake waits for further comment. None is forthcoming.

"So anyway, when Klaus told me about his interest in that deal you're working on, I told him we'd be happy to share our views on the matter, with him being such a friend of the DOT and all."

"What is your interest, Mr. Rise?" he asks, adding an element of formality to our little confab by refusing to use my first name.

"Well, Mr. Gunty," I say, getting right to it. "I'm a friend of the Norlands, owners of some private property surrounded mostly by state forest lands. As I understand it, the state plans to acquire and run a road through that property, opening it up to business uses."

"And your point?" asks Gunty. Jake looks embarrassed by his colleague's bad manners.

"My point, Mr. Gunty, is that I'd like to spare the Norlands, who are elderly spinster ladies, the upset of having their ancestral lands acquired by the state if I can. As I'm sure you're aware, they have no wish to be bought out by the government."

"Mr. Rise," says Gunty, "sometimes private owners must sacrifice for the public good. I'm afraid this necessary evil dates back to the earliest days of our democracy."

"Oh, certainly," I say. "Yet, given all the state land in that area, I can't help but wonder if there's a way of taking a small detour around their property. They will certainly be arguing for this kind of consideration when a court hears their concerns. No matter which route the DOT uses, it will need to acquire some wetlands to replace what is lost during the road construction. As a long-time partner of the DOT, I'd be willing to adjust my lease deal so that the state can, at little cost, replace lost coastal lands in the future."

As I knew it would, this suggestion intrigues Jake. If I'd be willing to sell or, even better, gift my land to them, Jake would be telling the tale of how he finally closed a deal with the heir of the infamous Troels Gravesin.

Gunty, on the other hand, looks distinctly uncomfortable.

"That would be highly unorthodox," he says, "and possibly illegal."

"But worthy of our consideration," Jake says, jumping in. He doesn't want to lose this deal just because of some pretentious neophyte with a stick up his ass.

In the end, we agree to adjourn and meet again tomorrow, giving them time to confer with their colleagues about a possible deal. We are hardly in the hallway outside Jake's office before Gunty pulls out his smartphone to make a call. He moves well down the hall away from us, and I'm wondering who's on the other end of the line.

When I enter his office the next day, Jake is wearing an uncharacteristically gloomy look, whereas Gunty seems annoyingly self-satisfied. Looks like the Norlands and I are shit out of luck.

Gunty explains that, after conferring with his superiors, my proposal was deemed "inappropriate." The moron's pretention pisses me off, but that's okay. They'd expect me to be irritated, and I need an air of surliness to pull off this next gambit anyway.

Jake makes a half-hearted attempt to engage in some other "horse swapping" around the land-lease deal. I tell him I've got no interest in other horses. Radiating impatience and anxiety about catching my plane, I yank out my smartphone and pretend to check on flight times.

My phone doesn't work. Little wonder. I've never tried to activate it. It's just a piece of junk I bought at a pawnshop last night.

"Shit," I say, "fucking iPhones. Can't hold a goddamned charge."

Gunty is one of those guys who likes to put his phone down on the table in front of him, ready to pounce on any message or email that he deems more important than the people with whom he's meeting.

"Could I borrow this a sec?" I ask, reaching over and grabbing his off the table. "Just got to check on my flight real quick."

He's outraged. Too bad. Rude little prick. His life could be worse. I could be ripping off his arms to teach him some manners.

I check his outgoing calls, especially the one he made after our meeting yesterday. Looks like he called that number a few times, but there's no name associated with it. Just some initials: GT. I memorize the number and hand his phone back to him.

"Got to go soon," I say. "Jake, can I talk to you in private for a minute?"

Gunty's offended again, but I don't give a shit. As he leaves, he shakes my hand, which I give a nice little squeeze, making his eyes pop.

Then it's time for me to see what I can learn.

"Sorry, Jake," I say after Gunty is gone. "I just wanted to get rid of numbnuts there. Before I go, I'm hoping you can give me a drink from the Wild Turkey you used to keep in your desk. I could use one."

Jake obliges. We shoot the shit for a while, talking about roads, trucks, fast cars and the sad passing of the tollbooth, which then leads us to the topic of asshole decision-makers. That's when we start talking about Gunty again.

"So, tell me true, Jake, why is Gunty so keen on pushing the Wela-coochee project through the front yard of my friends?"

"Gospel truth is I've no idea, Klaus. Not a single exec I know gives a damn about this project, but nobody is willing to rein in our Mr. Gunty. He's no higher up the organization than I am, but he's pretty much untouchable when it comes to Welacoochee."

"Some kind of politics?" I ask.

"Oh, yeah. The politics on this thing stink like the fart off a road-killed skunk."

"So, you know who's backing Gunty?"

"Not for me to say, Klaus. I don't need my nuts in a twister. But I will say that our Mr. Gunty's LinkedIn account is available for public display. Maybe his work history will give you an idea or two," he says, winking. "I'm thinking it might just."

Chapter Twenty-Nine

"Hunt him away, be wroth,
High Odin, heavenly powers!"
—*Egil's Saga*

Everyone said Alfr's escaped troll had committed the heinous deed.

Inge secreted me away in the manor's hidden cavities known only to Alfr's family.

Sunmane played the role of new king dedicated to avenging his father. Several bloody brawls broke out among the adherents of Sunmane and the Völsungs. Rumors of war spread. On the third day after the death of Bloodaxe, Inge and Halfdan Sunmane announced their engagement. Although this reduced the strain between the two kingdoms, many still suspected I couldn't have acted alone—that the Völsungs must have aided and guided me.

With Dofri's aid, Inge arranged for my escape by ship. It was a devilishly tricky thing to do under the circumstances. It would have been less risky to just kill me, signaling to the world that they had no role in the plot against Bloodaxe. In their positions, I might have gone that route. Especially because of the dogs.

The hounds were everywhere. Inge's servants had scrubbed the passages we had used during the night of our exploits. And Dofri had personally taken my bloody tunic and dragged it several miles through the underbrush before depositing it into a dark, deep hole in a cave that was renowned for having no bottom.

Even so, hounds would circle the Great Manor, sniffing in the air as their handlers looked up at the edifice suspiciously. If it were any other building, the trackers would have brought in the hounds and torn apart every floorboard to look for me. Those dogs haunted my nightmares as I lay hidden. Even now, over a thousand years later, they still do on occasion.

Despite the many risks, however, the Völsungs arranged for me to leave the country aboard a trading *knarr* headed for Iceland. Dofri handpicked the crew, only selecting men who detested Sunmane. They didn't want to live in a nation that had tied itself through marriage to Bloodaxe's spawn. Dofri asked if I had any crew suggestions from my time on *Ormen Vig*. Only two names came to mind.

On the third night after the assassination, Inge entered the small chamber where I was hidden. It was humiliating. I had been living like a rat in the walls, nesting in a shabby straw mattress, shitting and pissing into a covered bucket.

She pretended not to notice and quietly led me back to her chambers, where we made love for the last time. That first night had been a frenzy of ferocity and lust—she had still been in a carnal, killing frame of mind bent on extinguishing the gentle woman she'd been bred to be. On the last night, by contrast, she was tender and generous, savoring long moments of pleasure as if she were enjoying a sumptuous meal to be followed by a lifetime of fasting.

Afterwards, I held her, and we spoke intimately, as if we were friends and long-time lovers. We spoke of the past, not the future, focusing on the days when she served as audience to my training.

At the time, I hadn't appreciated how strange it was to have a weapons master spend so much time training a thrall, much less a troll. And then to have that slave train boys of noble breeding? Astonishing.

Amid the pillow talk, I finally worked up the courage to ask her about the symbols etched into my skin. I couldn't remember getting the original tattoos but had vivid memories of the times Mor examined them as I grew. She wanted to ensure that the words did not fade as my skin stretched. Those examinations were sometimes followed by a tortuous hour during which she meticulously and mercilessly punched ashes into my skin with needles made of bone.

"You mean, no one has ever read them to you?" Inge asked, tears in her eyes. When I assured her they had not, she told me that they were, in fact, difficult to read even for the literate.

"They are old runes," she said, "so their shapes are not quite the same as the ones we use today, and the spellings are different. But my father had them carved onto a wooden tablet. He brought in the best skalds and scribes to examine them. They are one reason he trusted you."

She bid me lie on my stomach. Then she straddled me like a naked rider as she read them from the back of my neck.

> *Forebear Völsung feeder of ravens,*
> *Bane of jotnar's kin,*
> *Spilling brotherly battle-sweat*
> *From this Hulder queen's brat,*
> *Horse-of-the-hanged retainer*

She spoke them as slowly as an incantation. This gave me the shivers, which from her perspective must have felt like the trembling of a horse.

"Are you okay?" she asked.

"I don't understand what it means."

"I don't think anyone does, Hallr. But you know the kennings, yes?"

"Most, I guess. Everyone knows that 'feeders of ravens' are warriors."

"And old tales tell of great Völsung heroes slaying the giants, or jotnar, in the mountains," she said. "Trolls are their kin."

"Yes, well, those tales are, shall we say, exaggerated. Anyway, battle sweat is just blood," I said, rolling over onto my back as she laughed, trying to maintain her position on top of me.

"I assume Hulder refers to your mother," she says, darkly. "The witch who killed my brother."

"My mother was no queen," I said.

"Not when you knew her," she said. "But when you were born?"

Mor never talked about the past, least of all her past. The few times she referred to my "soft" father, it was in passing and disparagingly. She didn't allow me to ask about him.

"No idea. It's hard to picture her a queen, though she had plenty of pride and arrogance," I said.

Inge punched me in the chest.

"'Pride is a royal's mantle,'" she quoted to me.

"Glad I am that you're naked, then," I said, making her smile. "I guess I'm the brat of the poem. That was the least of her insults. But I don't get what 'horse of the hanged' means."

"Odin's gallows."

"I don't know it," I said. "Mor mostly told stories about how Odin cheated and killed giants."

"She sounds so embittered."

"Embittered," I said, testing the word. "You could call it that. Tell me about Odin's gallows."

"He hung himself from the Great Tree for nine days in order to gain knowledge. Hung himself from a spear," she said.

"You mean Yggdrasil?" I asked, remembering Mor's confusing stories about the Great Tree. "That's the horse?"

"Of course."

"Makes no sense. How could I be connected to a mythical tree? Even if I were, how do I interpret the word 'retainer'? Am I its slave? Its barricade? Its possessor?"

"I do not know," she said, bending down and running her hand behind my neck while kissing me. "However, I think one day you shall."

On the fourth night, I was hoping to see Inge one last time. But it was Dofri who entered my hiding space just after sunset. He gave me a piece of slate and chalked a rough map into it.

"Memorize this, then leave immediately. I have cleared the hallways of guards and servants for a short time. Jump out the window of Bloodaxe's chamber. That way, if the hounds catch your scent, their trackers will think it's the track they already followed.

"Then run for the forest along this line," he said, pointing at the slate. "It's where we dragged your shirt to create the false scent trail. Deviate from that track here at the river crossing, and make your way to this small bay. It is fifteen miles or more, so you'll need to move fast. That's where the ship will be docked. Among the supplies to be loaded, there will be a large square crate into which you should be able to fit. Once it's loaded and the ship is away, you can emerge. The skipper knows the plan. Take this medallion. It declares you a freedman."

I examined the silver medallion, dazed by the notion that I was no longer a thrall. For some reason, I had a strong impulse to lick it, as if a metallic taste could make my liberty feel more real to me. I placed it into the pouch hanging from my belt. It would do me little good if Sunmane's trackers caught me.

"I have already sent along the crewmen you requested," he said. "Remember: if something goes wrong, fight to the death. If they capture you alive, they will torture you, making you say anything Sunmane wishes. He will use it against the kingdom, and he might well use it against Inge. She could suffer if you prove a coward.

"But I trust you will not, Hallr Halftroll. You did well to avenge your king and master. I only wish you'd killed his whelp, as well, when you had the chance. Too late for that. His death would only throw both kingdoms into chaos and war now."

Suddenly he drew his sword. For a moment, I thought Dofri had decided to betray me, after all. I remember being strangely at peace with it.

But rather than wielding it against me, he handed it over.

"A gift from the princess. On the day Alfr was stuck by that dishonorable turd of a merchant, he paid a small fortune for this sword. Ulfberht, the greatest swordsmith in history, created it. Inge had the hilt enlarged to match your grip.

"It is a princely gift," he said, sighing as he gave it to me. "A gift I begrudge you, because you'll never be half the swordsman I am. Inge has named it *Vidar*, after the god of vengeance. Do not disgrace me when you wield it."

Then Dofri gave me the scabbard, turned and walked away.

I badly wanted to go in search of Inge to say goodbye, but there wasn't time. I suspect that was part of her plan, or Dofri's. It was the season when nights were short, not much more than five hours.

So I did what I was told. Jumped out the window from which Inge had hurled the sorcerer's gonads. Cut off, discarded, thrown to the dogs.

I ran along the trail Dofri had sketched, still half expecting betrayal and ambush now that I was far away from the Great Manor.

Because trolls are terrible sprinters, the tales of humankind seldom mention that they are excellent distance runners. We are supposed to be slow of foot as well as mind. I proved that cliché wrong, running as if a demon were behind me. If there was to be an ambush, then I was going to try to blow by it so fast they wouldn't have time to react.

Only a half hour into my run, I came to the river on the map. In truth, it was more of a wide, deep stream than a river. I was going so fast and feeling so confident that I decided to cross it with one huge leap.

A serious mistake. I fell short of the far bank, coming down hard on some sharp rocks in the shallows. One pierced the boot on my right foot. There was no time to bandage it, so I just kept running, cursing myself for idiocy. My boot was squishing and sucking with blood. No hound could miss the scent. Hell, even a hunter without a hound could easily track me.

When I was young, Mor taught me that a wounded troll has two options when on the run: turn and fight, or flee while "earth-catching."

"What's that?" I asked.

"How can any troll not know earth-catching?" she shouted. "It's in your blood!"

"It's not in my blood!" I yelled. I almost never talked back to her, since it usually resulted in whacks and welts. But I was sick of her always making me feel inferior, as if I were not troll enough.

As expected, she raised her fist. I didn't flinch. She sighed, as if I were the stupidest child on earth, and decided not to club me after all.

"We earth-catch when we borrow strength of the earth and make it our own. The earth is of Arg. He gifts us his power when it's needed most. Do you understand?"

Of course I didn't understand, but I nodded anyway. Mor had made a kind of concession to me, a rare occurrence. I wasn't going to prove to her once again that I thought "like a human."

As I limped through the dark forest, I remembered Mor's words, not knowing if it was another of her myths. Focusing on my footing, I tried hard to siphon up strength from the moss, pine needles and stones beneath me.

Maybe it was just adrenalin or endorphins or whatever modern mumbo jumbo humans use to explain such mysteries. But I felt a surge of power. With every footfall, my legs grew stronger. The mosses radiated a bluish glow I'd never seen before. They were living springs pushing me along, as if I were a small ship surfing waves along the shore.

Then the ubiquitous beds of pine and spruce needles joined in, welling up in me like music, string instruments joining woodwinds in a symphony. Even the trees were players, pushing me along with invisible bands of force, handing me forward like arms in a crowd.

It was an ecstatic feeling, as if the universe were revealing itself to me for the first time.

Starlight fell through the forest in beams that crossed one another like woven threads of luminescence, a reticulum that did not catch but carried me.

Never before had I felt like anything more than an animal struggling to survive in a senseless universe. That night, though, I felt like something more, a true citizen of a realm I hadn't believed in.

Then slowly, like a receding tide, the glow of the world dissipated, the power faded. I was just another creature in the forest, prey or predator, limping along as stealthily as I could. I could smell the sea. The vast groves of square-needled spruce had disappeared, replaced by leafy trees that loved the warmth of the coast: giant gnarled oaks, great rounded ash, wide-leaved maples.

Stopping to listen, I could hear a nearby elk grazing on tender tree sprouts, and I caught the scent of a bear who'd rubbed up against a nearby elm to mark his territory. There were no chasing hounds.

I had travelled most of the distance over rugged country in just three hours. It was time to be extra cautious. There were guileful humans ahead.

As I approached the small bay, I heard the familiar patter of men working to load and prepare a ship, as well as of horses moving down the forest path I had avoided.

I told myself once again that it wasn't too late to head for the mountains, where I could survive while the fleeting lives of these men ran their course, turning them into dirt, along with any genuine memories of my existence. Although Sunmane would hunt me for decades, it would still be the smart, logical play.

So, why didn't I? I've asked myself that question thousands of times. At first, I was bound by my pledge to Alfr, then by my desire for revenge. But Alfr was dead, Bloodaxe was slain, and I was a freedman, not just by nature but by the decree of the Völsungs.

I still don't know. Maybe it was to please Inge, or to stick my finger in the eye of Sunmane, or to demonstrate to myself that I was just as good or better than any human being. Maybe I had no real choice, the Norns having decided my destiny long ago.

Or maybe I was just young. Young people, even troll people, do stupid things all the time. They embrace foolishness as a virtue. In my case, it was more of a bear hug.

I lurked on the edge of the camp. The winds were right, so there'd be no delays in sailing. If the captain were worth his salt, he'd be gone within moments of first dawn.

I could see the crate. It was square, not rectangular like the trollbox. Someone had told them to load it last, I guess, because it was one of the few large items not yet on the wharf. Compared to the sleek *Ormen Vig*, the docked merchant ship was a squat, though bloated, pig. Yet it had a kind of homely beauty. It was maybe fifty feet or so with a wide beam and lots of cargo room. The crew had already loaded huge amounts of stuff: casks, crates, armor and weapons, sailing gear, furs and pelts, wool, and even a few sheep and goats.

Time was running out for me to get into the box, but I was waiting for someone.

I'd almost given up, when the figure emerged from the forest. It was a huge, hulking being dressed in black, including a black hood hiding its face. It moved more like a mountain than a man, its legs stiff, threatening to teeter with every step. In front of the giant was a boy carrying a torch.

When the hooded colossus was no more than seventy yards from the dock, a blowing horn sounded from the outskirts of the woods, followed by twenty spear-carriers charging the figure. The hulk looked around it, seemingly confused, but the boy walking in front reacted quickly. Before the soldiers could reach them, the boy ordered the giant to its knees, threw back its hood and cast the light of the torch on it.

"It's only Ornolf," Kol yelled to the soldiers. "Ornolf the Oaf!"

Most of the warriors slowed to a walk. Some laughed, some looked disgusted, and a few looked relieved. But three kept charging. They were berserkers and not to be denied their bloodlust, smashing the oaf down with their shields, kicking him with heavy boots, whooping and bawling like a team of insane apes.

Had I been a hero, I would have charged in and defended the oaf. Instead, I was the one who requested he wear those black robes, hoping the ruse would draw out any enemies. Though I took no pleasure in his terrible beating, I knew this was often the way of the cunning man: gaining personal advantage at the expense of the innocent. Mor would have approved.

Shouts went up from the dock. Several men walked quickly toward the melee, shouting at the berserkers but keeping their distance. One of the approaching men was Dofri, who must have ridden a good horse hard to get there as quickly as I had.

"Ornolf is a freeman who has committed no crime," Dofri shouted. "I give you fair warning. Stand down or we shall defend him."

One of the berserkers, panting heavily, took a step back from the bleeding mess that was Ornolf. He shot Dofri a look of disdain. The other two continued. One hefted an axe over his head when an arrow took him through the throat. He gurgled horribly and yet still managed to slice into Ornolf's great back before dying.

The third berserker screamed in rage and took several steps toward Dofri and his three bowmen. "Stand down, I say," Dofri shouted again. The berserker slowed, then spat in Dofri's direction before going over and kicking the oaf one last time.

I used the distraction to make my way toward the crate, wedging myself in and pulling it closed with an internal handle and latches that had been made especially for this occasion.

I loathed it, feeling as vulnerable and restless as a caged wolverine.

Soon after I interred myself, I heard the voice. He was using his irritatingly pleasant yet complacent tone with Dofri.

"My apologies," he said glibly. "My men are on edge because your murderous thrall remains on the loose."

The two men walked in my direction.

"As you can imagine, Dofri, his escape has not helped my new position. So when hunters told me there were signs of him this night, I insisted on joining the pursuit."

"I understand, King Sunmane," said Dofri. "We, too, have been scouring for him."

"It would serve both our purposes to locate the creature," said Sunmane.

"But not to take him alive," Dofri noted.

"Oh no, of course not. Best to deliver justice swiftly," said Sunmane, standing only feet away from my crate. "I would reward such justice richly. With Alfr gone, the Völsungs need a new, wealthy leader with the strong support of Inge's husband."

Dofri said nothing, which worried me. He'd armed me and warned me to fight to the death if caught. Was this the moment he'd aimed for? He was a practical, unsentimental man who could always be counted on to coldly evaluate tactical advantages. He had to be considering the pros and cons of betraying me.

"You were always the better man, Dofri," Sunmane now whispered. "My father would not have dared challenge *you* to a holmgang."

"I too have a daughter, my lord," Dofri said.

I felt a wave of panic. I could see where this was going and prepared to explode out of the box. At the very least, I might be able to bite out the throat of the golden child before I was slain.

"Do you now?" asked Sunmane. "Of marriageable age, and perhaps with less fondness for monsters?"

Again Dofri hesitated.

"Alas, my lord, not yet of age."

"Ah, but we may yet be better friends," said Sunmane. "Who knows what the future may bring? I wish you to allow my men to search the ship."

"It would be unwise," Dofri said almost apologetically. "The crew consists of men who do not favor your cause, men you will soon be rid of. Going among them could cause an incident, threatening the fragile peace between our clans and kingdoms."

"You have so little control over your own men?" Sunmane asked with rising outrage.

"They are more Alfr's men than mine, my lord."

"I ask you plainly, Dofri. Is the troll among them? We have intelligence he was heading this way."

"I swear to you, Halfdan Sunmane, on the life of my clan, that the troll is not aboard that ship."

"For your sake, Dofri, I hope not. You'll find I have a long memory," he said and walked away.

After a time, Dofri muttered in disgust, "The viper would have betrayed Inge just to have you. Farewell, ogre. I hope that prophecy was more than a troll dam's trick."

I didn't make a sound, curled and quiet as a stone. There was nothing left to say.

Chapter Thirty

"The Florida in my novels is not as seedy as the real Florida. It's hard to stay ahead of the curve."
—Carl Hiaasen

I saunter as inconspicuously through *Snorri's* poorly lit parking lot as a seven foot troll can. The blue Jaguar in front of me reminds me of Olaf's, being another older model with a hood ornament. I wonder if he and Edmund had been in a perpetual pissing contest, or if they were such good buddies they enjoyed owning the same machine. Kind of creepy either way.

I nonchalantly bend down, jam my fingers into the metal between the hood and grill and yank up hard, shattering the latches. The car alarm goes off. An older couple getting into a Buick looks over, and I wave to them. "Battery died," I tell them. "Got a jumper cable?"

I doubt that makes sense. Would the alarm go off if the battery were dead? The man shakes his head, barely making eye contact. His wife jumps into the car so fast you'd think they'd just heisted a bank.

I reach in and pull loose every wire I see. That kills the alarm. I close the hood again, and then wave to the Buick just as it hits a speedbump far too fast. Tourists.

By the time I get back into the restaurant, Edmund is seated at our table, having a conversation with Hildy. His sandy hair is slicked back like Gordon Gekko. He looks less like the friendly frat boy I first met than a business-warrior wannabe gearing up for *Shark Tank*. He gives me a perfunctory handshake, which I try not to take personally, having been jammed with a knife in a bar fight on the behalf of this little shit.

It's a Tuesday night, and *Snorri's* is almost empty. Edmund's wearing a gray suit with a striped red shirt and no tie. Business casual, light on the casual.

"I told you I can't discuss that," he says to Hildy in response to a question I didn't hear. "I've signed an NDA. And I wouldn't discuss the Norland property with you, anyway."

"Because…?" she asks.

"Because they're members of your family," he says, giving her a smug look.

"So you've heard they're my aunts," Hildy says.

I wonder where he heard it. Hildy told me that relationship is not in any public records.

"Look, Hildy, I know you were playing me before, trying to pump me for information on this one stupid backcountry Florida swampland deal," he says. "You should have told me there was a conflict of interest and that you and big Klaus here were going to be working against us."

Backcountry Florida swampland deal. I've heard that phrase before.

Hildy, who has come armored in her own navy-blue business suit, says, "Your firm came to me, Edmund, and never mentioned a specific tract of land. Charlie just said you wanted to get an expert opinion on no-net-loss land-swap particulars related to a virgin tract of land."

Edmund's not conceding a thing. I don't think he knows exactly how Hildy and his deceased partner Charlie met. The truth is that Hildy reached out to Charlie first in order to find out who was behind the state's attempt to acquire Haven.

"Why am I here, Hildy?"

"Because I know who you're really working for. And I can make a recommendation that helps the state avoid future legal wrangling, even while acquiring properties that better ensure the public good and the good of your client," she says.

Edmund twists his mouth into a skeptical look.

"What are you talking about, Hildy? And, no disrespect, but what the hell are you even doing here, Klaus?"

I don't say anything, just slide a piece of paper across the table toward him.

He's back to smug. He thinks I'm not in his league, and my clothes don't help. I'm wearing a dress shirt with slacks but, compared to these two, I look more like a bumptious supermarket manager who's lost his nametag.

"What's this?" he asks, looking down at the paper.

"A phone number you should know," says Hildy.

He shrugs.

"Can you negotiate with us, Edmund, or should we call it and tell him you gave us the number because you were too busy to call yourself?"

Edmund thinks it over and then holds up a finger, signaling us to wait while he checks his contacts in his phone. Apparently, he relies on the machine to remember even his most important numbers. Typical.

After he compares, he stays cool.

"Go ahead and try to call it yourself. The person in question doesn't pick up unless he recognizes the caller."

"So, you don't even want to know our proposal?" Hildy asks.

"Not really," he says. "I don't trust you, Hildy. Not by a long shot. And I'm beginning to get a whiff of bribery here."

"Look, Edmund, I've given you nothing but good advice in regard to environmental policy, which you've never paid me for, by the way. Now that I know what the deal entails, I have every right to protect my family."

He shakes his head and stands up.

"You must really think I'm an idiot," he says before striding away like a greasy-haired cock-of-the-walk.

"I do believe he came here just to tell you to fuck off," I say to her.

"Could have been worse. Last time he saw me, he called me a dick-teaser," she says.

"He has a dick?" I ask, pushing my chair back and heading out the back door through the kitchen.

I sit quietly in this beautiful 1964 Lincoln Continental convertible—which Andre somehow dug up for this occasion—and watch from a distance as Edmund tries to start his Jaguar. Nothing. Then he tries to pop the hood. Again, nothing. Edmund gets out of the car, cursing. Right on cue, Fred walks by, supposedly headed toward his parked motorcycle.

"Oh, look who we have here," Fred says, strutting toward Edmund. "I remember you. You're the weenie who gave me shit at *Grimm's*. You and me, we've got some unfinished business."

"Look, man," says Edmund, "I don't even remember what we were arguing about. Whatever it was, I apologize, okay?"

"So, you come back into my neighborhood all dressed in your Men's Wearhouse duds and ask to kiss my ass? Is that how it is?" Fred says, pushing Edmund onto his car.

I jam down on the gas of the Lincoln, doing my best to make a Hollywood-esque tire-burning sound. I don't quite pull it off, but it's enough to make Edmund and Fred look my way as I pull up behind his car.

"You okay there, Edmund?" I ask.

"What the fuck, dude?" Fred says to Edmund, poking him in the chest with one finger. "You bring your goddamned ogre of a bodyguard wherever you go?"

Ogre? That hurts, though I've heard it once or twice before. I wonder if he was dreaming up the line while we were inside.

"Back off, Sabbath," I say. "Let's go, Edmund. I'll give you a lift wherever you're looking to go."

His Gordon Gekko swagger is gone.

"Thanks, dude," he says, trying hard to look calm as he comes around the Lincoln and gets in the passenger door.

"Hey, Sabbath," I yell. "Leave the Jag alone. I got your bike's license number."

Fred just scowls and flips me the bird.

Driving across the Bay Way with the wind in our hair, Edmund scooches toward me in the car's huge front seat. It makes me nervous.

"Hey," he yells, "this is sweet."

He sweeps his hand in front of him, pantomiming how much he appreciates all the chrome on the dashboard. He looks like a kid riding with his dad.

I nod appreciatively, trying not to look concerned. Truth is, I'm a lousy motorist. Years ago, through the flimflammery of a forged identity,

I got a Florida automobile license. I even taught myself to drive in the age when this car was new and people were trusting enough to leave their keys above sun visors. But that was half a century ago.

Once over the bridges, I pull into the parking lot for the tollbooth employees. Miriam sees me and gives me a wave from her booth.

"Nice ride!" she shouts.

Edmund looks nonplussed.

"What's going on, Klaus?" he says, a hint of suspicion in his voice.

"I've got to say hi to somebody," I say. "Come with."

"I'll just wait here," he says.

"Oh, come on, dude. I just pulled your fanny out of the flames... *again*. You're safe with me. If you want, give your wife a call, and let her know where you are. I just want to show you something cool."

He hesitates. On one hand, I work with Hildy and look like I might fit well into the cast of Texas Chainsaw Massacre. On the other, I keep saving his ass, have just parked in a government parking lot, and own the kind of car that he recognizes as a classic in mint condition. How bad could I be?

I grab a couple of flashlights out of the glove compartment, and we walk down the road to my property. As we trudge up the sandy path, I try to keep him calm with some soothing banter, as if he's a farm animal that I'm about to butcher. He complains about hiking in his dress shoes and suit pants.

We finally make it to the efficiency apartment, where there's light shining through a small window.

"I want to introduce you to someone," I say. "But, listen, don't worry if she seems a little touched. She's pretty old and not from around here."

As I open the flimsy little apartment door, I hear a voice shout, "Insects come. Stop up the door. Now!"

With one hand, I guide Edmund in ahead of me so I can get the door shut more quickly.

I give him credit. He's shown chutzpah tonight. I didn't think he'd willingly make it all the way through my jungle of a front yard while wearing his posh suit pants. Although these Americans may not know a troll when they see one, they've still got to sense something uncanny and dangerous amid the thorny vines, a predator out of nightmares.

But Edmund's kept it together.

Until now.

"Holy shit!" he says as he comes almost nose to nose with gigantic Aunt Urdy sitting in my humongous custom-made stuffed chair, knitting with needles that look large and sharp enough to stake a vampire. She's dressed in her black robes but has ditched the grayish shawl and white headscarf she usually wears, swapping them out for a black hood that hangs loosely over her forehead. Definitely some spooky, witchy, soothsayer shit.

Urdy doesn't say a word. She just leans in a little to see him better.

"I forgot how small they are," she says in the Old Tongue.

"Edmund, this is Aunt Urdy. She's visiting for a bit from, you know, out of town."

Edmund gapes at her. I think he's trying to decide whether he's being put on. What did the kids used to call it? Punk'd?

It's quite a scene. On the floor of the room, Urdy has spread out a circular rug riddled with rune patterns. It gives me the willies, reminding me of Bloodaxe's magic. There's not much else in the room: a 32-inch LED TV hanging on the wall, a side table with a remote and a wireless keyboard, and the kitchen stuff. The only other room, aside from the bathroom, is jammed with books.

Truth is, I don't use the apartment much, preferring my lair. Nothing like reading a good book in a lair. But if I want to watch the boob tube or surf the Net or play a bit of World of Warcraft, this is where I hang out.

The kitchen consists of little more than a white acrylic sink set into a Formica counter. On the counter is a microwave, toaster and a two-burner hotplate. Urdy has placed one of her own personal teapots on a burner.

"Are you putting me on?" he asks quietly out of the side of his mouth while still staring at Urdy.

"Show me hand," Urdy demands in her broken English. Edmund reluctantly lifts up his palm to her, as if he's afraid she might bite it off. I think of Hansel and Gretel. Urdy does look like she might pop dinky Edmund into a wood-burning oven at any moment.

"Yes," she says, looking at his hand. She must be doing the palm-reading bit for show.

"Your momma," says Urdy. "She is what is called a bitch, yes?"

"Hey," says Edmund, looking up at me. "That's my mom she's talking about."

"Yeah, well?" I ask.

"All right, we don't call her Hazel the Harpy for nothing, I guess."

"She make you feel not worth anything, eh?" asks Urdy.

"Well, I don't know…"

"So you like shiny things, shiny women," she says. "And cars and watches and rings, eh? Make you feel like worth much. 'Fuck off, Momma,' you think in heart."

"What are you, a shrink?" Edmund asks.

"I look shrunk to you?" Urdy barks.

"No, sorry, definitely not," says Edmund.

"You not so bad as you think," says Urdy. "We weave you better future, Orlog willing. You want?"

Edmund looks back to me again, more baffled than ever. I shrug.

"Uh, sure," he says.

"You take this," Urdy says, placing a small gold figure in his palm. "This remind you. You shiny in here." She points to her chest and, theoretically, her heart. How nice. Sort of a *Sesame Street* moment.

"That's beautiful," Edmund says, holding up her gift. It's an image of a man wearing a headdress from which extends blocky-looking feathers. Edmund lets me see it.

"It's yours, dude," I say. "For real, a gift from Urdy. She has some nice stuff and doesn't give much away."

"What is it?"

"Tlaloc. Be careful with him."

"Looks Mexican or something. Valuable?"

"Definitely worth a buck or two, but I'd hang onto him."

"Now, you do a thing for Urdy?" she asks.

"Sure," Edmund says, still studying Tlaloc.

"You make us tea. Water is in pot. You take care of water."

I point Edmund to the burners. He turns it on while I scramble around in the two small cupboards for something resembling teacups. The only things I can come up with are three novelty mugs I vaguely remember buying at a midnight sale at Wal-Mart: one proclaims the drinker a "Vintage Dude," another has a picture of Darth Vader, and the third is emblazoned with John Wayne's face and a quote: "Courage is being scared to death but saddling up anyway."

Urdy pulls a box of Earl Grey out of her robes. We stand around awkwardly while waiting for the water to boil. Nice get-together: an original, bronze-skinned Weird Sister, an average troll tollkeeper, and a yuppie-hipster whose four hundred dollar slacks are clustered with sandspurs.

When the water's hot, Edmund pours it into the three mugs, kidding me about my classy taste. As the tea steeps, we discuss the coming comet and the recent spate of hot weather. When it's ready, I toast, "To shiny stuff" as we click our mugs together.

Edmund is still cautious enough to let the two of us drink first.

"Now you make me promise," says Urdy.

"Promise what?" asks Edmund.

"Always to take care my water," she says.

He looks up at me, his once slicked down sandy hair tousled and sweaty-looking.

"What can I say?" I respond. "The lady loves her tea."

Edmund barks out a laugh.

"Sure, Ms. Urdy," he says. "I promise to always take care of your tea water."

"Good. You shine inside, pledged by troll's gold and the sacred waters of Urd's Well. You go now see my brother Máni."

"Yeah, I didn't understand a word of that. You've got an Uncle Manny around here, too?" he asks me.

"Kind of," I say. "Come on, I'll introduce you."

Still sipping our tea, we walk out in the direction of the bay and stand on the seawall. I'm trying to figure out the best way to make my pitch to Edmund. Tact and salesmanship aren't really in my wheelhouse.

"That's Máni," I say, pointing up to the moon.

"The Manny on the Moon, huh?" he says, chuckling at his own wit.

"Yep, it's a Norwegian thing."

"So, this is the DOT's property?" he asks.

"No. They lease a parcel of it down that way," I say, pointing. "You know where we parked? If you walk straight down the seawall, you come out right next to the parking lot. They lease that and about a hundred yards in this direction."

"Lease from who?"

"Me," I say.

"You're shitting me."

"Nope, I own about thirty square acres hereabouts, the largest tract of undeveloped land inside the city."

"Holy motherfucking hell, Klaus! Must be worth millions!"

"Oh, yeah. On the waterfront. Enough acreage for multiple gigantic condo complexes, and next to a major thoroughfare with easy hurricane evacuation. There might be, knowing the state's flexible standards, wiggle room in regard to whether some of it constitutes wetlands."

Edmund decides he has to sit down on the seawall.

"This wasn't..."

"Yes, it's the land Hildy was going to discuss with you. Look, you're a paid advisor to the governor of Florida, right? That's who's been driving this eminent domain push."

It turns out that Peter Gunty spent a decade working for Florida's governor before he went into politics. The governor is from a long line of real estate tycoons, so Hildy and I deduced that he must be the political force behind the DOT's plan to acquire the Norland property.

"I can't talk about that," Edmund says.

"You can at least tell me if you're consulting for the governor. You are, right?"

His eyes flick up to my face and then back out into the bay again. We're quiet a while. The lights along the causeway, reflected in the bay, look like quivering white and yellow candles aglow in dark waters.

"Let's say I am."

"Then the governor should get wind of how much land I have and am willing to, for example, deed to the state. Valuable land that could result in lots of new construction and jobs. I'm not talking about a bribe, mind you. You're an attorney, and I'll hire my own when the time comes, so we won't be engaging in illegal gift giving. I'm just making you aware of a citizen offering our leaders a rare opportunity to do some public good. And, on a personal level, I want the governor to know that I hope someday to be able to donate to his presidential campaign chest."

"Where'd you hear he's going to run?"

"He's a Florida governor, isn't he? Edmund, this could be your baby. You work out the logistics and the politics with him. You'll be able to sell this to the public a lot better than an eminent domain battle with little old ladies. And, show him that artifact Urdy gave you. In fact, I've got a gift that I'd like him to give to the Museum of Florida History in Tallahassee."

I pull the palm-sized golden medallion out of my front pocket. In the middle is an Aztec sun, surrounded by a circle of outward pointing arrow-like symbols. It's the gold orb I saw just before Hildy bailed me out of Helheim.

"Genuine Aztec calendar," I say. "I've read he's a history buff. He should enjoy it."

"You're seriously going to try to bribe the governor?"

From here we can see scores of lit boatdocks encircling the bay. They come in a range of Christmas tree colors: yellow, blue, green and even a violet or two. The bands of color in the water remind me of spectrums of light refracted through prisms.

"I'm giving it to the museum by way of the governor," I say. "It's a gift to the state, not to him. But he may want to look it over first, and he will never ever forget you were the one who gave it to him. Do I need to go through somebody else?"

He stares at the medallion. Urdy was right about his attraction to things that shine.

"No, I'll show it to him and see what he thinks," he says. "You've sure got some brass ones, Klaus. But Lam will hate the whole thing."

"Who's Lam?"

"Lam is the governor's secret weapon, a pollster as well as political advisor. She's pushed hard for the acquisition of the Norland place. But I can't say more than that. Lam's a stickler for secrecy."

We talk for another half an hour about the possibilities for my property, with him getting more and more excited, a kid dreaming of birthday gifts. I offer to drive him home, but he says he wants to walk the seawall and think. Says he'll call an Uber on the way.

"One last thing, Edmund," I add as he starts out on his walk.

"Shit. I knew there had to be a catch."

"No catch," I say. "I just want you to know that protecting the Norland property is good for everybody. It's the right thing to do."

"Sure, Klaus, I hear you. Of course, I also think you've got the hots for Hildy. But it'd be nice to be on the side of old ladies, alligators and angels for a change."

As he disappears down the seawall, I hear rustling behind me.

"Do you think it'll work?" Hildy asks, emerging from the brush.

"Let's see. We've got Urdy's spooky rune-induced voodoo, a couple of potent pieces of troll's gold I tried to magic with my rusty galdr skills, millions of bucks worth of waterfront property, a DOT looking for a deal, the desire to avoid a legal battle with your aunts, and good ole cloak-and-dagger, I'll-scratch-your-back-and-you'll-scratch-mine Florida politics.

"And, if worse comes to worse, that freaky old saboteur Troels Gravesin might just reappear. I think we've got a fighting chance. Now, if we only knew what kind of Powers within Powers, as Verda called it, are influencing the governor. We should find out more about this Lam character Edmund mentioned. Your aunts are sure the gov's just a run-of-the-mill mortal?"

"Pretty sure," she says. "Who really knows? Uncharted waters. Even if they're right, it's dangerous, you know. If we convince the governor to stop pushing for that DOT project, then whoever's been using him to get to my aunts is going to be mightily upset."

"Which might draw whoever it is out," I say. "Anger, revenge, desperation—those are hard to hide."

"So, Hallr, you're saying you want to trigger a frontal attack from somebody who's angry, vengeful, desperate and mighty enough to battle with the Weavers of Fate themselves."

"Well, when you put it like that..." I say. "Strategy was never my strong suit."

She smiles. I suppose I'd slay anything and anybody in any way and at any time for the sake of that smile. Oh, I know I'm an idiot. An idiot hundreds of years old who should know better. Certainly beguiled, likely exploited. Yet here we are.

"It's a lot to sacrifice, Hallr," she says, pulling in close to me and fingering my shirt. "Your home and all the rest."

"Yeah, well, I'll just have to give up my brilliant plans for a giant putt-putt golf course and ten-story water slides that plop sunburned kids into pissed-in pools. A real loss to western culture. Anyway, as you once said, sometimes sacrifices are necessary."

Chapter Thirty-One

"One should show oneself glimpse-wise, and pass like a dream."
—*Peer Gynt*

Just prior to launching the ship, they loaded the box into which I'd packed myself. Someone had bashed a few nails in to secure it, and I'd nearly cried out when one grazed my forehead. That would have been a pitiful end to my absurd saga.

But all went smoothly from there. We sailed on favorable winds and tides. I heard the lines tightening, a flag fluttering, animals scuttling on decking, a goat bleating, crew members chatting, the wooden hull of the ship gently groaning, and water rhythmically rushing by.

The men were enjoying the morning cruise when I knocked on the side of the box. I was in a lousy mood, feeling both banished and vanquished, not to mention ready to piss myself. I vowed I would die before being wedged into another trollbox, even if it meant braving berserker axes and the torments of sunlight.

I was preparing to smash my way out if someone didn't open it. But there was no need. A man soon pried it open with a wrecking bar. I must have looked a fool, all scrunched up like wadded cloth and squinting into the morning light.

Without saying a word, the man bent down to hand me a black cloak, tunic, leggings and hood. These were neither the battle clothes that had first been made for me nor the robes that had been ripped off Ornolf the night before. These were richly woven, the type of quality cloth worn by kings and jarls. The hood did not have the rough iron wiring of my previous one. It was more like a fine mesh woven of silver threads, a true work of art.

The man turned his back as I clumsily donned the clothing in the shadows of the crate. When I was done, I tried to stand up tall to impress and intimidate the crew but, not yet having my sea legs under me, only managed to trip and fall onto the deck.

To his credit, the man neither cracked a smile nor looked dismayed. He just reached down to lend me a hand. It was a small gesture but one that, except for Leos, no other person had ever made to me. I grabbed his hand and pulled myself out and up.

"Thank you," I said. "You're the captain?"

"No, sir," he said. "My name is Thorolf, and I'm your skipper."

I tried to keep my face impassive. His words implied that I was the captain and, therefore, owner of the ship. Inge had been true to her word.

Thorolf was our modern era's romanticized stereotype of a heroic-looking Viking, like an actor delivered by central casting. He was a large, blond-haired man in his mid-thirties, complete with blue eyes, a strong profile, and broad shoulders.

Ignoring the stares of the crew, he showed me around the ship.

"It is for you to name her, of course," he said. "Till now, we've just been calling her *Kaupmaðr.*" It was the word for trader, a generic name used as a placeholder.

"I like the simplicity," I said. "Let's keep it."

Despite their fine craftsmanship, the new clothes could not make me comfortable in the sunlight. In fact, the glare and burning were almost intolerable, but my pride would not allow me to seek shade or shelter. It was bad enough I had to dress like some cloaked ghoul in front of my crew.

"Would you care to take the steering oar, Captain?" Thorolf asked. I looked for a hint of parody in his voice, but found none. He was an altogether unique Viking, in my experience.

"Yes, thank you," I said. "I will after I speak with the crew."

We were sailing westward. The rising sun was still astern, so I stood as much in the shadow cast by the sternpost as I could. Removing my hood, I faced the crew.

"My name is Eirik Sturlung," I said. "You have no doubt heard the rumors that King Alfr's troll slew King Bloodaxe in an act of retribution."

There were some approving murmurings. Dofri had, after all, chosen men who hated the Bloodaxe clan.

"Because of my size and appearance, I am sometimes mistaken for Alfr's troll. As a result, I have been required to hide myself from the new king's soldiers. Just as they attacked Ornolf the Oaf last night, they would also attack me."

Ornolf, who was sitting up toward the bow, smiled through his puffy, badly bruised face at the mention of his name.

"As you can see, however, I stand here in front of you in the light of day. If I were a true troll, I would turn to stone in front of your very eyes. Isn't that true?"

A few of the crew nodded. Most just continued staring.

"I am, however, sensitive to the sun's rays on such a long voyage and so wear garments such as these. They are another reason some have mistaken me for Alfr's troll."

Although they didn't look convinced, no one argued or interrupted.

"Okay," I said, pointing to a man in front of me. "What is my name?"

"Eirik Sturlung," he said.

"Right," I said. "We will be traveling and trading far and wide together. If anyone were to believe I was Alfr's troll, we would all become suspect. King Sunmane's ships might give chase, and we would be hard put to escape from the fierce, fast, dragon ships. Does anyone here wish to be made a thrall to Sunmane or cut up like baitfish for the new king's amusement?"

"Nay," goes up a shout from maybe half the crew.

"Good," I said. "We have that straight. Now, do any of you have questions?"

No one said a word. They just looked at one another. A young man in the cargo bay piped up.

"Is it true you took a chomp out of the Bloodaxe head?" he asked.

Emboldened, the man next to him asked, "How did he taste?"

The others started chuckling, and even I had to smile.

"You two," I barked, pointing to the two men. "What's my name?"

"Eirik Sturlung," they answered.

"Am I Alfr's troll?"

"No," they answered.

"Remember that," I ordered. "I would guess he tasted like the maggoty corpse of a rabid skunk, the kind of filth no self-respecting troll could swallow."

I grinned, and most of the sailors laughed. It almost made the burning in my eyes and searing pain on the back of my neck worth it. I wished Inge could see us. Maybe, I thought, I wasn't a complete idiot to spurn the beckoning mountains after all.

Chapter Thirty-Two

"May I be a troll if I understand what it was that dazed and bemused me so."
—*Peer Gynt*

Time passes now, but slowly, slowly. Like hurricane season in the tropics. The days might be still, hot and sunny. The radar might be clear, and satellites as high as space might not spot a single cloud. Yet always there's that air of anticipation, the wariness of the grazing prey animal awaiting the predator, the fear of a great and terrible storm.

The court case against the Norlands is delayed until further notice, the DOT has reportedly shelved the plan for the time being, and the governor has stopped taking the calls of the once-confident and now-nervous Peter Gunty. There's been, however, no final decision.

It's as if two equally strong hands and arms were locked together, exerting incredible force, and yet the result is only stillness, the impression of rest made all the more disquieting by its utter falsity.

I receive a friendly note from Governor Tosser. Edmund and I have drinks together a few times. I sell a half acre of land and donate the proceeds to Tosser's newly created Might for Right political action committee. I'm even invited to a luncheon with the governor and several other donors to his PAC. We never discuss land or development. Everyone looks at me out of the corner of their eyes, fascinated and appalled.

I ask the governor about his advisor, Lam, but he only looks sideways into space, as if he were trying to remember something but just couldn't. He says the name is somehow familiar but he can't put a face to it. I'm not sure if he's being cagey or if something has been plucked from his mind like an orange from a tree. It worries me.

To me, the Great Tree seems greener of late. Every day, the two old jotnar reverently rub white clay onto its exposed roots. Yet many of the tree's leaves are still outlined in yellow, and some patches of bark still seem on the brink of decay.

Hild Brands continues its consulting work. Our little team—Fred, Misty, Hildy and myself—is not disbanded, but it meets less often. Hildy gives us access to all kinds of training materials—e-books, videos, online tutorials and the like—on the subject of Florida ecology and environmental law.

Fred and I learn the basics of state agriculture, the aquifer, invasive species, disrupted ecosystems, etc. We get the details of how Corps of Engineers projects have drained water out of the "river of grass" that is the Everglades and why Florida Bay has grown so salty. We watch time-lapse videos of evaporating seagrasses and coral reefs turning a bony, bleached white.

Misty, who studied some of this at university, takes pleasure in explaining things to Fred, who absorbs facts as readily as tropics absorb rainstorms. She says it's easy for him because all this information was originally baked into him as a bona fide Florida redneck. Still, I can see there's something bothering her. It's not sulkiness, per se. More like a distracted sadness.

Hildy spends much of her free time in Haven. I've been joining her on the weekends. I still don't quite grasp her role. She does household chores, but the truth is, Urdy and Verda are quite clean, orderly and self-sufficient. Hildy sometimes helps care for their enormous tree, but she's more of an apprentice than an expert. I sense her main role is to provide protection and perspective. Hildy understands the outside world better than they, even though they are, if I choose to believe it, helping to compose its very fabric. Hildy is a kind of bridge to humanity. And she is a warrior, of course, trained and bred for battle.

Today we are just going about our normally abnormal lives. The aunts are closely examining the bark of Yggdrasil, seeking patterns that were not there even minutes before. Hildy and I are dangling our feet in the spring, taking turns reading Seamus Heaney's translation of *Beowulf.*

The story pisses me off because you never find out about Grendel's murderous motives for attacking Hrothgar's banqueters. He's depicted as just a "prowler through the dark" who "nursed a hard grievance." Hildy laughs and points to the line about how "it harrowed him to hear the din of the loud banquet every day in the hall." She says that's explanation enough and that the story is the story—I shouldn't second guess it. I argue that I've got every right to second guess some anonymously written Norse epic handed down through the generations. I assert King Hrothgar must have done more to Grendel than just hold wild parties.

"Maybe Hrothgar was wrecking the local fens and the marshes," I say. "Ever think of that?"

"So Grendel was an eco-terrorist?" she mocks.

I'm about to counter with my Grendel-as-the-king's-illegitimate-son theory, when a commotion erupts in the hallway behind us. Aunt Verda and Urdy cry out in surprise: "Skuld!"

Surprise? Visitors never surprise the aunts. Few can locate them without a map and invitation. Once in a while, lost strangers stumble across the boundaries of their property, whereupon they develop a great uneasiness and promptly turn around.

No trespasser or guest in Haven goes unnoticed. The aunts always sense someone coming, as if they can literally feel the brush that visitors push aside and the path they walk. Even Hildy has learned to discern intruders from afar.

So, Hildy and I are alarmed when we hear the aunts cry out. We turn to see Verda and a considerably smaller person embrace one another. When they pull back, I see a youngish looking woman, maybe mid-thirties, with stylishly cut, dark, short hair. There are multiple layers of cherry-colored hues to her bangs.

Her clothes are startlingly chic. I imagine the labels inside have French and Italian names I've scarcely heard of. She sports a black cloak over a blue-and-black flowered blouse. Black leggings and fringy-looking ankle boots complete the outfit. But the most striking thing about her is the sunglasses, which give her a kind of Audrey Hepburn in *Breakfast at Tiffany's* look.

After Verda, Urdy also hugs her long-lost sister, though more formally, like a grandmother being polite to her granddaughter. Then Aunt Skuldy turns to Hildy, who has approached tentatively, looking as shy, star-struck and smitten as I've ever seen her.

"Aunt Skuldy," she says, warmly embracing her. "I'm so very glad and relieved to see you! It's been so long."

"Lovely to see you as well, Hildy darling," she says, though her smile looks tight and thin-lipped to me. Her accent is posh, as if she'd been educated at a Swiss boarding school.

When Hildy introduces me, I feel like a turd under a microscope. It's not that Aunt Skuldy is outwardly contemptuous. She just seems to be trying to mask her repugnance, holding out only the tips of her four fingers to me to shake.

Next, she approaches Yggdrasil.

"Still yellowing a bit, I see," she says, laying her palm on the Great Tree, which I could swear shivers in return. "Poor old thing."

"We do what we can," Aunt Urdy says with surprising coldness in the Old Tongue.

Verda smiles. "Now that you're home, all will be well."

"Oh, I don't know if I can stay, dear," Skuldy says, dismissively. "My studies continue, you know. I just wanted to stop by and see how things are getting along without me."

"You can't be serious," Verda says. "Yggdrasil needs you, Skuld, needs all of us together."

"Oh, nonsense Verda, we both know Yggdrasil was on the decline well before I left. I often doubt I make any contribution at all. Beside, you've got Hildr here now," Skuldy says. "I'm sure she's doing wonderfully."

"I could never replace you, Aunt Skuldy," says Hildy.

"No," she says, with a quick, prim smile. "I suppose not, but I'm sure you're doing your very best, dear."

There's an awkward pause. I can't decide if Skuldy is mocking Hildy, or just patronizing her. Either way, she's got my blood boiling.

"Oh, I know I've been a burden to my family," she says, directing her remarks to Verda. "But I am so enjoying life. Haven't I, haven't we *all*, earned a respite? I suggest going on a nice cruise and letting someone else tend the Old Tree for a little while. How about little Andre? Is he still in the neighborhood? Oh, there's this amazing Mediterranean voyage that is just to die for. Menus by Geoffrey Zakarianv, a splendid chef, and the wines are simply ambrosia."

Unable to take any more of this, Aunt Verda dashes away, nearly in tears. It's alarming. I've never seen Verda anything other than level-headed. Surprisingly, it is Urdy who maintains her cool.

"I know it is hard, sister," she says in the Old Tongue. "For you most of all. To weave a future of chewed roots and poisoned waters."

"Oh, such nonsense, old sweet Urdy. It's only hard because the inept mortals drag things out so. They can't even destroy themselves properly. It's embarrassing, really."

"You've always lacked patience, sister. Tides rise and tides fall."

"Have I? Or perhaps you've always had an overabundance. But let's not quarrel. All I really want is to soak in a hot tub for hours. Then we can have a bite to eat and catch up."

She gives us a little wave, grabs the handle of her designer luggage on wheels, and saunters away humming a tune. Wagner maybe?

Hildy and I strip the sheets off Aunt Skuldy's bed, make it up again, collect our things, and move them up to a smaller bedroom on the second floor. Hildy is silent except for the instructions she gives me about where to put things. Eventually, though, I can't take it.

"Was that as weird as I thought it was?" I ask her.

She shakes her head, not trusting herself to speak. Skuldy's condescension was hurtful, but I know that's not all that's upsetting her.

"Traveling can make people cranky," I offer.

"She can't leave them again, Hallr. She's needed here."

I nod. If they all believe she's needed, who am I to argue? A trollish nobody in a house full of gods and legends.

"She sure has flair," I say. "I know this is probably a dumb question, but why is she so human-sized? I once wore a bathrobe in her closet, and it was big enough to fit me."

"You think I can be changeable, even volatile?" she asks. "I'm nothing compared to Aunt Skuldy. She shifts shapes the way other people change clothes. And moody doesn't begin to describe her. She may seem capricious to others, Hallr, but her family knows her. We make allowances because, in the end, we love her and appreciate how indispensable she is."

I already knew I was way out of my league. This just confirms it. I should get out of here to let the divine jotunn types sort things out on their own.

I won't, though, at least not until I understand things better. Amid all this raw family emotion, I can't find a way to bring up the obvious point that Skuldy is one of the few beings that could take on her sisters. If she were the hidden enemy, would Urdy and Verda know? But why attack her own kin? It's worse than Grendel attacking the "lofty house" of Hrothgar. The motivation makes no sense.

Skuldy's been back for days now. Hildy took time off to be with her. I have a bad feeling about it. Maybe I'm just jealous; Hildy clearly has an acute case of hero worship. Or perhaps I'm afraid that Skuldy's repugnance for me will rub off on her.

I'm relieved when Hildy rings me and asks if I can visit again tomorrow, Saturday. She sounds melancholy. I suppose that means the ladies of legend haven't worked through their family issues.

When I arrive, Hildy is waiting on the porch, a large, straw, beach bag by her side. I don't know if this portends good or ill. She runs and embraces me, tears in her eyes. I ask what's wrong. She just takes me by the hand, and we walk deep into the forest. She pulls a blanket out of her bag, lays it down, and she makes love to me with a kind of volcanism, a release of magma-force emotions.

Afterwards, she questions me about what has been happening in the offices. I give her what little scuttlebutt I know, though I can see she's not truly interested.

Out of nowhere, she says, "Skuldy says I should leave."

"Leave Haven?"

"Leave Florida, Haven, my aunts, my job, you, everything."

"Why?"

"She says that, since she's back, I can be free. She doesn't want me to be a prisoner to my fate, as she has been."

"You feel like a prisoner?"

"Doesn't everyone sometimes?"

I let that statement roll around awhile. I've been an actual prisoner at times in my life. There's a difference between that and what she's talking about.

"The thing is, I feel less like a prisoner now than I have so many other times in my life. You'll think I'm going soft, but I feel needed and loved here."

"And so you should," I say.

With that, she rolls back toward me, and we make love again, this time without the hot embers and molten slag. Afterwards, I feel slightly reassured but am also apprehensive we may yet be fated for a deluge of cinders and ash.

Chapter Thirty-Three

"I have only one story left, and that one I dare not tell, and that is the
story of your travels."
—*The Tale of the Story-Wise Icelander*

I pondered whether I should kill my navigator Bjor as the *Kaupmaðr*
bobbed over the small whitecaps along the coast of volcano-ridden
Iceland.

A few days before then, he'd asked me to promise to spare him if
he helped us reach Iceland. I had told him I'd already made enough
idiotic pledges for one lifetime, and I'd be damned if I'd promise him
anything other than a quick death. He'd helped us anyway.

Everyone but Bjor was in good spirits as we approached Iceland.
The winds were still with us, and our skald Skylar Bard started chanting what had become the crew's favorite song: "The Fate of Thorolf
the Brave." I looked over to see if Bjor would grimace or roll his
eyes, but he gave no indication. Still, we knew he must secretly abhor
it. I'd stopped paying attention to the song after the first couple of
occasions, but as we approached Iceland and I pondered whether to
slit Bjor's throat, I listened hard in the hope it would help me decide.

Several days before, we'd been a half-day's sail northeast of the Orkney Islands when Kol had spotted a red sail. It belonged to the *Naorbita*, the dragon ship that Kol and I had narrowly escaped. Our current ship seemed like a fat, slow goose by comparison to Sunmane's *Naorbita*. Skylar Bard's song got that part right.

The sail of Sunmane's ship appeared
Sharp as a dagger on the sea.
Keen-eyed young Kol
First spotted the killer.
Kaupmaðr's crew cursed
The weak currents of wind.
As forty rowing warriors
Aimed their prow westward
Like a fleet hawk flying toward
A floundering, wounded goose.

I knew well that King Sunmane was not the forgiving type. I'd done him the service of slaying his father and bringing him to the throne, but I'd also infuriated him by profaning Bloodaxe's dishonorable corpse and then having the bad grace to escape with my life. It made him look weak. He would go far to murder me, including sending his flagship out to hunt us.

Stalwart Captain Sturlung schemed
with thoughtful Skipper Thorolf.
Fleeing would only signal fear,
they fatefully agreed.
Better to calmly crawl along
the flat ocean's cool edge.
A harmless wave horse
heedless of danger from dragons.
Even as our cunning captain
crept into the whale's home.

On the day of the battle with *Naorbita*, the water had been icy cold, sucking my breath away when I first dropped over the side of the ship.

But trolls can stand cold better than men. At the time, our skipper Thorolf and I were still hopeful that the Bloodaxe crew would search our ship and then, not finding a troll, would sail off to seek me elsewhere.

> *Our hidden hero awaited fate,*
> *hanging on an uncut thread.*
> *Soon Sunmane's ship Naorbita*
> *slithered darkly starboard.*
> *"Convey the king-killer troll*
> *from its wooden cave,"*
> *boldly cried Captain Bjor,*
> *bringer of Hildr's storm.*
> *The dread dragon spat forth*
> *determined children of battle.*

Bjor's boarding party had forced every member of my crew to stand up. When they saw hulking Ornulf, they thought they had their prize. Enraged by not finding me, Bjor decided to take our whole crew captive. That poor decision unleashed what Skylar called "Hildr's storm," the kenning for a bloody battle.

> *Yet Bjor's men met no mountain giant*
> *mightily though they searched.*
> *"Begone you bringers of bane,"*
> *shouted the Trader's brave skipper.*
> *The wroth soldier of the sorcerer's son*
> *unleashed his Surtr's blaze.*
> *"Plunder these poor men," he cried,*
> *"and punish them with thralldom."*
> *Outraged by odious injustice,*
> *courageous Thorolf onrushed.*

When Captain Bjor told my crew he was taking them captive, he'd drawn his sword or, as the song would have it, "Surtr's blaze." It was a mistake because it spurred Thorolf to charge him even though the only weapon our skipper had was a long knife.

Despite his size and appearance, Thorolf had not been the warrior type. He'd been a thoughtful man who loved sailing for its own sake, not as a means of pillaging. He had preferred trade to battle. I suppose that in another age, or given a different birth, he would have been a scholar or explorer.

In contrast, Bjor was a killer by both birth and nature. I doubt he was as sadistic and twisted as Grim had been, but he loved battle. He had long brown hair, a thin face and hazel eyes. He was lanky, tall and strong. Maybe Thorolf had an inch and a few pounds on him, but Bjor's training made him more than a match for our skipper.

As the shield din sounded,
the two ships split.
Strong and sturdy Sturlung,
mightily shoving them asunder.
Still swimming in whale's pond,
our captain grasped the serpent's tail.
His fist a fatal bone-break,
fearless Sturlung smote.
The worm's wood screamed
as the frozen sea flooded in.

Scores of Sunmane sailors
sang out in sorrow.
More blows bludgeoned the worm,
writhing in floods of Ymir's blood.
Fearful shield-gnawers screamed,
then sank as sudden shark's food.
Some swimmers kicked for Kaupmaðr,
but were clinched in Sturlung's kingly grip.
Soon all the serpent's sons floated
motionless in Ymir's slaughter dew.

When the two crew joined in battle, I pushed the ships apart to keep ours from being overwhelmed. Then I punched holes in their hull, a feat that would have been impossible for me if I hadn't been desperate and enraged. I didn't even try for stealth. I'm still astonished no one caught me flush with a spear.

Eventually, I'd been able to tear a hunk out of their hull. Once Bjor's crew was in the water with me, a couple of their berserkers slashed me with knives. But most of them carried axes, which were next to useless in the water if I swam below the surface. From there, I yanked down legs. They were surprisingly easy to drown.

Clashes coursed on Kaupmaðr
as Sunmane's crow-feeders raged.
Brave Thorolf drew his wound wand,
wielding against the blaze of Bjor.
The two warriors death danced,
both drinking wolf's wine.
Both bloodied they spilled
from the ship to bathe in the waves.
Moved by Thorolf's mettle,
Kaupmaðr's crew stormed.

Climbing the curving branches of arms
Sturlung reclaimed his wind-horse.
Clad only in red-lusting rage
the captain joined the death dance.
He yanked a wriggling arm from one worm son,
wrenched the weak neck of a second.
Though bathed in battle sweat,
the decks were cleared of worm babes.
As the valiant crew of Kaupmaðr cheered,
the captain searched for its skipper.

Aside from Thorolf, three of our crew had been killed in the battle. It could have been a lot worse if Bjor would have thought to bring on more men to search the ship. That, and underestimating Thorolf, was his biggest tactical mistake.

Closely scanning the swan land
Sturlung found only Thorolf's foe.
Half-dead he was from dancing,
weakly paddling in the drink of whales.
Cunning Sturlung snatched his shocks,
yanking the vanquished snake aboard.
"You've killed my counsel giver,
you contemptible dog," he yelled.
"A wise warrior that was to you
as the sun to a glowing bug."

The line about glowing bugs was just poetic license. I'm not too big on sun metaphors. I probably did call him a cur or something, though. I was incensed. Not only did I need my skipper Thorolf to navigate, he was among the few human men I'd liked and admired. It's a miracle I didn't kill Bjor. If he'd been more than semi-conscious, I would have. Still, there was that little inner voice—my mother's, no doubt—urging me to be cunning. An astute troll values his assets, and that son of a bitch Bjor was an asset.

After Thorolf had been killed, we had no navigator. Our best option, young Kol, didn't know the waters north of the Orkneys. Bjor had not only been up as far as the Faroes but, he claimed, had spent time conversing with skippers and captains who had been to Iceland.

As we approached Reykjavík, though, Bjor was no longer of value. In fact, he was a threat. I never admitted to him that I was Alfr's troll, and he never claimed I was. There was no doubt in his mind, however, of my identity. He'd tell the Icelanders who I was, and he'd be able to send word to Sunmane that I'd survived.

Of course, my identity would be an open secret anyway. The men of Iceland were not naive Americans who, a millennium hence, would not even believe in trolls, much less recognize one. If nothing else, Skylar Bard's song would give me away. I suppose I could have slain the skald as well, but where would the killing stop? Men drink and tell stories. There's no power in the world that can keep them from it.

As for Bjor, he was a jarl by birth, had been the flagship captain and, like Grim, was a navigator. In other words, he was smart, proud, dangerous and not to be underestimated. I knew it was best to kill him but it was also tempting for me, a former thrall, to humiliate him, taking a modicum of vengeance on all his arrogant kind.

So, before we landed, I called Bjor to the bow. "I am Eirik Sturlung, not the one you were sent to seek. You will not tell me or anyone else otherwise. Do you agree?" He nodded and swore an oath.

In the end, I let him live. I wound up selling him to a landowner who had fled Norway to escape Bloodaxe. The man was amused by the idea of keeping the jarl as a thrall, and he agreed to keep the disgraced captain for at least two years before ransoming Bjor back to his family. That was my small gesture to the memory of Thorolf the Brave. As it turned out, killing him would have been the wiser course.

Chapter Thirty-Four

"Gluttony is not a secret vice."
—Orson Welles

I've been invited for dinner. Though I've spent a lot of time with the aunts already, we've never had a formal sit-down, complete with china and silverware. In fact, now that I think about it, I've never seen the aunts do more than drink tea. I imagine it's Skuldy's idea, another habit picked up during her travels among mortals.

Maybe the habits of Urdy and Verda have rubbed off on me. Trolls love to eat, live to eat. We have huge bodies to fuel, so the legends are well founded. We do consume whole goats and horses and, when feeling surly, human beings. Of course, we also eat fruits, grains, vegetables and the other trapezoidal building blocks of the food pyramid, but what we crave most are those dense, energy-rich pockets of protein known as meat. Lovely, lovely meat.

On top of that, trolls are the original stress eaters. Try being shunned and hunted by ignorant, giant-hating humans all your life. Not to mention dealing with sundry other magic-wielding members of the family of fae. Trolls were never the cool kids in that group. In fact, the many sins of the imps, elves, pixies, sprites and the like are often blamed on innocent trolls. Oh, I'm not saying trolls are angels, but they definitely serve as the proverbial (and often actual) whipping boys of Midgard.

Then there's the good, honest employment of toll collecting. Everybody hates paying tolls. So trolls tend to be about as popular as lawyers and tax collectors. It's a hard life, and food is one of the few recompenses.

Yet, since I've gotten to know Hildy and her aunts, the urge to binge has dropped away. That could just be a result of the humming seidr in this house of weirdness. But maybe it's something else: a sense of belonging or purpose or ardor for a vanquished valkyrie. Regardless, the flabs of belt-stressing fat have receded like a tide, leaving behind a svelter version of the troll stereotype.

So I'm surprised by how hungry the smell of cooking lamb has made me. Aunt Skuldy is waltzing around the kitchen like some dancer from The Nutcracker, literally swishing past me in an elegant Parisian-style apron printed with stylized black-and-white phases of the moon. There's the slightest whiff of perfume as she moves. I'd say she was flirting, if I didn't already know she detests me.

As the four of us sit at a long table covered with starched white linen, she serves us wine in silver chalices, the likes of which I haven't seen in hundreds of years. Thick, heavy chalices that actually have a few dents in them, indicating they're the real deal. I'd never been to a decent Norse feast where somebody didn't toss their silver chalice at somebody.

The wine is red and thick as blood, and even sweeter to the palate. I've never tasted anything quite like it. I'm not, however, much of a wine guy. In the Northlands, real wine was rare because grapes seldom grew at such latitudes. We imported it, making it an expensive libation only the jarls and hersirs could afford.

"How do you like the wine, Hallr dear?" asks Aunt Skuldy, standing next to me. She insisted I sit at the head of the table because I am, as she calls me, their honored guest. I sense sarcasm, though it's hidden deep as darkness.

"It's, um, fine," I say.

"Oh, yes," she says, speaking disconcertingly close to my right ear. "Very fine indeed. From the Rhinelands, as an old one like you remembers. Yet it's something new from the clever mortals. They call it Trockenbeerenauslese. They deem it a dessert wine, but why wait till our appetites are dulled? Besides, I have something even more toothsome planned for our last course. It's quite luscious, don't you think?"

"Very sweet."

"Very sweet," she says, standing up near my shoulder again. "You see, the berries were dried and shriveled and rotten with botrytis. You know it? A necrotrophic fungus that slowly kills. So slowly. If the berries are crushed in just the right state of death, they can be made into this nectar of the gods."

As she speaks, I can nearly see the plump grapes wither before my eyes.

"Intoxicating," she says, laying her hand on my shoulder. "Don't you think, Hildy dear?"

Hildy. I'd almost forgotten about Hildy, who sits one chair removed from me on the left. She's upset. No, she's angry. Or something. It's becoming harder for me to tell as Skuldy whisks in and out of the room, bringing in the various dishes. Oysters as big as a human palm. A steaming cream of barley and mushroom soup served in delicate-looking glass bowls, which are painted with silver highlights in the style of the gripping beast. I know it's irrational, but I fear the glass will break before I can eat my soup. I scoop quickly, my spoon ringing against the glass. Glancing up, I see Skuldy beaming like a happy mother. Urdy watches as if I were a crawling bug. No, this must look bad. Slow down. I try hard to slow down.

"Sister," says Urdy. "You make Hildy unhappy and the troll more befuddled than is his wont. Put away your arts."

"Oh, Urd. You've always been too serious. Mortals enjoy their intoxications," Skuldy says, looking into the eyes of Aunt Urdy, who is as tall sitting as Skuld is standing. "You are enjoying yourself, Hallr, yes?"

The smell of the lamb is making me ache. Oh gods, the spices! I smell every sliver of garlic, fleck of pepper, leaf of rosemary. I'm salivating so hard that I hesitate to speak for fear of drooling.

"Yes," I say, after some delay, though a part of me senses it's not the right answer.

Finally the meat arrives. As she serves the leg of lamb on a large silver tray, Aunt Skuldy manages to rub her breasts against my left shoulder. Those warm, soft breasts and the lovely, large leg of lamb are so beautifully fused in my imagination, I almost weep at the sublime art of it.

Someone calls my name. Several times, I think.

"Hallr!" Hildy says loudly, nearly shouting.

"Yeah, here I am," I say, dazedly. "Sorry, what was that?"

Hildy stares. Is that menace in her eyes? Why would she ruin this wonderful moment with her thunder? They've asked me to carve. Oh, yes, carve. I need to share this meat. Share with others. The concept strikes me as so cruel, another slight against trolls everywhere. But I do, of course. I take up the silver serving fork and push it deep into the leg. The gorgeous reddish essence of the lamb spurts and trickles out of the impalement. I'm tempted, sorely tempted, to bend down and suck at those holes to draw more out, to drain the leg dry of the melding of blood and fat.

I don't, though. I'm in control. I'm civil. I cut several slices, letting them fall to the side of the great silver platter like vanquished foes. Foes whose hearts I must eat. Mor would want me to gorge on them. Refusing would be disrespectful, churlish even. So I stab at the thickest wedge, heaving it to my plate, cutting it and finally, oh finally, bringing it to my lips. Arg help me, it is beyond delicious. Skuldy is a generous genius with stunning legs and breasts like fresh baked bread.

I eat, and eat, and eat.

There's a voice in my head now. Shut up voice, can't you see we are feasting, that this is an occasion, that I am an honored guest? But Mimir's ill-timed whisperings will not relent.

Troll, he says. *Poor, paltry excuse for a giant, the dregs of a once-great race. Look around you, you ridiculous relic. See how their eyes mirror your gluttony back like burnished bronze.*

Slowly, reluctantly, I turn my face up and away from the exquisite, enchanting meat. Their plates are still empty, pristine as old bones in the desert. The right corner of Skuldy's lips are twisted up in a subtle simper, Hildy's face is turning a disquieting crimson, Urdy still stares stonily, and Verda is doing her best to politely avert her eyes by rearranging the napkin on her lap.

Suddenly the meat turns to ashes in my mouth. I take a drink of the wine just so I can swallow.

"I, um, guess I forgot to serve," I mumble, but the tone is all wrong, like a resentful child, not at all what I intended.

I begin to serve what's left of the leg of lamb onto their passed plates, shuttling them back to the women whose appetites I must have already ruined. A troll at the dinner table of gods. How did I get here?

Calling up every reserve of discipline I've managed to acquire over a long, harsh life, I serve the ladies and then stand up, forcing my chair back clumsily.

"My apologies," I say slowly, determined not to slur. "I find I'm a bit under the weather. You must excuse me."

No one says a word. Verda gives me a small, forced smile for the sake of politeness. I turn away, headed for the room Hildy and I share, but then turn back.

There's so much left to say. That I am not the clod I appear to be, that Hildy must not be sent from her sanctuary, that the wine is too damned sweet, that necrotrophic fungus harms the souls of trolls, that Skuldy is a terrible artist bitch of unholy beauty, that the Great Tree may yet be saved, that the spring is cool and lovely and alive.

Instead, I bow my head slightly to Skuldy, saying, "Thank you, for the excellent meal."

Time for bed. I just need to doze a while. Sleep cures all.

I'm sitting alone at a table in a crowded, noisy restaurant. It's a round table with a white linen tablecloth. A fancy set of silver forks, spoons and knives are all laid out. A white napkin has been folded like a pyramid and placed so it stands in front of me.

For some reason, I have an erection. A big one, which is embarrassing in a public place like this. It pushes up the edge of the tablecloth, forming another linen pyramid above the table. I push it down, which smarts like hell, so that it's wedged up against the underside of the table.

But then the table itself begins to rise. I don't know what to do. Before, I thought I saw a cooked pheasant under glass. Now I recognize that it's Mimir's head. He's trying to get my attention, but I'm still focused on the erection. People in the restaurant are starting to look.

The table is seriously tilting now. Mimir's head is shaking back and forth. I can't hear what he's saying from inside the glass but his words are easy to make out, "No! No! No!" No to what? I stand up, intent on lifting the dome from over his head. Stupid, because when I stand up, the table falls over onto its side.

Suddenly it's dark except for a spotlight shining down on the round table. Table? It's not a table at all. It's a woman's rounded, white buttocks pushed up toward me.

A gorgeous ass presented to me, Hildy waiting for me to enter from behind, a balm for my still aching hard-on. I penetrate her with great relief, placing my hands on her hips to draw her toward me.

She moans, but I can't see her face. It's turned downward and is in darkness. I enter again and again. It's bliss and yet… something's wrong. Who is this? Who do I want it to be?

As she arches her back, her head comes up and I see Skuldy's hair, complete with cherry-colored hue on top. Then a strong beam of light shines in my face. It's a door opening. Someone is in the doorframe watching us.

There's a scream. I jolt awake. The light is real. It blazes down on Hildy and me as we make love. I am on my knees, while her head is bowed down toward the foot of the bed, gasping. The scream becomes a roar. I'm trying hard to understand, still dazed, still in the grip of the erotic dream when the blow comes. I'm smashed in the face with a fist of iron, thrown back hard against the oaken headboard of the bed. That I'm under attack is clear but the who and the why isn't.

I hold up my arms, trying to shield myself from the blows and, if I'm being honest, the reality of what's happening. There's Hildy standing over me and shouting, yet there's also Hildy kneeling on the bed. I'm bashed again as if by a thunderbolt. I'm barely maintaining consciousness.

The door slams and the wood explodes, splintering.

Then there's laughter, the kind where a person is having an uncontrollable fit but trying to do it quietly. Skuldy. She's standing naked at the foot of the bed. It was her. Her in the dream. Her in the bed.

"Why?" I ask.

"Because you're a troll, of course, an unrestrained brute, no more human than a rutting moose. The poor girl was thinking you were something else. She needed to be shown otherwise. And you ably did so. Now, if you don't mind, I have some troll stink to wash off."

Chapter Thirty-Five

"Bard had prepared there a banquet for the king; and there was to be there a
sacrifice to the guardian spirits."
—*Egil's Saga*

Iceland was my halfway house for learning how to pass as human.
The heaps of silver from Inge helped. When I first arrived, I was
able to gift a number of the most prominent Icelandic chieftains in
the Southwest with precious metals, jewelry and practical trade goods
(tools, livestock, seeds, etc.). This encouraged them to overlook the
rampant hearsay and trollish features.

Most publicly welcomed me as a freeman of means, even if derid-
ing me in private. Some, though, seemed legitimately friendly, view-
ing me as a living symbol of rebellion against the growing power of
Sunmane. Every time he won another battle in Norway—and he won
many—chieftains, jarls, and hersirs scattered like coveys of ravens
startled into flight. Many flew to Iceland, where they nursed their
grudges for decades.

Of course, a few referred to me as the Halftroll and resented the
fact that a known outlaw and suspected king-killer was permitted
to acquire farmland and fisheries. I tried to avoid their animosity by

claiming land further north at a time when most of the colonists craved the green lands south and east of today's Reykjavik.

My lands, located near the Eldborg crater, contained rich, volcanic soils. And I had some unique advantages as a farmer. For one thing, I could work all through the dark winter months, when most colonists were still huddled in their halls and huts. In fact, I relished going out into the bitter cold of darkness to haul the large rocks out of my soon-to-be fields and build large cairns with them along the roads and paths I blazed. I had plans to charge tolls along those roads one day, having learned the business from Mor.

It was the first time in my life when I was truly on my own and in control of my destiny. No mother to protect and demean me, no king to command or condemn me. It was both thrilling and confusing, as I strove to find my way even while hiding aspects of my true nature.

I strove to be a good neighbor to my fellow westerners, as we called ourselves, most of whom were hard but hearty men willing to strike out on their own. I liked such men. They reminded me of the trollfolk of my youth: strong, reclusive, bull-headed and brave. Though they liked their solitude, most were willing to help in times of need, even if their neighbor did bear an unsettling resemblance to the kobolds of their homelands.

One of the first of these farmer-chieftains I got to know was a middle-aged man named Asmund. We met during the long, dark winter nights when the temperatures seldom rose above freezing. I had dug and hauled stones for hours, pulling along a sledge to one of the largest cairns I'd built. I reveled in it: the snow and ice crunching under my boots, my breath steaming like the vapors over hot springs, my back and shoulders growing hard with the simple, brutal labor. I was piling rocks and boulders on the cairn when Asmund appeared.

He had no wish to surprise me. Surprising a man in the wilderness could be deadly in those days. So he stomped his feet as he approached. I was surprised to see a lone man out in the middle of my lands amid such darkness. He wore fine fox and mink furs, a rich cloak and expensive brooches, so I knew at a glance he was no thrall or common workman.

Nor was he the type to waste time on flowery greetings.

"I'm your neighbor, Asmund," he said by way of greeting. "You're the Halftroll."

I wasn't pleased with the Halftroll tag, since I'd gone to great lengths to put it behind me.

"Eirik Sturlung," I said.

We stood there in the frozen wastelands for a time, not saying a word. I went back to slinging rocks off my sledge as he watched. Although he wore a sword, I felt no menace in the man.

After some time in silence, I asked, "What brings you out so early in the morning?"

"Needed the air," he said. "Don't sleep much anymore."

"Huh," I said. He'd must have walked twelve miles by himself through a hazardous landscape.

"Come to my farm on Yule," he said. It was an offer from a man accustomed to giving orders. I considered it at length as I worked. It was an honor but also a potential trap.

"Thank you. If I come, I must sacrifice to Ymir," I said, not looking at him as I tossed an especially large rock up high onto the nine foot cairn.

Asmund also took his time responding, as if our conversation were set to the pace of the local glaciers. He bent down and threw a stone onto the cairn, which I took as either a sign of politeness or an aggression. Maybe both.

"And Odin," he said.

I thought about this. Could I sacrifice to that tricky, well-traveled murderer of giants? If I really were half-human, a prospect I still didn't entirely accept, then my father would have worshipped the one-eyed Aesir king—as did all my neighbors in that new world.

"All right," I said.

Asmund nodded, our negotiations at an end.

"Farewell," he said.

I nodded in return, and he walked off into the icy darkness.

Chapter Thirty-Six

"Angry at this insult, Skuld proudly rose and declared that her sister's gifts would be of no avail…"
—*Myths of the Norsemen*

I can't find her. She's not at her apartment and hasn't checked in with the office. After a few days without hearing from her, her Chief of Operations called the police and reported her missing. They've come up empty as well.

I've asked Fred and Misty to do what they can to find her. Misty's been spending every day at her computer looking for some kind of electronic trail. Fred has been playing detective, riding his bike all over the city, speaking with Hildy's landlord, chasing down business partners, staking out Snorri's.

Andre has taken a leave of absence from the restaurant and insisted on staying with the aunts. For some reason, he thinks they now need his protection. He says he'll call me if she shows up there. I wonder if that's true.

I don't want to go back to Haven, ashamed to face Urdy and Verda. As for Skuld, how can I meet her again without losing control? I fantasize about twisting her fashionable little head off, though

I know there's no chance of harming, much less killing, a creature of such power. Yet, I must go back. I've run into nothing but dead ends. The aunts are my best hope now.

When I pull my bike up near the front porch, Andre's there leaning against a wooden support post. His transformation is astonishing. He's still short, by troll standards, and looks around sixty years old, but he has been transformed from scrawny to brawny. I'd known he was more than human, but I never thought he could pull this off.

He smiles at me, showing me a golden grill of teeth. I signal for him to spin around, which he does, showing off a flashy vest of silver mail armor over a bright white t-shirt.

"Dude, nice makeover," I say from inside my helmet. "Bulking up for the ladies?"

"You could say that," he says.

I step into the hallway and take the helmet off.

"You, on the other hand," he says, "look like shit."

"Yeah, well, baking all day in a black suit in the Florida sun may not agree with me."

"I thought trolls slept in the daytime."

"The sleeping thing's overrated."

"Well, you made a long trip for nothing. She's not here. Haven't heard a peep."

"I came to talk to the aunts."

Andre shrugs. "Not sure they're in a talkative mood."

"Mind if I try?"

"Would you take no for an answer, big man?"

Andre has been sandbagging all along, only pretending to be intimidated by the likes of me. After all, he helped haul me out of that swamp, a feat requiring great strength. He probably could have kicked my ass anytime since the first day we met.

I shrug and walk in, not wanting to extend this conversation now that he's doing his best Heimdallr impression. Shit, for all I know, he is actually the gold-toothed horn-playing god of rainbow bridges or whatever. Or is he just having ironic fun with the whole Marvel Universe movie mania these days? Either way, I don't care right now.

It's quiet. In the main hall, Urdy and Verda are doing their thing, which I've never taken time to study in detail, figuring it's way beyond an ignorant troll. Still, on the surface it seems simple enough. They take long, sharp needles and write into the gray bark of Yggdrasil. How they can carve runes into something that moves and shimmers is beyond me.

Once the runes are carved, they creep upwards, the tree bark carrying them like a sluggish river. As far as I can see, there's no telling what the tree is going to do with the runes. In some cases, it stretches them beyond recognition; in others, it squeezes them together into what looks like a single line. Maybe a quarter of the time, though, I can still identify the runes even once they've moved up the tree a ways. For me, it's progress. The first time I encountered the tree, I'd not recognized the runes at all.

Sometimes the aunts turn away from their carving and do a bit of weaving instead. Urdy uses a spinning wheel to make thread out of what looks like wool. Verda takes the thread and makes bits of cloth of varying sizes and shapes. I have no idea where the colors come from. Then one or both of them takes the bits of cloth and lays it over patches where the tree bark is degraded or missing altogether. The cloth always matches those patches perfectly, which is incredible considering there's never any measuring.

After carving and weaving and patching, they take white clay from the wide pool set in the stone floor and rub it on the bark as well as the roots extending above ground. The aunts never seem impatient or rough in their work. They treat the tree with a practiced reverence, as if it were another old and highly esteemed woman, beloved and needing care.

I've been transfixed a long time. They must know I'm here but haven't so much as turned their heads toward me. The fact they haven't told me to scram is at least a minor point in my favor.

When they finally stop to have a cup of tea, I approach them.

"Good evening, ladies," I say.

At first, just crickets. I try to wait them out.

"Hallr," Verda finally says, the barest possible concession to civility.

"Verda, Urdy, I apologize with all my heart. I can't expect you to accept that apology but I was hoping you might help me find Hildy. I'm frankly at my wit's end, though I suppose my wit wasn't very long to begin with. That's what got us into this mess.

"I'm begging you, if you know where she might be, please tell me. She probably doesn't want to see me, but at least I could apologize to her. I love her, ladies. You know I do."

"This is not about love," Urdy says, still not deigning to look at me.

"Of course it is, Urdy," I say.

I'm expecting to be dismissed or worse, but they just finish their tea, put their things away, and go back to their work. I suppose I'll need to wait till they're done and try again. I'll do whatever I need to.

"What in Odin's name is he doing here!" demands a voice from behind us.

It's Skuld, of course, but a different version of her. As tall as her sisters now, perhaps a little less chic but still wearing expensive-looking clothing. Her hair is longer blond, her sunglasses are huge and round.

Urdy and Verda did not banish her. Why did I think they might? They need her for the sake of Yggdrasil, and that trumps whatever she might do to me, or even Hildy. Besides, I'm sure Skuld has argued it was for Hildy's own good. Was it? She has me doubting and even loathing myself.

I suspect Urdy and Verda dislike what she did, knowing that I was drugged or magicked or whatever, but they will not turn against their own sister for my sake. I want to scream to them that Skuld is their enemy as well as mine, but I have no proof.

I need to keep cool. She's going to do everything in her power to make me lose it. In fact, just the size of her makes me ache to attack. It would, at least, give the appearance of a fair fight.

"I'm here to apologize to your sisters."

"Get the hell out!" she yells.

"Why do you hate me so much? You despised me from the moment we met. Is it really just about me being a troll?"

"Get out!" she screams, pointing toward the door.

"It is because she cannot see you," says Urdy quietly.

"Shut up, you old hag," Skuld says, almost growling. "I see just fine. I see everything. See too much."

"Yes," says Urdy. "But not the troll. His future is shrouded."

"He has no future," says Skuld, growing right in front of me, becoming a true giant, the likes of which I've never seen except, if it was real, in my toxic tête-à-tête with Surt hundreds of years ago.

It's not just Skuld. Everything is growing: the furniture, the foundation, the Great Tree itself. She must be at least thirty feet tall now. This is nuts. She tries to kick me with her gigantic designer sandals. I nearly laugh at the absurdity.

I try to spin away but she deals me a glancing blow, in earnest about killing me. I wobble on my feet behind her, sure I'm about to die. Maybe if I got hold of one of those giant needles of theirs, but the table on which they placed them is too tall for my reach.

Hallr in Wonderland. This time I actually do laugh, which I can see enrages the giant.

Screw it. "Use what's at hand," Dofri used to say in our training. "And if nothing's at hand, use your brains."

I feign a frontal attack, then dodge around her. In that moment before she can turn, I hurl myself at the back of her knee and am gratified when I feel her stumble. Up goes her heel. I push that as well, trying to topple her like a tree. When she actually goes down on her giant ass, I roar a troll roar, acutely aware it'll be the last victory of my life.

"Enough!" says Verda. The entire hall snaps back to normal size. "Skuld, we know your pain. Who knows it better? But this is improper and offensive."

Then Verda, who has always been so cordial, says to me, "Return at your peril, Hallr."

Still breathing hard, I nod solemnly, wondering how I might salvage one last shred of dignity.

"Again, please pardon me, Mistresses Urdy and Verda. Even if I never see you again, you have my everlasting respect and gratitude."

I bow the courtliest bow I can remember, turn and walk out of the hall. Andre's just outside the door, smirking at me.

"I thought you were supposed to guard people around here," I say.

"Them, not you," he says. "But you've still got a few warrior moves for an old guy."

"Will you still call me if Hildy comes back?" I ask.

"Sure, but I'd keep your distance from her. It's an understatement to say she can hold a grudge."

He escorts me to the front door. As I walk out onto the porch, he says, "You know, troll, Hildy feels humiliated. I know her as well as anyone. She'll go somewhere to punish herself and try to forget. It might be the last place you'd expect."

The last place I'd expect. I nod to him and start walking my bike through the brush. It gives me a chance to think before I hit the pavement. When I do, I reluctantly map out a route to the one place I least want her to be.

Chapter Thirty-Seven

"Toward winter there should be a blood-sacrifice for a good year, and in the middle of winter for a good crop."
—*The Younger Edda*

Asmund had already been in the land for two years and had brought with him a large family as well as a sizable collection of thralls. By contrast, my farm originally consisted of me, Kol, Ornolf the Oaf, Skylar Bard, and another sailor from *Kaupmaðr*. We eventually recruited seven freedmen who were either artisans or tenant farmers. I forbade anyone from keeping thralls on my lands.

Of my people, the only ones who came with me that night were Skylar and Kol.

I discovered that Asmund was not only a local chieftain but temple priest, or *godi*, in the old Norse tradition. It made sense he would over-see the celebration of Yuletide, which was a bloody affair in those days.

The festival to which Asmund had invited me started just after sunset. A small crowd gathered outside a thatched barn that was still in the process of being transformed into a temple. One muddy wall had been torn down so that everyone could easily approach a roughly hewn wooden carving of Odin.

Old one-eyed Vetgam sat on a throne holding his spear like a scepter. He had ravens on either shoulder and wolves sitting on both sides of the throne. My mother's son, I imagined the two crows taking a shit on him, even as the two wolves lifted their lupine legs to the throne.

I had brought a sheep, goat and calf along with me. I couldn't really spare any of them in the middle of winter, but it was unthinkable to arrive without decent offerings. Besides, somewhere in the back of my mind, I worried that this was all an elaborate ruse to murder me in front of Odin, who was also known as Ygg the Terrible. My irrational thought was that bringing good livestock somehow increased my chances of survival.

I think Asmund appreciated my gesture. Because it was my first winter in the land, I could probably have gotten away with bringing an older, sickly cow. He nodded solemnly in my direction as I gave the leads of my animals to one of the three white-robed young men who awaited.

Other guests had also brought offerings. Asmund himself brought forward an impressive range of animals, including one enormous bull that would have gone for a small fortune in settlements down south. Ultimately, there were fourteen animals, all of which were eventually tightly bound by the sons.

Asmund also wore white ritualistic robes that went well with his closely cropped but graying head and beard. The impression was one of grave simplicity. He called for other volunteers to participate in the ceremony. Asmund wanted at least as many men as there were animals, so that everyone could strike at once. This not only made for better theater, it prevented the noisy panic that would ensue if the animals were killed a few at a time.

As several guests stepped forward, it dawned on me that I was expected to volunteer. I hesitated but could see no way to gracefully bow out. In anticipation of the event, the chieftain had had white robes made for each of the major landowners in the region. Impressively, based on our one meeting in the darkness, he had accurately judged my dimensions. Two women from his own household helped me into the robes.

Once everyone was properly attired, I stood over the large sheep I'd brought to the feast. I was offered an axe but declined, instead calling to Kol to deliver my sword, Vidar, to me. I guessed the gorgeous weapon flashing in the firelight would be a crowd-pleaser, and I wasn't disappointed. The spectators started whispering to one another the second I unsheathed it.

Before the sacrifice, Asmund stepped forward to speak.

"Since ancient days, good men have offered up thanks to the gods. Tonight, I bestow this black bull to great father Odin, Lord of the Aesir, victorious spearman, battle heightener, awakener and chooser of the slain. My household also sacrifices to the god Freyr, bringer of virility and prosperity. We thank him for the richness of last year's crops and beseech a fertile season in the coming year.

"We also offer thanks for our honored guests. Each of them honors Odin as well as other great ones to whom they owe allegiance. Our neighbor Ulfar the Good would have us know he sacrifices to the new Christian gods, one of whom hung himself on a Great Tree, as did the Allfather himself.

"We have learned from the gods that sacrifice is a great good. Warriors sacrifice themselves, not just for honor, but for the glory of their kings. There are the humbler sacrifices as well. The fathers who lash themselves to the plow each spring for the good of their families. The mothers who too often perish giving birth. These are honorable, if difficult, acts. Sacrifice is not just our duty but our privilege and, among great men, our joy. Thank the gods for it. It connects us to the Tree of Life and tells us who we are. Without sacrifice, there can be no springtime. Without it, the waters of the wells run dry, and Midgard itself withers unto dust."

His sermon delivered, he made the signal for us to make our cuts. In my case, it was a simple affair. The greatest blow was required of Asmund himself, who nonetheless killed the huge bull with a single swing of a two-headed axe. We death-dealers placed the animals so that their blood would pour into stone bowls known as *hlautbolli*. Once they were filled, Asmund took some special sacrificial twigs, placed them into the bowls, and used them to sprinkle blood on the walls of the temple and the various carvings. Then he used the twigs to sprinkle us as well, the blood slightly shocking me as it showered over my face, head and shoulders. I hoped I didn't flinch too noticeably.

Only later did I realize this was a kind of test. Some of the attendees were curious as to how holy blood would affect a troll. Would it burn me? Would I run screaming from the temple? I wonder if I disappointed them.

It was after we'd all changed back into our clothes that ten men showed up on horseback. As they approached the cooking fires outside Asmund's Hall, the biggest one leaned over to his comrades and said something. All of the men laughed uproariously.

The big man's name was Keel-farer the Giant, a former berserker who made his fortune by challenging his betters to holmgangs and then collecting weregild after he'd bested them. More than one wealthy family in Norway had hired men to seek out and kill him, so he'd fled to Iceland. He had a large, round head and a red face, and he was taller than I was at the time.

"Have we missed the sacrifices?" he yelled to no one in particular.

No one spoke. The friendly banter around the fires died.

"They are all as deaf as the god Höðr is blind," quipped one of the riders, causing another bout of laughter. They'd started their Yuletide drinking early.

"Where is neighbor Asmund?" Keel-farer asked.

Asmund came striding out of his Hall.

"I bid you welcome, Keel-farer," said Asmund.

"We'd have felt more welcome if we'd been invited," smirked the giant, dismounting his black and white horse.

"All neighbors are welcome," responded Asmund, still cordial and calm. "And all bring offerings for Odin this night."

"We forgot to bring our big, fat sheep with us," winked Keel-farer. "Only us wolves."

Asmund said nothing, just stood there, his arms folded, staring at the mounted men or, rather, at their mounts. Keel-farer followed his gaze.

"Are you shitting me, Asmund?" he said.

The chieftain remained silent and shifted his gaze to Keel-farer's horse. Because they were so hard to transport, horses were not yet common in Iceland at that time. To have ten was an arrogant display of opulence.

"You know, Asmund," said Keel-farer, drawing his sword. "Someday you and me will likely dance amid the stakes."

Asmund remained a rock.

Keel-farer smiled. He raised his sword high above him, then swiveled and swung around, catching one of his men's horses in the throat. It was pandemonium as the terrified horse fell back, then tottered over. The astonished rider managed to jump off just before the horse came down on top of his leg. The other horses panicked—bucking, rearing, dashing into the shadows as people scattered to get away from them. Keel-farer's face, which was naturally ruddy, turned crimson as he howled with laughter.

"How's that for a sacrifice?" he asked the crowd.

Asmund hadn't flinched during the chaos. As the horse died, he called over two of his sons.

"Butcher and boil our guest's offering," he said. "And show his men to our stables once they've calmed their horses."

Chapter Thirty-Eight

"Grendel was the name of this grim demon haunting in the marches, marauding round the heath and the desolate fens."
—*Beowulf*

Andre said she'd go to the last place I'd expect. Vandriller Junction sprang to mind. She held contempt for this whole place, and she reacted with particular—and uncharacteristic—fear and repulsion to the swamp where Brad Lauder was killed.

But now that I'm here at the lip of the swamp, I can't envision Hildy going into it. Nevertheless, I stand at the edge and yell her name anyway, feeling like an idiot. Nothing. What did I expect?

I go back to the bike and tour up and down whatever highways and byways I can find, feeling like a lost soul amid the virtually empty spaces.

I've had time to think during the two-hour ride. That second night at *Grimm's*, Hildy discussed a land sale with that noxious, little drug dealer, Lucky. She knew how to contact him if she wanted.

But Hildy wasn't actually interested in buying swampland. It was Edmund who'd wanted to find a considerable swathe of cheap land that could be, under the no-net-loss policy, legally swapped for the wetlands of Haven.

Hildy knew there was someone who referred Edmund to Lucky. She'd wanted to understand that connection.

Could this nasty fen out of nightmares be the land Lucky was trying to sell? Hildy said she'd look into who owns it, said she might "have a line" on them, but she never told me if she found out. That in itself disheartens and rankles me.

So this is a long shot. I'm operating more on instinct than logic. But maybe Lucky has his operations somewhere out here.

I decide to take the country roads around the perimeter of the main swamp and the phosphate mines. I do a full circumference, seeing practically nothing, not getting even a twinge of intuition. Yet I've come this far, so I slow way down to speeds where I can barely keep the bike upright.

Hildy took her own bike when she left. I've stopped at various biker bars along my travels, looking for her sky-blue machine. Misty has made calls to others. In this area, I see no biker bars or clubs. Once in a while, I do spot a couple of hardcore MC bikers passing me on the road but I figure they're just making their way home or are doing a little midnight joy riding.

I pull over and check my smartphone. I have one text from Fred telling me *Snorri's* was a bust tonight and another from Misty just asking how I'm doing. Her text was from a few minutes ago, so I give her another call, telling her where I am and asking her to check to see if there are nearby places that might cater to motorcycle crowds.

I hear her clicking away on her computer. She's capable of doing a lot more than plugging a couple of words into Google. She not only taps into the usual search engines but has access to some government databases through *Hild Brands*, plus she knows how to navigate the IRC channels and, more importantly, the Darknet.

It surprises me when she comes up empty. There's always something, no matter how unpromising. Then she tells me she has a lead. A friend of Hildy has posted on Facebook, saying that a chum from out of town has unexpectedly popped in. She lives up in the Florida Panhandle. That might be how Hildy is staying off the radar, Misty says.

It sounds thin to me, and I can hear Fred in the background arguing that it's not a great lead. I tell her to look into it more before I ride all the way up there. She argues with both me and Fred, saying I should head north now. Practically insists. I suppose she's just worried and frustrated, but it makes me leery nonetheless. I ask her to give me the address and tell her I'm on my way.

But I'm not. I continue to ride along the backroads circling the swamp as if I'm a satellite caught in the gravitational pull of something massive and malevolent.

I pass another couple of bikers. Not the same guys as before, so I switch off my headlight, turn my Harley around and follow from a distance. They swing into the driveway of what I assumed was an abandoned, down-on-its-luck McMansion from before the last Florida real estate bubble burst.

The riders don't park in the driveway but, rather, take a dirt path around the back. Should I follow them on my bike or get off and walk in? Screw it. I'll ride the bike. Fortune favors the bold, right?

Around the back of the building is a large cement terrace that looks like it should be packed with garden furniture. Instead, it's littered with broken bottles, crushed beer cans, and, of course, a string of motorcycles. There are also two shitty-looking vans and a truck. From this side of the house, you can see some shards of neon light leaking out of shaded windows.

I look for Hildy's bike. One is the same model but red. I check the chrome and, sure enough, there's a little red on the edges. Crappy recent paint job. I scratch the paint with my nail. Looks like blue underneath. I also see that somebody's removed the sparkplug.

The only entrance is up a set of stairs leading to French doors. There's a guy wearing scuffed up khakis and a ripped polo shirt sitting on the top stair. He's got cloudy junkie eyes and tries to cadge a few bucks off me. I consider showing him a photo of Hildy and asking if he's seen her, but my gut tells me that's a bad idea. Best to just fly under the radar for now, if that's possible.

The panes of glass in the French doors are covered by cardboard that was once the thin skin of a case of Molson's beer.

I pull open the left-hand door and step into a large room that looks like a posh hotel lobby, complete with stuffed chairs, sofas, a long bar, and even a spiral staircase. Except this lobby is anything but posh. The stinking stuffed chairs are ripped all over, the sofas look like they're going to cave in. There's cheap plastic furniture wedged in between the chairs and sofas.

The room's very dark, lit mainly by lights around the bar and three flat screen TVs showing the same strange music video. There's a guy, no more than twenty years old, sitting on a stool next to the door watching me.

"You're not a member," he says.

"Not yet," I say.

"Got to check for weapons, or you can't come in."

"Sure thing."

He gets up off the stool and frisks me, which is quite a sight because the kid's a little height challenged, maybe five foot six. I don't smile, though. He's got huge biceps for his size. I figure he's a steroid user and probably perennially testy.

As he pats down the front of me, I look at his t-shirt, which has a picture of a wolf with razor sharp teeth. The beast is gaping at me with open jaws, already on the attack. Under the image is a couple of stylized letters: FD. If that's a motorcycle club, it's not one I know.

"You're not wearing colors," he says to me.

"Nope," I say.

"Okay, you've got to stay here in the main room. The rest of the house is for members only. A member invites you in, or you don't get in."

I nod, pay him money, then head directly for the bar and order a Jim Beam. The bartender is wearing the same t-shirt. I take my drink and head for the darkest corner of the joint I can find, intent on disappearing into the woodwork.

I sit back and watch the music videos. This time around the song is Lou Reed's *Heroin*. Up comes documentary footage of an atomic bomb going off, followed by that cowboy riding the bomb scene in *Dr. Strangelove*, then some horrific concentration camp footage from the movie *Night and Fog*. After that, a film showing kids shooting up heroin in a crack house, then a scene from *Apocalypse Now*, then a newsreel of the Twin Towers falling. It continues like this: one scene after another of war, disease, terror, pestilence, drug abuse, violence, porn, prostitution, torture, murder, mayhem, etc.

At first, I figured it was the same images set on a five-minute or so loop. As I settle in, though, I realize it's a much longer loop, if it's a loop at all. Somebody spliced together extravagant, voluminous heaps of hopelessness, a massive digital download of despair.

I sit up sharply when I recognize a face amid the digital chaos: Skuld's. A black-and-white photo of her standing behind the Florida governor during a ceremony. Then a color video clip in slowmo of her embracing the governor just after his last election win was announced. Lam. *That* is the proof I need to convince her sisters. For some reason, there are a few scattered cheers among tables after the clip runs.

The music isn't specifically linked to the images, but the photos and videos pass by faster or slower depending on the tempo of the music. *Heroin* segues into REM's *It's the End of the World as We Know It* which dissolves into *Wish* by Nine Inch Nails, which bleeds into The Cure's *Killing an Arab*, which leads into *Bad Moon Rising*. I've lost count of the songs by the time *Smells Like Teen Spirit* rolls around.

It's the weirdest collection of bikers I've ever seen. Some are just sitting at their tables stoned out of their minds, so focused on the screens that you would think they were ensorcelled. At other tables, people are playing cards, doing shots, shooting shit, hardly seeming to register the media liquid in which they're submerged. Some aren't bikers at all. They're junkies who, I'm guessing, were ferried here in those vans.

I'm so transfixed by it all I don't even register when the lights go up on two wired cages in which strippers dance. They look clumsy, stoned and unprofessional. I think it's a kind of stripper karaoke. The men hoot and shout, throwing half-full bottles of beer at the wire. A guy with a Mohawk haircut stumbles up to a cage and hollers at one of the women in it, telling her to stop. She flips him the bird, so he goes around to the front of the cage, grabs her and starts beating.

She's pretty bloody by the time this other guy intervenes. Huge dude by human standards. A good six and a half feet and built like an NFL linebacker. He grabs Mohawk-head with one hand, yanks him out of the cage, and flings him off the stage.

The crowd starts chanting, "Fenrir! Fenrir! Fenrir!"

Fenrir. It's the name of one of the most terrifying creatures in Norse folklore, an unstoppable giant wolf. Fenrir kills Odin at the battle of Ragnarok, which is the Norse version of the apocalypse. In a biker bar, that kind of nickname would usually represent bravado, a swaggering trope to go with a cool tattoo and an impulse toward violence.

"Gracias, Fenrir," says a voice from a microphone.

It takes me a second to recognize Lucky, who has taken center stage. He still has the spiky black hair and black leather jacket but I see he is wearing a new patch. The same wolf as on that other kid's t-shirt. There's a full name spelled out on his jacket: Fendwellers.

Suddenly Lucky's neck tattoo makes sense: that stylized merging of a runic F and an English or, more accurately, Latin D. Fen Dweller. I recall where I first saw it a millennium ago: on the neck of the murderous Bloodaxe. Did I? Can I trust such an old memory? At the time, I wasn't even literate. But, yes, I'm sure of it now. Which raises the question of why the Norse king Bloodaxe would have combined a Runic F and a Latin D in a neck tattoo. It's almost as if the tattoo had, from its beginnings, been an emblem of fate spanning past and present.

This, though, I need to puzzle out later. Lucky is doing some kind of shtick, which I struggle to make out because the speakers are distorting his words. It's clear, though, that he's introducing someone named Lamia.

Lam. I don't breathe, my heart drubbing like a hammer. Wearing a crimson hood and cloak, a woman ascends the stage. When she throws back her hood, I breathe again, relieved to see the pieces fit together. It's Skuld, of course, although she has natural-looking red hair that is unfashionably long, and she's no longer model-thin. She's full-figured and strong looking like the ninth century country girls I knew in Risør, except she's dressed in burnished mail, like a warrior or, to be more exact, a valkyrie. I've an impulse to rush the stage and demand to know where Hildy is. But that'd be suicide. This time, her sisters would not be around to save my sorry ass. Trollish caution and the instinct to skulk prevail. So much for being bold.

Urdy said Skuld couldn't "see me." Clearly, she can literally see me, so I assume Urdy meant in a different way—a Norn-like way that I can't imagine. I pray that's true or I'm surely dead.

Skuld commands the room in a way Lucky couldn't. She makes sure the sound system is working correctly before she proceeds.

"Thor," she says.

"Thor," a few people respond.

"Not the blond comic-book boy with girly good looks. The real one, the red-haired hammer-wielding god of storms, Thor!"

"Thor," the crowd responds, this time with greater numbers and almost in concert.

"Thor and Tyr went to the home of the dreaded giant Hymir to borrow a cauldron. The giant was so awesome that he could explode massive rafters with nary a touch. Hymir grudgingly offered his hospitality to Thor."

"Thor!" they said, this time in true unison.

"The terrible Hymir slew three oxen to feed his guests, and the lusty Thor ate two. The giant was amazed and muttered, oh how he muttered, that he must go fishing the next day to feed his ravenous guests. Thor said he would come fishing as well. The rude giant Hymir bade the great god to find his own bait, so Thor slew the monster's largest ox and cut off its head for bait. He did this, Thor."

"Thor!" they shout, more loudly this time.

"In the boat, Thor disdained the giant's shallow, safe, fishing grounds and rowed them into the deepest water where sea serpents dwell. The giant Hymir caught two whales on his great fishing hooks but Thor was unimpressed. He angled for larger prey and soon he found it. The Midgard snake, Jormungandr, which holds the world together by circling the Earth and biting its own tail—yes, this largest of all serpents—took the colossal, bloody bait of Thor."

"Thor!"

"Thor braced his legs so mightily on the boat's burden boards that his feet went through the hull itself. Thor then stood on the bottom of the sea and hauled up the horrible snake, straining every muscle and tendon and tissue and sinew. Then, at last, he pulled the head of the ugly, world-spanning beast to the surface. He did this, Thor."

"Thor!"

"Thor lusted after victory, no thought for anything but honor. He raised his great hammer and was about to smite the great serpent dead when the ignoble, cowardly giant Hymir—fearing the end of times and the destruction of his own useless life—cut the line. Thor, deprived of his prey, smashed down the giant, who disappeared into the sea. Thor had not cared if the Earth itself spun apart like a spool of thread, flinging mortals to the skies. He cared not if he himself would perish in Ragnarok. No, the god of storms only cared for one thing, the only thing, the great honor of Thor."

"Thor!" they scream, now in perfect unison. They throw chairs and broken bottles. They push, pummel and kick one another. They go berserk in a way that's primal and familiar.

"Thor," they shout. "Thor, Thor, Thor!"

At last, the patrons have simmered down. Skuld has disappeared like mist. Lucky is at a table near the stage, talking to guys who seem intent, as if there's business on the line. One of them is Professor Jormund dressed in biker clothes. Fenrir is also with them. He's probably the one Hildy and Andre saw at the swamp.

Did they somehow sic that giant gator on Brad Lauder?

There's still much I need to do: find Hildy and, if possible, get a hold of that video file. But after Skuld got offstage, when the lights were brought up a couple of notches, some guys sitting at a table in front of me turned their heads in my general direction with looks of stoned curiosity. My gut tells me I need to get out of here. Fortunately, the lights grow dimmer and the deranged film starts up again. When it looks like no one is paying attention, I slip out the back. Only the short, blond-haired kid takes any notice.

Now what? If I'm smart, I get on the bike, ride away and regroup. Maybe come back with Fred and Andre for support. I've been extraordinarily lucky so far and shouldn't push it.

But I'm not smart.

I wheel my bike behind a copse of nearby scrub palms, trying to keep it from being seen and recognized by Lucky or Skuld. I pull my old seax and scabbard out of a side-bag and strap it on.

It's just like me, I think, to bring a knife to what could easily become a gunfight.

Then I start to investigate the grounds. No sliding glass doors anywhere, but there are several windows I might pull myself into. It's not exactly a fortress. I cautiously peek into several of the windows but there are people everywhere I look. How can I enter the place unseen?

The house is up on a knoll. That's not so unusual in central Florida, where some houses even have basements. But I doubt this knoll is a natural formation. I'm betting it's built on one of the dirt hills left over from the phosphate mining operations. I walk across the spongy, overly fertilized St. Augustine grass making up the lawn. I hate the stuff. It's like walking across a lumpy old mattress saturated with heavy dust.

As I'm walking, though, the feel of the ground changes. It becomes harder and hollower, as if there's a space under the surface. It takes me a while but I finally discover that there's a covered canal running from beneath the house to the swamp. I push through a dense thicket of cattails to find the opening into the water.

I imagine this was originally just a lead-out from the house, carved into the land so some yahoo could motor his boat from a dock near the house into the swamp. Then the idiot realized he'd cut his property in half with a foul, stinking trench. So, having more money than sense—this has to be a stupid flood risk—he decided to cover it and plant grass.

I've no idea if the story is true. Still, it makes me feel better to think of it as a vanity project built by some dumbass who viewed this horror show as waterfront property. Somewhere in there, I hope, is a seldom-used pathway into the McMansion crack house. The fetid tube is probably my best bet, though the last thing I want is to wade into alligator territory again.

If I stay to the side of the tunnel, the water shouldn't get very deep. My hand goes to my side to check for my seax, which might be a relic of another age, but beats any of the crappy little knives of this era.

I'm trembling as I start into the tunnel. Vertigo hits, and I'm suddenly re-experiencing the terror I felt when that goddamned reptile pulled me under. I start backpedaling into the cattails, intending to get as far away from the evil cavern as possible.

Little art thou like thy kin in stoutness of heart, says a voice in my head.

"Easy for you to say, Mimir," I growl. "You're long since dead."

I go back to the opening and take my first step into the goo oozing along the sides of the tunnel.

"Fuck it," I whisper. "Trolls love caves."

Chapter Thirty-Nine

"He is given forth to be a wolf in holy places, and may no more abide in the
land with his father."
—*The Story of the Volsungs and the Niblungs*

Asmund had built a modestly sized hall. Once the feasting started, it
was crowded with family, guests, and servants. In addition, there were
five men who were obviously warriors—Asmund's housecarls. Such
men are expensive to keep, so it impressed me that a chieftain just
two years in the country could afford them. King Alfr had kept thirty
housecarls, but his lands were centuries old. Iceland, by comparison,
was still just a wilderness.

Another surprise was that Asmund seated me at the high table.
I suppose it would have been a serious offense to seat one of his
neighbors elsewhere, but I had lived most of my life among humans
as a thrall. I was accustomed to standing in dark, drafty corners during
feasts, assuming I was allowed in the Great Manor at all. I was seated
between Ulfar and Keel-farer, who made a show of examining me
from head to toe with a condescending look on his face. I ignored him.

Before the drinking began in earnest, ritual required that we guests
make three toasts with blessed wine. Asmund began with a toast to
Odin, asking his guests to drink to the wisdom and leadership of the

Icelandic founders. Next was Ulfar, who spoke of Christ's resurrection but also urged everyone to drink to Frey and Freyja in order to "bring back the long days of sun, fine harvests and lasting peace among the chieftains." Keel-farer sneered at the mention of lasting peace, saying under his breath that it was a virtue of women and Christians. We all pretended not to notice.

The third toast was raised by a guest named Karl, bidding us drink to the health of Asmund our host. Everyone in the hall responded with vigor to this toast, loudly echoing the sentiment. Just as we began drinking, however, Keel-farer let loose a shudderingly loud fart, one that sounded as if it were ripping the wood from his chair.

"I beg your pardon," he said, as his men first snickered and then broke out into howling laughter.

Asmund's face turned red, though he waved off his sons and his housecarls, who had jumped to their feet.

"Never mind," Asmund said loudly. "We have all encountered foul winds before."

As if it were a witty retort, Keel-farer grinned and said, "Yes, my winds are most foul."

After the toasts were complete, the boiled and roasted meats from the sacrificed animals were served, making everyone merry for a time. We drank ale and mead from silver cups and bowls, toasting the good health of our host multiple times to make up for the vulgarity of Keel-farer.

Once the men gorged themselves, the drinking started in earnest. Asmund's wife had us draw lots to determine who our drinking partners would be. The idea was to match up men and women as much as possible. In those days, the women drank a little, but their main purpose was to have a civilizing influence, playing to their partner's vanity, talking them down from homicidal rages, guiding them in the direction of games, culture and flirtation.

I was paired with the woman who helped me don my sacrificial robe. Solveig was Asmund's niece, an orphan whose father had been killed in one of Bloodaxe's kingdom-expanding wars. She was a blonde-haired, blue-eyed Scandinavian woman with an unusually triangular face and sharp chin. She wasn't a conventional beauty but had a unique attractiveness. She was quietly observant and, as I learned, highly intelligent.

She showed no fear of me, for which I was grateful. She asked me questions about my farm, stock, fisheries, and ships: all the things Icelanders loved to discuss. I was trying to lead her to talk a little more about herself and, by extension, Asmund, when the drinking games began.

Yule was, of course, a solstice feast. On this longest night of the year, the story goes, Odin leads a throng of ghostly riders and hounds through the night sky, causing a racket of pounding hooves, howling dogs and raging winds. Seeing them ride, or even hearing it, presaged doom, so it was up to us carousers to deafen ourselves to the wild ride through songs, stories, toasts, drumming and, of course, drinking. Lots of drinking.

Skylar Bard was in his element. At the request of the woman with whom he was matched, he agreed to quietly sing "The Death of Thorolf the Brave." As he started, several other guests gathered round, urging him to chant more loudly so they could hear over the noise of the hall. Soon they were beating on the tables and stomping on the floorboards to the beat of the verse. Other conversations quieted as people leaned in to hear.

When he finished, there was much cheering. Those who only heard the end demanded he repeat the song, which he did with even greater gusto and drama. The man was not only skilled but a natural ham.

After his performance, Keel-farer the Giant shoved his way through the crowd to Skylar.

Fairytales for fools are laid,
Steaming on feasting tables
Looking savory on the solstice
Spiced so well with guile
Yet soon the stink of lies
Strikes the nose hard as Mjölnir.
The crowd recoils realizing
It's steaming crap in feasting bowls.
To prove his perverse prevarications
the bard spoons up the mess, then pukes.

Keel-farer's men went wild, cheering for their chieftain, pronouncing him a great man for having bested a bard at his own game. "The bard is a liar," said one. Some guests booed, others urged Skylar to defend himself.

It's at this point that I moved closer to the bard. He was a witty man and, based on my experience, no coward, but he was obviously no match for Keel-farer physically. I wasn't sure that even I was.

Many a man can testify truly
To my tale of woe and courage.
Methinks the ale has made thee ail,
Your eyes abused, your nose confused
The fae folk fly in circles round
Your flushed and flaming face.
You stumbled on toward shithouse
bound, so sadly vision doubled
You do mistake your ass for mouth,
Your butt does speak, your lips do spew.

At first, Keel-farer look confused, letting the lines bubble around in his sopped brain. Then his red face turned an appalling shade of purple. He tried to conjure up some devastating rejoinder but only sputtered half-formed lines.

It dawned on me that he probably came to the feast knowing that someone would sing "The Death of Thorolf the Brave," which had grown popular on local farms in the idle winter months. He or one of his comrades had likely formulated the lines in advance. Given his size and dangerous reputation, he must have been accustomed to winning these games through sheer intimidation.

Everyone could see it coming, especially Skylar, but no one could stop Keel-farer's attack any more than they could hold back an avalanche. Keel-farer tore into the bard, smashing him to the straw-strewn floor, which was now foul with spilled ale and other detritus. By the time I got to them, Skylar's face had been hammered multiple times. He was already unconscious, but Keel-farer, a berserker by both training and nature, had no intention of stopping.

I could see from the amused expressions of his men that they were not going to haul him off, so I grabbed him from the back and yanked him up, trying to pin his arms to his body. Very few humans could have broken that grip, but Keel-farer was among them. He raised his arms, shook me off without even bothering to turn around, and then dove back onto Skylar. One of his men lamely tried shoving me, no doubt hoping his fellows would join in. Indeed, they punched me a few times, but otherwise couldn't be bothered, being crocked and wobbly on their feet.

I backed up, then ran at Keel-farer, knocking him sideways off Skylar. This time he took serious notice of me, elbowing me in the head as we wrestled on the floor. I crab-walked away, trying to gain enough distance from him to stand. By the time I did, he'd sprung up at me with a knife in his hand. I stumbled backward, trying to recall Dofri's training. I pulled a wooden pitcher off a table and used it to fend off the knife, then side-kicked him to gain a bit more distance.

"Enough," Asmund shouted. "This is a holy day. Do not profane my manor with blood this night." His five housecarls surrounded us, each holding a halberd, their iron spikes pointing toward our necks. I vaguely remember being impressed by the weapons themselves, which were unusual at the time.

Keel-farer started to surge toward me but stopped short to avoid impaling himself. This showed he wasn't in full berserker mode, which meant I'd probably gotten off easy. I nodded, raising my hands, signaling my willingness to settle down. Still furious, Keel-farer stalked off, flipping a heavy table and benches on his way out the doors.

By Norse standards, the episode with Keel-farer was not a big deal. If you shove teams of men renowned for violence into the same room, serve all of them as much alcohol as they can consume, and then encourage them to play drinking games in which the point is to ridicule one another, well, the outcome is all too predictable. So, after bringing Skylar to and propping him up on a bench, we all went back to our carousing.

Toasts were drunk to me for being stupid enough to step into the middle of a fight that included a giant whose entire fortune had been made in killing, maiming and intimidating people. My host and fellow guests forced one drinking horn after another on me. The secret behind the horn is that you can't rest it on a table or the brew will spill out, so you must drink all the contents at once, a surefire recipe for blackout drunkenness.

When they ran out of ale and wine, they broke out the mead in earnest. The horns kept coming my way.

When the dim morning of the day-after-solstice dawned, Keel-farer's gang began stumbling around looking for their master. Their horses were still in the stable, but the giant was nowhere to be found. His men assumed he was holed up somewhere on the farm with a woman, but though they waited around, he never turned up.

Eventually Asmund organized a search party, which finally found him in the waning minutes of that short, gloomy day. He was dead, his throat ripped out and his body mauled by some wild animal strong enough to haul him hundreds of yards past the perimeter of the farm.

This struck everyone as incredible. The largest predator in Iceland was the Arctic fox, yet this looked as if it'd been done by a large animal, probably a bear. In those days, there was the occasional report of polar bears floating in on drifting ice, but they were rare. A few Icelanders had captured and caged bears, though none in the immediate area that anyone knew of.

Because it was snowing, identifying the animal tracks was impossible. Only vague indentations could still be seen, and they led away from the body toward some marshes.

Keel-farer's men were soon mumbling about the murderous Halftroll in their midst. One went so far as to say that it was well known that trolls could change into other deadly creatures. It didn't help that I couldn't remember anything past the endless horns of mead. There was a point at which I myself wondered if I were the murderer.

Solveig ultimately came to my rescue, vouching that I'd never left the feasting hall before curling up on a wooden table near a hearth to sleep it off.

Keel-farer's men could not find anyone else to accuse. They had to haul his heavy corpse away, their thirst for vengeance unslaked.

Once they were gone, I hung around the scene, pretending to look for tracks. In truth, I had caught an interesting scent amid the carnage.

I hiked over to the marshes toward which the footprints, now virtually invisible, had been headed. In the frozen marsh, by the light of the rising moon, the animal's tracks were more visible. As I followed, the ice cracked and popped beneath my feet. At one point, my leg went through the ice, but the water was only a few feet deep. I finally came to a more open place in the middle of the marsh, where the tracks disappeared altogether. Following a hunch, I turned in the direction of Asmund's farm and, where the dead reeds and grasses were thickest, I spotted human tracks.

By the time I got back to the farm, most of the guests had left. Family members and servants were busy clearing and cleaning things up. Kol tended Skylar's wounds when he awoke, but not much could be done for his badly swollen and discolored face. They wanted to go home, but it had grown too dark to travel. I said we should take advantage of Asmund's hospitality for one more night.

I asked his wife, Ragnhild, if I might speak with her husband before he retired. She showed me into his chambers, where Asmund sat erectly in a large chair, unsuccessfully trying not to look fatigued. I doubt he'd slept at all the night before. When he asked about the marshes, I told him of the two types of tracks I'd found.

"Interesting," he said. "I compliment you on your tracking skills. What do you make of it?"

"To me, there are several possibilities. First, the two sets of tracks are completely unrelated to one another. Second, someone was waiting for a well-trained animal to return to him in the marsh and then somehow carried the animal away, perhaps in the direction of your farm."

"The second seems unlikely, given that the animal must have been a large one."

"I agree. But there is another possibility."

"Which is?"

"That Keel-farer was killed by a shapeshifter."

Asmund looked skeptical.

"The stuff of legends," he scoffed.

"As are trolls," I said.

"Have you ever met such a creature?"

"Not until recently, my lord."

Asmund tried to speak, though his voice was raspy. He cleared his throat and took a drink of water from a bowl next to him.

"Explain," he finally said.

"In the place to which Keel-farer's corpse was hauled, I could smell a scent that was familiar yet foreign."

"Ah, the renowned noses of trolls," he said.

"Yes, sir."

"The familiar scent?"

"With all due respect, my lord, it was yours."

"And the foreign one?"

"That of a wolf. Judging from the tracks in the marshes, a large one."

"And so now you have concluded that I myself, your host and neighbor, am a shapeshifter?" Beneath his rising display of anger, I heard an undertow of true menace.

"I have no proof, of course. Nor would I share any if I had it. In my opinion, Keel-farer was a man who needed killing."

There was a long pause between us. I wondered if it was a mistake to confront him, but I'd judged him to be an honorable kind of murderer.

"I trust this story of yours will not become another of your bard's songs?"

"I will never mention it again to anyone. But I have one question."

"Which is?"

"Was his death part of the Yule sacrifice?"

"No," he said, no longer trying to hide his weariness. "No, not in the way you mean. I am not such a monster. This was just a dirty job we decided needed doing."

"We?"

"That may be a subject for another time. Good night, Eirik. You and your friends are safe here this night."

"I had no doubt of it, my lord."

Which wasn't exactly true, but when speaking to a shapeshifting godi on a holy day, it pays to be cordial.

Chapter Forty

"With all the might and main of a dragon must I strive"
—*Volsunga Saga*

The philosopher Plato asserted we are all like people chained in caves, able to see only the flickering shadows of passersby as they walk past a fire behind us. Or maybe they're walking outside the cave in the sunlight. I can't remember. Anyway, the idea is that we go our whole lives mistaking shadows for reality.

But what if he had it backwards? What if the shadows are the reality, the daylight parts of ourselves just superficial reflections? Maybe the shadows are where the real action is, the place where we, our true selves, crouch.

What if life in this fetid tunnel is the true expression of who I am, alone, lost and stumbling through the muck in a sucking, mangled parody of progress?

I tell myself to get a grip and breathe deeply. Though this place stinks like a sewer, breathe.

I must be at the halfway mark by now. A quote comes: "Stepp'd in so far that, should I wade no more, Returning were as tedious as go o'er."

The Bard? Screw him. Screw Plato, too. And, while we're at it, screw weird sister Skuld. She can't see me in this darkness. Right? I make my own way.

The water has gotten shallower. The canal's more of a big muddy ditch at this point, with pockets of water here and there.

I stop, listening. Behind me, there's a barely perceptible bellowing I recognize as a gator call. Nothing to worry about. If a gator were actually in the tunnel, it'd be a lot louder. It's out in the swamp somewhere. Far away. Far, far away.

That vet who stitched me up said gator attacks are highly unusual. That was her phrase: "highly unusual." I know that's true. I've been around gators for hundreds of year. I've hunted them, eaten them, turned them into stew and steak and waterproof boots. They are troll prey, not predator.

The vet also said it must have been a very large gator, based on the wounds. No, maybe it was "extremely large." She speculated a fifteen- or sixteen-footer, a record-breaker, a heavy weight, a granddaddy dragon of a gator.

I shudder.

Gators don't scare me. Gators in a hellish, seidr-soaked, sacrifice-bent, malevolent fen of a swamp—well, that unnerves me a bit.

I take another plodding step, then reflexively crouch and freeze when there is a deafening response to the gator in the swamp. The deep-throated growl that raises all the hairs on my arms. Imbecilic, idiotic, moronic me! Walking right smack into the dragon's den like some knuckleheaded Mario Brother. A loud slapping sound, gator tail on mud. A warning. Then I hear it move toward me. Lucky for me, there's not enough water here for it to swim. I turn to run back down the tunnel, then think better of it. Gators move fast when after fleeing prey. Getting caught from behind would be dumb and cowardly both, not a good way to go.

So I do what comes naturally, roaring in return, trying to give the big lizard second thoughts. And it works, at least for a second or two. I get a low-throated growl-hiss, but I don't hear it coming forward. The gator is close, but not that close; I'd say forty yards or so.

A sliver of starlight reflects off the water and into the tunnel, giving nocturnal monsters like him and me the barest glimpse of one another.

I can just make out his red eyes and, I'm thinking, he can at least see my silhouette.

What did Urdy call the beast? Malice Striker? That has a ring to it.

"Calm down, ole Striker," I whisper. "Maybe we both can still get out of this unscathed. What say you?"

The beast just hisses again.

Keeping my eyes on it and holding onto the handle of the seax on my belt, I step backward once. Good. No movement from Striker boy. Another step. This time I can see him crawling forward slowly in stalking mode. That won't do.

"You dimwitted worm," I say. "You can't get the drop on me this time around."

It stops slithering forward.

So, I can't go forward and can't go back. I'm basically screwed.

Next to me there is a serious dip in the mud, as if there used to be a piling buried here that got plucked out like a rotten tooth. It gives me a bizarre, desperate idea. I sidestep into the dip, sinking up to my knees in a stagnant pool. Striker just watches, growling low like a threatening dog. I'm right smack in the center of the tunnel.

I conjure up every bit of instinct I can muster, trying to sense the ground beneath me. As I said earlier, trolls are natural diggers. Maybe I can put that talent to use. I pivot my feet and twist my legs side to side, keeping a close eye on Striker. I'm sinking, first down to my thighs and then my waist. This may be the stupidest strategy ever. If Striker attacks right now, there's no way to retreat.

Sensing some advantage, the wily old worm starts creeping forward again. It's now or never. Letting go of the hilt of the knife, I use both hands to dig out space to either side of me even as I'm swiveling like a corkscrew. I'm sinking into this muddy hole quickly now, but the gator has picked up speed. I yell one last time to see if that'll slow it again. It doesn't.

The hole isn't yet as deep as I am tall, but my hands have dug out enough room for me to crouch down and bring the sandy sludge in over my head. Just before Striker gets to me, I've disappeared under the mud. The basilisk bastard can run right over me and out the tunnel, if he's just looking to escape into the open. Most gators would, I think, so that's Plan A.

But, true to his name, he's a malicious one and starts clawing at the mud over my head. I'm trying to dig my way down further, but gators are diggers too, and he knows I'm just beneath the surface, a pre-buried but lively corpse. Easy pickings.

I can feel the terrible weight of him up there. He scrapes the top of my head with his claws. No choice now. Aiming up behind the frenzied claws, I stab into his belly but hit something solid. Rocks, I think. Gators eat rocks to help them digest food.

As he twists, I damn near have the knife wrenched out of my hands. Even though I'm still under the mud, I hear and feel the nightmarish hiss of the beast. It jumps backwards to get away from the knife, which is not what I want. He's still between me and the end of the tunnel.

Striker's fucking furious now. He lunges forward again, this time thrusting his lower jaw down at me, trying to sink his teeth into something. In fact, he succeeds in ramming my head, dazing me. But if I go unconscious, I'm done for. I thrust the knife up between his front legs this time, hoping to hit his lungs or, if I'm lucky, heart. Another huge bellowing roar followed by thrashing.

I'm expecting him to run forward or back. He thrashes some, then less, then the huge and heavy monster inconveniently decides to die directly on top of me. I'm good at holding my breath, but not while fighting for my life in some low-budget Jurassic Park knockoff. I need a breath. Right now.

I dig as quickly as I can to my right, trying to tunnel out from under the malevolent son of a bitch. Shit. I'm in mud. There's just nothing to push up off. It might as well be quicksand.

My only hope is to use Striker himself for leverage. I thrust my right arm as high as I can, driving the knife into the side of his head, then pull myself up. I'm seeing spots in front of my eyes by the time I can finally poke my head up to grab the most delicious lungful of air in a long, hard lifetime.

Chapter Forty-One

"Most virtue is a demand for greater seduction."
—Natalie Clifford Barney

Since the death of Keel-farer, Asmund and I had become something akin to friends. He'd come over to my farm one month, and I'd revisit his the next. It was a signal of legitimacy for me since Asmund was the godi and foremost chieftain in our region. We would talk crops, fishing, hunting, management methods and, as we grew to trust one another, the more dangerous topics of politics and religion.

He helped me get my farm in order, recommending the best planting schedules, informing me which crops grew best in which areas, sharing his secrets for animal husbandry, and telling me where he thought the best pastures were. His advice played a major part in the richness of my first harvests.

I thanked him with gifts of ale, a new breeding cow, furs, and jewelry I'd acquired through trade. As the days grew shorter the following autumn, I started spending long nights at his hall playing strategy board games and listening to stories. His eldest son was abroad, wintering in Dublin and determined to go on raiding expeditions in the spring.

That left his two sons, Magnus and Mar, at home with his daughter Signy and niece Solveig.

In our region, Asmund was the undisputed champion of the board game they called *hnefatafl*. The game was akin to modern chess, except the king was in the center of the board and had the goal of escaping to the peripheries, chased by raider-like pieces bent on the king's capture. His sons learned the game, but as young men, were not very interested in spending their time mastering it. Signy was indifferent to the game, but Solveig was an excellent player, having learned at the hand of her uncle.

When I first played with Asmund, he would quickly pummel me and then hand me over to his niece for a somewhat gentler pummeling. She and I would sit on a bench near the fire and play for hours. She didn't instruct me per se, though she did often shake her head and smile when I was about to make a stupid move, encouraging me to try something more sensible.

In time, it became clear that she wasn't just humoring me for the sake of her uncle. She genuinely liked me, a development that, judging from her expressions, Signy found distasteful. Asmund, however, never showed any concern that we might be spending too much time together. His wife followed his lead, though probably reluctantly.

In the early summer of the following year, Asmund did me the honor of asking me to watch over his family as he traveled to meet with fellow godi further in the south. This was in the years before the emergence of the famous Althing, the general assembly during which the top leaders of Iceland made new laws and judged legal disputes. Asmund's meeting was something much smaller and less formal. It was more of a fraternity of some of the founding godi.

After he returned from that meeting, he became more likely to travel to other parts of Iceland, which was beginning to fill up with landowners. Before he left on those trips, he quietly asked me to look in on his family from time to time. Magnus and Mar were eighteen and sixteen at the time and determined to go raiding with their elder brother. They left the farm the following spring.

Asmund was proud of them but didn't entirely approve of raiding for raiding's sake. Unlike many men on those such ventures, his sons did not need to supplement their farming incomes with the spoils of battle. They were quite comfortable on their huge farm, and there was more land in Iceland for the taking. Although he'd been a raider in his younger days, the godi hadn't enjoyed the pillaging of monasteries and villages, the raping of women, the suffering and destruction.

In that era, there was a certain breed of sadistic men who gloried in all those things, much as Grim had. The culture embraced their stories in songs and sagas. When such men came to Iceland, sometimes they turned into solid citizens, understanding that the Viking way was not the way of living at home. But others were like Keel-farer. They viewed Iceland less as a new home than as a new frontier ripe for exploitation.

Asmund encouraged his sons to join in real battles against armed soldiers in Ireland and Britain. He felt those were more honorable and lucrative engagements, though also more dangerous.

At any rate, Asmund came to rely on me to keep an eye on his family and lands. I did so as unobtrusively as I could, not wanting to antagonize his daughter, who was, I think, humiliated to be connected in any way with the infamous Halftroll.

Sensing my reluctance to offend, it was Asmund who approached me about a match with his niece. By the standards of those days, she was getting older. She'd turned down several middle-aged suitors. Asmund felt she might be waiting for me to court her. So I did. We married early in the following spring in a modest ceremony.

What can I say about Solveig? She was slender and taller than most human women I'd known. Her ears were unlobed and vaguely cuspated, giving her an elvish look. Her breasts were rather small, though this didn't detract from her beauty in my eyes. It gave her a more athletic and regal look.

Unusually for that time, Asmund had given her and Signy some basic weapons training in case there were any emergencies out there on the Icelandic frontier. The Norse seldom killed or raped their own women, but Iceland also contained what we'd today call men of Irish and Scottish origin, some of whom had been brought to the nation as slaves. In Asmund's eyes, such men could not be trusted.

I had never quite let go of the absurd dream of being with Inge again, though she had already reportedly given the ever conquering Sunmane his first son and was well on her way to becoming a kind of empress. So being married to Solveig was strangely jarring, as if I were a lottery winner who'd never thought to buy a ticket. She suddenly was in my home and my bed, a friendly acquaintance who had, without my comprehending it, become integral to my life. It took my heart months to catch up with the reality that I loved her—loved her with an unanticipated intensity.

I didn't think I deserved her, or any other part of my good fortune. I was happier than I'd ever expected to be, yet that in itself made me nervous. There had to be something wrong, another shoe to drop.

Then, about the time I started to believe I could be well and truly content with my life, the other shoe did drop—hard and heavy, borne by the person I trusted more than any other in my new world.

That summer Asmund asked me to go on a pilgrimage to Vík í Mýrdal. There, he said, he was meeting with old friends, fellow godi, who could be important to my future prosperity. I was reluctant to leave my wife, who was newly pregnant, to go traveling during the excruciatingly long summer days during which I had to travel in my thick robes and a densely meshed mask covered by a wide-brimmed hat. Sailing to Iceland this way had been a misery. Still, I considered Asmund not just my friend but my mentor and benefactor. I couldn't refuse him.

In one of Asmund's ships, we sailed down and around the southern peninsula, then southeast all the way to Vík í Mýrdal. It was a small but important village because it was the first habitable land on the southern tip of the island. When first arriving in Iceland, we hadn't stopped there on our way up the coast, but we had taken in the eerily magnificent Reynisdrangar rock formations, which rise up from the sea like three giant ships with raised masts. The legend is that these are the remains of three trolls who'd been caught by the dawn as they were hauling their ships onshore.

I didn't believe the legends, of course. No trolls I'd ever met had been quite that large. Still, I nodded in respect to them as we passed.

Vík í Mýrdal was bowed like a devotee beneath the great Mýrdal-sjökull glacier, which rests atop the fierce Katla volcano. When we beached Asmund's ship, we were met by four men who, one at a time, embraced him with a mixture of joy and solemnity. Each was a godi in his own right. After Asmund introduced me, we all adjourned to a large, earthen cottage up on a hillside. There we were greeted by another man, Regis, who wore ceremonial robes and appeared a few years older than the rest, around his mid-sixties.

We enjoyed refreshments inside the cottage, standing at the unglazed windows and admiring the view of the local cliffs, sea and rock formations. Afterwards, a servant cleared away the food, closed the shutters and left us. At first I assumed they did this to make me more comfortable, but once Regis called the meeting to order, I realized it must be part of their annual ritual. The godi wanted their privacy. We took our seats around the long, roughly-hewn wooden bench on which our ceramic drinking bowls still sat.

"It's hard for me to believe that yet another winter has gone past so rapidly," Regis said. "It seems they fly ever faster as a man grows grayer. This only serves to underscore the urgency of our purpose here.

"This year we welcome Eirik Sturlung, who must be wondering why a group of old men has bid him to come so far to speak with them. We begin by welcoming you. Through Asmund, we have followed your career with great interest. Now that you are a member of his family, we feel we can fully take you into our confidence.

"We six, as well as several others not here present, have embarked on a mission. It is one we hold sacred in order to forge a great new nation from this wilderness we call Iceland. The ultimate success of our enterprise will depend, as you can imagine, on the character of the men who found this nation. We have no king or assembly to select these men. Each comes of his own accord.

"Once they arrive, however, we have leisure to judge their characters. Are they worshipful, hard-working men of distinction and honor? Or are they selfish and lazy men intent on thriving at the expense of their neighbors, men with no honor who wish to rule through the kind of self-serving violence that still plagues our motherlands? We wish, above all, to spare ourselves the plague of kings like Halfdan Sunmane. Do you agree this is a worthy goal, Eirik?"

I did, of course, but I also sensed trouble. I was not so much in the thrall of my mentor Asmund that I couldn't see the bubblings of human conniving.

"It seems a worthy goal to me, Lord Regis," I said, granting him the title more to demonstrate respect than because any godi warranted it. "How do you go about achieving this goal?"

"We assassinate," he said. "Asmund said you are a man for blunt talk, Eirik. That is the common word for what we do. That is what happened to the berserker Keel-farer during your first winter solstice. Asmund killed him so that the nation would be spared his irrational, irresponsible violence and his bald-faced ambitions."

Somehow I wasn't surprised. Part of me had expected something like this. Asmund had dropped hints that he was working with others after he killed Keel-farer. Nonetheless, it made me feel so sad and weary that I yearned to place my forehead down on the bench.

"I see," I said, striving to stay expressionless. "And who decides on the targets for assassination?"

"We do," Asmund interjected. "It is a grave responsibility—one we do not take lightly."

"I'm sure of that, Lord Asmund," I said. I realized he had put great faith in me by bringing me to meet with this cabal. He had staked his reputation and, very likely, both of our lives on my wisdom in that moment. But I also recognized that my beautiful Solveig had been a lure into a trap. Asmund had wanted to ensure that I was his kinsman so that any betrayal of his secret society would also be a betrayal of family, which was the blackest type of betrayal in those days. Had my new wife, who had just announced she was pregnant, known she was playing the role of honeypot?

"Solveig?" I asked him, my throat catching.

He shook his head. "She knows nothing of this. Her affection for you is genuine, Eirik. I have been shrewd but not devious, my son."

I nodded, praying he was being honest with me. He had never called me "son" before. I felt simultaneously honored and resentful.

Regis sighed. He and Asmund hadn't been sure how I would react. They were over one of their two big hurdles. Now that I understood the game, I could easily see the second hurdle.

Asmund could read much of this in my face. He knew me better than anyone since Leos.

"Can you guess why we have summoned you?" he asked.

I nodded again, still not trusting myself to speak. Yet it was critical to my survival that I did.

"I'm no godi," I said. "So, you must need another assassin."

I almost used the word "killer," which would have instantly shaken their confidence. I needed time to think things through.

"Yes," said Regis. I almost wished Asmund had not told him to speak bluntly. I could have used a little more ambiguity in that moment. Because I now understood that I had not escaped my fate, after all. These men knew I was a king-killer, the person behind one of the greatest assassinations of our age. That made me just the kind of talent they needed. I had been carefully recruited.

"And who," I said, trying hard not to allow sarcasm to creep into my voice, "do you feel needs assassinating for the good of the nation?"

Chapter Forty-Two

"Him only would she have who should ride through the flaming fire that was drawn round about her hall."
—*Volsunga Saga*

At the end of the tunnel is a dock standing five or six feet above the muck. I imagine that before the tunnel became filled with silt, and the local droughts brought down the level of the swamp, there were two or three feet of water in here, enough to float a fishing boat. Now, there's this rickety mess of a dock made of rotting wood. Where there should be a boat is a scattering of rotting bones. This must be how they kept their pet Striker in the tunnel when they wanted, feeding him as much meat as he'd take. Up against one wall is the hairy leg of an ungulate. Wild boar, I'd say. I wonder how much meat started out alive down here.

I pull myself up on the dock and walk along it to the end, where there's an aluminum fish-cleaning station tinged with brown spots and streaks. It looks abandoned, a tool hardly ever used. I wonder if the original owner caught a single fish in that deathly sedge. On the side of the cleaning station is a fragile-looking, green plastic hose that I use to rinse myself off. I suppose the sound of running water might draw somebody out here, but I'm beyond caring.

The apathy builds into a wave of despair, as if the mud itself has leached me of hope. I've no idea why I'm here. I want to curl up in the muck under the dock and await my own slow decay. Even if I find Hildy, which strikes me as the longest of long shots, she'll still detest me. I'm nothing more than a polluted beast born of a conjured lust between a furtive creature of fae and a gullible Norse hillbilly stumbling through the woods. A congenital loser from the moment the mortal sperm wormed into the hulder's egg.

I sink to the dock and lie down, willing my life to be over already. To just end.

From far away, I hear a small voice. It's saying something over and over. I want it to stop. "Hero," I think it's saying. "Hero, hero."

The voice grows louder, though still muffled.

"I'm anything but a hero," I say aloud.

Thanks for the news flash, it says. *I've been saying 'hello,' not hero. Your mind is turning to mush, and I can barely get through.*

Mimir?

Do you have any other voices in your head?

I can always hope.

Shut up, you pitiful excuse for a jotunn. Listen to your betters. This place reeks of despair. It oozes in from that swamp and pervades every nook and cranny of this place. Impressive bit of Boyg enchantment, actually. Skuld is so talented. Harnesses the depressive Zeitgeist of the Great Recession and weaves it in with...

"I get the drift," I whisper. "You're telling me to get up off my ass."

Close enough, he says. *Stay vigilant. Don't let the place get in your head.*

"Like you are?"

Entirely different, he says. *Move.*

The door leading out to the dock is locked. I put my ear to it. All's quiet. It is a steel door that, although growing rusty, has rims and seals around the edges to keep out water if there's a flood. I grab the lever handle with both hands and pull. The door groans. I'm afraid I'll tear off the handle, leaving me stuck outside, but it comes open with a kind of loud pop that alarms me. For over a minute, I listen intently for approaching footsteps.

When I don't hear any, I creep inside. There is a tiny vestibule and short flight of stairs, above which is a hallway. The first room I come to is, or was, some kind of game room. The walls are painted a robin's-egg blue, though they've been chipped, cracked and marred with black skid marks from clumsily moved furniture. There's a crooked photo of a short, brown-eyed man wearing Bermuda-green slacks, a sport shirt and a toupee that doesn't quite match his natural hair color. He's posing with this cue at the pool table, which was once a major feature of the room, though it's long gone. He's looking up at the camera with a smile that is so contrived it's creepy. His eyes are brittle little BBs set amid taut muscles that are desperately straining to look happy. For a moment, it brings back the wave of despair that overwhelmed me a few minutes ago.

On the east wall is a standing bar that looks like something out of the Rat Pack era. It's trashed but was once a work of art, being carved from what I think is walnut. Where the framing along the bar top still exists, it's split and splintered. One corner looks like it's been sheared off by sharp rock. But the bar still functions. There is a bunch of whiskey, vodka and gin bottles, all with off-brand labels. Most are empties lying on their sides, though a few still stand and hold their dregs like worn down men holding only bad memories.

On the west wall is a huge stone fireplace complete with a gas-fed blaze. Must be at least six feet high. It's weird that they should keep a fire going here. The rest of the room has an abandoned air, a place of last resort for desperate stoners seeking out the last booze in the house. The fireplace should be dark and littered with broken glass, or it should frame a pitiful little blue flame that sputters. But this is a red, orange and yellow inferno, a fierce spirit caught in a dead zone. Are those really gas logs, or maybe a kind of giant gas-log sculpture?

I know I should move on to other parts of the house but I'm transfixed. Aside from the sheer size of it, there's something wrong. For one thing, the back of the fireplace is sunk so far back that I can barely see it. Correction, I can't see it. That makes no sense.

I squat down in front, trying to stare through the tendrils of flame. Not a tunnel, thankfully. I couldn't bear another tunnel. It's a space of some sort. I can just make out the light flickering on the wall.

But if this fireplace stands between two rooms, how do I get to the other one? About twelve feet to the right of the fireplace is a column of tacky orange brick about the width of a door. It's not an entrance. Maybe it used to be.

I look for some way to turn off the gas. Nothing. There must be another entrance from somewhere. I slip back into the hallway to check on a couple of other nearby rooms. One's a small bedroom and the other an unused utility room. Both are filled with trash, used hypodermic needles, blackened spoons, burnt candles and filthy futons. Neither one leads to the mystery space behind the fireplace.

So I go back to the game room, crouch down and, feeling like a moron, whisper, "Anybody in there?"

Nothing.

"Hildy, I know you're in there," I say. It's stupid. I have no idea where she is. But I remember her mentioning someone who walked through a fire in one of her stories. I call again. Still nothing, so I give up. I have most of the house to search.

As I'm turning away, I hear something. Maybe some kind of muttering.

"Hildy?"

"Fuck off," someone slurs.

"Hildy!"

I get nothing back but a kind of mumble and moan.

"You hurt?" I ask.

Silence. I need to get in there. I could just try kicking the phony gas logs to crap. That should stop the fire... if it doesn't result in a massive fireball. I tell Hildy to turn off the gas from her side. Just more silence.

Between the burning logs and the top of the fireplace, there's room enough for me to crawl through, if I happened to be fireproof. Which I'm not. Not even a little.

Maybe this flame is enchanted like in the sagas. Usually, I'd be able to sense that, but this whole house is engorged with dark hoodoo. It's like trying to sniff out one needle in a stack of needles.

"Hildy, if you can hear me, get out of the way. I'm coming in."

I back up to the other wall, sprint toward the fireplace, and try jumping forward head first through the flames. Let's just say I have mixed success.

I am, somehow, the eponymous outcast Peer Gynt dancing madly on a stage in a dilapidated theater. A drunken young man, I go crashing headfirst into a forest of tree flats.

I shake my head to clear it, only to find I'm now a middle-aged human. "Well, I'll be a troll," I say, "if I understand what it was that dazed and bemused me so."

My long-dead wife Solveig stands over me, hands on hips.

"You left me high and dry in a half-built hut, you schmuck," she says.

"Flaking out is what he does best," says Hildy, drifting down from the catwalk on a wire connected to a winged hypodermic needle. She takes her shining spear and sticks me with it once, twice, thrice. "Not a true troll at all."

"What difference is there twixt trolls and men?" I ask her in a whining voice.

"Big trolls will roast you," she answers, burning me with a torch. "And small trolls will claw you," she continues, clawing my left arm.

"With men," she concludes, "it were likewise, if only they dared."

I wake up, unclear if I'm actually waking, or if I'm waking into another dream. Or, as it happens, a nightmare. Hildy's still here, cackling ominously.

She's sitting cross-legged on a concrete floor, dribbling a bottle of one hundred percent-proof vodka onto my smoldering leather jacket. She's delighted when it flames up. I wave my arm, trying to put it out. It's hard because I'm all crumpled on the floor. I've got a wicked though receding headache, but it's nothing compared to the pain in my right leg, which I vaguely remember smashing on the artificial pile of gas logs. It turns out those are welded into place.

"Will you stop already?" I howl.

"Probably not," she says. "Look at you, singed head to toe. You know, when Sigurd walked through the flames for me, he wasn't singed at all." She's slurring her words, clearly stoned out of her gourd. I'm feeling woozy myself, having smashed my head. But maybe there are other factors at work; hypodermic needles are scattered on the floor.

"Yeah?" I say. "Then what was the fucking point?"

"That he was fearless, that's what. The fire couldn't touch him."

"Nice for him," I groan, trying to prop my head up with an elbow. "Bet he made a damned fine prom king. By the way, did you maybe stick me with something?"

"You stuck yourself, moron, by jumping into a room full of needles. But I might have helped just a little," she says, holding one up and threatening to jab me with it. I flinch, causing her to guffaw. It's smack, I guess, though I haven't indulged in any kind of opium product for almost a century.

"Well, then, thanks for the first aid," I say, almost meaning it. I'm starting to feel warm and relaxed. Now that I think about it, my leg should hurt more than it does.

"Fuck you. You stink," she says, putting her face right down in front of mine. "Literally."

"Not my fault you buried yourself at the end of the sewer from hell," I say, looking around. This room is little more than a cement cell, complete with scurvy futon, one of those little Japanese tables, a toilet, sink, and paraphernalia spread all over the place. I spot two florescent orange tourniquets, the kind made of tubes, both laying there like limp, dead snakes. There are several stainless steel spoons with blackened, burned crud caked hard in the center, perdurable as original sin.

"You should have taken a hint, asshole," she spits.

I'm an idiot for baiting her. I need to take it down a notch or three.

"Okay, so we're not off to a good start here."

"Really?" she says. "What gave it away?"

"Look, let's begin again." I try to sit up cross-legged like she is, but I can barely bend my right leg. "First of all, I'm sorry. Really, really sorry."

"You're right about that. One sorry son of a bitch."

"I didn't know what I was doing, Hildy. I wasn't even awake."

"No? At the time, you looked pretty aroused to me."

"Not till I... Damn, Hildy, I was magicked. You've got to know that. First at the meal, then in bed."

I am, in fact, feeling sleepy again. I try to concentrate. If she truly turns against me, I'm done for. Not only could she kick my ass, she could cry out and bring Lucky's goon squad down on my head. As messed up as I am, I don't like my chances of fighting my way out of here. No, if I'm going to make it, Hildy's going to need to save me, not vice versa.

"Poor baby got roofied with a potion, eh? Why is it every time some asshole cheats, he says it was because he was crocked and bewitched?"

"In this case..." I start.

"In this case, you were a pig. Are you telling me you didn't have the hots for her as she twirled around in that goddamned apron?"

"That's not the point."

"No? Remind me what the point is again," she says.

"Okay, so let's say I'm a rotten bastard..."

"Good idea. You're a rotten bastard."

She's not slurring as much now. A little anger might be good for her at the moment. I'm hoping demigoddesses have a high tolerance for recreational drugs.

"That's still no reason for you to wind up here, Hildy. This place is foul."

"Fair is foul and foul is fair, and you can kiss my derriere."

"Classy, but wrong. In this case, foul is just, well, foul."

"It suits me," she says.

"Bullshit, Brynhildr. Maybe it suits a moldy, has-been assassin like me. I'm sure it suits your cracked candy man, Lucky, or Skuldy, doing her Vegas shtick for the losers upstairs, preaching the thrills and joys of Armageddon. But it doesn't suit you a bit."

"Wait a minute. You brought that bitch here?"

"Brought her? She runs the fucking place, Hildy. I figure she's got Lucky on a chain. *She's* the one. The hidden enemy."

"You lie. A topsy-turvy, decked-out-in-garish-plumage stinking corpse of a lie."

"I don't even know what that means, but I'm telling the truth, and I think you know it."

She's still fuming but silent, finally trying to focus despite the cobwebbery of her inebriation.

"I doubt," I say as gently as I can, "I was the only one magicked, my love."

"I'm not your love, old troll," she says defiantly.

"So help me God, you are. But, to be honest, that's not the real point."

"Again with a lost point. You should really work to keep your points in your pants."

"The point," I say, calmly, "is that your aunts need you. Skuldy has lost it and..."

"She hasn't!" Hildy says. "She's just tired. Very tired. You live long but are still mortal. You don't know what it's like, especially not for her."

"No, guess I don't. But I think she's more than just tired. She's a Norn with a plan. That's why you can't stay here. 'Cause it's exactly where she wants you."

I take the chance of putting my hand on her shoulder.

"Take your hand off me," she snarls. I do. Fast. I've been maimed enough already. But I can't think of anything else to say.

After a couple of minutes, she looks down and whispers, "I don't know if I can leave."

"You can," I say softly. "At least trust me that far."

"Right. Because you've proven so trustworthy."

"Hey, look, I just slayed a slimy dragon for you. Did Sigurd ever do that?"

"As a matter of fact…"

"Sonovabitch. I just hate that guy."

I get the most feeble of smiles out of her. Not much. Maybe enough.

"By the way, I don't suppose you know how to dial down the fire a little."

She reaches over to a metal latch and turns off the gas. The flames die down, then fade completely.

"Um," I say.

"I just wanted to see what you'd do," she shrugs.

Chapter Forty-Three

"Kill a man, and you are an assassin. Kill millions of men, and you are a conqueror. Kill everyone, and you are a god."
—Beilby Porteus

The word *thing* was used by Germanic peoples of the time to demark a legislative body where important issues could be discussed and decided. It is the root of the word *Althing*, the ancient Iceland assembly that still exists in a much-evolved form. The men who recruited me, using the word *thing* in their own way, called themselves the No-*thing*.

It was a self-effacing title, even a dark joke, broadly hinting at the fact that they did not represent a true and legitimate assembly of chieftains and priests. They were a secret sect of self-selected judges and executioners, men who knew they did wrong in order to make things right.

And I was their tool—or at least one of them. Asmund was also an assassin as well as one of the founding members of the No-thing. I don't know how many other assassins there were, though I doubt they were more than a handful. They had to be supremely careful to find men with the right set of qualities: trained murderers with a strong sense of duty who could trust the No-thing to make the right decisions.

My first assignment came the following winter, which was the perfect time for a darkness-loving troll to stalk his prey. My target's name was Rezso. He had a farm north of mine up in the area of Buoadalur.

People seldom traveled far in winter in those days. By January, most of the nation was literally an ice land. I, however, was uniquely qualified to traverse the rough country inland. It took me about three days to get to Rezso's farm, though that was the easy part.

Once there, I had to scout the landscape and determine the best way to get to him. In Rezso's case, it was difficult, because he was a hard drinker who seldom wandered out of his house, even to relieve himself. Instead, his servants had to empty his stinking chamber pots into the snowbanks. In the end, even I grew very cold and impatient. To draw him out, I wound up leading one of his cows into a nearby bog where I broke the thick ice, hobbled the animal, and then pushed it in. I made sure it was close enough to the house for them to hear its calls.

A burly, Scottish male slave was the first to investigate. I'd made sure the animal was well and truly stuck. Any rescue of the beast would require several men and some ingenuity.

He assessed the problem, cursed, and reluctantly went back to the house to get help. I could hear furniture being tossed around and a man shouting. I was perversely gladdened by his ravings. In a small way, this supported the No-thing's claim: that Rezso was a villain who not only raided the animals of other farms—a crime that some Icelanders considered worse than murder—but had killed people in his region, including one of his own sons during a smashball match.

The master finally showed himself. He didn't look so much dangerous as pathetic, drunk and stumbling through knee-deep snow, wearing only his undertunic and a pair of loose boots. He had a look at the cow, started screaming and waving his arms, then motioned the Scot and another man over to the barn to gather some farm implements.

Soon after they left, I ambushed Rezso, breaking his neck before his dulled mind even registered me. Then I threw him into the bog along with the poor cow. I hoped that the two other men wouldn't notice my footprints. It was dark and moonless, and I'd chosen a time when the snow was falling heavily.

As I started homeward, I felt nothing but a sense of grim satisfaction. I'd done the ugly job for the greater good, and I'd done it with professional economy. As the miles grew, however, so did my misgivings. Had I been sure it was the right man? Was the No-thing's intelligence accurate or based on hearsay?

These doubts slowly accumulated on me like grime. In the world of trolls, calculated and cold-blooded murder was uncommon. When trolls attack, it's usually because they're hungry, enraged, jealous, or, occasionally, greedy.

Miles from nowhere, I removed my fur mittens and rubbed my hands hard in the snow, scouring them until they started to bleed. It wasn't enough. A half-day removed from my farm, I took off all my clothes and rolled in the snow like an arctic bear. This time I scoured my whole body, even tried to rinse my hair with the falling sleet.

When I got home, Solveig greeted me with delight, asking how my journey had gone. I barely responded, telling her I needed a bath and bed. She offered to scrub my back. I told her I wanted to do it myself, then proceeded to poach myself in near-scalding water.

The murders got easier over time. I hardened myself. I couldn't view the assassination as a sacred duty in the way Asmund did, but I could resign myself to my lot. I tried to put away my surliness around Solveig and our two young children, Alva and Ying. Sometimes I even succeeded.

In the fourth winter after I'd begun my string of killings, I was sent on assignment to the same farm where I'd broken the neck of Rezso. Regis had had little to say about this man, except that he was Rezso's brother and was carrying on the family tradition of drunkenness and violence.

"Drunkenness and violence are the birthright of every Icelander," I said.

Regis hadn't liked being questioned.

"We have credible reports," he said stiffly, "that the man is a menace to his neighbors."

I nodded, though was not convinced. I had been in the country long enough to know that neighbors often quarreled, questioning one another's ownership rights, courting the same local beauties, coveting each other's coves and anchorages. Were the reports coming from a neighbor who couldn't abide anyone else on those lands? Was that neighbor a friend or relation of one of the No-thing members?

I went away without asking, but the questions plagued me when I revisited Rezso's farm, now run by his brother. The brother was an easy victim, coming out for the short span of daylight hours to care for his animals, shovel snow off his roof and other daily chores. And, unlike his brother, he used an outhouse. I could have, perhaps should have, murdered him as he was moving his bowels and shoved him down the hole.

Instead, for several days I hovered around the farm like an evil spirit, watching, listening, and looking for evidence that the man was a menace. Yes, he drank. But so what? Occasionally he yelled for his wife to serve him, though there were no signs of beatings or bitterness. He even played with his children, a pastime that many a Norseman disdained.

One night, while it was snowing and moonless, I wrenched the man out of the outhouse, threw him in the snow and sat on him, my hand over his mouth.

"Don't sing out or I'll kill both you and your family," I said. "Do you understand?"

He nodded, breathing hard and heavy, the terror in his eyes bringing me no pity, only the craving to crush out his life.

"Do you have a quarrel with any neighbors? Speak the truth. Just nod or shake."

I could see the wheels turning, his eyes darting back and forth. He didn't know which answer I wanted, though knew his life depended on it.

"Just speak the truth," I said again. "The gods favor those who speak truth."

The man nodded.

"Who is your quarrel with?" I asked, uncovering his mouth just enough for him to speak.

"Olaf," he said.

"A most common name," I said suspiciously.

"He is the godi in this region. My brother insulted him, and he has not forgiven. He wants our pastures."

These were facts I could check on, if I wanted to go to the trouble. Though it would have been much easier to kill him and be done with it. There he lay at my mercy, his pants still down, his bare ass in the now-shitty snow.

"Settle the dispute," I told him. "Make him gifts. Apologize for the acts of your brother."

He nodded. Of course, he was in no position to argue, even if he'd already tried his best to make peace with his godi. But it didn't really matter anymore. I couldn't bring myself to kill him.

"I am the wraith of justice," I said, almost smiling at the absurd fiction. "Do justice, or I will return."

He nodded again. I stood up, backed into the darkness and then jogged for miles through the lightly falling snow without stopping. I wondered if I'd just made the worst mistake of my life. I could hear my mother berating me once again for being soft.

Chapter Forty-Four

"What path should I choose? Many paths lie before me."
—*Peer Gynt*

Buddy's is a barbecue shack with a gravelly parking lot cut into the perimeter of the forest. There's no indoor seating, just a handful of half-rotting, green picnic tables strewn around the property. Only locals have the sense to eat here.

I sit on one of the benches facing the road and wait for Hildy. I've been anxious about her all week, despite checking in with her by phone several times since she went back to Haven.

After I found her at the McMansion crack house, we got out of there relatively unscathed, though we'd had to lurch through the tunnel's muck—and around the enormous corpse of Striker—like a couple of drunken and cantankerous vaudevillians. We got on my bike, found a park where we could clean ourselves up, and then went back to Haven after Andre confirmed Skuld was gone.

Urdy and Verda offered us tea and listened to my story, though their eyes kept flicking back to Hildy, who was still sallow and ill. I didn't mince words, telling them Skuld was Lam and had been working against them the whole time. I didn't have the video file to help prove it, but they didn't argue. Nor did they seem especially dismayed, just downtrodden and wistful. The four of us were a sad lot: me bashed up and burned, Hildy already in withdrawal, and the two aunts brought low by Skuld's betrayal.

"Thank you, Hallr," Verda had said, taking my hand in hers. "You've done well. It is best we have this in the open now. We will speak with our sister."

"That's it?" I'd said. "She sics the government on you, nearly drowns Hildy in enchanted pond scum, tries to turn me into toe jam and…"

"You think we're stupid, troll?" asked Urdy, her mood suddenly swinging from lethargy to ire. "Blinded, yes."

"And in denial," said Verda, almost to herself.

"But not stupid," continued Urdy. "We understand. Understand more than you, like a forest knows more than a seedling. We must now decide, but you must go. Hildy is protected here. You are not. You leave now."

"I won't," I swore.

In the end, though, I did, after Hildy agreed to call me to confirm all was well. Then, yesterday we agreed to meet here at *Buddy's*, a place where we've been several times before. Neutral territory.

Around dusk, Hildy pulls up on a new bike, a dazzling blue Honda Gold Wing. When she pulls off her helmet, she looks calm and clear-eyed, if not exactly happy. The gravel crackles under her boots like low-grade thunder.

Buddy's is about as close as she wants me, or I want to be, to Haven. She walks up, and we kiss cheeks like the platonic friends that I'm deathly afraid we've become.

"Nice bike," I say.

"Yeah, a gift from Andre," she sighs. "The new Valkyrie model."

"Subtle."

"That's what I said. He claims he bought it because it's a rocket."

"He's looking out for you."

I don't bother mentioning that someone, I'm assuming Andre, stole my old bike and replaced it with a gleaming black and gold Harley CVO Road Glide, complete with a new registration. The Glide is still a mighty piece of machinery with tons of torque, but it's faster and lighter than the Electraglide. It came with a note saying, 'For our leaner, meaner gator-slayer. Thanks for bringing her back.'

Hildy doesn't say anything, just stares at the menu. Since it consists of only four entrees, I expect we're done making small talk about bikes.

"So?" I ask.

"So, Aunt Skuldy is back and they've been discussing things," she says. "How's the pulled-pork sandwich here?"

"You mean the pulled-pork sandwich you eat every time you come here?"

"Yep."

"I hear it's tasty," I say. "What does 'discussing things' mean?"

She shakes her head without looking up from the menu.

"Honestly, it's beyond me, Hallr. Much of their conversation is wordless. The earth shakes, the Great Tree blows back, yellow leaves come raining down. They're trying to work things out somehow, but it's hard. You might be right."

"About?"

"You said she'd lost it."

"And you said she hadn't."

"I don't know. Skuldy's ignoring me. No explanation or apologies. After they confronted her, she told them they'd left her no choice, that she'd done what she'd thought was right."

"What the hell does that mean?" I ask, raising my voice. The people sitting near us look in our direction, startled, then look away. I've been stewing for days about how passively Verda and Urdy had accepted the news of their sister's treachery.

"They refuse to make any of the changes Skuldy wants," Hildy say, leaning forward and almost whispering. "They're still doing things the same way they have for millennia."

"But that's good, right?" I say.

"Sure, it's the way the whole thing was designed. But Skuldy wants to run what she calls experiments. Some of it sounds crazy to me."

"Like?"

"Like embedding titanium into some of the carved runes."

"Weird. And why's that?"

"So the runes won't twist as they rise up the tree."

"You're saying the twisting is good?"

"Yggdrasil is alive, Hallr. It doesn't really distort the runes. It allows them to fit with one another, to adjust to new circumstances, to make room for an infinitude of complex events and individual choices. What she's talking about is taking that away, making Yggdrasil do exactly what she wants it to do."

"Why now?" I ask. "Like you said, they've been at this stuff for an eternity."

Hildy shrugs and stands up. We go back to the shack and grab a couple of Miller High Lifes, which is the only beer *Buddy's* serves. Then we order two pulled-pork sandwiches with a side of spicy fries and go back to our bench.

"Did you know the Norns turn up in Shakespeare's *Macbeth* as the three witches called the weird sisters? But it's not really weird as in strange. It's weird as in *wyrd*, which is usually interpreted as *fate*. It comes from an older word *wert*, which means to turn and rotate.

"Those turns in Yggdrasil are key, Hallr. Destiny's not linear, like an iron track a train follows. One fated event affects another in unexpected, interwoven ways that not even my aunts can perfectly predict. These days, Skuldy can't accept that. She thinks humanity needs stronger guidance, that they're out of control and upsetting the balance of nature, killing Yggdrasil in the process."

"But her sisters want none of it."

Hildy nods. We get up again, grab our sandwiches, and Hildy tells me how Skuldy has spent years studying quantum mechanics, determined to poke holes in the underlying notions of uncertainty and unpredictability.

"She's obsessed with the idea that if, as some physicists theorize, there are an infinite number of universes, then her entire existence is pointless," Hildy says. "The other night she was literally screaming, saying that if they can't do a better job of directing wyrd, then they might as well tear reality apart so they can finally see what's behind the 'veil of Yggdrasil,' as she calls it. Or, at the very least, be freed of their meaningless lives."

Hildy's not touching her sandwich. The once-glistening barbecue sauce grows duller as it starts congealing, reminding me of blood hardening on battlefields.

"I think, though she denies it, she has something to do with the comet Loge. It's getting close to Earth now, and it's preoccupying Verda. The scientists say nothing will happen, but..."

I push my plate away. I know things are bad when I stop wanting spicy fries.

"So you're dealing with a dangerously desperate Norn on the edge of ontological despair," I conclude.

Hildy sighs deeply.

"Well, it may not be quite that bad," Hildy says, gamely trying for a smile. "The three of them were having a conciliatory cup of tea when I left. Maybe the worst is over."

I move our conversation away from Skuld. Hildy has taken an official leave of absence from *Hild Brands*, having explained to her board members that she's in the middle of a family crisis. And she's convinced Andre to stick around Haven, at least as long as Skuld remains.

All of this makes me feel a little better. Dope-fiend Hildy seems gone, though maybe I'm seeing what I want to see. Regardless, I take the risk of telling her about my suspicions of Misty as well as how I sent Fred up to Vandriller Junction to spy on Lucky's creepy-ass crack house.

"That's dangerous," she says. "Lucky knows Fred and could spot him a mile away."

"Fred's not going inside that dump, just watching the comings and goings from a distance. Lucky and Skuldy are connected in ways we don't understand. Lucky and company are not just dealing smack. There's some of kind of bizarre indoctrination going on."

Hildy stares down at the table, which is riddled with initials that kids have carved into the wood over the years. I don't know if she's just ashamed of whatever happened there or troubled by the fact that she was so oblivious to the Skuld-Lucky relationship.

"It's still dangerous," she finally says.

"No doubt it is, but I can't think of anything else to do," I say.

She looks up from the table and into my eyes. "You're right. It's a good idea for now, at least until Urdy and Verda can get Skuldy calmed down. They're patient with her. She's always been the high-strung one. They'll figure it out."

It's completely dark now. Estelle, who is Buddy's wife, or at least his long-time girlfriend, comes around and lights the citronella candles on all the tables. Families have taken up most of the other tables, and I'm sure Estelle would like us to hit the road to make room for new arrivals.

I walk Hildy over to the parking lot. I bend to her and she gives me a quick, dry kiss on the cheek.

As I wave goodbye to her, the aridity of that kiss lingers. A relationship gone to ashes. I'm suddenly filled with a black wrath and an impulse to destroy something in this worthless universe, one that even Urdy and Verda won't properly defend from the very bitch trying to destroy them.

Rather than getting on my bike, I turn and walk in the direction of a family at one of the picnic tables. I remember Captain Grim and how he furiously chopped up children during his raids, and I'm suddenly, inexplicably desperate to do the same. To raze, slay, annihilate. To pull the arms and legs off these inferior, enfeebled humans.

As I get close to the family of four—a plumpish mother with two towheaded young kids and their lean, dark-haired father still wearing some work shirt with his name stenciled onto it—they swivel their heads toward me, alarmed. At the last second, I swerve by them and tromp directly into the forest beyond, smashing through the foliage until I find a young oak, grab it by its gray trunk and pull the whole thing out of the ground, roots and all. Then I start swinging it like a club against the trunks of the larger trees—mostly longleafed pines—until the oak is splintered and shredded into a thousand pieces.

Finally, the storm inside me quiets and I weep. I weep for my present and past and future. I weep for all the things I've lost and all the things I will never have.

When I emerge again from the dark forest, my phone rings as if on cue. It IDs the caller as Misty, whom I've been brooding about since the night I finally found Hildy. Reluctantly, I answer it, only to hear a voice that is definitely not Misty.

"What'd'ya say, big man!"

"Who's this?" I ask, though I already know.

"How's the head? Still a pool-cue-sized dent thereabouts?"

"No," I say.

"So listen, fat-ass. Oh wait, Lam calls you a troll. I like that. It's a good way to describe a big, mutant-looking giant with a potbelly and a dead-end job."

"Get to the point, pissant."

"First point is this. Lam has been making noises about wanting you to join us. She's read her tea leaves or whatever and said you might finally be ready. The planets aligning, some shit like that. Are you, big boy? Ready to let go of your death grip on your loser life and join the *übermensch* once and for all?"

"I'll think about it," I say, realizing that Skuld might even be right about me, descendant of giants and kin of Grendel. Destroyers. "What's the second point?"

"Second point is I've got little Miss Girlie right here in front of me, giggling as I tickle her with my favorite karambit. If you're still being all gallant these days, I thought you might want to come back out here and give her a little rescuing."

"Put her on the phone," I say.

"Don't tell me what to do!" he snaps, his smart-ass, smirking attitude suddenly falling away. "I'm in control here!"

I say nothing. The boy is clearly unhinged. By and by, he puts Misty on the phone. She's weeping.

"Can it, Misty," I say. "I know you've been working with them, so I doubt you need a lot of rescuing. But I don't know why you'd help the dickweed that pointed a gun at you for the sheer pleasure of it."

She's trying to speak through tears, choking on either real or pretend phlegm.

"You tried to steer me away from Lucky's place when I was closing in," I say. "And Edmund knew way more about us than he should have. Fred didn't want to think you were the leak, but he checked and found the texts on your phone. This week, I asked Edmund about it and he confirmed you'd fed him information."

"I had to, Klaus. Lucky said he'd hurt Fred."

In the background, Lucky says, "Damned right I did. And I would, too."

"He's not *normal*, Klaus. He's some kind of..."

She's gone. Lucky has taken the phone from her.

"Oh, tis true, troll boy, that she was supposed to spy for us, but she did such a shitty job of it, I've got to reprimand her. That's just good management, after all."

"Fine, so you're in Vandriller, I take it."

"Surely, surely am. We'll put out the welcome mat for you. And bring little Miss Hildy, too, why don't you? I hear tell she's a fighter, though so far I've only seen her on her knees begging for a fix."

That's not true. Can't be true. Stay cool.

"It'll take a few hours," I say.

"Oh, we're all about the patience, tollkeeper. All about the patience."

I go back to *Buddy's* and sit down under a nearby live oak, no doubt making the locals nervous. It takes me a while to reach Fred by phone. When I finally do, he's just a few minutes away from Vandriller Junction. I tell him about Misty.

"I don't know what to believe, kid," I say. "Maybe she was telling the truth, maybe parts of it, maybe it's all bullshit. Maybe your psycho ex-buddy is just looking for payback, or maybe he's up to something else. Whatever's going on, you'd be an idiot to just barge in there alone playing the hero."

"He's messed with her mind, Klaus," he says. "She thinks she's protecting me. But don't worry, I'm not an idiot."

He says he can quickly get the local cops involved without bringing in the Feds, who would usually take over and complicate a potential kidnapping. I tell him to give me a call as soon as he knows something. Not for the first time, I wonder if I can trust Lucky's former pal.

Should I ride up there? Should I call the cops myself? I try Hildy's cell, though I know that's a long shot. She has to leave Haven to get a cell connection.

Lucky's a tricky little thug. My gut tells me to go to Haven. But then I wouldn't be able to get Fred's call, which might be crucial. If it's true that there is no such thing as fate and that universes really do split apart during key moments of decision, then this moment would be one of them.

I get up and grab another Miller High Life from *Buddy's*, then lean back up against the tree to watch the locals. Estelle has lit bamboo tiki-type torches, which cast long shadows of the men, women and children huddling around their picnic tables. There's laughter, conversations, kids playing with the candles on the table. It's primal, barely different at all from how humans lived over a thousand years ago: bread, meat, fire, comradery, stories. Always more stories, woven and interwoven like the webs of fate.

My phone rings.

"Klaus," Fred says. "Nobody's here, the house is empty except for some trash on the floors. The cops think I'm a crazy crank."

"Okay, we got played. Let's try…"

The call drops. Just as I'm about to dial Fred's number, the phone rings again. The ID says "Urd," which is impossible. Aunt Urdy's about as likely to use a cell phone as I am a spinning wheel.

When I answer, there are only two words weakly spoken in the Old Tongue. "Troll, come."

Chapter Forty-Five

Bjor had me dead to rights. The tip of his knife pricked at my jugular when I awoke to his whispering. He could kill me with the barest flick of his wrist. I stayed very still.

My main concern, aside from staying alive, was remaining quiet enough that Solveig and the children wouldn't be wakened. She was sleeping with our youngest, Alva, to make her feedings more frequent. The little girl had trouble taking the nipple and, as a result, was not gaining weight quickly enough.

I didn't know how much of this Bjor knew, but I had to assume everything. He was never a stupid man. He was, however, very bold to enter our home. Working as an assassin, I always waited for my victims to come out into the open air.

"Hello, Bjor," I said softly.

"Hello, Hallr," he said. "Still deny it's Hallr?"

"Would it matter if I did?"

"You might be dead faster."

"Then, no," I said.

"Why did you let me live when we got to Iceland, Hallr?"

"I'm asking myself that very question."

"Then I'll tell you. Because you have a semblance of honor. That bothers me. I find it unnatural in a troll, as if you were a talking dog or flying snake."

"Yes, rather creepy."

He pushes the blade in just enough to draw blood.

"You're not taking me seriously, Captain Troll."

"On the contrary, I'm taking you deadly seriously. You must want something besides killing me, or I'd be dead."

"Maybe I want a bit of conversation so I can enjoy your terror and regret, getting my fill of vengeance," he said.

"Could be."

"So, Alfr's Troll, are you overcome with anguished contrition?"

"Not exactly, but you've certainly gotten my attention."

"It's very tempting to kill you. Think of how nice a twist that would put on 'The Death of Thorolf the Brave.'"

"Yes, maybe I'd even get my name in the song title this time."

"But, no, I want a more complete yet honorable revenge, Hallr Half-troll. Have you realized the No-thing has decided you should die? Not because of anything you've done, mind you. They fear what you know, your skills, and what you might do in the future."

"I guess I should have seen that coming," I say. "They're the paranoid and proactive types."

"Indeed, and on this particular matter, they and King Sunmane are in complete agreement. Alfr's Troll must die."

"They say great minds think alike. But I take it you have a different plan."

"Indeed I do. Here's how it works. You legally turn over all your lands to me, leave Iceland, and never look back. In exchange, I forget about Sunmane's reward for your head, take credit with the No-thing for disposing of their troll problem, and swear to you on my life that I will protect your family as long as I draw breath."

"Why would anyone need to protect my family? They've done nothing, and Solveig is the niece of one of their most esteemed members."

"Actually, no. I'm sorry—though not very sorry—to be the bearer of yet another piece of bad news. You see, Asmund has recently passed on."

I'd seen Asmund just a few days before, when he'd seemed well. I thought of how devastated Solveig would be.

"When, and how?" I asked.

"Keep in mind that I absolutely will kill you, Alfr's Troll. I'll have no compunction. It would probably be the best for everyone, anyway."

"You'll have to kill me quite soon if you don't tell me when and how."

Bjor sighed.

"Asmund passionately argued that the No-thing should leave you in peace. They began to worry that he would ultimately side with you, and that would shift the balance of power in Iceland. If their two best assassins suddenly turned on them... well, you can see how they might want to take measures against such a possibility."

I already knew the answer, but I asked him the question one more time, wondering if I could still kill him after he'd sliced my carotid. I thought it might well be possible. I'd heard of trolls raging several minutes after having their heads cut off.

"You've already figured it out, haven't you, Halftroll? Yes, I slew him just a few hours ago, demonstrating my skill set to the skeptical No-thing. And they will look for his killer quite nearby. You see..."

That was when Solveig smashed Bjor's head in with a household hammer I had been using to do repairs in the nursery. Although she was no shapeshifter, Solveig had learned the art of stealth from her uncle. And the art of striking a death blow, as well. She'd heard what Bjor had said about her uncle. Once the would-be assassin fell, she kept her hammering with two hands, smashing one hole after another into his skull.

She only relented when she heard Alva's crying in the room next door.

Although I couldn't fault Solveig, I wished she had dispatched Bjor after he'd finished his explanations. There was something in his last words that didn't sit right with me.

The first thing I had to do, of course, was figure out what to tell Solveig. She kneeled over Bjor's corpse, still holding the hammer high. As I moved slowly to take it out of her hands, she suddenly swung the hammer in my direction. As gently as I could, I grabbed her hands and pried it out of her bloody fingers. Then I picked her up and embraced her, though her arms had fallen lifelessly by her sides.

"You're an assassin," she said.

"I was. No more," I said.

"And uncle, too?"

"Yes."

"Why? He was such a good man," she said, pushing out of my arms.

I hesitated, searching for the right words. Or maybe just the right set of lies.

"I must wash," she said, briskly turning away. "Then I must nurse Alva, or Ying will soon be up. We can't let him see this."

So I was left to clean up the bloody killing, while she went on to nurse our hungry child.

It was not long after I'd placed Bjor's body in our barn that we heard the horsemen coming.

Magnus, Asmund's second son, had become a man. Not a stupid one, but not overly bright, either. He assumed the world was as it seemed, coming at life in a straightforward manner.

So, when he found my sword, Vidar, standing like a Christian cross in his fallen father's back, he came to the obvious conclusion. Vidar was among the most well-known and admired swords in the region. I'd wear it to all festive and formal occasions. Men would lust after it as if it were a beautiful woman, a fabulous Freya of tempered, strong steel.

Magnus was joined by his brother Mar and four others. They rode hard to our farm, their hearts pulsing with vengeance.

The moment I opened the door, Magnus threw bloody Vidar at my feet as if it were the corpse of Asmund itself. When I jumped away from the blade, Magnus swung his favorite engraved hand axe at my head. With my left hand, I caught his arm as it plunged toward me, though he still managed to slice my forearm. With my right hand, I punched him. I had the presence of mind to hit him in the chest rather than the face, which might have killed him.

I turned and fled from the men, flying out the back into the icy gloom. There was no way to talk to them. If I stayed, I'd either kill my kin or be killed by them. Killing kin was the ultimate sin among the Norse.

As I ran, the sight of the bloody sword flashed again in my mind. Before Solveig killed him, that was probably going to be Bjor's next bragging point: that he'd slipped into our house not once but twice—the first time to steal Vidar, which I'd kept displayed on a wooden rack over the fireplace. I cursed myself for my complacency.

Magnus and his men immediately began the hunt, having brought along two dogs. My best advantage was familiarity with the landscape. By then, I knew every crevice, boulder and snow-hidden stony wall. I strangled the over-eager dog that got too close and smashed the hind-quarters of the other with a large rock. Though I escaped, I knew they'd come for me again when the weak, winter sun finally rose.

They wouldn't hurt Solveig or the kids. In fact, I still held out hope Solveig could eventually convince them of my innocence. Certainly, Bjor's corpse was evidence in my favor. She could tell them at least part of the truth—that Bjor sought to frame me in revenge for his years of thralldom. But that would take time.

Weighing my options, I made for Eldborg crater. The distance to it was so great that they probably couldn't track me all the way there in the few hours of daylight available. Even if more dogs were able to track me all the way to Eldborg in the darkness, I'd have the precious high ground.

These days, I hear that Eldborg is as dead as an old bone, its circular crater rising seventy yards or so above the frozen lava fields. Back then, though, it was a long simmering and smoking furnace, threatening to detonate and spew hot ash and brimstone for miles.

That night, I scrambled up the windward side of the volcano so as to avoid the smoke as best I could. Still, here was no escaping the rotten-egg stench. It was toxic and acrid, badly inflaming my nasal cavities.

As I crouched among the flaking igneous on the rim of Eldborg, I thought of how similar and yet utterly different I was from my kin hunched amid the granite mountains of Norway. Cold, stoic, solitary creatures nearly melded with the crags themselves. I envied the ones who, tiring of their long lives, lingered through the dawn in order to finally become true stones themselves, hardened into a restful oblivion.

I didn't have that option. The sun would sear my mind and scorch my body, but never give me peace. Eldborg, however, offered me a similar end. In the crater below was an orange-red circle of flowing fire, a foundry in which I could unmake myself, become as one with the liquid stone.

Was that my intention when I decided to slip down the crumbly rim a few yards? Centuries later, I'm still not sure. Eldborg's molten lake was not a bubbling cauldron throwing up gobs of lava, but more of a glowing stew set to a low simmer. Even so, the air was baking hot and carrying enough chlorine and sulfur dioxide to make me dizzy. It would have been a simple matter for me to slide off the ledge and out of history.

"Shall I scrape you into the fire like a scrap of rotten meat?" a voice asked.

If I hadn't already been muddled by the gases, he might have startled me off the ledge. As it was, though, the appearance of this impossible being barely surprised me, as if he were just a character in one of my dreams.

He was big. Bigger than any troll I'd seen, even among the ancients of Jotunheim. A true giant. His skin was as charred as the black crust on slow-moving lava, though crimson glowed through cracks and patches. Sitting naked on a nearby outcropping, he appeared comfortable. He'd stabbed a huge sword into the cliff, which he used to anchor himself. It was his sword, which glowed like hot coals, that gave him away.

"You're Surt," I said, remembering the myths of a kingly fire giant destined to defeat the gods and destroy the world in fire.

"And you are Sveigðir-volsungr."

I'd never heard the name before, though the ring of "Völsung" within it vexed me.

"No," I said, feeling stubborn for reasons I couldn't name.

The giant grinned, his large teeth a glaring white. The scorched man had implausibly noble features, even without a particle of hair.

"We do not choose our true names," he said.

"I do."

Surt's smile slowly faded as he realized I was serious.

"Show me your markings," he commanded. I could feel the broiling heat radiating off his face as I bowed and he leaned over me to read the runes. As the giant pondered, I felt my fate swing to and fro like a weathervane before a storm.

"It's true, your destiny is finely wrought, though strangely obscured. There may come a day when, small though you be, great things hinge on you. Will you be ally or foe? Both aspects are yours."

I squinted up at him, my slowed mind struggling to grasp his meaning. He scrutinized my face, then sighed.

"On this day, we'll let the sword decide," he said.

With that, he pulled what the kennings called "Surt's blaze" from the cliff head and tossed it nonchalantly into the air. The enormous weapon swung end over end like a juggler's torch. It must have risen hundreds of yards above the rim of Eldborg. I was transfixed by the deadly beauty of it and the awesome power of Surt. It was only when the blade began its downward arc that I realized it was going to cleave the ledge on which I was braced.

I scrambled madly upwards, the loose rocks sliding under my hands and feet as if I were an insect caught in the pit of an antlion. It was only by gouging my thick fingers into the stone body of the crater that I managed to gain enough traction. Just as I reached the rim, Surt's sword plummeted past, roaring as its flames tore through the air. Adrenalin pumping, I virtually threw myself down the jagged rocks coating Eldborg's flanks, trying to maintain my footing but sometimes tumbling down on my knees or sliding on my back. There was a cacophonous report of the sword clanging down the throat of the volcano. When it hit the fiery lake, an explosive plume shot skyward.

It wasn't an actual eruption, more of a gigantic molten burp spewing ash and cinders. Several fist-sized pyroclasts fell like burning hail onto the black-and-white mink cloak I threw like a hood over my head and shoulders. I had to beat my flaming clothes with bare hands.

After the immediate dangers passed, I plodded back in the direction of my farm through a shower of thin, black dust. I laughed to myself like a lunatic. I didn't know if Surt had been real or just a vision brought on by the noxious miasmas of Eldborg. Either way, though, I'd faced down and survived the Lord of the Fire-Giants. I'd be damned if I was going to run from the callow, petulant children of Asmund.

Chapter Forty-Six

"Vision is the art of seeing what is invisible to others."
—Jonathan Swift

As I straddle my bike in the parking lot, I hear a scream and turn to see Buddy, his greasy apron ablaze, running from the smoking hut where he does his barbecuing. The rest of his clothes instantly catch fire. Buddy explodes like a scratched match, then falls to the ground, rolling and writhing. Just beyond him, the hut itself erupts into a conflagration, then immediately dies down into an ember. It all happens in a flash, as if I were watching a film on fast forward.

Impossible. What I've just seen is impossible. Yet I can't take time to puzzle it out. Urdy has called. Called without a phone.

I turn out of the parking lot onto the dark county road, which cuts through thick woods. This is usually a quiet ride, with few cars on the road. Just me and woods and the sound of the bike. But now there's crackling behind me, as if I were being hounded by a skeletal beast with popping bones. I check the rearview mirror and see that the asphalt road behind me is being churned up.

Insanity. My bike and I are somehow ravaging the road behind as we pass over it, a plow of annihilation. Or are we being stalked by an invisible destructive force? Although I'm already speeding too fast down this lonely road, I throttle up even more, striving to leave the destruction behind.

"Mimir," I say aloud into my helmet, "what in the hell is going on?"

I suppose you'd deem it a psychotic break, troll.

"So I'm hallucinating."

Not precisely, Mimir says. *It's what the seers call 'norn sight' or 'norn vision.' Odin put great stock in it.*

"I heard Urdy's voice on the phone before. Is she plaguing me with these visions?"

In a way. Though they're not exactly visions in the plural so much as vision in the singular.

"Wait. You're saying this is how a norn sees the world? All the time?"

The three Great Norns do, yes. Temporality has only passing significance to the three sisters. What is, what will be, what was, what could be, what signifies as. These are all of a piece, troll. How did you think they viewed the universe? Certainly not with your tragically circumscribed sense of reality, almost human in its paucity.

"Why is she doing it? If she wants me to get to Haven, this is not helping a damn bit."

Oh, I very much doubt she intended it. I assume it is a side effect.

I decide not to give him the satisfaction of asking, "Side effect of what?" The visions themselves have me distracted enough.

From here, there are two ways of reaching the entrance to Haven. One is via a diagonal bypass to Route 9; the other is the main junction of Route 9, which T-bones with this road in another mile. I am preparing to take the bypass, drifting from the center of the road into the right lane, when the bypass blinks out of existence. There is nothing there but a wall of trees, indistinguishable from the rest of the forest.

"What the fuck?" I yell, swerving away, nearly ditching the bike, which would likely be fatal at these speeds.

Mimir explodes into hilarity.

"It's not funny. I could have been killed. Was the bypass actually there?"

Well, that depends on how we think about the arrow of time and entropy, among other things. Now if we assume that the arrow...

"Forget it, you freak show."

I wonder if there's logic to this. I'd prefer not to smash into a real-life, kill-you-stone-dead truck that I don't happen to register while having a vision. Yet I need to take the risk of riding. There's no time for caution, assuming I didn't hallucinate Urdy's call in the first place. Which seems all too possible.

Suddenly I'm flying. Or, rather, the bike is. Maybe a hundred feet below me is the path leading to Haven, crowded with various types of animals. Sheep, rabbits, wolves, lizards, snakes. As if in a fairy tale, they're all human-sized. Two wolves race ahead of the others along the path. They attack Andre as he stands guard. One snatches his arm, the other his leg, snarling as they try to delimb him.

Then the vision fades. I don't need to ask Mimir the meaning. I got the gist. Haven is, or soon will be, under attack.

Just as I am approaching the T-bone with Route 9, I see a phalanx of bikers cruising by, heading north. There are maybe fifteen of them out in front of a couple of ancient minivans and a black Ford pickup truck, and another fifteen or so riding behind. I arrive at the intersection just in time to see the patches on the back of their jackets. Fendwellers.

I've got to assume these men are real and on their way to Haven. So, how does one stop thirty to forty guys plus whoever's in the vans and trucks? Beats the hell out of me. I'm just going to follow them from a distance while I think.

Maybe these bikers are the animals in the vision. They're planning to invade Haven in order to... what? Kill Urdy and Verda? Burn their manor down? I've no idea. They could be planning a pajama party with Skuld for all I know. I could call the cops but, assuming they could even find the place, they can't do anything until this little menagerie breaks a law.

I decide on a straightforward approach. I speed up to catch the phalanx, and then pull alongside one of the two bikers bringing up the rear of the cavalcade.

"Hey man," I shout to him. "You guys going to party somewhere around here?"

He looks like a genuine MC type: thirty-something, denim vest, tattoos, mustache and goatee, jeans, a black bandana with a gold snake design. I've seen guys like him ride by the tollbooth countless times. Nice people most of the time. This dude gives me a deadpan look with deep-set, brown eyes, then asks if my name is Klaus. I tell him no. He says nothing, just nonchalantly reaches his right hand into his jacket.

As I watch him, another vision clamps down on me. The biker's head transforms into the head of a diamondback rattler drawn back for a strike. I hit my brakes as hard as I can without flipping, catching Snakehead by surprise. He tries to swivel to shoot the gun that he's whipped out, but I've plunged myself into darkness.

I pivot the bike by throwing down my legs, picking it up and turning it the other way. Not a smooth move, though it works for me. I'm throttling in the opposite direction as fast as this new bike will take me, which is considerably faster than the old one would have. I make a note to thank Andre if he and I happen to live through this night.

I switch off the headlamps. No point in giving Snakehead a target if he follows. When my lights are extinguished, I see to either side of me long, linear swaths of greenish bioluminescence. We called it *foxfire* in the forests of Norway. Based on how it's glowing, it looks like honey fungus. However, that stuff grows on dead trees, not on the asphalt of Route 9. As Urdy's visions go, this one seems pretty straightforward. I follow the dark path that unfurls between the dual swaths of ghostly glow, trusting there's a method in her madness.

I slow as the luminescent path veers off the pavement to the left, but take it without question. By all rights, I should be headed into a gruesome death that involves being shattered by the trunks of pines and oaks. Instead, the glowing path leads me into a mouth of an impossible cave. Not just any cave. The cave where I lived with Mor.

I wind down the bike. The vision implies I'm safely ensconced. Outside the cave, I hear the reverberation of motorbikes blasting past. As I turn my bike around to face the cave opening, I'm startled to see someone in front of me, then shiver as I recognize her.

"Greetings, Mor," I say shakily.

She reaches up to put her hand on my shoulder. This gesture is as close as we ever came to an embrace.

"Sorry I never went back to the caves, Mor. I should have checked."

"You didn't want to know," she says.

"No."

"It was the cunning thing to do," she says, smiling. That's unlike her. She's smaller than I remember. Her arms are thin, though tough-looking and sinewy. Her hair is wiry, black and gray, forming a wild mane. Like mine, her nose is aquiline rather than the stereotypical broad, spatulate, troll-type. Her cheeks are high and full, as if someone had used them to sharpen the edge of their blades. I see a glimmer of the fiercely fair woman who wooed my father, whomever he was, out of the safe straits of Norse normality.

She motions for me to lower my head to her. I anticipate a slap or maybe a whispered message. Instead, she kisses my cheek, something she never did in life.

"Go now," she says, walking past me and into the darkness of the cave. Her voice is joined by Urdy's and Verda's. Together, they say, "Do not waver."

The cave disappears. I'm standing in the woods between two huge banyan trees, their roots spread around me like a cage of tentacles. Facing the road, I hear two motorcycles approaching. Stepping out from between the banyans, I see the long, broken trunk of a fallen, half-rotted pine tree. It's leaning up against one of the banyans like an actor killing time in the wings before going on stage. This is your moment, tree. As I pull it, the opposite end falls to the ground, exploding in a puff of leaf detritus and dust. I position it so that one end points out toward Route 9.

The bikers who chased me are coming back this way. There are two headlamps. I sling my entire arm span around the end of the trunk. Just about the time I can clearly identify Snakehead on his bike, I catapult the trunk into the middle of the road. As their front wheels smash into the beetle-bored bark of the rotting log, the men somersault up and over it, unwieldy and unwilling victims of ruthless physics. Snakehead's bike crashes down on top of him like a sudden slap from a hostile universe. The other biker is thrown higher into the air. He reaches his apogee, windmills gracelessly, and belly flops into the implacable pavement.

I move quickly before another vehicle comes. I push the tree trunk mostly out of the road, then check on the men. Snakehead's corpse is mangled, one eye turned to pulp. I strip him of his jacket and bandana. The other man is unconscious and wheezing. Something has punctured his lung, I'd say.

I should just put him out of his misery. He would have shot me without a second thought. Hell, it wasn't long ago I killed Olaf just for being a dickhead. I prepare to break his neck with a swift kick. But don't. Instead, I pull them and their bikes to the side so they're out of the road. No need to cause another accident.

I hate it. None of it is clean, either morally or, speaking as an assassin, professionally. If he lives, he might tie me back to this. But that's not something I can worry about right now.

I catch up with the cavalcade surprisingly quickly. They've slowed down, I suppose, to await the return of their comrades. The pickup truck and some of the bikers, however, are gone. I assume they've raced ahead of the main group.

There's no time to overthink things. I take Snakehead's bandana and tie it over my nose and mouth like a bank robber in old films, or like a biker who is sick of cleaning lovebugs out of his teeth. I throttle up and blow by the guys in the back, past the vans, then past the riders at the vanguard. I crouch low to disguise my height as best I can.

My hope is that, even if this seems suspicious, Snakehead's jacket will confuse them long enough for me to get well in front. It's only another fifteen or twenty miles to the turnoff onto the path that leads to Haven.

I'm running the Road Glide full out, praying that a deer or bear doesn't suddenly cross my path. Unless one of the Fendwellers is riding an absolute crotch rocket, I should be able to gain a few miles on them. But how to stop or slow them? I can't very well throw dead trees at them all night.

Five miles or so before the turnoff, I spot a rusty, 1960s-era, black Buick Riviera in a driveway, no doubt somebody's weekend restoration project. I pass it fast but go back around to have another look. What was once a grand, almost heroic automobile is now a decayed hulk. The passenger door isn't locked. I lean in, put the hulk in neutral, and push it backwards as quickly as I can, considering the tires are not just flat but rotting off. I soon have it spanning across both lanes of the road. I yank off the strips of chrome and anything else that could be reflective. Next I roll my Harley out in front of the Buick relic, turn on the bike's high beams and wait. It doesn't take long for the Fendweller caravan to show up.

My plan is to blind them long enough with my high beams that they don't spot the Buick till it's too late. This new bike comes with dual

LED headlamps that I hope will do the job, but I know the beams are focused forward. The light may not be broad enough to blind them all.

It's like a game of chicken, except I'm a sitting duck. I can't yank my bike away till they're too close to stop. They're coming, coming, coming. When I see the first barely visible glow of brake lights on pavement, I flip off my lamps, wrench the bike away and gain as much distance between me and the collision as I can.

I feel a surge of victory when squealing tires sing out like a flock of mortally wounded violins, followed by sickening concussive thumps and explosions of tempered glass. I'm running the bike barely fast enough to stay prone, listening hard so I can judge the damage. Men shout and curse.

My euphoria quickly fades. While slowing down this group, the other one has left me far behind. I have wasted precious time. As I throttle up the bike, I'm so desperate I resort to prayer, beseeching Arg-ending Odin to call off his fucking wolves.

Chapter Forty-Seven

"In the feud He rejoiced not, but far away drove him
From kindred and kind, that crime to atone for,
Meter of Justice."

—*Beowulf*

They sentenced me to exile for two years. In the end, it was either that or a holmgang with Magnus. He still believed I was ultimately responsible for his father's murder, as indeed I was.

The holmgang was sorely tempting. Not only would I have prevailed, I probably could have used my greater bulk to force him beyond the ox hide's perimeter, thereby winning without seriously injuring him.

I chose exile for several reasons. First was Solveig's worry for her cousin. She knew how much Magnus yearned for my death and doubted I could avoid harming him in a duel.

More importantly, the No-thing survived. I yearned to kill Regis as much as Magnus did me, yet the leader of the cabal was slippery prey. There were rumors he had fled Vík í Mýrdal to parts unknown. He would recruit more assassins. Even if I caught him, there were the other members, some still unknown to me.

Bjor thought the No-thing might settle for my exile. Would my family be safe? I'd never heard of it targeting women and children.

Rather than trying to explain the No-thing to Asmund's sons, Solveig and I blamed everything on Sunmane. We told Asmund's son Mar, who was wiser than his brother, that King Sunmane might still send more assassins. He agreed to take over the farm in my absence and protect my family.

Ultimately, though, the primary reason I allowed the local chieftains to exile me was my conversation with Solveig.

Solveig sat in front of our hearth on a low plank chair I'd constructed for her using driftwood from a wrecked ship. She was nursing Alva. I sat cross-legged nearby, both of us staring into the fire.

"You've barely spoken to me for a week," I said quietly.

She nodded.

"I must know your mind, Solveig. You are the wiser of us two. In fact, the wisest person I know."

She dropped her gaze to Alva, unwilling to look at me.

"In truth, Eirik, I no longer know with whom I speak."

"I am the same, Solveig."

"The same what, Eirik? I am not a fool. I've always known you were the Halftroll of legend."

I sucked in my breath. Though an open secret, it was not something we'd ever discussed.

"Yet I also saw you as a man. Marred as all men are, but also perceptive and resourceful. In this land, we may all remake ourselves, even heroes from tales."

Heroes. The word baffled me.

"Or monsters," I said.

"Yes," she said, her eyes finally finding mine. "Even monsters. But perhaps monsters cannot be unmade. Perhaps I was a fool to believe it."

"Perhaps you were," I said, trying to contain my resentment. "Or maybe assassins can serve the good, Solveig. Your uncle thought so."

She lowered her eyes again to Alva. The child had fallen asleep.

"I loved him," she said, barely above a whisper now. "Yet I also knew the secret of his shapeshifting, Eirik. I was the only member of the family who did, aside from my aunt. Now I wonder if he, too, was fated toward darkness."

I thought of Surt's words about a "finely wrought" fate.

"Do you know the Roman word *redimere*, Eirik?"

"No. One of Ulfar's words?"

"Yes, he taught me some tenets of the new religion he follows. *Redimere* is much like *gjalda*, meaning to repay. But it also means *rétta*, to atone. Ulfar believes anyone can be 'redeemed.'"

"And what do you believe, Solveig?"

"That the Halftroll would duel Magnus, but Eirik Sturlung would exile the monster for its sins and then return to his family a redeemed man."

In that moment, I yearned to explode like Eldborg itself, arguing that trolls were no more monstrous than men. Quite the contrary. Men, not trolls, invented the No-thing. I was only their tool. I ached to quarrel with her assumptions, biases, and sanctimonious dogma. Ultimately, though, I held my tongue. Whether I was troll or man, something in me craved her absolution.

"Then, my wife, exile it shall be. When I return, Alva will be speaking and I will tell her tales of villains and monsters slain."

Chapter Forty-Eight

"More serpents lie under Yggdrasil's ash than any one
would think of witless mortals."
—*Poetic Edda*

Battles are for suckers. Men lining up for slaughter. Spear lines, musket lines, infantry lines, front lines of all sorts. Poor bastards being mowed down in droves because that's where some chieftain or jarl or king or general or president tells them to stand.

Trolls don't battle. They attack, assault, clash, contend, crush. They impale their prey in charges down mountains, or smash them in canyons with boulders, or club them as they march along wooded, dark trails.

At times, I have played the game of human battles, lined up like a pawn on a chessboard. There's an exhilaration to it, a rush of adrenalin, abandonment, and bloodlust. Fight for your comrades, die for them, too. Honor, glory. It makes a kind of sense if you believe, as many do, that humans descended from bands of sharp-toothed apes waging war in treetops.

No, I've had enough of human battles. I'll fight and die like a troll, not like those men casually dying in droves.

So, I fall into stalking mode rather than battle mode when I arrive at the decrepit billboard—with its faded reds and yellows weakly proclaiming the virtues of a Remington chainsaw long since defunct—and see the scratched, black Ford pickup parked there like a dark omen.

On the path behind the billboard, there are tracks stinking of gasoline. Thinly treaded roadsters and cruisers have rolled past recently, along with some sport bikes with bigger tires. There are a few deeper treads telling the tale of what must have been in the bed of the truck: a three-wheeled ATV, a type of monstrous machine befouling American forests from sea to shining sea. And, I think, maybe a couple of dirt bikes thrown into the mix.

I dump my own bike in the woods, knowing it will be less than useless from this point onward. The fact that the Fendwellers took their machines into the jungle bodes well for me. I'm licking my chops, thinking of these night-blind morons crashing through the brush. Time to go hunting.

I rush down the paths I've come to know well, a true fendweller intent on prowling for pretenders. It's only minutes before I catch up with the moaning, groaning dimwits shoving their hogs through vines and slashing saw palmettos. Wielding flashlights, they're scurrying about, seeking the tracks of the ATV that has left them in the dust. Despite the leather jackets and tats, most are fresh meat, barely more than children.

I wonder about weapons or, more precisely, firearms. Even a scared kid, barely trained, can pop off a lucky shot in the dark. Combat was better before gunpowder, when the skilled and the strong prevailed, barring a chance arrow or lucky swing of a Dane-axe in a melee. But screw it. I'm way too old to believe there was ever a Golden Age of violence.

I could kill them all. Snatching them out of the dark, bending their little chicken necks, then going back for more.

Yet, even on these seidr-soaked borders of Haven, we live in an age of laws. Better if I don't kill too many. I'm already past a modern troll's quota for the evening.

So I stride toward these boys, who are the sheep and rabbits of my original vision, and yank one toward me. A bald, stocky kid with a swastika on his cheek. I immediately designate him Adolph Penis Head.

"Evening, boys," I say, now holding Adolph in front of me in a headlock. "This is private property. You're trespassing and, according to the yahoo laws of this backwards state, I could now shoot you dead with impunity."

That's not exactly true but it's a reasonable bluff in a state where a kid was legally shot on a public sidewalk for the crime of carrying Skittles.

"I already called the sheriff. They're on their way, and the backwoods cops around here don't play. I recommend pushing those hogs back out to the road and calling it a night. That-a-way."

I'm doing my best to loom over them, conjuring up every primal, run-away-from-the-giant instinct they have. I step sideways off the path, still hanging onto the red-faced Adolph, motioning for them to leave the way they'd come. Which, amazingly, they do, passing by me one at a time. That is, up until the last guy, who I recognize as the mini-bouncer at Lucky's crack house. Just a couple of feet before he passes by, another vision descends on me. The boy's face morphs into that of a hooked-beak, sharp-faced Florida snapping turtle. I don't know exactly what that signifies in the lexicon of Urdy, but I can't imagine it bodes well. I chuck chunky Adolph right smack into Turtlehead. They both go tumbling down while I move behind Turtlehead, haul him up by the scruff of his leather jacket, and snatch a snappy little .22-caliber aluminum gun out of his right pocket.

"Goddamned kid," I say, pulling him up. My adrenalin pumping, I'm primed to literally tear off one of his shoulders, Beowulf-style. Instead, I give him an old-fart lecture.

"Wake up, kid. The world is wondrous and life is short. Don't be suckered by the likes of loony Lucky. Go be somebody, somebody who's worth a shit, who does some good in this weird-ass universe."

"Fuck you, freak," he says, walking away with the rest of the pack. As he does, though, the hideous turtlehead dissolves into something human. I hope to hell he doesn't come back.

The annihilation of the cosmos begins with all the slightly sleazy, vaguely pathetic drama of one of those reality-TV cop shows. There's a drunken thug yelling at a darkened house, claiming he was invited in by some woman of dubious character. The thug in question is, of course, the dangerous little shit Lucky.

"I'm telling you, bro," he's shouting from behind a tall, longleaf pine. "We are official invitees of little Miss Skuldy. It's a special-delivery-type situation." His words are slurred, but I've been down this road before. It's an act, a way of lowering the expectations of his enemies.

"Go home, boys," answers Andre, who is crouched behind the balustrade on the roof of the porch. "Rednecks will be shot on sight in these parts."

Lucky motions to others who are, even to my nocturnal eyes, just shadows among the trees. That's unsettling for a couple of reasons. First, they're much better coordinated than the other dimwits I've seen tonight. Second, these particular humans are somehow able to see one another in this darkness. Not your average, everyday home invaders.

Lucky has the look of an icy elf. Spiky black hair, pallid skin, oval jawline, turned up nose, cold-yet-amused eyes. He reminds me of Sunmane. A certain cold fire. An artistic flair for leadership and deceit.

Almost like brothers, says Mimir.

Brothers born a thousand years apart—no, not likely. I've no time to consider Mimir's latest riddle.

Lucky is not lying about the special delivery. Attached to a hitch on the ATV behind him is a small dump trailer loaded with a steel drum. Oil barrel? There are also a couple of chainsaws, an axe, and several rifles, including an evil-looking assault weapon. And he has a scoped rifle slung around his right shoulder. I can smell its oiled gunmetal, dark, lustrous and deadly.

Yet the chainsaws are even more ominous. Just bringing them into Haven is a desecration beyond reckoning, stoking my rage.

Lucky unslings his rifle, leans it up against the tree, and says, "I'm coming out from behind the tree with my hands up."

As he does, an arrow smacks into the wood near his head. Lucky ducks back behind the tree, smiling to himself. It was a feint, of course. The men he's leading moved when he did. They're trying to flank Andre, who should have stuck that arrow in Lucky's eye. Warning shots are not going to cut it with these guys.

So what am I waiting for? While he's still facing the porch, I stalk the little cretin. As I'm pulling back my fist, planning to end him with a blow to his spiky head, I'm hammered with another Urdy vision. Lucky transforms into a giant owl, its head swiveling one hundred and eighty degree to look directly at me. I swing but he easily ducks the punch, then sweeps out his left leg to trip me. Down I go, cursing my incompetence. Never even considered this Bruce Lee shit.

I do, at least, manage to snatch at his rifle strap, yanking him down with me. On the ground, I roll and kick him over my head. He's more alert and skillful than I anticipated, but he's also a lot lighter, and the laws of physics still pertain. He goes flying as I wrench the rifle strap off him, leaving me with the gun.

Lucky tumbles but rolls to his feet, quick as a panther. I'm only up on my knees when he comes charging forward. When he sees me raising the muzzle of the rifle, he ducks away, scrambling into the brush. I try to get off a shot but it's too late. I'm crap with guns. On impulse, I crack the rifle over my knee, breaking it in two, then throw the pieces into the dark where Lucky disappeared. Snatching up the other weapons out of the dump trailer, I smash those against the trunk of the pine tree. Truth is, Lucky is smart and fast, so I don't trust myself to keep control of these glossy hand-cannons. What happened at *Grimm's* could happen here just as easily.

It doesn't take long for regret to sink in. A bullet smacks the pine tree at head level, sending splinters into my left cheek. I dive toward a large thicket of palmettos I'd spotted before. Two more bullets whiz by as I make my dash into the shrubbery, followed by a foreboding silence.

Think, troll. At least three people. Could be just one with a gun. Best guess: two with a rifle, Lucky with a pistol in his pocket. Even worse, I suspect they're packing magic as well. Although it's well hidden, I got a whiff in my tussle with Lucky. Makes this even harder. I need to come up with something fast or die, die, die like a cornered possum in the scrub.

Jesus, Hildy, where are you?

Then another vision wraps itself around my mind.

Kept at bay by a circle of enchanted runes, Hildr, whose very name means battle, can only watch as Skuld contends with Yggdrasil. Urd and Verðandi lie prone on the stone floor, dazed by poisoned tea, as Skuld prays silently, then pleads shamelessly, resolute to bend the Great Tree to her celestial will.

When incantations come to naught, a goddess scorned, Skuld unsheathes a keen blade designed by dwarves in ages past, forged for deadly furrows. She carves the Tree with broad, deep strokes that, within the vision, I can read clearly. She blazes the runic words "I Rule" into the lustrous stem of Yggdrasil. The deity's dictate rises up the sacred wood as boldly as a conquering battalion till the runes begin to turn and swirl like smoke on a breezy day.

Further up the silver stock, the runes finally fuse into the equivalent of "U Rile", causing the goddess of Wyrd to scream in furious frustration, screams that carry upward through the shivering bark and branches, shaking each leaf, each tendril tolling like bells for the dead.

The vision dissipates, bringing me back to myself. Not a good place to be. A cringing, frightened bird hiding in brambles. Gunfire. My first thought is that they have me surrounded, are raking the boscage with bullets, an ignominious death at hand.

No. It's more distant than that. I suddenly realize they don't give a crap about me, a craven beast escaped into the undergrowth. Invading Haven is their only goal.

The firing continues like a stream. Must be cover fire. Move.

Rushing back to the dump trailer, I see the mysterious steel drum is gone. Idiot. I'm an idiot. It was so obviously crucial to their plan, whatever that is. And I just left it there like your classic nitwit troll.

Up ahead and moving fast are two people carrying the barrel toward the front porch. Another figure, this one standing in the notch of a live oak, is blasting away at the roof with a rifle, keeping Andre at bay. It's Lucky's snake-faced cousin, Jormund. This is the sonovabitch who's going to pay first.

Sister Skuld brandishes irons, burning bark with writhing runes, pouring molten metals in, then cooling alloys to hardened steel. "Skuld Decrees" read the runes upon the making. Yet, as the words rise, the adamantine metals crack, bend and blend, double, treble and more, propagating like rumors in a city besieged.

When the letters finally rise and fuse, they read as a litany: "Cureless reckless deluder seducer seceder." Skuld is stunned, then grins and chortles madly, convulsed as a world in seizure.

Jormund coils in the branches. I see him as a giant, black cobra spitting venom at Andre in long, thin pulses. I know there is a man with a rifle there. Moments ago I glimpsed him. But the Norn sight discerns only the serpent now. What makes it even weirder is that, when I train my eyes on the roof, it's bullets I see splintering the carved wooden balustrade behind which Andre hunches.

Old Andre is desperate to stop Lucky and the one named Fenrir. Jormund keeps firing. I'm sprinting now, trying to reach Jormund before the invaders make the safety of the porch. But Andre decides he can't wait any longer. He raises his head and shoulders high enough to get off a shot with his bow, only to be smacked backwards by a bullet. Lucky and Fenrir make it to the porch unscathed and start kicking in that thick wooden door. That's when I finally reach Jormund, who senses me too late. I yank the cobra tail as hard as I can out of the tree, hoping to rip Jormund in two.

Instead, the whole serpent cascades down around me like twenty feet of slick, thick, scaly rope. I battle my body's urge to flee, desperately seeking the cobra's head, hoping to grab it from behind to keep it from striking. All I see are terrifying coils of black, gleaming plates. I draw my seax, intending to slice the damned thing like so much sashimi. But, shit, there's the head rising in front of me, its hood expanding like ebony despair. In this critical moment, I struggle against the upwelling of Urdy's vision, to no avail.

Professor Jormund sits erect behind his huge, lustrous black walnut desk. He's a mesmerizingly grotesque man. Thin lips stretch nearly all the way across a triangular jaw, giving me a feeling of dread as he speaks.

A term paper I wrote sits on the desktop in front of him. I am his anxious student, clutching nervously a No. 2 pencil and twelve-inch ruler.

"What I fail to understand," he says, "is why, given not only your family heritage but your personal history, you seem to have utterly missed the point of the readings in this class. For example, there is this young Inge, eh?"

The professor leans in a bit, saliva forming around the corners of his mouth.

"She is a wondrous heroine, driven by her Will to Power to ruthlessly destroy everything, even her archaic sense of morality, for the one true goal of grasping the mantle of her own greatness. Slaying Bloodaxe to become a bloody queen, then wielding her husband like a sword to become the empress of Norway. Yet you, it seems, have failed to respect her utter rejection of convention, her eagerness to destroy anything, even her entire personal universe, in order to become fully herself.

"Your own mother would have understood her, yes? Ah, she was a strong woman who tried to cleanse you of your weak moralities as acid washes away feculence.

"And then you were fortunate enough to have become apprentice to the No-thing, a band of men willing and able to become true Nietzschean supermen, potent leaders who recognized your potential as a razor with which to strip away weakness."

For a mesmerized moment, I see it—Jormund's vision. The strong wiping away the weak, like flecks of useless meat off a cutting board. Me joining them, leading them, a creature of power defying ancient Urd, a disciple of black Surt slicing through this thinning, rotting veil of existence, purging it with fire. So beautiful.

Jormund leans in closer now, the saliva nearly a drool. I blink and my hand tightens on the wooden ruler with its shiny edge of copper.

"Yet you have, I see, failed to learn from your mentors. They would be so disappointed. To forget one's purpose is the most egregious form of obtuseness. One should die when it is no longer possible to live."

The professor darts forward, his mouth widening into a dark vacuum that threatens to draw me in. A drop of his saliva spurts into my right eye, making me cry out. I lash out with my ruler, slicing a sudden, red smile into his throat.

Bloods fills my right eye, which Jormund jabbed with a black combat knife. Don't know how bad it is. It burns like a mother, but I guess I'm fortunate not to have a bullet lodged in my brain.

"Asshole," I say as I kneel over his body. The front of his t-shirt is soaked in blood from his slit throat, so I flip him over and rip strips of cotton from the back. I wad up some of the strips and put them over my eye, then tie the rest in a diagonal bandage. An ugly improvised eyepatch. No time for anything fancier.

I told you there'd be more to lose, Mimir says.

Chapter Forty-Nine

"Hung with hard ice-flakes, where hail-scur flew,
There I heard naught save the harsh sea
And ice-cold wave, at whiles the swan cries"
—Ezra Pound

"Cold, eh? Like the streams of Elivagar!" shouted Skylar Bard in my ear.

He sounded so jolly, I nearly chucked him into the sea. Even as ten-foot waves washed over us, the damned skald was composing songs. I could practically hear this one already:

*Out of the cold, crashing wastes of Niflheim
the freezing rivers of Elivagar flooded
Eirik's ships like icy sleet engulfing Ginnungagap.*

None of it was poetic to me. The vicious storm had come howling out of the northeast not long after we'd left Iceland for the Orkney Islands.

Of the four ships in our motley little fleet, Ivar's knarr labored most in those waters. His crew had not shortened his ship's sail enough.

When I'd been able to spot the knarr through the rain and sleet, the ship swayed recklessly amid the whitecaps.

We'd reefed the square sails hours ago, but things were getting worse. I signaled the nimble *Valdyr*, my longship, to come within hailing distance.

Though I owned the ship, Kol was its master. He'd designed it, overseen the shipwrights who'd crafted it and had chosen its crew well before I knew I'd be exiled. The ship had cost me a fortune, but it was the price I was willing to pay to keep Kol around.

I stepped out of the cockpit I'd installed on *Kaupmaðr* and threw back my sopping black hood. Sól burned me even amid the grayness of the rain and sleet.

"Let's furl the sails," I shouted.

He nodded, though I sensed he was reluctant. If anyone could maintain raised sails in such a storm, Kol could. Yet he knew it was the proper move. First, though, he'd agreed to sail over to inform Captain Ivar of the plan.

I'd had misgivings about Ivar from the start. He seemed more ambitious than intelligent and was still new to the trading game. Even worse, he hailed from one of the territories now controlled by Sunmane. But when it came to trading vessels, it was wiser to sail with as many ships as possible. As Sunmane conquered more territories, more traders originated from his lands. I couldn't very well avoid them all. Besides, we were only sailing as far as the Orkneys together, and Ivar didn't strike me as the dangerous type. His crew and passengers, however, were not to be trusted since they were ultimately bound for what we now call Norway. I tried to have as little to do with Ivar's ship as possible.

Even though it was a tricky business in such winds, my crew was happy to bring the woollen sail down. They could crouch under it for added protection from the storm. But it meant we needed to make greater use of the oars to keep us from a calamitous roll or pitch.

Sailing to starboard was the *Grágás*, a heavy-laden knarr owned by a Swede trader named Nasi. He'd grown wealthy sailing between England and Iceland and was a skilled captain. The *Grágás* furled its sails as well, and it kept pace nicely with *Kaupmaðr*.

When the *Valdyr* finally reemerged, I knew there was bad news. The normally lithe ship was trudging through the seas. Kol hadn't found Ivar's ship, only the wreckage of its demise, including several sailors and one passenger who'd survived by clinging to casks, crates and other flotsam. As well as rescuing the people, the *Valdyr's* crew salvaged many trading goods out of the swells, an enterprise that was bold to the point of recklessness in such perilous weather.

We agreed we'd haul the salvaged casks onto the knarrs when the storm died down.

"It will soon wane," Kol yelled.

He was wrong. For another week, the northeaster only grew fiercer. Our crews were dying of exposure amid brutal, heat-sucking waves that rose to twenty feet at times. We were hard put just to keep the water bailed and the bows pointed in the right direction.

There was little opportunity for genuine sleep, but everyone dozed.

One afternoon, I dreamt I was an eagle as large as a mountain. Soaring over the ocean, I never flapped my wings and yet maintained an effortless spiral. South I flew, then bent to the west for hundreds, maybe thousands, of miles. Spotting a great land mass below, I felt the currents carry me north and then northeast until I spotted the Irish coast. From there, I arced south and southwest again, over and over in a great spiral.

Looking back, I suppose it was the first prophetic dream of my life, or maybe just the first symptom of an unhinged mind. Regardless, I awoke knowing what needed to be done.

The gale-force gusts had receded, but the winds continued to blow steadily south by southwest. We were badly lost. This was long before the days of compasses, sextants, chronometers and the like. Although Kol was a navigational prodigy, he could do little more than guess at our location.

We all knew, of course, that northeast was roughly the way homeward, and we would have set a rough course in that direction if the winds had allowed. Our best option was to sail close to an easterly direction and hope we'd hit a landmass eventually. This was Nasi's counsel and Kol's preference when we discussed the situation in the stern of *Kaupmaðr*.

"I wish to follow the winds themselves," I said.

"Madness," shouted Nasi, who was a beefy, red-faced man. "There is nothing in that direction, and our stores of food will not hold out forever."

I tried to make logical arguments but ultimately had to confess, "The gods sent me a dream." It was idiocy to admit it. Only women were expected to receive prophecies or deliver proclamations.

Nasi moaned as if he couldn't believe what I'd said. Kol was silent, but I'd known him long enough to sense he was excited at the prospect of sailing to parts unknown.

"Aboard my ship is a spaewife we rescued from Ivar's knarr," he said. "She may be willing to sing us a *wyrd* song to help guide us."

Nasi scoffed but agreed to confer with the woman. After all, he did not want to make an uncertain voyage with a single ship.

She was a comely woman, not stout but still ample and curvaceous despite the hardships of the voyage. It was unusual that she was already in her late twenties and not yet married. In the case of Thordis, however, it seemed the least strange thing about her.

Some men of the age had tattoos all over their arms and shoulders, but few women bore more than a smattering of tattoos, mostly runes or lacy images of leaves, vines, fruit or birds. Thordis, however, bore images of Yggdrasil on each check, with the descending roots from each one intertwined under her chin.

Although they had seen better days, her clothes marked her as a wealthy woman. She wore a green cape that was inlaid with gems, though some of those gems had gone missing. On her head, she wore a black hood of lambskin edged in white ermine fur. Her eyes were a grayish blue and her hair a sable black.

Using furs and pillows, we tried to create a seat of honor for her in the stern of my ship. Kol was attentive to the point of solicitousness, a side of him I'd never seen. Of course, he'd grown up without a mother and, on my farm, with few women within a day's walk.

"We know you are still recovering, Thordis. Thank you for agreeing to this," Kol said.

She nodded, keeping her eyes on his. She'd nearly died when Ivar's ship was swamped, of course, and Kol was her savior. She barely glanced at Nasi and dropped her eyes entirely rather than look at me.

Her song was not what I expected. It was a sweet and melodic retelling of the fall of Idun, the Norse goddess of spring and rebirth. The gods needed Idun's apples to maintain their immortality.

Thordis's song was different from the version I knew in which, through great strength and cleverness, the storm giant Thiassi kidnapped Idun. It was a tale Mor told to illustrate the greediness of the gods, who refused to share Idun's apples.

In Thordis's version, Idun was already married to Bragi, the god of skaldic poetry. He was sitting in the sacred ash Yggdrasil when she suddenly felt faint. Losing her hold on the Great Tree, she plunged into and then through the Well of Urd, down into the realm of Helheim. There she fell into a terrible lethargy.

Bragi journeyed the cold depths of Helheim to retrieve his wife. Covering her with a white wolfskin, he played his harp and sang as he had never done before. After much beautiful striving on the part of Bragi, Idun awoke and together they ascended to the branches of Yggdrasil.

We were all silent after Thordis's song. We still awaited her prophecy.

"The sea spirits were pleased to listen to the song," she said. "They have told me that either direction, east or south, is perilous. However, only southwest is favored by the One-Eyed god, seeker of wisdom, champion of sojourns."

Her words settled nothing. Nasi practiced the new religion, Christianity, as well as the old one. He was quite willing to disappoint the wandering god if eastward might still bring him home again. Meanwhile, I was having second thoughts, knowing that Odin—kin killer of Aurgelmir—was behind my eagle dream. Kol, though, was now convinced we should sail southwest.

In the end, I swallowed my misgivings about Odin, trickster though he was. Besides, following the winds would place me far beyond the reach and rule of Sunmane, as well as the No-thing. So Nasi headed east alone, taking several of my sailors who placed no trust in me. Of Kol's crew, however, not a single one joined Nasi.

Chapter Fifty

"A daughter is born of the sun
Ere Fenrer takes her.
In her mother's course
When the gods are dead
This maid shall ride."
—*The Younger Edda*

By the time I stumble through the manor and into the anterior part of the main hall, Hildy is in full battle mode. She has thrown iron chainmail armor over her black leather riding gear and she's donned a burnished steel and brass helmet. She holds a thick wooden shield that is black with a stylized yellow eagle emblem. In her right hand is a seven-foot spear with a long, deadly looking blade inlaid with copper and silver.

She's quite a sight, even with just my one eye. There's nothing of the comic-book valkyrie about her. No deep cleavage, boob plates and bare skin. Hildy would cut up those bimbos like fish bait in seconds. She's the real fucking deal.

Lucky has already gotten a taste of her. He's sitting on his black steel drum, trying to smirk through his pain when he spots me. He's cradling his right forearm and there's a bloody gash in his leg. You really shouldn't screw with a woman whose very name means "battle" in the Old Tongue.

Fenrir is in better shape. He and Hildy circle each other. He must have pulled a sword off the wall. He holds the long, bronze hilt with two hands in a way that looks practiced. Maybe kendo training.

Hildy spins her spear in a nonchalant way, almost unconsciously, like a cat flicking its tail. She smiles, for the moment forgetting about her catastrophically crazy aunt.

Fenrir is even bigger than I thought when I saw him from a distance at Vandriller Junction. He has a wolf image tattooed onto his forehead. He'd be a genuine menace if Hildy weren't so good. Fenrir tries to use his superior height to come up over her shield. She deftly ducks under and slices his thigh with the razor edge of her spear.

"Mother!" he swears.

Truth is, in the hands of an expert, a spear is a better weapon than a sword. If you can keep the tip from being hacked off, its reach is far superior and it can slide into small openings in a way a sword can't. Fenrir keeps charging her, hacking at her shield in an attempt to overwhelm. Every time, she jabs or cuts him somewhere, and every time he yells, "Mother!"

I almost laugh. I know Hildy's using this match to vent her intense frustration with not being able to stop Skuld. But she should just end this thing. The sooner, the better.

Of course, I'm not one to talk. While these two are dancing, I should slip by and wring Lucky's scrawny neck. My back against the wall, I move in his direction. He's already staunched his wounds and is now brandishing one of those curved folding knives, a karambit, and watching as I approach. He puts his hand in his pocket as if he still has a pistol. I'm not buying it. If he still had one, he'd have used it already.

"Mother," Fenrir screams, this time taking the spear point in his ribs. That one must have really hurt, maybe even sliced into his liver or spleen. The dude is a bloody mess now, moving slowly and slipping in his own blood.

I'm maybe ten feet from Lucky when Skuld appears.

This is bad. I've not forgotten her fee-fie-foe act. Can even Hildy battle one of the Great Norns? But Skuld doesn't take giant form.

Instead, though still recognizable, she becomes a middle-aged woman, plump and maternal-looking.

When Fenrir spots her, he breaks away from Hildy and rushes toward her. He gets down on his knees and hugs Skuld around the waist. "Mother," he whimpers. I realize with a jolt that Fenrir hasn't been cursing all along. He's literally been calling for his mother.

Skuld looks down at him with concern.

"Oh, poor baby," she says. "Did your big sister give you a boo-boo? No tears now. Remember, you're the strong one, the one helping—not hindering—mommy. Oh, baby, it's okay. Tonight, we rule or destroy. Either way, your pain will be gone. Go on, now, show that bad girl who's Momma's favorite."

Hildy's shocked. She didn't know. Never even suspected that Aunt Skuldy might be her mother or that she might have siblings. But it makes sense. If it's a lie, it's a damned good one. The fight is suddenly sucked out of her, indecisive as she ponders battling her mother, harming her brother.

Skuld places her hand on Fenrir's scalp and strokes his forehead with her thumb. As she does, his forehead recedes, as if he were made of clay. The meaning and horror hits me when, stroking her son's nose, it elongates into a muzzle. She moves quickly now, dexterously molding the man into a wolf. An enormous wolf. A yellow-eyed, black-furred cur from Helheim.

Mimir?

Yes, my puerile pupil?

Is what I'm seeing part of the Norn sight?

Oh, no, mon cyclops. This is something much rarer. Genuine therianthropy. It was once common among the gods. And not just the Norse deities. I don't suppose you've read your Gilgamesh. But therianthropy has faded along with most of the gods themselves. This is the power of the Great Norn Skuld even in these waning days. Her ability to manifest the players of the Ragnarok mythos even now... just stunning.

"Yeah, stunning," I say aloud. "Not great news, is it?"

No, says Mimir. *From your narrowly circumscribed point of view, it is quite bad news indeed.*

Chapter Fifty-One

"Love is whatever you can still betray. Betrayal can only happen if you love."
                              —John le Carre

Odin the Raven God must have had himself a good cackle about the time we finally made landfall on the coast of what would later be called Florida. We were a wretched mass: scurvy-ridden, loose-toothed, dehydrated, sunbaked, half-starved and sporting an assortment of sores, scabs and infected cuts. Although not as prone to many of these ailments as the humans, my enemy Sól had nearly burned and taunted me into madness.

My hood and robes—along with the small, wooden cockpit I built for myself in the stern—had kept me alive, but it could never offer me full protection from the despised radiation blasting down on us like an omnipresent furnace. The only good news was that the days grew shorter, though hotter, as we sailed further south.

We first landed on barrier islands several miles north of today's Miami, then found our way into an intercostal bay. We soon located a stream of brackish water good enough to drink. Afterwards, the men stumbled into the shade of a dense mangrove forest, lying amid the cool, encrusted roots as if they'd reached the halls of Valhalla.

Over the next several days, we found plenty of fish, shellfish, birds, seaweeds, sea grapes and other edibles to sustain us. For a time, we thought we'd discovered a lush version of Iceland, empty of all human beings.

Within the week, however, we caught a glimpse of indigenes. We called them the *Njörðrbarns*, after the Norse god of seafaring and fishing, because they carried fishing spears and casting nets and wore necklaces of shells. They were, in general, shorter than our men but lithe and strong-looking.

There was no friendliness in them, however. Though they observed us, they would not come near. When we approached, they threaded their wooden arrows and made threatening gestures, so we left them alone.

Kol used the longship for exploration and found that the Njörðrbarns had a large settlement to the south near the mouth of a wide river. He said they were thriving but he couldn't spot field crops of any sort.

"Perhaps we could farm this land and trade with them," said Kol.

"Or use them for slaves," said Bork, who served as his second-in-command aboard the *Valdyr*.

Others nodded. The Vikings not only used the Irish, Scots and others as thralls, they sold them in a systematic way. Many a trader had made his fortune capturing and selling slaves to the east, west and south. Having served as a thrall myself, I could too easily see the fate of the Njörðrbarns in years to come.

Finding little shelter from the inferno-like Florida sun, I dug myself a pit away from the camp we'd established. With relief, I discovered the limestone that underlies so much of the place. It wasn't true stone, in my eyes. Not like granite, marble, quartz or feldspar. No, it was just compressed cakes of skeletal remains, the detritus of long-dead oysters and clams, conches and corrals, sea urchins and sand dollars. Still, it was the closest I could find to the kind of cool rock on which a troll might lie in peace.

Yet the pit was a mistake.

I should have realized it the first time Thordis happened upon me. She came to the edge of the pit and looked curiously downward. When she saw me in the darkness there, her eyes widened in alarm, and she instinctually made a gesture of protection against wickedness.

I knew I frightened her. While Solveig had mostly seen the man in me, Thordis could see only the troll. With her discovery of my pit, her fear turned to dread.

She was about to dart away when I said, "Don't be frightened, Thordis. I just wanted to get out of the sun for a time."

She stopped, seeming indecisive, then looked around to see if anyone else were in the vicinity.

"You seek darkness, I know," she whispered. "Always in your dark hood. In darkness you slaughtered a great king."

That shocked me. I thought she merely feared me as a troll and had no idea she was a Bloodaxe adherent.

"A great and bloody tyrant, you mean, devious and cruel," I finally responded.

"No, the father to an even greater king, a brilliant light to your darkness."

I laughed despite myself, knowing it was no way to win her over. "You mean Sunmane the Blazestarter," I said. "A fiery glow indeed. You don't know him the way I do, Thordis."

Despite her facial tattoos, I could see her color darken with rage.

"He is my cousin!" she hissed, likely confessing more than she'd intended.

"Ah," I said, "and he sent you to Iceland to see the sights. Did you come with Bjor, Thordis? Did you speak with Regis?"

But my words, or maybe my budding rage, had sent her flying away.

Our relationship with the Njörðrbarns evolved. On a nearby beach from which they often watched us, we started leaving bits of colored cloth, bronze and copper coins, and some fragments of broken glass. In return, they left us shell jewelry, smoked fish, venison, deerskins and fruits.

It was the summer doldrums when the winds were changeable and faltering, so we made good use of the oars as we continued south. *Kaupmaðr*, of course, had fewer oars and was less streamlined than *Valdyr*, so we took the lion's share of supplies, while Kol scouted ahead in the longship.

In this way, we explored the many cays on which the Njörðrbarns were settled. We found they were expert canoeists. Their deft little dug-outs were practically an extension of their own bodies. Watching them glide by like human-shaped dolphins gladdened my heart. It felt like a kind of wholesome magic.

Kol came into his own. He'd been born for it, seeing the poetry in the motions of the seaborne Njörðrbarns, in the sound and fullness of *Valdyr*'s sail, in the blueness of the Caribbean. His growing love for Thordis heightened those joys. I did not tell him she was, I felt sure, a Sunmane spy. I'd killed Kol's father and he'd forgiven me. He would not forgive again if I murdered his first real happiness in life.

The winds grew steady again, and we sailed northwards up the west coast of Florida. As the seas grew white with foam, I noticed that *Kaupmaðr* was taking on more water than usual. When I stepped into the cargo hold to investigate, a beam began to crack. I could feel the sponginess of the wood beneath the ballast stones and was lucky not to have put my leg clear through the strakes.

I signaled Kol, and we beached both ships on the inside edge of a barrier island. As Kol carefully inspected the hull, I feared the verdict.

"Shipworms," he said.

"How bad?"

"Bad," he said. "We can try wedges and patches, but the keel is tainted and the hull riddled. She needs to be rebuilt. We might find lumber ashore, but it could take days to restore her, if we can manage it at all."

I should have kept my temper. These things happen on ships. But I missed my family and the constant sun and heat were taking their toll.

"Damn it, Kol," I shouted. "How could this happen?"

I'd placed him in charge of maintaining *Kaupmaðr* after we'd first arrived in Iceland. He should have maintained it better, I thought. The longship had distracted him.

"It's been a long voyage, Eirik," Kol said.

"And you have been much diverted," I said, looking toward his ship. In my line of sight was Thordis, as well.

Kol reddened.

"Yet my ship is whole," he said.

Frustrated and enraged, I took a step toward him. In days past, he would have stood down, conceding my authority. Now, he held my gaze, even as the hands of many of his crew felt for weapons on their belts.

I stopped, aware I'd been a fool to thoughtlessly challenge him in front of his men.

"Yes, Captain Kol," I said, "it is whole for now. But worms may come for any. We must guard against them in these wild lands."

I walked away down the beach, afraid of what I might do if I stayed.

We found a river inlet, grounded the *Kaupmaðr*, built supports on which to raise her, and began to make repairs. It was even worse than we thought. Shipworms are the termites of the sea, except even more insidious. Though called worms, they are bivalves that bore though wood with sly, sharp shells. They enter the ship's body through microscopic holes, then grow and burrow like festering resentments.

Everyone grew anxious. Food was the most obvious problem. The local seas had turned a brownish red, which Thordis claimed was a sign that Aegir, the sea jotunn, was angry with us. Since the seafood was making us sick, and shipworms had infested my ship, it was easy to believe her. None of us knew that red tides caused by algae blooms were common in the Gulf of Mexico.

Thordis struck me as increasingly unhinged, making her protection-against-evil gesture every time I came within a few feet of her. Everyone noticed, of course. Some sailors began mumbling that I was bad luck, shooting me uneasy glances when they thought I wasn't looking. Thordis would sometimes huddle with Kol's sailors, including his second-in-command, Bork, watching me under hooded eyes.

Their fear and scheming made me anxious, weary and extremely homesick. I badly missed Solveig. The children too, of course, but especially my wife, who had once accepted me as a man, not a monster. I wanted the exile over. I wanted to be in my own bed holding my wife. Most of all, I wanted to ask her what I should do, to receive her judicious, quiet wisdom.

I finally requested that Kol walk with me along the shore and away from our ships. At first we said nothing, both of us harboring resentments from our last encounter. Little birds scurried in front of us on tiny legs, darting back and forth in mild, foam-filled waves, probing the wet sand with their bills. Eventually, though, I told him of my conversation with Thordis, telling him of my suspicions that she was a spy, and I warned that the gesture she made at me was sowing seeds of discord among the crews.

His expression remained blank, which angered me. I'd expected more. Maybe surprise or hurt, betrayal or denial. But I was the surprised one.

"I knew," he said, "that she is kin of Sunmane. One of the rescued sailors from Ivar's ship had heard the rumor and she admitted as much to me. I asked her to keep quiet about it. I know how you hate Sunmane."

"With good reason," I said.

"Yes," he admitted, "though he also has reasons for hating you, and we cannot expect Thordis to take your side."

"*Our* side," I said.

He chose not to respond to that but reassured me she was not a spy, that she had been called by the gods to go on a voyage for reasons she herself did not understand.

"That seems convenient," I said.

He sighed like a grown son beleaguered by an ignorant parent.

"I will ask her not to make that gesture near you," he conceded. "But I cannot change what is in her heart."

Thordis was only a part of the problem. The crew of the *Valdyr* was afraid that, if the knarr couldn't be repaired, everyone would be dangerously squeezed into a single longship never intended to hold so many. What's more, the knarr stored most of our remaining goods and equipment. Losing it would mean we'd have to make hard choices about what to leave behind.

We grew even more anxious when the *Nóttbarns* appeared. They spoke, looked and acted differently than the Njörðrbarns of the south. They blackened their faces, especially their eye sockets, with charcoal, and they tended to visit us at night, which is why we named them after the Norse goddess of darkness.

We tried to develop trading relationships with them in the same way we'd done with the Njörðrbarns, but they ignored anything we offered. Instead, they made threatening gestures, insisting we leave their territory.

We would have retreated from the area if we hadn't already removed many of the strakes and ribs from *Kaupmaðr* in our rebuilding process. Every night, more Nóttbarns gathered like darkening clouds.

On the fourth night after they first appeared, the Nóttbarns attacked, raining down arrows as we slept on the beach. Although we had our shields with us, our lookouts didn't give us enough warning. Three men died in that first volley.

As a precaution against the Nóttbarns, Kol had anchored the *Valdyr* forty yards beyond the beach. It was a good defensive strategy but it also meant that those of us on the beach had to fend for ourselves while protecting the *Kaupmaðr*.

In my hubris, I was secretly glad of the attack. I yearned for action and felt certain that, if I could display my prowess as a warrior, I could win back the loyalty of those who had adopted Thordis's poisonous prejudices.

But I underestimated the Nóttbarns. Their bows were nearly as thick as a man's arm and more powerful than any comparable weapon used by the Norse. As I charged into the forest after them, two arrows came ripping through my shield. One punctured my left bicep and the other grazed my skull at eye level.

With my sword, I managed to kill one warrior and maim another, but the others retreated. Although I lusted to pursue them, Dofri had taught me well. Aware I'd be heading into a classic ambush, I back-tracked, intent on keeping *Kaupmaðr* safe from destruction. Once near the ship, I shrank into the shadows and crouched, eager to draw in any unwary Nóttbarns.

Hearing the whispers of our crewmen behind me, I stayed where I was, assuming they were there to defend the ship.

"Where is he?" one whispered.

The other hushed him.

"Sturlung is here," I whispered back, "awaiting the enemy."

A knife sank deep into my back. Instinctively, I stood and swung my sword backwards toward my attacker, then rushed into the forest headlong. I must have made it a hundred yards or more before blood loss rendered me unconscious.

For the first time since becoming a freedman, I awoke in manacles. I was coughing, trying to get liquid out of my mouth and throat. I spit it out onto the ground, then wheezed as I drew in breath.

The four people standing nearby turned toward me.

"The evil seed still lives," said Thordis.

Kol came and bent over me. My back was to a pine tree and my arms chained behind.

"Hallr," he said.

I looked up into his face, trying to focus my scattered thoughts.

"Why, Hallr? Why did you kill Skeggi?"

"Skeggi?" I asked. He'd been a member of Kol's crew, a man I barely knew.

"With your sword, Hallr. You cut him in two, then Bork stabbed you."

"Was attacked," I said weakly, the pain in my chest excruciating.

"After you killed him, monster," said Bork.

Thordis nodded, even though she'd been on Kol's ship the entire time.

"I warned you, Kol, he would bring down death on us," she said.

I could only shake my head. I didn't have the breath to argue. My chest felt as if there was still a knife in it.

Kol turned to Bork.

"Are you certain? That Skeggi didn't attack first?"

"Yes, captain," he said, glancing at Thordis.

Kol looked back and forth between them. He must have known, or at least suspected. He and I had lived through this before, with his father and Leos.

I could see his thoughts. If he spared me, his crew might turn against him. If I recovered, he knew I'd seek revenge on Bork, and maybe Thordis. So, it didn't matter whether I was guilty or not. He had to be practical.

"Come," he said, turning away from me. "Let's finish the repairs."

Thordis looked down at me. She was going to argue but then thought better of it.

In the glare of the sun, I didn't bother trying to watch them hammer the last strakes into the knarr. All I could do was concentrate on taking one shallow breath after another, trying to live through the next ten seconds, then ten more, then ten more after that.

It was afternoon when they finished and launched the *Kaupmaðr*.

Once the seals had been tested, Kol waded to the beach. Thordis splashed after him even after he waved her back to the ship.

"Kol," she shouted as he approached. "You must finish him. The beast must be buried. I've seen it. Or he will slay us all."

Kol didn't respond. The sun was at his back now, his shadow looming over me.

"He will destroy us!" Thordis shrieked in frustration.

Kol touched the haft of the knife in his belt, pondering her words.

"Perhaps we would deserve it," said Kol. "But he will not. He will die alone here in the wretched swelter of this foreign wilderness. Forgive me, Hallr. I was, after all, raised by monsters."

Then he turned away, grabbing Thordis by the inside of her arm. He would not let her go, however much she wailed.

Chapter Fifty-Two

"He was too strong. There were women behind him."
—*Peer Gynt*

The Fenrir wolf stands at least five feet tall at the shoulders, a demon even the giant trolls of old would have feared. My Icelandic chieftain Asmund had been able to transform into a large wolf, but nothing like this monster. Fenrir must be twelve feet long.

"Now," says Skuld. "Go romp with your siblings. Momma has work to do."

Lucky looks stunned but delighted. The battle tide has turned, yet Lucky makes no sudden moves. There's no knowing how much of Fenrir the man remains in the beast.

Hildy and I instinctively back away from the giant black wolf, who has begun to growl, its gaping mouth open as it bares its fangs. I'm fascinated by how the pulled-back skin on his muzzle rises and shivers like rippling ridges. Goldenrod eyes glow beneath furious, beveled brows, its ears pulled back flat against the sable head.

Neither Hildy nor I attacked Skuld when we had the chance. Should we have? Could we? What happens to the fabric of existence if we harm, never mind slay, one of the Great Norns? And, for Hildy, there's now the added horror of matricide.

I slowly pick up the sword Fenrir dropped before his transformation. Hildy's coming back to herself, girding to do battle with her brother. I pray she won't hold back. She shifts her eyes sideways toward me, then makes a subtle movement with her hand, which I take to be a sign for me to grab one of the nearby shields.

As I creep toward the wall at a glacial pace, Fenrir watches me, snarling so loudly I can feel the vibrations on my skin. Hildy makes a subtle adjustment with her spear, which I think is intended to draw the wolf's attention. Despite our astonishment, we should have attacked straight away, while its mind was still dazed from the transformation. Too late now. Fenrir is planting its feet, preparing to pounce.

Everything happens at once. Fenrir leaps toward Hildy who, despite lancing the animal in its breast, is thrown to the floor. I snatch down the shield and then charge directly into the massive beast in order to knock it away from Hildy. Lucky, meanwhile, takes advantage of my new focus by rushing past and slicing his karambit into the right side of my back. It's a deep cut, a mortal blow if I were human.

Down I go in a jumble of teeth, fur, blood, and muscle. As I protect my head and torso with the shield, Fenrir seizes my left leg with knife-like teeth and shakes his head in a frenzy. I feel my flesh tear away, then hear the hound yelp as Hildy digs her spear into its side, saving my life.

The good news: the spear goes deep. The bad news: it's wrenched from Hildy's hands, leaving her with only the shield. Fenrir goes berserk, leaping onto Hildy, crushing her into the stone floor. Its jaws close around her waist even though she smashes its snout with her shield. She's moments from being ripped into pieces.

Out of the corner of my eye, I see Lucky rolling the black barrel in Skuld's direction. I manage to stand on my shredded leg, haul back the sword, and swing with everything I've got at Fenrir's back right leg, severing it at the hock. I let the momentum of the sword turn me in a complete circle, coming around to stab as deeply into his right quarters as I can, intent on slicing vital organs.

Fenrir releases Hildy as he yowls, whimpers, and tries to scuttle away on three legs, the spear still sticking in his side. Hildy rolls, springs up and gives chase.

"Let it go, Hildy!" I yell, exhausted and bleeding heavily from multiple wounds. I want no more of the monstrous mutt. We need to find Lucky.

She ignores me, of course, so I hobble after her like Stumpy following John Wayne in *Rio Bravo*, cursing all the idiotic heroes of history. She's backed Fenrir into a corner, using her shield to batter him. The giant wolf, fighting for its ebbing life, barks, growls and lunges with a desperate viciousness. Hildy dances forward and back. When she sees me, she says, "Keep him busy for a sec. I need to get my spear back."

Feeling almost as desperate and destroyed as the woeful wolf, I take over, poking at its head with my sword as it lurches. The sound of its cacophonous, hollow-sounding snaps fills me with dread, making me realize how fortunate we've been so far.

Hildy's intent on pressing our luck even further, circling around to Fenrir's side. While it snaps at me, she leaps in to grab her spear. Not just yanking it out, as I'd hoped. She throws her weight and speed into it, jamming the spear further in, twisting, then jerking it free. Fenrir yelps again and rounds on her. I bellow, trying to keep its attention, but the beast is past caring about me. It whimpers as it loses its footing. Hildy struck a mortal blow in that last thrust.

She looks at me grimly. Only now do I realize she'd wanted to put the hound out of its misery. Mercy amid the battle bloodlust.

I'm so out of breath I can barely speak but manage, "Lucky got the barrel through."

She looks at me alarmed, as if I've let her down in some critical way. Which I suppose I have. She sprints back down the enormous hall, and I'm once again relegated to my role of muttering Stumpy slipping in his own blood.

Lucky stands inside the circle of runes, prying open the lid of the steel drum as Skuld watches. He's placed it next to the stone pool into which the marble fountain flows. On the side of the drum facing Hildy and me is an aluminum sign that reads "DANGER" in white block letters on a red background. Beneath that are bold, black letters reading, "HAZARDOUS CHEMICALS."

"Aunt," Hildy shouts from outside the perimeter of enchanted runes she cannot cross. She pauses, starts again in a voice tight with emotion. "Mother, the battle is over. Enough blood has been spilt. Please, let us make peace."

Next to Skuld is a workbench littered with tools, potions, cords and sundry other items she has used for her experiments. There's even an emergency generator. It's been turned off, so I guess the power tools were no more effective than anything else at bending the Great Tree to her will.

"Oh no, daughter," says Skuld, with an eerily quiet voice. She looks in our direction, yet her eyes don't focus on us, as if she is in a trance. "The battle is yet to be truly waged, a battle far beyond you and your spear and your absurd pet troll."

As Hildy and I try to physically force our way into the circle, Skuld turns again toward Yggdrasil. Hildy tries a spell of her own, but her galdr is no match for her mother's. We can only watch as Skuld's fingers transform into claws with which she carves an incantation into the flesh of Yggdrasil.

> *Bow to your betters, Old Tree,*
> *Bend or be broken.*
> *Fate must be finely threaded or*
> *We Great Ones are finished.*
> *Menacing mortals threaten all.*
> *Better to utterly end Midgard*
> *Than idly rely on ignorant luck*
> *Or Orlog ingloriously creeping*
> *Trunks of truculent trees*
> *Untrustworthy as quantum dice.*
>
> *I pledge my power will prevail*
> *Mine own self supreme*
> *Or I shall righteously rip*
> *Your roots from Ginnungagap,*
> *Let them finally burn or freeze*
> *Revealing sweet, fatal darkness.*
> *Relinquish all capricious control*
> *Or cruel poisons shall be poured.*

The runes slowly rise, though they remain otherwise unchanged. I wonder if this means the Great Norn has finally broken the will of her foe. A short poem appears beneath Skuld's:

Fate and freedom must merge and turn,
Or only fixed death and tyranny remain.
Long ago love ignited the universe,
Only love today may save it yet.

Still in her trance-like state, Skuld motions for Lucky to pour the contents of the black drum into the marble pool.

"Only a quarter," she says.

Hildy backs up and makes a run for Skuld, hoping to physically leap over the rune barrier. That doesn't work either. As she tries to spring, she falters as if all the power has been drained from her.

Whatever's in the barrel pours out dark and slick. It blackens and fills the pool. I'm transfixed as it flows down the floor toward the spring.

I look around for something that might penetrate this barrier. I try throwing the sword, but it only drops to the floor as if its momentum suddenly disappeared.

If nothing's at hand, Dofri would say, use your brains. I'm still bleeding from multiple wounds. Remembering when Bloodaxe froze me with his spell in Alfr's Manor, I actually try to mar the runes with my blood, but my blood makes no more headway through the barrier than the sword did.

I study the stone floor, focusing on the individual runes themselves. It's very old language that I couldn't have made out prior to the recent Norn visions, but now I can see that certain words are used again and again: battle, valkyrie, will, fierce, power, strive, primal. And the name Hildr occurs prominently once in each quadrant.

A small earthquake roils. The few green leaves that grow inside the great hall fall from Yggdrasil.

Hildy looks desperate, glancing around like a caged animal. She needs to fight something.

"Hildy," I say quietly, nodding toward the floor. "Look at the runes. They've been aimed at you like a weapon."

Skuld is focused on the Great Tree, liking what she sees. The bark has lost much of its sheen, the runes on it rise slowly and unevenly, stuttering and sometimes halting. There is little twisting, turning and blending of letters, as if the runes themselves had become old and arthritic, reluctant to bend.

"I don't understand," Hildy says.

"You're large, Hildy. Immense. You contain multitudes, remember? She can't keep all of you out, only the parts she needs you to be now, in this moment. Maybe Fenrir wasn't supposed to stop you. Maybe he was only there to make you more of who you are at this moment: Hildr, whose name means battle."

Skuld smiles, closely monitoring Yggdrasil, using a hand gesture behind her to tell Lucky to stop pouring. She believes she has finally defeated the Great Tree. Lucky continues pouring. She turns around, annoyed.

"Stop. I said stop," she says impatiently.

"Oh, yes, I heard you, Mommy," Lucky says. Dust is starting to shower down around us. The shuddering of the building grows more intense.

Hildy stares into my one good eye, then closes her own.

"Thank you, Hallr," she says, holding a hand up to my right cheek. Closing her eyes, she steps slowly into the circle of runes. She looks so peaceful and content, a woman walking along the bank of a river on a sunny day. She carries the spear not like a weapon but a walking stick.

"I said stop pouring!" Skuld shouts to Lucky. "I command it!"

"Oh, I'm stopping," he sneers, then kicks over the rest of the barrel.

The world goes mad. The earth is sucked out from beneath us. We plunge down, then are struck hard as the ground slams upwards again. It's the kind of earthquake that never happens in this part of the world. Yggdrasil cracks down one side, and a massive pillar of water erupts from the spring, followed by the hissing sound of receding waves. All of us have been thrown to the stone floor.

Skuld shrieks at Lucky, who is laughing his ass off. It's not one of those maniacal laughs like in a horror movie. It's a deep belly laugh, as if he's just carried out the best trick in the history of everything.

Hildy is the only person among us who has risen to her feet again, having pulled herself up with the spear. She is, despite all logic, utterly serene. Outside, something enormous streaks through the sky and smashes into the earth miles away to the west. There's a flash, then a rising mountainous cloud of orange and red flame. It billows higher and higher before fading into a molten red that dissipates into blackness like cooling lava. The western horizon becomes orange embers, lighting that section of the sky.

Hildy has reached Yggdrasil. She leans the spear against the roots, then pulls off the iron mail as if she's removing a nightgown. She picks up the spear again, using it like a hiking stick as she climbs up the thick coiling roots of the Great Tree. I'm baffled, yet growing anxious. At the last instant, as she puts the tip of the spear under her sternum and grabs the hilt, I understand.

Just as I open my mouth to plead, she plunges the spear through her body and into the tree.

Knowledge-craving Odin hangs by a spear on the wind-rocked tree, having sacrificed himself to himself. From high in the Great Tree, he peers down into the spring, seeking the wisdom of the Great Norns. Watching the silvery fish turn and bend, he has a flash of insight, grasping the great secret of the Sisters: the runes.

Odin shares his knowledge with the descendants of Ask and Embla. The Sisters warn it is a dangerous gift. The runes are two-edged swords, brandished for duplicity as well as divination, tyranny as well as freedom. Not just for science and art but as mighty engines of destruction and blight.

The Great Tree is brought to the precipice of annihilation.

Only Hildr stays the final extinction, hanging in place of Father Odin, discovering an even deeper knowledge, the ancient, ineffable wisdom of roots and leaves, earth and sky, stone and rain. A bringing together, a binding, a rapture beyond the lessons of runes. Now one with the Tree, her blood flows down the branch of her spear into the poisoned pool. The black liquid slowly clears. The shuddering of the earth quiets.

When the vision fades, I crawl over to the base of the Great Tree and pull myself up. Hildy is bleeding heavily, each beat of her heart pouring blood down over the roots of Yggdrasil and the hilt of the spear. She's dazed, staring out at the spring as the sun rises, but still conscious.

"Hildy," I say quietly, "I'm going to remove the spear now."

"No," she says, slowly focusing her eyes on my face. "We both know you can't. You are, after all, the retainer of Yggdrasil."

I hear Lucky screaming in outrage nearby, cursing me and Hildy, all his amusement vanished. I pay him no heed. If he attacks, death would be a mercy. Then his howls are gone, replaced by a gurgling sound that holds no interest.

"There has to be another way," I tell her.

"There isn't, not one that leaves all this intact. But it's okay, my love. Making choices is what I do, remember? This is the easiest one I've ever made."

"Return to us, Hildy. Even Odin got to dismount this damned horse." She smiles, though weakly.

"I'll both stay and go, Hallr. You now know that's possible, yes?"

There's no response to this. I'm not sure I know a goddamned thing anymore.

Chapter Fifty-Three

"His origins are become remote as is his destiny and not again in all the world's
turning will there be terrains so wild and barbarous"
—*Blood Meridian*

The Nóttbarns saved me. Hearing me whimper, they buried me
beneath scores of palm fronds. For days on end—for reasons I never
understood—they would bring me fresh water to sip out of a large
shell as I sat manacled to the tree. Then, one day, I was able to pull
the chains apart.

But instead of offering thanks to the gods, I petitioned for
vengeance.

"Hear me, great Ran, devourer of men. If I am indeed born of
giants, grant that Kol may never reach his home alive. Pound his ships
with waves thick as blood, drag them down with whirlpools, drown
them in seaweed strong as iron chains, then retch them up in stinking
fragments of half-digested spume."

I poured every particle of my begrimed soul into the curse, not
caring if I damned myself in the process.

And my curses were heard. A hurricane blew into the gulf. Two
days later, the bodies of Kol and his crew were cast up onto the sands

of my new domain. I picked through the debris, snatching a necklace of coral gemstones from the corpse of Thordis, a seax from Kol's belt. Once it was done, I knew I too had perished, my soul no more than another bloated corpse rotting to blackness in the sun.

Yet my body endured. Through the centuries, I was more phantom than fact, more observer than actor. A parody of an immigrant and a farcical set of contradictions: free yet a slave, alive yet deadened, betrayed yet betrayer. I'd braved the jagged crystalline seas to wash up, abandoned, unwelcomed, in a settled land that was rich and hostile and destined for conquest. There I lived like a heedless brute, forgetting the meaning of time.

Hundreds of years later, I witnessed the end of Eden and the era of hard, bright, Spanish steel slicing through a profusion of lost cultures like Thor's lightning. There were huge, black and brown barrel-chested horses smashing through countless camps and villages, places already putrid with disease. The invading Old World microbes acted like catastrophic shock troops carrying apocalyptic pestilence, decimating indigenous innocents in advance of rage-eyed warriors. The bitter seeds of the American age were sown.

I watched, a true evil troll of human lore, feared by aboriginals and conquistadors alike. With no more compunction than a lion, I once killed and ate a Manasota man just for the crime of trespassing. Another time, I hunted four passing Spanish soldiers because of the lovely smell of their war-steeds. Afterwards, I turned choice cuts of men and horses on a huge oaken roasting spit over a bonfire, stuffed myself, then danced with elation under a gibbous moon. I took their iron box of Aztec gold and made it my hoard.

I had gone quite mad.

Only in dreams did I catch unbidden and unwanted glimpses of who I'd once been. I'd wake up terrified and howling like a wounded animal.

Finally, I drifted back toward a pain-wracked, fragile sanity. I grew aware of what I'd lost and become. Despondency drove me into long sleeps that would last weeks, sometimes months, maybe even longer. I've no way of knowing now. I would crawl from my hole so emaciated as to be barely able to feed myself. In those times, I became a carrion eater, waving away bands of noxious turkey buzzards to feast on sun-rotted meat.

Even when I became relatively heathy in body and mind, I lived like a man marooned. I could have made my way to the Appalachians, a place more natural to trolls, yet I didn't. The horrid, hot jungle and endless tangles of barnacled mangroves became not just my home but my fate. And there was always my watery, dark cave, my living tomb.

Chapter Fifty-Four

"Darkness cannot drive out darkness; only light can do that. Hate cannot drive out hate; only love can do that."
—Martin Luther King, Jr.

I've been underground for weeks, since the day Hildy finally died. Is died the proper word? Less died than disappeared. No, not disappeared, either. *Transfigured* is the closest word. She somehow became one with Yggdrasil itself, a hideous sublimity that plunged me into prayer and tears.

I should also be dead. Truly dead, slain by the baneful Lucky. I would indeed have died if not for the astonishing Andre, who survived his devastating wounds long enough to put an arrow through the neck of that perilous, nihilistic son of a bitch. In the end, Lucky was even more dangerous than Skuld herself, mother of monsters and heroes. Skuld, bearer of so much pain and venom and scheming. In the end, Hildy's sacrifice saved all of us, but her mother most of all.

Skuld wept, wailed, and keened for long days and nights. She was inconsolable in the face of her daughter's death. Something in her cracked, an impenetrable shell that had long bound her tight with a festering ego. At first, I assumed she was mourning the failure of her own schemes, or was putting on an act to avoid retaliation and punishment. Indeed, I despised Urdy and Verda for their apparent forgiveness of Skuld, for not reaching out with all their incomparable power and turning that bitch to ash.

But the Norn sight hadn't ended abruptly when Urdy awoke. For a time, I literally felt their grief, and they mine. I caught glimpses into memories, events, dimensions and realities of each of them, including pain-ridden Skuld. It was surely just a fraction of what the Great Norns were feeling and remembering about Hildy, but it was more than enough to overwhelm a lowly troll. Over the course of the nine days of Hildy's transfiguration, I could finally see how the sisters were part of a single being contending with a great grief. Not just grief, though. They also felt honor, humility, and gratitude. Hildy had gifted these all-knowing creatures with a new knowledge that could not be scribed even with the most sacred of runes.

So, yes, Skuld was both remorseful and chastened, perhaps for the first time in her ancient life. Whatever cracked inside also deepened her. There were times, eerily, when she took on the form of Hildy. It wasn't an exact transformation. From what I could sense, it was an involuntary response to her bereavement. I abhorred it, seeing Hildy right there, yet infinitely far beyond my reach.

When I was finally able, I left Haven without a word.

Few had noticed my absence in the outside world. It had much larger concerns, the world being itself in a kind of recovery. Whatever happened at Haven, there were reflections of it in the whole of Midgard. There were deadly meteors calved from the comet, earthquakes on every continent, volcanic eruptions that resulted in darkened days, like black drapes drawn in a room of mourning. The humans don't understand what happened. How could they? How can I?

Yet the crisis passed, their civilization still intact. The phones and Net are working again. I got several texts from Freddie. He found Misty alive and bartending in Atlanta, still claiming she'd been coerced by Lucky. I'm beyond caring at this point.

Edmund left a voicemail, wondering about moving forward with our agreements. Chen left one, as well, wanting to know if I'd be willing to take on some part-time tollkeeping again.

I've mostly stayed alone in my lair, dreaming of her. A thousand different dreams during long hours of torpor, yet Hildy haunts every one of them. Even when awake, I can't shake the sense she's here. I talk to her constantly in my mind, and often aloud.

Today, I finally decide to emerge from my den, open the shed and unlock the fence gate. I'm naked and sodden with spring water. Naked except for the black eye patch Urdy made me.

It's twilight outside. In my fugue state, I don't know if this moment exists before sunrise or after sunset. Am I soon to be chased back into the darkness of my refuge, or will I be able to savor a long walk in the soft Florida dusk? A beginning or an end?

Then I see that the light is in the east. I've timed things all wrong. It disappoints. Feeling stubborn, I stand here outside the gate, unyielding no matter what comes, my mother's son. This is Act V rather than Act I, yet I don't want to leave the stage.

As the sky brightens, I'm stupefied by a rising flood of color. All around me in a wide circle are beach sunflowers and blanket flowers, a surfeit where none had been just a few days ago. I bend down to them, touching the soft petals. The colors are astonishing. Brilliant and blazing hues I've never seen before. Pinks and reds and oranges and yellows. But the words can't do justice to their range and vivid variety. So many pinks. I don't know their names, which one is coral or carmine, carnation or crimson.

I have the uncanny sense of being embraced.

As I kneel here, I'm suddenly aware of a pleasant warmth. Looking up, I'm astonished to see Sól well above the clear horizon. She shines on me. Except at Haven, or through the filtered glass and woven screens of helmets and masks, I've never seen a sunrise before without cringing in pain. So many hundreds of years without this.

It terrifies me, the absence of pain. Surely, it will take hold again. It always takes hold. Always, always. Even without the inevitable agony, I lose my nerve and cower back to the safety of the shadows.

But that stubborn feeling remains. I look east, then again step out of the shelter of my sad little shed, through this mad embrace of wildflowers, and finally out into the soft sunlight.

Acknowledgements

Many thanks to those who have taken the time to critique various drafts or portions of this work. Thanks especially to Lane Robins, Rhonda White, Mary Lippitt, Miles Overholt, Jenn Mondello, John Biesecker, and Scott O'Connell for reading and critiquing earlier drafts. Also thanks to my workshop fellows and teachers at the Writers in Paradise conference at Eckerd College conference, with special thanks to codirector Les Standiford for his encouragement. I also send my appreciation to Amanda Rutter for proofing the book—though I am, of course, responsible for any proofing errors or imperfections (if you see something, say something). During the writing process, various readers on the Scribophile platform were of great help. Support was also there from my family, including Will Vickers, Louise Cadwalader, Justin Vickers, Tim Vickers, Beki Martin, and Carroll Vickers. Finally, thanks to Cyndi Vickers, without whom the book could never have been written.

Mark R. Vickers

If you enjoyed this book:

I would be very grateful if you would rate and review it on Amazon. com, Goodreads, or wherever you tend to write your reviews and commentary. That greatly helps spread word of mouth about the book.

Also, please feel free to visit **thetollkeeper.com**, where I blog on the topic of myths, legends, literature, tollkeeping and sundry other matters related to the book.

34553144R00214

Made in the USA
Lexington, KY
25 March 2019